is the heart's peril . . .

MaryKate's head snapped up. Harry was standing before her. Her pounding heart stammered in her chest. "You frightened me!"

"I'm sorry."

"I thought you little folk."

"Hardly that," the large man replied, smiling a little. The shadowy light winked between the branches of the ancient oaks.

"Somehow I imagined that nothing could frighten you." He hesitated, and then: "I visited this place riding the other day. I saw you running as if pursued."

"Pursued?" she asked quietly.

"Yes." He stood where he was, two feet away from her.

"Only by you," she told him.

"Yes. Well. Then you're in no danger."

"Am I not?" she asked softly, staring up at him . . .

Kathleen

Books by Sheila O'Hallion

Fire and Innocence
Kathleen
Masquerade of Hearts

Published by POCKET BOOKS

Most Pocket Books are available at special quantity discounts for bulk purchases for sales promotions, premiums or fund raising. Special books or book excerpts can also be created to fit specific needs.

For details write the office of the Vice President of Special Markets, Pocket Books, 1230 Avenue of the Americas, New York, New York 10020.

Kathleen

Sheila O'Hallion

POCKET BOOKS
New York London Toronto Sydney Tokyo

This book is a work of historical fiction. Names, characters, places and incidents relating to non-historical figures are either the product of the author's imagination or are used fictitiously. Any resemblance of such non-historical incidents, places or figures to actual events or locales or persons, living or dead, is entirely coincidental.

An *Original* Publication of POCKET BOOKS

POCKET BOOKS, a division of Simon & Schuster Inc.
1230 Avenue of the Americas, New York, NY 10020

Copyright © 1988 by Sheila R. Allen Inc.
Cover art copyright © 1988 Jim Avati

All rights reserved, including the right to reproduce this book or portions thereof in any form whatsoever. For information address Pocket Books, 1230 Avenue of the Americas, New York, NY 10020

ISBN: 0-671-63840-8

First Pocket Books printing December 1988

10 9 8 7 6 5 4 3 2 1

POCKET and colophon are trademarks of Simon & Schuster Inc.

Printed in the U.S.A.

Kathleen

Prologue

THE ROOM WAS SHROUDED in silence. It hung as heavily as the velvet drapes that were closed across the enormous windows. Outside, morning had begun, but in the ornate master suite night still held sway.

The sounds of the London hawkers, calling out their wares beyond the thick stone walls, could barely be heard. Horses and carriages clip-clopping around the Mayfair square hurried on past the street vendors, hurried on about life's business, unaware that death was nearby.

Inside the dark room the smell of the old man's medicine hovered over the lace coverlets, tinging the air with the smell of a sickroom.

Beside the bed a younger man dozed uneasily, slumped back within a tall wing chair. The chair, the drapes, and the thick Oriental carpet beneath his feet swallowed the small sounds of their breathing until the old man suddenly hacked violently, clearing his throat.

Henry Charles Richard George, better know as Harry to his friends, heard his father's distress, his eyes opening as he sat forward, leaning toward the bed. He peered intently at the still sleeping Duke of Exeter, the light from the

KATHLEEN

bedside oil lamp guttering away into the folds of ornate cloth that spread across table, bed, and walls. The room was engulfed in shades of forest-green.

Forest-green velvet and silks complemented the thick green rugging figured with deep blues and wines and browns. Green materials shot through with gold threads clotted across all the tables in the room, covering them and hanging down around them to fall against the patterned rug.

The room was overstuffed with overstuffed furniture. With knickknacks and furbelows and great potted ferns that spread their dark green fronds across tables and dark mahogany dressers, adding to the forested gloom.

Harry watched his father as the old man slept, trying to gauge whether to call for the doctor. Again.

He felt oppressed by the room, by the cloth, and the darkness, and the sickroom smell. And something more. At thirty-seven he had never considered his own mortality. Until this last fortnight, when illness felled his father, he had never truly faced the fact that one day he would become duke.

In obligations, and responsibilities, as well as in title. The thought was sobering to a man who had spent his youth doing as little work as possible. Crockford's and the other London gaming halls knew him much better than his retainers and dependents did. His father had always taken care of the estates. Now he stared at his father's wrinkled brow and realized that he, himself, had passed the midpoint of his life.

If he lived to be as old as his father was now, he had less time left than he had already spent on this earth. The thought left him uneasy. He wasn't ashamed of his past. He had never been less than a gentleman should be, Harry told himself. But neither was he particularly proud. He had accomplished nothing.

A soft tap at the wide hall door brought Mrs. Billings around its dark-stained oak panels. She hesitated, just inside, adjusting her eyes to the gloom. From the hallway behind her, morning light spilled across the carpet, backlighting her ample figure and haloing her gray hair.

She spoke as she came closer. "How is he this morning?"

"I'm not sure." Harry's voice sounded as if it came from deep within his six-foot frame. "He's been coughing."

KATHLEEN

Mrs. Billings stepped around the bed, adjusting the satin coverlet as she reached to touch the old duke's forehead. "He's got the heart of a young man and the stomach to match it, Your Lordship. He'll be right as rain again. Mark my words. You needn't worry so."

Harry stared at her, his hazel eyes dark in the gloom-filled room. "I pray you're right." He rubbed his stiffened neck where he'd lain against the leather chair. "Will you stay with him while I change?"

"I'll stay longer than that," she told the Earl of Lismore, Baron Lichfield, and one day to be the fifth Duke of Exeter, though God willing, that day wouldn't come soon.

Mrs. Billings had raised young Harry after his mother had run off to Italy with her poet, taking over for the lost mother and the father who buried himself in Parliament, unable to come close to his son until the boy was grown. Mrs. Billings liked to say she knew the young master better than he knew himself. "I'll stay until you've had a proper rest. And a tub bath to fix those long muscles you've curled into that chair all night."

Billings always spoke plainly. She was no lady, as she herself would tell anyone who asked. She believed the good Lord gave us bodies to use and not to be afraid to mention in mixed company. Queen Vickie herself had all the same equipment as everyone else, was Billings's motto. Harry remembered his first disastrous forays into polite society when he had spoken whatever came to his mind, any which way he felt like it. Such things as body parts, my dear, are *not* discussed in mixed company, his aunt had told him quite firmly. There was, of course, the exception of hands and face, but never feet, swollen, tired, or otherwise. As to the rest, it was better left unmentioned altogether.

"His Lordship will be just fine," Billings was saying as she watched Harry. "The doctor said to send round for him this morning, and I already have, so off with you. Until we know what's what, there's nothing you can do here."

Harry hesitated and then slowly stood up, looking down at his father for a moment before he turned toward the door. It was useless to fight Billings. His father had told him that when he was eight, and it had held true every since. One way or another she always got her way.

KATHLEEN

Most women did. No matter who paid the costs. His tired brain told him he wasn't being fair to Billings. And then it shut down, balking and thinking about anything until he had sleep. Particularly women. A fleeting memory of his mother crossed his mind before he could dismiss it. Only when he was very tired, or very, very drunk, did he ever think about his mother.

It was close to the midday meal when one of the footmen came to wake Harry. The doctor was staying to lunch and word had been sent round from Buckingham Palace that the prime minister would be arriving within the hour to look in on his old and ailing friend.

Waking from a troubled sleep, Harry stared at the boy, unfocused for a moment. "What's your name?" Harry asked.

The boy saw the earl's intent expression and mistook it for anger. "Robert, Your Lordship." The boy stumbled over the words.

"And how old are you, Robert?"

"Fifteen, Your Lordship." Robert's pale blue eyes were widened with worry over what he had done or had not done to incur the earl's wrath.

"Have you worked here long?" Harry asked.

"I need the job, sir!" the boy burst out. "I mean, Your Lordship. My ma will kill me dead if I don't do her proud. She says it every time I see her in the kitchen."

Harry sat up. "There's nothing wrong."

Robert stared at the taller man as the earl stood up and reached for his dressing gown. "I was promoted from the kitchens last year, Your Lordship. My mother spoke to Mr. Peeves. She said I did good work even if I was her very own."

"I can manage, Robert. Tell Peeves I'll be down directly I've looked in on the duke."

"Yes, sir, thank you, Your Lordship, I'm sorry, your— Your Lordship."

"What are you sorry for?" Harry turned back to stare at the boy.

"I don't know, Your Lordship."

"Never apologize before the fact, Robert. It will lead

people to assume you intend to do something you must apologize for. Some say it's wiser never to apologize at all."

Robert didn't know if he was expected to reply. He stared at the Earl, watching him turn away. He hesitated and then left, closing the door quietly, leaving Harry alone with his thoughts as he rang for his valet.

Lunch with the doctor was a quiet affair, Harry asking about his father only to be told that we must all trust in God.

"That's all well and good," Harry told the man, "but in the meantime, since we are here on earth, isn't there something *you* can do? Or one of your brethren?"

The doctor's opinion that God giveth, and God taketh away, sent Harry into monosyllables. The sounds of their silverware and china were soon the only sounds to be heard between the two men at the table.

The doctor had a healthy appetite, filling his ample body steadily to the accompaniment of the steady, deep, ticktock of the huge rosewood grandfather clock that sat at the far end of the side parlor.

Since the duke had leaned back from his dinner, complaining of the heat, and then fallen forward, Harry would not step foot in the dining hall. He had told Peeves to put a table anywhere he pleased, as long as it was not in the room where his father had nearly died.

The doctor made an attempt at conversation, asking about the parlor, but Harry only said he preferred it this way. The doctor looked toward the footmen, motioning for more food.

One of the footmen who served the cold roast and hot steamed vegetables was Robert. Harry didn't notice, and Robert stayed back from the table, handing over the covered silver servers from the sideboard that had been imported from the dining hall to another lanky youth.

Peeves came to the door, bowing slightly. "The prime minister is arriving, Your Lordship." The butler's sonorous tones made the words seem freighted with importance.

Harry reached for his napkin. "I'll be there directly."

The doctor looked up from his cabbage and roast. "Please carry on, Your Lordship. Don't consider me at all. I'll finish alone."

KATHLEEN

"Yes. Well." Harry turned to leave and saw Robert by the sideboard amid the silver salvers. "Thank you, Robert."

Robert's companion was surprised. He leaned in to whisper after the earl left the room. "Since when did you get so chummy with the swells?"

"Leave off," Robert hissed back, embarrassed.

"Boys?" The doctor's voice rose behind them, turning them round. "Is there any pudding to be had?"

Sir Robert Peel had spent his life in public service and it showed. Nearly sixty years of age, he had survived long years as Her Majesty's chief secretary for Ireland, the coming of the railroads, the going of the Chartists, and even an assassination attempt that had claimed the life of his private secretary, whom the murderer mistook for Peel himself.

Peel walked into the main hall of Exeter House with the steady stride and assurance of a man who ran governments and ran them well. Though not a popular man, particularly with the queen, he still managed to win the votes and the confidence needed to get the work of England's government done.

"Well, Harry—how are you holding up?" Peel came forward, taking the younger man's hand and staring steadily into Harry's eyes. "How is he? What do the doctors say?"

"Damn all, is what the doctors give us." Harry spoke easily with the man he'd known since birth. "Come along up, and we'll let him know you're here."

They climbed the wide mahogany stairs toward the second floor of the huge four-story house, Harry leading the way to the duke's suite of rooms.

In the sitting room Mrs. Billings, dozing by the fire, was startled by their sudden appearance. "Oh!" She stood up, half-curtsying. "Your Lordships—"

"Why aren't you with him?" Harry demanded.

"Ask him. He ordered me out," Billings told Harry flatly. "There's no arguing with the man when he's like that."

Harry walked past the housekeeper, Peel coming more slowly behind, giving Harry a chance to open the door between the ornate chambers and look toward his father's bed, his concern obvious.

KATHLEEN

"Stay out!" the old man barked, his voice thin with age and ill health.

"Sir Robert's here," Harry told his father, moving on into the room.

Sir Robert stopped in the doorway, staring across the wide chamber at his bedridden friend. "I say, Charles, what do you propose to do about anything if you keep to your bed?"

The duke relaxed back against his down-filled pillows. "Women! Never could stand them. Always poking around into everything and fussing about as if they knew what they were doing. What are you doing standing over there? Come here where I can—" The duke's words were lost in a coughing fit, the prime minister coming forward to sit in the wingback chair Harry had slept in the night before.

"—see you," the duke finished his sentence, clearing his throat. "Bloody damn cold," he said.

"I thought it had been rather warm for April," the PM replied.

"Got a bloody damn cold, man—on top of whatever else is wrong with me. Harry, find my brandy. That infernal woman was hiding it away when I caught her at it, but she won't tell me where."

Harry went in search of the brandy, leaving the two old friends to themselves for a few minutes. The duke glanced toward the open door to his sitting room and then leaned toward Sir Robert, speaking softly. "I have to beat this, Robert. He's not ready."

"Harry will do all right for himself."

"At a gaming table or in some woman's withdrawing room. Or drawers. But not at running all this," the duke replied. "I know Harry's good qualities, but I'm not blind to his faults. He needs time. And I don't have it to give him."

"Aren't you borrowing trouble? You look much better to me than you did that night at dinner."

The duke's eyes lit up. "Gave you all a fright, did I?"

"Yes. And I must say you don't look the least bit sorry for it."

The duke's expression sobered. "I'm sorry enough about what it will mean when I'm gone. Harry has to learn."

"Harry has to learn what?" Harry himself asked from

7

KATHLEEN

across the room. He came forward carrying a brandy decanter.

"We were discussing Parliament," the prime minister replied smoothly. "We could use young blood on the floor."

"Perish the thought," Harry said. He set the decanter down, reaching for brandy glasses from a silver tray on a table near his father's bed. "I'd rather it was someone else's young blood you spill, please. I'm not cut from the right cloth to be a politician."

"Is that a polite barb, dear boy?"

"Hardly that. Merely the truth. I simply can't imagine putting forth all that work and energy laboring on about banker's rights and foreign money. Or sitting through more discussion about Ireland."

The duke watched his son carefully. "Ireland's future is tied to the dukedom's own, Harry. Our Irish holdings have been in the family for over a hundred years."

"Brandy?" Harry asked the prime minister, handing a glass toward the duke.

"No, thank you. I must have my wits about me for this afternoon's session," Sir Robert replied.

"There's no use changing the subject, Harry," the old duke told his son.

"I'm sorry. What *is* the subject? Ireland?" Harry tried to convey respect and boredom in the same breath, hoping to end the discussion. It came too near his own early-morning recognition of how ill-prepared he was to handle the estate for his father until he got well. Harry did not want to think about having to handle it alone one day.

Sir Robert was standing up. "I'd best get back."

"I'm thinking of sending Harry to Ireland," the duke said, surprising both of his listeners.

"Really?" the prime minister said. He looked toward Harry, who was staring at his father. "If you do, I shall ask for a firsthand report on this latest crop failure."

"Ireland's crop is always failing."

"It would seem so," the PM replied. "I shall call round the first of the week, shall I? Do you feel up to a bit of cards?"

"Probably cure me. I always feel better winning from you," the duke told his old friend.

KATHLEEN

The prime minister's eyebrow rose. "We shall see." He looked toward Harry. "If you decide to go to Ireland, come round and talk first."

Harry shook his head. "I am beginning to think both of you are quite mad. I shall hardly be traveling in the near future. I shall be here where I am needed."

Sir Robert said his farewells, Harry turning toward the door to walk him out. The duke spoke, stopping them. "I need you here, Harry. Robert can find his way."

"Of course," the prime minister said as he left father and son to themselves.

"Come sit," the duke said, a fit of coughing interrupting his words.

Harry did as his father asked, falling back into the wing chair and staring at his father's ravished face. The duke swallowed more brandy, the coughs subsiding. He took several deep breaths before he looked over to meet his son's gaze.

"Harry, I'm not well. Let me speak plainly. I'm not getting younger, and I may not be getting better. It's time things were straightened out." He watched his son's face. "I mean between you and Amelia."

At the mention of his wife's name, Harry's face turned to stone. His father saw it.

"You have responsibilities to our people, Harry. You *must* make amends with Amelia."

Harry stared at his father, his face a mask. "I'm not sure it is even possible."

"Then you must annul the marriage. Harry, there is no succession. There is no one to come after you. You *have* to have a son." The duke watched Harry's face, trying to read past the wall he had put up. The older man did not know how to ask his son the right questions; he longed to help, and he did not know how. Or if his son would let him. "You have obligations. Responsibilities."

"I am aware of that. You have never had to tell me that," Harry said stiffly.

"Well, I'm telling you now. I have always done my duty. You are my son. You will, too." The duke paused. "You must reconcile, or you must end the marriage and be free to marry elsewhere. I never should have let things drag on this long. But now it is vital." He watched his son. "You tell me you want to help. This is the one thing you can do for me now, Harry. If I am to die, let me die in peace, knowing that I did not waste my entire life rebuilding the family inheritance only to have it pass on to others after my son."

Harry sat erect, his shoulders back, as if ready for attack. "Divorce is unthinkable."

The duke let his son's words hang on the air between them, not replying. Finally Harry spoke again: "When you are well, we can discuss travel plans."

"And if I never am?" the duke prodded. "It must be now."

Harry stared at his father.

"Now," the duke repeated. And then was silent.

1

A RAINSTORM FLATTENED the green-sided ocean waves, the sun blotted out by thick black clouds. Rain poured down onto the decks of the English packet ship, drenching the ship, the sea, and the Irish coastline ahead.

The storm moved faster than the ship, cracks in the cloud cover letting a few of the sun's rays fall toward the waters of Dublin Bay, light and shadows changing the colors of the sea and the lush green mountains that rose beyond. Leaving the ship behind, the black clouds raced inland, spreading rainbows in their wake.

"I say, Harry, don't you have sense enough to come in out of the rain?" Leo's languid voice came from the passageway behind the tall man who stood by the rail, staring out at the changing light patterns of sea and sky and coastline. Leopold, Lord Cumberland, ventured out from the protection of the passageway, coming nearer his friend. "What is it you're staring at?"

Harry did not immediately reply. He glanced back at his friend and then nodded toward the interplay of sunshine and storm clouds ahead of the ship. "What do you see out there, Leo?" Harry asked finally.

KATHLEEN

Leo looked out toward the lush emerald-green land that fanned out across the horizon beyond the bay. The port of Dublin lay protected by the soft-looking hills, wharf after wharf filled with grains and produce being loaded into English vessels, their sails furled, their crews reaching and hauling.

"I see Ireland, old man, what else am I to see?" Leo replied. "It's what we've been aiming at, isn't it?"

"Look at the amount of grain . . . these people say there's a famine going on here."

"Oh, well . . ." Leo yawned. "The Irish are always bewailing something. No one ever listens."

The Earl of Lismore straightened up, turning toward Leo. "I talked to Peel before we left. He said Parliament has been brought to a standstill by all the debate on the famine issue. By God, Leo, look!"

"I'm looking." His distaste showed. "But you shouldn't ask me to any sooner than I have to, you know. If the old duke hadn't been so determined I accompany you, all your pleading would have been for naught, I assure you."

"You have told me," Harry replied dryly. "Over and over again."

"Why he wanted his son and heir to tramp all the way over to this godforsaken island is quite beyond me. He's bed ridden after all. What if something should happen while you're gone?"

"What if it should happen while I'm there?" Harry replied, his eyes clouding over. "I had the same discussions with him. He wouldn't listen."

"What is so blasted important over here?"

"Amelia," Harry told his friend, turning back toward the passageway.

Leo stared after him. "Have you lost your mind? Harry, wait up a bit, there!" He hurried toward the passageway. "You did say Amelia, didn't you?"

Harry was almost to his cabin. Leo was hard put to keep up with the taller man's long strides. "I did hear you correctly, didn't I? Have you been in touch with her?!"

"No." Harry opened the cabin door, Leo following him inside. "We haven't spoken since she left ten years ago."

Leo stood across the small room, watching Harry reach

for a decanter of port. Staring at the man with whom he'd grown up. They had gone to school together, had cut a wide swath through the London ladies together. Harry's expression was grim as he stared back. "What on earth is going on?" Leo asked. "My God, don't tell me. Is she in Dublin?" he asked, preparing for another shock. Harry sat down in a teak chair placed before a large teak desk. "She's been living on our western lands in Cork. At the Priory."

Leo sat down hard. "Are you telling me your wife has changed religions and become a nun?!"

"Hardly. Lismore Priory is the family estate."

A tap at the door brought Robert inside a moment later. Promoted from footman to valet for the earl and sent on an adventure to Ireland, Robert's enthusiasm even included Leo's man Archie, who had taken Robert in hand to teach him the ropes. So far most of what Archie was teaching Robert was how to be irreverent to the nobility without losing your job in the process. Moving past the two English lords, Archie motioned Robert toward an open trunk of clothing.

"You see, I told you there'd be room left in there," Archie said to Robert.

Harry threw his soaked greatcoat toward the two valets, its green and black checked wool dripping water onto the polished wood floor.

"And that's a sorry enough mess," Archie said, catching it.

"You have no idea how apt those words are," Leo told Harry's man. Leo continued: "Robert, has your employer told you we are soon to be confronted with a hysterical woman?" Leo turned back toward Harry himself. "Just what do you propose to do with Amelia once the two of you meet?"

"Amelia?!" Archie looked shocked. Robert, to whom the thought of joining in the conversation was as foreign as France, turned back toward the trunk, pretending he could not hear their words.

"Yes. You remember—his wife," Leo answered his own man. "Bloody simpleminded idea. If the old duke had asked me, I would have told him," Leo said as Robert closed the steamer trunk.

KATHLEEN

At first Leo's words didn't register. Then Robert straightened up, his eyes rounded with surprise. "He has a wife?!" After the words were out Robert realized he'd spoken out loud. No one else seemed to pay any attention.

"Coming all the way out here on a wild goose chase is what this is," Leo went on.

"Wild goose? Or wild wife?" Harry tried to make it light, but years-old anger welled up under the five short words.

"You can't want to see her," Leo said. "It can't have been your idea. I know you too well. But why on earth would the duke want you to, either? What's to be gained? I mean, why are you doing this?"

"Because my father is dying," Harry said quietly.

Leo's chastened expression spoke for him.

"He's never recovered from last winter. You know he hasn't, Leo. He may not have long to put things in order."

"All the more reason not to leave," Leo said, watching Harry. "I say again, what's to be gained?"

"An heir," Harry replied.

Leo stared at him. "You can't mean it—I mean, you can't plan—I mean, what *do* you plan on doing?"

"When he thought he was dying, my father's last wish was that the marriage should either become one in truth or that we 'end the farce,' as he put it." Harry took a long swallow of the port. "When he recovered he felt the Deity was giving him a chance to see that the dukedom was secure. He wants me to come to terms with Amelia, to mend the breach, and to bring her home. Hopefully with child. Boy child."

"My god." Leo took the port decanter from beside Harry.

"My sentiments precisely," Harry replied. "But I can hardly say no. If I cannot come to terms with her, one way or the other, I am not free to pursue any other. Not and make the issue legal in any event."

"You can't be serious," Leo said.

"He's as serious as a casket," Archie replied, seeing Harry's look and leaving. "If you ask me, it's a fool's errand," was his parting shot. Robert hurried after him.

Harry stood up. "My father's ease of mind means more to me at this point than any other considerations. Any other." Harry repeated the words, as if still trying to convince himself. He looked down into the glass of port in his hand, swirling it a little.

"You make me awfully glad there's no dukedom in my future." Leo reached for the decanter, filling another glass, and swallowing quickly. "I wish one of you had confided in me before we sailed."

"You wouldn't have come."

"That's the point," Leo replied sourly, reaching for more port. "I abhor family scenes. You see what a distance I keep from my stepmother and her brood."

"What did my father say to you?"

"He said I was needed. That you had to come and that all of Ireland was up in arms and full of starving people and that he'd rest easier knowing you had someone he could trust with you."

"He didn't!" Harry almost smiled.

"Yes, he did. I was quite flattered," Leo told his friend. "It wasn't until I was on board that I began to think about what might happen here. I imagined the worst. Especially since the Irish blame every ill wind on us English in the first place. Or at least I thought I had imagined the worst. Until you dropped this news upon your unsuspecting friend."

Archie came back in. "If you want to be changing anything, Lord Leo, you'd best come with me now. I'm closing up your trunk next."

Leo stood up, reaching to place his glass on the table. "You are a martinet, Archie. I might just as well have joined the army, you order me around so much."

"Someone's got to keep you in order," Archie said placidly, heading toward the door. Leo followed him out, Archie turning back once he reached the passageway. "We'll be docking within the hour, they tell me. Robert's gone to see about the rest of the belongings."

"Thank you," Harry said. One more hour, he thought to himself. Watching them leave, his heart hardened within him. He would do what he must. But none could make him like it.

A dark edging of storm clouds still lay low along the horizon when the hired carriage rounded the cobblestoned corner and clip-clopped past the rows of red brick and white-

KATHLEEN

windowed houses that lined Exeter Square in the center of Dublin. A stout gray church tower rose above the nearby roofs, the city stretching out all around in shades of gray mixed with the soft green of trees and parklands.

Exeter House sat along the southern edge of the city square, larger than most of its neighbors. Archie stepped down from beside the cab driver to pull out the step for the passengers, opening the door before Robert could reach for it.

Harry came out first, staring up at the house he had never before seen.

"No one in my family has been here since my grandfather. He only came once, and that was fifty years ago, according to my father."

"Excepting Her Ladyship," Archie added, watching Harry's grimace.

"Is she here now?" Leo asked Harry, dreading the answer. "To meet you or something?"

"Amelia would not find it convenient to leave the western properties. Or so the letter she sent in reply to my father's said. We shall go to her." Harry started up the steps, a butler opening the front door and standing back, waiting for the newcomers to enter.

"You're quite sure you wouldn't rather have privacy when you meet? I could wait for you here in Dublin," Leo said hopefully.

Harry turned back to grasp his friend's arm, bringing him forward. "You'll not desert me after coming all this way, will you?"

Leo sighed, handing his top hat to the butler. "Have I the choice?"

"No," Harry told him genially. "Why do you think I brought you along?"

"I shudder to think," Leo replied, but he followed the others into the front parlor, where a cheery fire and afternoon tea awaited them.

Nottingham lace curtains hung at the windows that looked out toward the square. Heavy plush side-curtains in darkest crimson surrounded the lighter lace, tied back with velvet cords in the same dark crimson. Dark fringed cloths covered the mahogany tables that stood around the room, stuffed birds under glass domes placed upon each table. A horsehair upholstered sofa covered in navy blue velvet sat near the fire, other chairs scattered around the room, another sofa near the doorway.

All was in perfect order, the fire was blazing merrily, and yet the room, the house, felt unused. Unlived in. Cold.

Harry turned toward the butler. "You are Scotsmith?"

"I am, Your Lordship." The man looked to be in his fifties, his face and body rounded with years of soft living. "We, my wife and I, have taken the liberty of engaging a gentleman's gentleman for your guest and several household staff. We do without when we're alone, of course."

"Yes. Whatever is necessary." Harry spoke carelessly.

"And are we to know how long Your Lordship will be in residence?" the butler asked.

"We shall be leaving immediately for the west. When we return I have no idea how long it shall take before Her Ladyship is ready to travel home to England. I assume she will need to procure a new wardrobe before venturing to London. In any event, we will leave as soon as possible."

The butler bowed himself out, moving toward Robert and Archie, while Leo threw himself down onto the sofa nearest the fire.

"Has Amelia evinced any interest in seeing you again? Or in England, for that matter?" Leo looked toward where Harry leaned against the fireplace mantel, staring downward toward the flames.

"None whatsoever," Harry replied.

Leo's sigh was prodigious, a wide yawn accompanying it. "I have a feeling you're going to regret not having listened to Archie's sterling advice before this ordeal is over."

"If I had a choice I would not be in Ireland, let alone ready to propose sharing household and life with a woman I should never have married in the first place. Nor would have, left to my own devices." Harry scowled. "Even the duke admits he made a mistake asking me to do so."

"How can you possibly get a child by a woman you can barely tolerate?" Leo asked his friend.

"Others have done so," Harry replied. "And as soon as there is an heir, she can retire again to her Irish retreat, for all I care. Once I have an heir, my duty shall have been done. And hers." Harry stared into the fire, lost in his own gloomy thoughts, Leo left to wolf down the dainty tea sandwiches by himself until Archie walked in carrying a pile of visiting cards.

"All the local gentry's wanting a chance to chat you up," Archie told them irreverently. "And a card about a dinner dance that's set for tonight, in case you've got the wind to make a leg this soon after that misery they called a crossing."

"You really had mal de mer, Archie. I've never seen you look so pale." Leo grinned. "While I, on the other hand, was tip-top the whole way over."

Archie scowled. "It wasn't pale you saw. I was as green as the bloody sea itself. My innards are still heaving and shaking."

"Please. Not while I'm eating," Leo told him.

"Should I send round to give regrets?" Archie asked Harry. "Or are you going to be foolish and go?"

Harry pulled at his cravat, loosening it around his neck, scratching at his chin. "Let Robert learn how to do it, Archie. You have no social graces whatsoever. There's still hope for him if you let him alone."

"Well, I like that, after all I've done for the both of you over the years. I'm the one who's cleaned up your boyish messes, my lads, and don't you forget it."

"How could we?" Leo groaned. "Go away."

"As soon as I know what to tell them. Are you going to be foolish or what?"

"I'm on a fool's errand in the first place," Harry said. "And if I take your employer out, he may be less fretful. In any event, I might as well complete the folly, and let the locals get a chance to look at me, as they must be talking of nothing else. Ask Robert to check and see if all is ready for us to leave tomorrow?"

"Tomorrow?!" Leo groaned. "Please—tell me my hearing's off. You can't possibly want to set off on a cross-country carriage ride immediately upon landing. It's not cricket, old man, I tell you right now. I refuse to budge until at least long enough to have some country tweeds ordered."

"No one shall care what you wear in the west. No one goes out there except estate agents and rusticating squires."

"Even more reason to allow me a moment's respite and some polite conversation before I have to traipse after you into the lion's den."

"Polite conversation, bosh! It's the ladies you're after and don't deny it," Archie told Leo tartly. "Always was. Always will be. With both of you." Archie cast an eye in Harry's direction. "And don't deny it."

Leo stood up. "Show me where I'm to lay my head. If we're on the town tonight, I want to look my best. After all"—he grinned across the room at Harry—"this is, as one could say, virgin territory for us, old man."

"One could say it. But one would hope one would not." Harry had to grin back at his friend, some of the heaviness of heart and mind lifting as always when around Leo.

"I'm here to give my life and all, yours etcetera, of course," Leo told Harry. "But I must have a bit of fun before you pack us off to all those estate agents and rusticating squires. Not to mention a wife who wants none of you and will probably take out her ire on poor me."

"Archie will protect you," Harry told him.

"Archie'll protect himself, thank you very much," Archie told the two of them. "You two have to be on your own. I don't have the knack for dealing with women."

"Truer words were never spoken," Harry said. "Look at all the poor maids who've fled the house in tears after trying to work for you."

"Well, now," Archie said, "are we to stand here talking about me, much as I like the topic, or are we going to get things ready for an evening out?"

"An evening out's what I vote for," Leo said.

Harry started toward the door. "We might as well. Otherwise we'll only be sitting here, staring at each other all evening."

"What a horrible thought," Leo replied.

Harry motioned Archie on through the door into the parquet-floored hall beyond. "Lead us to our chambers, Archie, and then send Robert up. I'm sure the whole of Dublin is bursting with curiosity about our arrival, the whole sordid story dusted off and making the rounds again here as in London."

"No one cares about what happened between you and Amelia anymore. Except perhaps you and Amelia," Leo said.

"Are you willing to wager on that?" Harry asked softly.

"I'll take any bet you'd like to make."

Leo did not reply. He followed Archie up the unfamiliar stairs, Harry coming slowly behind.

The hall was chilly with more than the cold spring afternoon. It was chilly with emptiness.

Much like my life, Harry thought as he grabbed the banister and started up the stairwell. Empty and cold.

The dinner dance that evening was being held at the Dublin residence of the Clarences, the former mayor of Dublin introducing polite society to his daughter Honoria, newly back from school in England. The tall brick house blazed with candlelight and conversation, the rooms overheating with too many people crowded within them. Musicians wiped their damp foreheads in between German quartets, and the household help carried platters of food back and forth from kitchens to parlors; heavy silver trays hoisted high above the crowd as they circled their way past the guests.

The music and light spilled out into the street in front of the house, greeting Harry and Leo before they reached the door. At the sounds and smells Leo visibly brightened, straightening his posture, glancing at Harry's cravat as they descended to the roadway from the hired coach.

"Is my cravat absolutely impeccable? I don't want to let the English side down in front of wild-eyed Catholic heathens," Leo said.

"You'll be lucky to find an Irishman in the house, outside the kitchen help. And I'm sure this far from London there'll be none to compare with your knowledge of the thirty-two lessons on how to tie a cravat."

"Laugh all you like, these things are important to a gentleman."

"I wouldn't know," Harry told his lifelong friend. They entered the house, handing hats and topcoats to the man

KATHLEEN

who stood reaching out for them. "I hardly think the subject of cravats worth the bother."

"You hardly think anything worth the bother," Leo told him.

"You're right. I don't," Harry replied, fixing a polite smile in place as a gentleman in evening dress came toward them, smiling profusely.

2

In the west of Ireland four days later, the blue distances were alive with birdsongs, the moist air turning the sun's rays into a tender pearly light peculiar to the region. The soft light shone down across a hundred shades of green.

Hills covered with heather and oak rose higher and higher and then fell steeply toward the sea. The cliffs that lined the jagged shore were pocketed with caves and covered over with dainty mosses and luxuriant ferns. The sea washed between two hills, the long inlet lined with cliffs, and the oak groves that drew down toward the salty tang of the ocean waters. Goats ran wild on the sheer cliffs, nibbling at greenery, gulls and gannets swooping down past them into the sea.

Nestled into the lee valley of the inlet, the ancient stones of Lismore Priory rose high above the tiny village of Beare at the edge of the waters. Tiny thatched cottages enclosed the end of the west road, only the sea and the light boats of the fishermen, their curraghs, beyond.

The west road curved back around the Priory, forking into two prongs and continuing eastward toward Cork and far Dublin beyond.

KATHLEEN

The Priory's farmlands stretched back across one of the roads, crofters' thatched cottages dotting the countryside here and there, their rough-built thatch and stone weathered into soft grays and browns. Purpled with heather, more hills rose to the east in the distance; between them and the western sea were country fields carpeted with yellow broom and crimson loosestrife. Between the fields dark green hedges overgrown with the creamy froth of meadowsweet marked boundaries, fields of corn and barley and potatoes nearby, other fields nestled into nooks and crooks at the base of the hills across the valley.

"Mary-Kathleen! Mary-Kathleen!" A woman's voice called out toward the young woman who walked purposefully across a field of young potato shoots, the first tiny green sprouts peeping out of rows set a foot apart from boundary line to boundary line. A small black dog romped across the rows, angling back and forth across his mistress's path.

The young woman, Mary-Kathleen O'Hallion, did not stop. The dark red of her home-dyed petticoats flared out under the dark gray gown she wore, her feet bare against the damp-smelling earth.

"MaryKate—please—" The other woman caught up with her. Out of breath from running, Sophie O'Hallion took great gasps of air. "He didn't mean any of it. You know what your brother is like."

"I don't want to talk about it."

Sophie walked along beside her sister-in-law, reaching for her arm. The little dog stopped, waiting for them to catch up.

"It's just after the bad crop last year, and all the worry, he's touchy still. That's all." Sophie was still out of breath.

MaryKate snorted. "He can be as touchy as he pleases. Sure'n after twenty-six years of listening to him bellow, it doesn't mean so much as a sneeze to me."

Sophie stared at her. "But, then, what are you angry at?"

A shadow of defeat crossed MaryKate's emerald eyes and then was banished, the fight showing through. "I'm angry because he won't believe that the seaweed and fishguts and shellfish he's using for manure are damaging the land just

KATHLEEN

because it was an English farmer in an English book that said it! I'm angry because he won't plant the turnips I told him about, no matter that when the blight hit the potato crop last year it didn't hit the turnips! His skin won't turn yellow from eating swedes, he says!"

"A man has to do what he thinks best," Sophie said philosophically.

"And you and the wee ones are just to starve?"

"MaryKate, don't go exaggerating. We've had lean years before, we'll have them again. It isn't worth all the fighting, dear girl."

MaryKate stared at Johnny's wife. Sophie was only four years older, only thirty, and already had six children. Her oldest boy was thirteen, the baby boy still at the breast, and four girls between. "Sophie, go back to my stubborn brother and tell him I'll give no more advice."

"That will be the day," Sophie said, grinning, watching until MaryKate herself had to smile back.

"Off with you!" MaryKate told her sister-in-law. "I'm late back for Lady Amelia."

Sophie lost her smile. "It's that, you know, that's the real cause of all your brother's worry about you. Your working for the English. It upsets both your brothers, MaryKate. It just isn't right."

"Not right to repay kindness with loyalty?" MaryKate's chin jutted out, the stubbornness of the O'Hallion clan visible in her pretty face. "She schooled me and now she needs help schooling others. All Irish lasses, Sophie my dear, all to get educations and good husbands. Now, isn't that something my brothers would think a right and proper thing to do?"

"Johnny thinks it's wrong for any Irish to take an Englishwoman's charity."

"Yes. He's made that plain."

MaryKate began walking again, this time more slowly. Sophie stayed beside her. "I'll walk with you to the fork and then head back." She drank in the soft spring air. "It's nice to be walking and not have one or another tugging at me skirts for a bit."

They went through a break in the hedge, the narrow track of road cutting into the west road a little farther up. They

24

walked in silence until MaryKate stopped to pick a wildflower, handing it shyly toward Sophie. "Truce, then? At least between us?"

"Always. You know I love you as if you were one of my own," Sophie said, touched. She took the flower and stuck it into her thick dark hair. Twirling around, she struck a pose. "And how do I look, then?"

"Like a princess in a story," MaryKate told her.

They reached the fork in the road, Sophie walking backward, a few steps ahead of MaryKate, as carefree as if she were a girl again for a few precious moments.

Just beyond the fork one prong curved sharply back around a rough-hewn rocky hillock. The sound of thundering hooves came at the two women almost in the same instant that a rider rounded the curve, heading straight toward them. Directly behind him a coach and four loomed, traveling just as fast.

MaryKate saw the coach in the same instant that Sophie turned toward the sound. MaryKate reached for Sophie, shoving her into a heap at the roadside, safe from the pounding hooves. Just as he would have felled MaryKate herself, the rider yanked on the reins. The horse reared, taken off balance by the sudden human obstacle and the wrench on its bit. The rider grabbed at MaryKate, one strong arm lifting her alongside as the horse lost its footing, falling toward the marsh.

Horse, rider, and MaryKate spilled into the bog, cold water splashing up to soak them, the ground giving way beneath the weight.

Mud spattered them all as the coach braked, the sound of the brakes grating loud over the sounds of rippling wind and distant birdcalls. The coach driver was swearing to himself as a head appeared at the coach door, lowering the top half to stare out at the mess.

"I say, Harry—what are you up to out there?"

The man's English accent hit MaryKate's ears with almost the same impact as her body had hit the ground. She pulled back away from the mud-spattered rider, pushing her disheveled red hair back from her eyes. "English, is it? How *dare* you?!"

In that moment a small, mud-spattered dog splashed out

KATHLEEN

of the boggy marshland, barking and biting at the leather-gloved hand of the disheveled rider beside MaryKate in the cold mud.

It took the rider a moment to register that the disheveled wench was speaking to him. He had never been addressed with that tone of voice in his life. "I beg your pardon?"

"And well you should! Just who do you think you are, careening around the countryside, ready to run all of us into early graves?"

The Earl of Lismore stared at the impudent chit. Mud spattered her cheek and her freckled nose. Masses of red curls tumbled every which way about her head. Blazing green eyes glared at him. "Madam—I just saved your life."

"From what, but your own foolhardiness? And don't you go madam-ing me. Help me up." The imperious tone went with the stubborn little chin. 'If you've hurt Pugs, you'll *really* have something to answer to!" She reached for Pugs, holding his muddy fur close.

Harry glanced at the coach and saw Leo leaning out, grinning. Grimacing, the earl got to his feet, mud seeping down inside his riding boots. He reached for the girl, not taking the hand she had raised toward him, but pulling her up by the shoulders, staying far back from the yapping dog.

"Unhand me!" she yelled at him.

"You told me to help you up!" he snapped back at her, his patience lost. The dog growled deep in its throat.

"Tut-tut, Harry old boy, what will the lady think of our manners?" Leo asked. He was grinning hugely.

"I don't see you moving to help the other wench."

"You'll not touch me!" Sophie said, standing near the front of the coach. Gingerly she walked around the horses, coming nearer MaryKate. But she kept one eye on the coach in case the driver decided to finish the job and murder them both. "MaryKate, are you all right?"

"Do I *look* all right?!" MaryKate lifted her soggy, mud-soaked skirts, a flash of creamy white ankle and calf seen until she reached the road edge and stepped onto firmer ground.

"If you've lost me my horse—" Harry was saying grimly, reaching to help the horse up, praying its legs weren't broken.

"I?! And now with the threats!" MaryKate flared.

"MaryKate—" Sophie spoke softly, looking from the rider dressed all in black to the coachman and the English fop within. "Your tongue will get you hanged."

"They can't hang us for speaking the truth," MaryKate replied defiantly.

"Actually," Leo looked toward the tousled redhead, "in the course of human events that's very often happened, you know."

"By you English, no doubt!" MaryKate spit out the words.

Harry had the horse to its feet, leading it out of the water, watching for signs of limping. It favored its right front foot, but could put weight on it. "God's teeth, another ranting Irishman. Is that all there is in this godforsaken country? Are even the women infected with this need to blame everything on someone else?"

"MaryKate"—Sophie was edging away—"let's be off."

"You go on," MaryKate told her.

"And leave you with four Englishmen?!"

"I'm Welsh, meself," Archie said from beside Robert on the driver's seat.

Harry Beresford, Lord Lismore, spoke through gritted teeth. "I assure you, there is no need for concern. This meeting is at an end."

Leo watched Harry reach for his horse. "You do look a sorry sight, old boy."

Harry swung up onto his horse. *"Shall* we?" Harry said pointedly to Archie.

"You're just leaving them here, then?" Archie asked.

"It's their country. I'm sure they have places to go," Harry said.

Archie ignored his master's words, looking down at the taller, feisty one. "You're all in one piece, are you?"

"No thanks to you!" MaryKate told him tartly.

"If she's well enough to have a shrew's tongue, she's well enough to walk," Harry said. With that he was off.

The coach followed after him.

"Slowly!!" MaryKate called out. The coach slowed. Harry did not. "Of all the arrogant, self-centered, English fops!" MaryKate spoke more to herself than to her sister-in-law standing beside her.

"Come home with me," Sophie said. "You look a terrible sight."

MaryKate looked at Sophie's own disheveled hair and gown. "You've got a tear in your apron."

"Better that than in me hide. Come along now."

"I've got to get back. Her Ladyship will be waiting already. At least I have a good excuse," MaryKate said grimly. "If that sorry pair stop anywhere near, I'll have Lady Amelia straighten them out for treating our roads as racetracks!"

"Don't be counting on it. The English stick together, just as much as we do. It might be their only trait I like." Sophie was already moving up the narrow road. "I've been gone too long; Johnny'll be going daft watching the bay."

"Go on, go on. I'll see you at Tuesday market." MaryKate waved her brother's wife off, then set out in the opposite direction, disheveled and angry, Pugs at her heels.

3

THE FOUR-STORY GRAY stone walls of Lismore Priory stood sentinel on a promontory overlooking the village and the sea beyond. Rising above the surrounding countryside, it dominated the landscape.

It had been built over two hundred and fifty years before, built in the time of Queen Mary Tudor, Bloody Mary, by the Catholic Church. It had housed a nunnery then. The English prioress had taken in both Irish and English girls. And all somehow had managed to live together, under God's grace, in harmony and peace.

Until Queen Elizabeth sent Lord Essex to straighten out "the Irish problem" that had grown worse and worse ever since.

Essex had confiscated the land, sent the nuns back to England to be dealt with, and begun the wholesale slaughter of Irishmen and Irish land rights as well.

The Priory had come into the Lismore inheritance by marriage in 1744. Since then it had been one of the hundreds of absentee estates the English had peppered the island with, run by estate agents even more greedy than their employers. And much less honest.

KATHLEEN

Until Lady Amelia arrived.

MaryKate came flying across a field of purple heather behind the Priory, using a shortcut into the kitchen gardens. She headed for a footpath that led up stone stairs to a wooden gate in the priory wall, quickly crossing the flower-strewn path that meandered around the grounds toward the great front square.

Cook was startled as MaryKate burst through the kitchen door, two student helpers looking on, surprised. "Lord, and you gave me a fright!" Then Cook took a better look. "You look as if you've been fighting banshees."

"Very nearly," MaryKate said, heading toward the back stairs.

"What happened?" Cook called out after MaryKate's departing back.

"We were nearly run over by a crazed Englishman!" And with that MaryKate flew up the stairs, Pugs at her heels.

"And what are you standing around gawking for?" Cook asked the girls. "Is it more work you're looking for?"

MaryKate reached her attic room, quickly stripping out of the torn and muddy gown, pulling off her petticoat and standing in her mud-spattered white shift. Muttering darkly to herself she reached for a clean shift and began washing off the caked mud, praying Lady Amelia wasn't upset with her.

In the nine years she had worked, and then lived, here, MaryKate had never seen Lady Amelia angry. Pugs laid his mud-caked carcass down on the wood floor, wagging his tail once, and then just watching his mistress.

While MaryKate changed her clothes, far below within the Priory's one hundred rooms Lady Amelia sat quietly to tea, a book of sonnets on her lap. With her were two of her students and a minister.

The Right Honorable Reverend Mr. Grinstead sat across from Lady Amelia, sipping as quietly as he could at his steaming cup of China tea. He managed to look both interested and ecclesiastic when she finished speaking.

"Oh, I quite agree, Your Ladyship. Mr. Shakespeare's sonnets are quite wonderful. For temporal art. But, for me,

30

the most lovely poetry of all remains in the Bible. The Song of Ruth, for example." He smiled at the two silent school girls.

"The Song of Solomon," Lady Amelia agreed.

"Solomon has always bothered me. It seemed so explicitly sensual. Although, of course, it was not meant to be taken in that light. Still and all, I fear that for most of my parishioners, reading the Song of Solomon is much more interesting than perusing Mark or Deuteronomy." He sipped at his tea. "I am sorry your assistant could not join us today."

"I can't imagine where Mary-Kathleen's gotten to," Lady Amelia replied. "She's always most punctual."

"How unusual. The Irish are so forgetful of appointments. Rather like children, I always say." He spoke as if the two Irish girls were not there.

"Not Mary-Kathleen. Nor, I think, anywhere near the amount we so recklessly assume. In these ten years, I assure you, Mr. Grinstead, I have learned much about the Irish. And all to their credit."

"I hope you will help me to know them better," he replied.

"I hope so, too, Mr. Grinstead. For everyone's sake." She spoke softly, a melancholy twinge to her words.

Sounds of a loud commotion came faintly into the quiet room. They all looked toward the closed door, which flew open to reveal the butler, Wallace, and a mud-bespattered giant.

Dressed in black and already striding past Wallace, the giant dripped mud in his wake across the dark red Turkey carpet. Behind him a thinner man and two servants hesitated and then came slowly forward.

"Your Ladyship—the Earl of Lismore and Lord Cumberland," the butler said.

Amelia froze, staring up into the hazel eyes and strong-featured face of her husband.

"Amelia." Harry glanced toward the man across from his wife, who quickly stood up.

Amelia found her voice. "This is Reverend Grinstead, our Anglican pastor, recently arrived from London."

Harry nodded slightly. Leo came closer, bowing and then staring when he saw Amelia's fragile blond beauty up close.

Recovering, he reached for her hand. "It's been much too long, dear Amelia." He lingered over the kiss, his lips moist against her hand.

She withdrew it as if stung. "I did not expect you."

"As I see," Harry said. He was stripping off his cape and gloves, throwing them in Robert's general direction.

"You did not tell me you were coming," she said.

He shrugged. "You would not come to England. There was no choice."

She hesitated, giving a fleeting glance toward the cleric. "We had just begun tea. If you care to change first, I can ring for more."

But Harry was already looking around the room. "I need none. Robert, Archie, shift around and find where they hide the brandy."

The Reverend Mr. Grinstead smiled uncertainly at the tall, broad-shouldered man who somehow seemed to take up the whole room. "A tiresome trip, I take it, Your Lordship?"

"The entire miserable way," Harry replied, "capped by my nearly being unhorsed by one of your local heathens. Unbelievable tongue on the wench. No respect for herself or anyone else."

Archie had reached the hall when he stopped in his tracks. He grabbed Robert's arm as the boy came up behind him.

"What is it?" Robert asked. And then looked in the direction Archie was staring.

The young woman descending the steps from the upper regions of the huge house was much cleaner than the last time they had seen her. Archie reached behind himself to close the parlor door, a huge smile forming. "Oh, gor, but this may be a bit of fun after all."

MaryKate glanced toward Robert and then saw Archie. She stopped in mid-stride.

"Is there brandy about?" Robert asked innocently.

"His master has need of some double quick," Archie put in, not so innocently.

"Double quick, is it?" MaryKate came forward, down the steps, and across the wide hall toward the man. "Like all else he does, no doubt."

"He's in there." Archie pointed.

"Arch!" Robert protested, but Archie was already speak-

32

ing again, enjoying himself. "You're going to add no end of amusement to our stay, I'll wager, young lady."

"I am, am I? And stay, is it, you're thinking of doing?" MaryKate looked grim. "I'd not unpack if I were you. When I finish telling Lady Amelia—" She saw his expression, sudden concern bringing a frown to her face. She looked from the younger man to the older and then looked back at the quiet one. He didn't look to be more than eighteen. "He's not her brother or some such, is he?"

"No, ma'am," Robert told her.

"No, indeed," Archie added truthfully. "Nothing like."

"Good. Because that would be rare trouble." And with that MaryKate headed toward the drawing room. The two students came out past her, their eyes wide, moving as if the devil himself were behind them. MaryKate looked grim as she went through the door.

"Ah, Mary-Kathleen, there you are." Amelia spoke quickly, glad of an excuse to end the silence that filled the parlor. Harry refused to talk, Reverend Grinstead hesitated to intrude, and Leo was not bothering to help.

Leo glanced toward the girl called MaryKate, standing bolt upright once he recognized her. "What kept you so late?" Amelia asked, seeing neither Leo's reaction nor Harry's. Angry surprise brought Harry a step away from the fireplace.

"This sorry excuse for a man, that's what kept me, Your Ladyship." MaryKate saw Amelia's startled expression. "Nearly ran over both me and Sophie and Pugs as well, with never a 'by your leave' or an 'I'm sorry.' Just 'Get out of my English way before I knock you down!' "

Harry advanced toward the girl, angry brows knit together. "Who do think you *are*, addressing me in such a fashion?!"

"Harry!" Amelia came to her feet, standing in the way of her husband's angry advance. He towered over both women, glaring past Amelia at the Irish chit.

"Mary-Kathleen," Amelia said quickly. "This is the Earl of Lismore. My husband."

MaryKate was stunned. Lady Amelia had no husband. Had never had one in all these long years. "I don't understand."

KATHLEEN

"Please, let me help you," Harry said sarcastically. "If I am to assume you work here, then, my girl, you work for *me*. If you live here, you live on *my* property. And at *my* sufferance!"

"The Priory belongs to Lady Amelia—"

"By marriage. And also by my sufferance," Harry said coldly.

Amelia turned away from him, sitting down heavily. As she did, the minister caught her eye, his face full of questions. She looked away.

"We were married ten years ago," Lady Amelia said. "A—a family arrangement. Before I came here. It hadn't occurred to me to mention it—it hadn't seemed—"

"Important?" Harry asked. The butler brought a silver tray in, a crystal brandy decanter and four glasses upon it.

Robert hung back in the doorway to the hall, peering toward Archie, who walked in as bold as brass, beside the butler, enjoying himself. Harry reached for the decanter before the butler could set the tray down and pour.

"I wouldn't mind some, too," Leo said. "Remember me? The forgotten party."

"I'm sorry," Amelia said faintly. "Tea?"

"Who is she?" Harry asked his wife, deliberately ignoring MaryKate.

"She is my companion."

"Not for much longer," Harry said. "We will be leaving for Dublin immediately."

"What are you saying?" Amelia cried out before she remembered the others in the room. "Why?"

Harry ignored the others. "To get us an heir and get home to England. Archie—find out where the blasted hell Robert is and get him to find my rooms and draw me a bath. I'm beginning to stink." Harry saw the flash in MaryKate's eyes and met them with angry ones of his own. "Have a care what you say and do, girl, or you'll be out of here quicker than we are." And with that he left the room.

Leo stood up. "Charmed to have met you, Reverend. And to see you again, Amelia." He turned toward MaryKate. "And—you. Is there someone who can point me to my chambers? I'd best change before dinner, too."

34

KATHLEEN

Amelia motioned to the butler. "You'd best make ready the green suite. And His Lordship's rooms."

"Very good, Your Ladyship." Wallace bowed and left, his face a mask. Leo glanced back once toward MaryKate before he followed.

The Reverend Mr. Grinstead glanced toward MaryKate. "I fear I may have intruded at a bad moment—I hope you will accept my humble apologies."

Lady Amelia tried to force a polite smile as he stood up, reaching to kiss her hand. "Please forgive my—my husband's—rudeness. And his language. It must have been—a tiring trip."

"Of course. Please don't give it a thought. Travel can so deplete one. I only hope you can convince His Lordship to tarry at least a while longer in Cork. All will sorely miss your presence if you are to go. None more so than I." He glanced again at MaryKate. "I don't know how I would have got on when I arrived had you not leant me your aid and support. If your husband finds Ireland to his liking, perhaps he'll wish to stay," the reverend said.

"I have no wish to leave," Amelia spoke faintly.

"Nor shall you have to," MaryKate said defiantly.

The Reverend Grinstead stopped beside MaryKate. "I hope to see you in church, Mary-Kathleen. It would mean so much to Her Ladyship."

"I have my own church," she told him. But her tone was subdued.

"An open mind, child, and a little conversation is all I ask." He bowed slightly and left, leaving Mary-Kathleen to stand across the room from Amelia, the two at last alone.

Amelia sank back on the petit-point chair. "Oh, Mary-Kathleen. What are we to do?"

MaryKate came forward slowly, kneeling beside the woman who had befriended her since childhood. "Why did you never tell anyone you were married?"

"It just . . . never came up." Amelia spoke with a little sob to her words, the back of her hand against her mouth for a moment before she let it fall back into her lap. "In truth, I think I had forgotten myself. It had been so long, I thought he would leave me in peace."

"Why did he not? Why come now, after all these years?" MaryKate asked.

"I don't know. His father wrote . . ." Amelia trailed off.

"You knew he was coming?" MaryKate's surprise showed.

"No! I thought if I didn't agree to come there, they would forget about me again."

MaryKate straightened up, looking toward the tall windows and the Priory grounds beyond. "What will happen to the girls here, to the school?"

"He doesn't know about the school." Amelia could not put her thoughts together. It was too sudden a shock.

"You were married ten years ago and came here. He wasn't with you." MaryKate was trying to understand.

Amelia's eyes filled with tears. "I'm sorry, forgive me, I can't seem to help it. You see, he sent me away."

"How could you marry such a loathsome brute?!" MaryKate blurted out.

"It was arranged between our fathers." She stopped, thinking of the man upstairs, in her house. He was demanding his marital rights and an heir.

"Your father sold you?" MaryKate asked bluntly. "I mean, that's what it is, isn't it? Whatever the English call it with their fancy words. How could your own father do that to you?"

"Fathers just do," Amelia replied. "We were no more than out of the church before I was packed off here." Amelia's tear-stained eyes appealed for understanding. "We never even touched."

"God's eyes!" MaryKate burst out. "Of all the bloody, bad-hearted devils! Just thank you very much for your land and your riches and off you go! Did your parents not object at least to that?!"

Amelia shook her head. "I can't talk about it. About any of it. I think I shall lie down for a bit."

MaryKate stood up. "Of course. I'll sleep in front of your door, if you like. I'll not leave you to the likes of him!"

Amelia leaned against the girl, accepting her strength as they walked out into the hall and up the great stairwell. A small sad smile turned Amelia toward MaryKate as they walked.

KATHLEEN

"At least I never used the master suite." She shivered, thinking about having to walk in there and face him. "I don't know what I shall do," she said faintly.

"You shall fight. And you shall win what you want for yourself," MaryKate told her. "None should live except as they wish. You'll not be forced away if you've no wish to go."

"But how can I fight him?"

"We'll find a way," MaryKate said grimly.

Amelia's hand touched MaryKate's, finding a warm port in a storm-tossed sea. She was still holding it when MaryKate opened the door to Her Ladyship's rooms.

Once they were inside MaryKate closed the heavy oak door and reached for the ancient, rusty key. Turning it, she locked them both inside.

Away from the reckless Englishman who had just invaded Lismore Priory.

4

MORNING BROUGHT PALE SPRING SUNLIGHT to warm the icy Colleycomb River, melting the last vestiges of winter's snow. In the distance white-peaked mountains stood eastern guard beyond the low rolling hills of County Cork.

Inside Lismore Priory the halls felt chill, the household staff staying out of sight. Waiting to see what would happen next, they whispered to themselves, the gossip already passing around the village.

MaryKate woke from a fitful sleep on a pallet in front of Lady Amelia's door. Yawning, she turned over, stretching muscles stiffened by the hard bedding.

Across the room an ornately carved wooden bed filled almost the entire wall. Within it, sitting up and staring out the window at the morning sun, Amelia looked as if she had not slept the whole night long.

MaryKate scrambled to her feet. "Are you all right, my lady?"

Amelia turned listless eyes toward the Irish girl. "What?"

MaryKate bit her lip. "Never mind. How could you be? . . . I'll be getting you some tea and toast."

"I don't want anything."

KATHLEEN

"Something in the belly always helps," MaryKate replied.

"Does it?" Amelia stared at the girl with new eyes. "You've known hunger, haven't you?"

"I've been lucky, my lady. I've been here with you almost as long as I can remember. And I've been able to help my brother's family because of your kindness. But there are many others who went hungry last year when the potato crop failed."

"But all else was fine."

"All?" MaryKate stopped. "Oh, you'll be meaning the other crops?"

"Yes."

"Ah, but the other crops belong to the landlords, my lady. The only crop the poor tenants own is the potato."

Amelia watched the girl. "That must change."

"Aye, it must. It's in the how to change it that the problem lays." MaryKate smiled a little. "You look so tired. Let me bring your tea and then you try to rest." She saw the woman's expression change. "I'll keep him away until you're up to seeing him."

"Will you? Please? Tell him—tell him anything."

MaryKate nodded, reaching for the doorknob and opening the door.

Harry stood there, filling the doorway. He glanced down at MaryKate. "Do you sleep in your clothes?"

The Irish in her flared. He saw her eyes flash, her voice deliberately calm when she replied. "I did last night, Your Lordship."

Harry stared at her. Somehow she managed to say "Your Lordship" so disparagingly that the words sounded insulting.

"You are in my way." His irritation underlined his words.

"Yes. I am." She spoke defiantly, glaring up at the man who stood almost a foot taller and who was glaring back at her. "Her Ladyship is not well."

Harry glanced past MaryKate toward Amelia on the bed beyond. Amelia saw his glance shift and shrank back against her pillows. "Perhaps it's from missing her supper last evening."

"She was already unwell then," MaryKate said tartly.

39

"And is she so unwell she cannot speak for herself?" Harry asked coldly.

"Of course, if you want to force your presence upon a sick person—" MaryKate's defiant stance still barred his way.

He hesitated, MaryKate preparing for him to thrust her aside. Harry saw her stiffen. "I have never forced my presence upon a lady in my life," he told the Irish maid. "My wife can attest to that. Can you not, Amelia?"

"Please, I shall feel better in a little while. This is all so . . . so unsettling."

"For both of us, I assure you. But I *shall* expect you to supper this evening. You have a guest." Harry turned away, walking back down the hall toward the main stairwell.

Amelia watched MaryKate. "Has he left?" she asked faintly, afraid he would reappear around the open door.

"Yes, he has." MaryKate reached for the key. "If you like I'll lock you in."

Amelia hesitated, then softly spoke. "No. It won't be necessary."

Unwillingly, MaryKate left her employer behind the unlocked door and went in search of tea and toast.

Downstairs, the huge cold rooms lay silent, MaryKate's footsteps echoing around her as she hurried toward the kitchens.

Two of Lady Amelia's students were huddled together at the large rough-hewn kitchen table, falling silent when MaryKate walked past them toward the black iron stove.

MaryKate could hear them whispering as she reached for the china teapot on the shelf above the bubbling kettle. She busied herself measuring the tea as the younger girl, Bridget, came up beside her.

"MaryKate, is it leaving we'll have to be?"

"I don't know what you're talking about," MaryKate snapped. "Have you nothing better to do than sit and gossip?"

"MaryKate, that's not fair." The taller girl stood up, "Have you our books ready, then, Bridie?"

"You're just trying to get rid of me so you can talk alone," Bridget accused the older girl. "You're not fooling me. He's

KATHLEEN

come to take her away and we'll all starve, that's what's to happen, isn't it?"

"Bridget O'Malley, no one's going to starve and that's a fact." MaryKate tried to smile. "Now, off with you. Do as Siobhan says or you'll have more to worry about than just starving."

Unwillingly, Bridget left the kitchens. The smell of strong dark tea filled the cold morning air. Siobhan reached to help with the tray MaryKate was preparing as Cook walked in, tying her apron strings tight as she moved.

"And how is it all, then?" Cook asked the girls.

"That's what I'm trying to find out," Siobhan said.

"There's nothing to tell," MaryKate said.

"He wants her to leave. You can't deny that," Siobhan added. "He said it loud enough last afternoon for people in the next county to hear."

"She doesn't want to go," MaryKate replied.

"I can't see how she can stay," Cook said. "I mean, if he wants her gone, then where is she? Gone."

"She doesn't have to go." MaryKate's stubborn little jaw stiffened.

"What choice does she have?" Siobhan asked.

"I don't know," MaryKate replied. "But there's got to be a way. He can't do this to her!"

"And aren't they famous last words, then?" Cook turned away from the girls, reaching for her pots and pans.

The morning hours lengthened toward noon, spring sunshine warming the old stone buildings of the Priory. In the annex, which had once housed noviciate nuns, the large common room was now used as a schoolroom, fifteen young girls seated at the long trestle table that filled the center of the room.

At the head of the table MaryKate led the penmanship class as the girls tried to keep their whispers down to an inaudible background noise. They did not succeed. MaryKate, already irritable, tried to keep the rumors at a minimum, but the girls would not be still.

"MaryKate, you have to tell us what he looks like!" Rose looked for help from the girls to each side, imploring

MaryKate with her eyes. "Please. They say he's ever so big and handsome."

"He's big all right," MaryKate told the girl. "He's as big as the devil, and the devil is what he is if he keeps you all from your work. And me from mine!"

"Ah, but is he handsome, then?" Margaret asked, her eyes wide and round.

"Handsome? Have you ever seen the Englishman that was handsome?" MaryKate asked. "Of course, if you're willing to think that any enemy of your people, of your country, is handsome, then there's nothing I can do about it, is there?"

"But MaryKate, you've always told us that it's not the English to fear but only our own stubbornness. You said there are English that are good as well as Irish!"

MaryKate's cheeks flamed with color as she answered, "Of course there are English who are good and kind. You would not be here if not for the Christian kindness of Lady Amelia."

"Then what are you saying?" Margaret asked.

"I'm saying you should be studying your penmanship and not fretting away over English lords."

"Has he been bad to her, then? Why have we never heard of him? You said she had been here since you were small and you've not seen him, have you?"

"I've seen him now," MaryKate replied. "And what's between them is neither your business nor mine. What *is* our business is whether your lessons are done or not." MaryKate looked around the long refectory table. "Are they?"

Twelve heads of red and reddish brown hair bent to their tasks, quill pens dipped into inkwells and making dark splotches across the sheets of rough paper before them.

Other sounds outside took MaryKate's attention from the scratching pens around her. MaryKate glanced unwillingly toward the nearest window as the sounds of horses and men's deep laughter floated in on the late morning air.

A flash of a dark rider seated upon Lady Amelia's favorite chestnut crossed the courtyard past the window and was gone from view. MaryKate looked back at the girls, only to see Siobhan staring up the length of the table at her. MaryKate looked away, afraid the extent of her animosity toward the man who was Lady Amelia's husband showed in her eyes. She had no right to animosity, nor to ask the English lady to stay on for that matter. If she wanted to go.

But she didn't want to go; MaryKate knew it as well as she knew God was in Heaven and the sun would come up tomorrow. Perhaps now, finally, in this way, she could repay Lady Amelia's kindnesses. How, she wasn't yet sure. But somehow there must be something she could do to prevent his taking her away.

When she looked back up, Siobhan's eyes were still upon her.

A sudden hush deepened the silence in the room, the pens stopping their motions. MaryKate, lost in her own thoughts, didn't notice it immediately. Looking up after a moment she saw fifteen pairs of eyes staring toward the front of the room.

MaryKate turned in the heavy oak chair, looking behind her toward the door. Which was open, the large frame of the Earl of Lismore filling the doorway. The sight oppressed her, as if he were taking up all the air in the room and leaving none for anyone else. She knew it wasn't fair, her irritation growing with the knowledge. Irritated at herself, she wanted to take it out on him.

"I was looking for the countess," he said stiffly, aware of the multitude of Irish eyes gazing toward him.

"As I assume you can see, she is not here, Your Lordship," MaryKate replied, applauding herself for her calm tone of voice. Not hearing what he did: the edge of ridicule that colored the words *Your Lordship*.

He stared at the Irish chit. The girl goaded him past all endurance with her attitude. "I say, you do everything about the place, don't you? Servant, teacher, whatall." His snide tone brought a nervous giggle from Bridie's lips. The girl beside Bridie kicked her under the table to shut her up.

The earl glanced toward the girls and then dismissed them all with his gaze, turning away, the doorway empty. Cool spring air floated in toward MaryKate, who suddenly realized she was still staring after him. She turned back to find fifteen pair of Irish eyes staring up toward her end of the table now, questioning.

"Are you through with your lessons, then?" she asked, staring them down.

5

Night came more swiftly than MaryKate had ever known it to. Lady Amelia had been fretful and vague through the day. The earl retired to his rooms after racing with his friend Leopold. They had ridden the horses hard. Her Ladyship called the stableman up to her rooms, telling him to take special care of her poor darlings, telling him to feed and water them himself after they'd been cooled down.

All the stableman's assurances gave her no peace; she still worried over her horses and found herself slipping into tears at the merest thought of what was to come next.

MaryKate sensed her employer's agitation and tried to bring her thoughts away from the giant brute who had stormed this female citadel and devastated Lady Amelia's peace of mind. But Amelia's distraction would not brook any help; her fear of what was to come overshadowed all else.

"All is lost," Amelia spoke fretfully as MaryKate combed her hair, readying Her Ladyship for dinner. "He will win. Men always do." Tears spilled down her pale cheeks. "Oh, Mary-Kathleen, why do we have to be born female and weak? If I were a man, I would fight him tooth and nail!"

KATHLEEN

MaryKate stopped brushing Amelia's soft curls. "Why not do it now?"

"Now?" Amelia looked vague. "But how? I have no weapons."

"You have all the weapons any could need. He must love you or he would not be here demanding you respond."

"Love me?!" Amelia looked in the mirror, staring at MaryKate behind her. "Love me? He doesn't know the meaning of the word. He is here because the family estates are in jeopardy if there is no heir." Amelia watched MaryKate's expression in the mirror. "Love! We've never even *kissed!*"

MaryKate stared in earnest now, watching the woman who had befriended her when she was still a child. Amelia had offered her a job when none were working and gave and gave gladly to all who needed grain and food.

Amelia looked down at her own shaking hands. "I'm afraid to be alone with him."

"He said he wouldn't force you—" MaryKate began, only to be cut off in midsentence:

"And you *believe* it? He wants to *force* me to his *bed*. To gain a son and heir and then to throw me away again, as he did before. As he's done all the others."

"The others?" MaryKate asked.

"Oh, not for heirs. He'd be cautious about that, never fear. But for his own selfish pleasure. He'd take anyone who was unwise enough to get close. Ask Leo. Or any who know him and his reputation."

MaryKate stared at the mirrored reflection of the woman who had befriended her, her eyes angrier the more she thought about what Amelia was saying. "How could you have married him?" MaryKate burst out, the words escaping her lips before she could stop them. She saw Amelia's expression and softened her tone, feeling the older woman's anguish. "I know your father wanted it, but even so."

"I didn't know," Amelia said simply. "I had no idea what marriage meant. Until—" Her words stopped. "Until . . . then," she finally added. "My hair is fine, Mary-Kathleen. Thank you. But I can't do it. I can't have dinner with them, no matter what he says!"

MaryKate put the brush down on the narrow mahogany

45

dressing table amidst all the crystal pots and enameled eggs filled with powders and jewels. "Then you won't and that's that. I'll bring you a tray."

"Could you stay the night again?" Amelia asked quietly.

"Yes," MaryKate replied, "of course."

Harry did not send up to his wife's suite to ask why she did not appear for dinner. The sounds of Harry's and Leo's revelry filtered up the steps and through the thick walls of the Priory, muffled and indistinct.

Lying on the hard pallet near Lady Amelia's door, MaryKate could feel the draft coming in under the thick oak door, could hear their loud voices, shouting, arguing, laughing, reminding her of her own brothers at the village pub.

MaryKate found herself listening for the various sounds, identifying them one by one; footsteps, argument, laughter, and then the swift sharp crack of billiard balls from the game room off the main hall.

MaryKate did not remember a time it had been used before. Drifting off to sleep she dreamt of English lords who cracked people's heads together to get their attention.

Nothing woke her later. Nothing she could ever remember. Her eyes opened to the sounds of silence within the house. Only the winds hitting against the windows, rattling them behind their heavy drawn drapes, edging her toward consciousness.

She could feel her stiffened back against the hard pallet, nearly as hard as the wood floor beneath it. The bedding was bunched beneath her, her blanket entangled with her nightgown. She sat up, pulling the blanket out from beneath her.

Sleepy-eyed, she glanced across the gloomy room, lit only by the dying embers of the fireplace, seeing the large bed against the far wall. And the tiny figure that rested upon it, one arm flung wide.

Winds hit the windows, rattling the glass, disturbing the drawn drapes nearby. Surprised it was open, MaryKate got up, reaching through the drapes for the sill.

The night air was fresh and cold. MaryKate stood, enveloped by the heavy drapes, shivering. Reaching to latch the window, she glanced down toward the moon-splotched lawn out beyond. Shadows and moonlight played tag across the grassy incline, a black ghost of a figure pacing toward the end of the lawns where the formal English gardens began.

MaryKate stared at the moving figure, trying to focus her eyes, realizing finally that it was the earl, his black riding cape pulled back behind him with the winds. His head down, he paced to the edge of the rose garden and then turned, retracing his steps.

But he did not continue inside. He hesitated and then turned back, retracing his steps from the edge of the lawns to the rose gardens.

Back and forth, over and over, he paced. MaryKate watched him, the moonlight picking out his thick crop of dark hair and then losing it to the shadows, until he paced farther and the moon won out again.

When MaryKate realized she was staring at him, she latched the window, pushed back beyond the drapes, and sank to her narrow pallet. When her eyes closed she could still see him walking.

6

THE SOUNDS OF thick Irish brogues brought Harry fully awake in the large front bedroom. He blinked against the sunlight streaming in the window nearest his bed, yelling for Robert, who slept on a pallet in the sitting room next door.

The sleepy-eyed Robert appeared a few moments later. Opening the door, he scratched at his bare chest.

"What's all that commotion downstairs?" Harry asked. Robert shook his head. "Well, go find out, man!" Harry continued, with an irritability that had not gone away since the moment he arrived in the west country.

He didn't wait for Robert. He stood up, pulling on his trousers before walking to the large oak clothespress. He yanked the door almost off its hinges, staring in at the array of soft cotton shirts hanging neatly beside wool and tweed jackets. He grabbed the nearest white shirt as Robert walked back in.

"Tenants, Your Lordship."

"What do you mean, tenants?"

"The butler says they're here to see . . . the, ah, that girl." Robert dreaded using her name, seeing Harry's brow

KATHLEEN

darken further as he understood. Harry reached for his boots.

"Help me on with these." Harry's expression was grim as he finally finished dressing and headed toward the second-floor hallway and the wide stairs to the main floor.

Leo was halfway down the stairs when he heard Harry's approaching boots and stopped. "Isn't it early for you to be up?" Harry asked.

Leo shrugged. "In town I'd never live it down. But out here the air doesn't seem to agree with sleep. I tossed and turned all night."

"I know the feeling," Harry said grimly.

"You look fit to be tied," Leo responded, walking with Harry into the front hall. Near the huge front door several men waited, swapping stories until they saw the two Englishmen come closer. Their conversation petered out into a dead silence, one of them taking his cap off. Another nudged him, giving him a dirty look.

"What's wrong?" Harry demanded of the strangers.

They kept their silence, staring at him.

"Who's the spokesman here?" Harry asked.

Still there was no answer.

Leo stepped closer to Harry. "Perhaps they don't speak English."

"They bloody well speak English," Harry said. "If you are tenants on this property, one of you at least had better speak up sharply, or I shall consider this disrespect. And I do not tolerate disrespect from my tenants. I am the earl and this is my property."

The men's thick, country boots shifted on the polished floor. One of the men finally spoke up: "It's a duke who's to owning the Priory lands."

"The duke is my father," Harry said impatiently. "What is it you want?"

Another of the men spoke: "I'm Brian Sweeney, Your Lordship. I've come to ask petition for a mite more time, as my rents are due and the crops haven't come in."

"You must make an appointment," Harry said.

"Ah, but that we have, Your Lordship," Sweeney said, smiling ingratiatingly at the English lord.

"Put your cap back on, man," Tom Cullen spoke to

KATHLEEN

Sweeney, his face a mask of rebellion as he stared defiantly at Harry. "There's no need to be groveling when it's only common justice we're after."

"Justice, is it?" Harry stared from one man to the next, gauging them. "All I heard in London was about the crop failure here. And all I saw in Dublin and the entire way across this godforsaken island was field after field of corn and barley. This country is groaning with salable food!"

"Ah, but that's the landlord's crops, Your Reverence," Brian Sweeney said. "It's the poor potato that's ours and that's failed again this year. It looks to be coming up strong and powerful this new season, but it won't be in until midsummer—not enough's so you could notice. All we're asking is a little more time."

"Your rents are due now?" Harry asked.

There was no immediate answer. Leo lounged against the thick stone wall, his head still aching from last night's brandy. "A strange time for rents, isn't it?" he drawled.

"As you'll be finding out anyway," Tom Cullen started, "it might as well be straight between us. MaryKate's already given us a wee space of time."

"MaryKate has given?" Harry asked, his voice becoming deceptively soft.

"With Her Ladyship's permission," Brian Sweeney quickly put in.

Harry glared at the four men. And then singled out the two who had not spoken. "And you're here for the same, I take it? Your names are?"

The younger man looked toward his older brother, who glared back at the tall Englishman before him. Both men were tall, broad-shouldered, and angry. "It's O'Hallion. This here's Patrick David, I'm John Joseph."

It took Harry a moment. And then the names registered. "O'Hallion, is it? And you, of course, are related to MaryKate O'Hallion."

Johnny O'Hallion didn't like the man's usage of Mary-Kate's nickname. "It's Mary-Kathleen O'Hallion who's our sister." He stared straight at the earl.

"Your sister," Harry said. He turned on his heel. "Wait here. *Wallace!*" the Earl of Lismore bellowed the butler's name. Robert, starting down the stairs, heard Harry holler-

KATHLEEN

ing and stopped. He retraced his steps and disappeared back upstairs to avoid Harry's wrath.

Harry strode down the hall, bellowing Wallace's name out again, and the butler arrived at a half trot from behind the green baize door to the kitchens. "You called, Your Lordship?" he spoke quickly.

Harry's each word was distinct and freighted with a tone his servants in London had long since learned was not to be trifled with. "Where is *Kathleen* O'Hallion?!"

"Behind you, Your Lordship." MaryKate's voice poured out icy cold and as quiet as his was over-loud.

He turned on his heel, staring down into defiant green eyes. "I take it you've been helping Her Ladyship with the rents," Harry said, his eyes hard.

"I help Her Ladyship with all that I can," MaryKate replied.

"I'll just bet you do," Harry said as Leo came close behind him, grinning at MaryKate, who paid no attention to the earl's traveling companion. Her eyes never left Harry's own and never lost their defiance.

"Tell your *brothers* and their friends that they shall have to come back tomorrow. I have not yet had the *pleasure* of going over the tenant account books. But I *assure* them, *and you,* that I shall do so immediately after breakfast. Have them ready."

MaryKate stared at the tall Englishman, wanting to snap out at him but forestalled by the look in his eyes. She nodded curtly, turning away from him.

"Do you understand?" Harry asked her back.

She turned to look back toward him. "I understand English, Your Lordship, as you already know. I have gone neither deaf nor stupid overnight."

He started to reply and then stopped. It was beneath him to argue with a chit of a servant girl in front of servants, friends, and tenants. "Leo!" Harry glared at his friend.

"Good grief, what have I done?" Leo spoke lazily, his smile fading as MaryKate passed by him. "I wish you wouldn't shout so in the mornings, Harry. It's a beastly habit when one's not only been sleepless but hung over as well."

KATHLEEN

Harry was already striding toward the dining hall. Leo looked toward the front door and then followed.

At the front door MaryKate stopped beside her brothers, not looking toward Johnny. To the other men she spoke softly. "There's no problem. I'll talk to Her Ladyship and all will be well."

"Oh?" Johnny shook his head impatiently. "And since when does a wife tell her husband how business is to be handled?"

"I shall *handle* it myself," MaryKate told her oldest brother.

Paddy touched her arm. "Johnny's been right all along, MaryKate. You'd best be coming home with us and not staying here."

MaryKate's chin lifted. "The likes of him aren't scaring me, whether they do you men or not!"

"Scared, is it?" Johnny almost laughed at her. "You have a wicked tongue, MaryKate, and always did. But scared is the last thing any of us feel when looking at English dandyboys."

MaryKate heard her brother's voice rise, as if deliberately baiting the men who had walked through a door at the far end of the main entryhall. "There'll be no problem," she told them all.

"You're sure of that?" Brian Sweeney asked.

Tom Cullen looked grim. "I say I'd rather go into hock then ask a favor of the English."

"And just what will you be hocking?" MaryKate asked tartly. "Your wife or your poor children? For there's little else any of you can call your own after last year!"

The silence that met her words brought their meaning home to each of the four men. "There's little choice," Sweeney told the others. "Pride's a costly thing to have, these days. I for one will grovel as much as he likes if it will feed my family until the crops come in."

"We noticed, Brian," Johnny said curtly.

"And we don't need to be fighting amongst ourselves, either," MaryKate told her brother, who started to reply and then turned away, reaching for the door handle.

"There's naught to be done here," he told the others.

"I'll send for you," MaryKate promised.

KATHLEEN

"Don't go promising things you can't deliver, MaryKate. It's an English trait you've picked up." Johnny spoke harshly.

MaryKate bit her tongue, not answering as she watched the men leave. When she turned around she saw Wallace staring at her.

"There's nothing wrong with the record books, is there?" the butler asked.

"No!" she told him. "Of course there's not!"

"Good." Wallace sighed and turned back toward the green baize door that led into the servants' hall and the kitchens. "I can't imagine what he'd be like in a bad mood."

MaryKate grimaced. "I didn't know he had any good ones!"

In the dining room Leo was helping himself to a plateful of eggs and kippers from the covered dishes laid out on the sideboard. Archie walked in from another door, bringing papers with him and then reaching for the dishes.

"There's no hope for getting a London paper. You'll have to make due with the Dublin ones and them five days old at that," Archie said.

"Bloody backward nation!" Harry spoke from between clenched teeth.

"What's happened now, then?" Archie asked with the familiarity of long association.

Leo groaned. "Don't ask or you'll get him started again. Neither my digestion nor my head could stomach it."

"Is your stomach the only thing you ever think of?" Harry asked his friend.

"Don't start on me, now. And no is the answer to your question. As you bloody well know, I think of a great many other things."

"Mainly gambling tables and ladies' skirts," Archie said.

Leo shrugged. "I defy you to tell me more worthwhile occupations for a man of independent means. And you forgot clothing. I am quite noted for my sartorial elegance."

"Stuck on ourself this morning, aren't we?" Archie put in, bringing a pot of scalding hot tea to the table for them.

"One day I shall have to fire you, Archie. You are utterly impossible. What do you think, Harry?"

KATHLEEN

"Hmmm?" Harry looked up from his contemplation of his plate. "What?"

"Good grief, now you don't even listen to me! I shall go immediately back to Dublin."

"Oh, no, you won't."

"What do you think you are doing? Inspecting that plate for answers? Your food's gone cold, and you don't listen to the conversation around you. You must get a grip, old man."

"I'd like to grip that chit's neck," Harry said.

"I can think of other places on her anatomy that I wouldn't mind gripping." Leo grinned at Harry, who looked stonily back. Leo lost his grin. "Oh, all right. Stay in your snit."

"Snit?!" Harry was offended. "I've just found out that I'm probably being robbed blind and you call it a snit?!"

The door to the main hall opened, a pale Lady Amelia standing framed in the doorway. She hesitated when she heard the last of her husband's words. He stared down the length of the table at her.

"I . . ." she faltered. "I didn't mean to intrude—"

"Intrude?" Leo smiled at her, standing, his napkin tucked into his cravat. "How could you possibly?"

"Yes. I have a question for you," Harry added as she started forward and then stopped at his words. "Sit," he said, the word coming out sounding like a command.

She slipped into a chair across from Leo, halfway down the table from Harry. A young girl came timidly through the other door, looking toward the occupants of the table and then toward Archie.

"Come along then and fix your mistress up," Archie said to the girl. She ducked her head and complied, skirting wide around the Englishmen at the table. Archie left the room, taking a slice of oven-toasted bread with him.

"Just exactly what are this MaryKate's duties?" Harry asked his wife.

Amelia's bent head came up a fraction. "Why, whatever has to be done," she replied vaguely.

"And who oversees her tasks?" Harry asked.

"Well, why, that is to say, that, of course, I—"

"In other words, no one does," Harry answered for Amelia. "In other words this household is at the mercy of a chit of a girl whose contempt for everything and everyone English is as apparent as the map of Ireland across that defiant face of hers."

"I think she rather likes me," Leo said. "She's no reason not to."

"Don't flatter yourself," Harry said crisply, still staring down the table at his long-lost wife. "Well? Isn't that rather the color of things?"

"She is totally honest and totally devoted to me," Amelia spoke up for MaryKate, her voice quavering.

"As far as you know," Harry replied. "Well, we shall soon see just how honest and how devoted she is, shan't we?"

Amelia watched her husband's angry eyes. "What's happened?"

"That is exactly what I am determined to find out," Harry replied.

~7~

HARRY'S MOOD HAD NOT lightened by the time breakfast was over and he walked toward the small parlor Amelia told him was used as "MaryKate's" office. Amelia would have accompanied him inside, but he stopped her, telling her since she had not done it before, there was no reason for her to start checking up on the girl now. He would handle it, and they would soon be gone in any event. The girl, however, might be gone sooner.

Amelia watched him walk inside, waiting for a moment by the doorway, almost going near enough to listen and then stepping away as Wallace came down the hall. She nodded to him and quickly walked on past and out toward the schoolrooms and the girls who were waiting for MaryKate to appear.

Harry opened the study door to find MaryKate already waiting for him, large account books spread over the working surface of a small carved desk. He stared at her, gauging her brazenness, and then came forward to sit at the desk and open the first book.

The chair was fragile, his frame looking too big for it.

KATHLEEN

MaryKate started to suggest getting another and then bit the words off. If he crashed to the floor, it would only serve him right.

"This is the most current book," she began, "with the exact state of the current account tallied at the end of each monthly sheet. The books go back to before I started working on them. I can't vouch for accuracy on anything before my time." She spoke crisply, standing almost at attention, ready for his onslaught.

"And how far back do your own accounts go?" Harry asked.

"Five years," she told him.

"That's far enough," Harry replied. "And who kept the books before you so *generously* took over the duty?"

"It was Higgins," MaryKate said. And then at the earl's look: "But then, you don't know who Higgins was, do you?" She spoke with satisfaction, as if re-proving his lack of any rights here. "Higgins was the butler before Wallace. He had been a schoolteacher and did double duty, as I do now," she added. "Wallace wasn't very good in school," she finished, answering before he could ask the next question.

"I see." Harry looked down the open double page at the neat, orderly rows of figures for supplies and wages, crops and rents. "I need pen and paper," he told her.

She moved to get them, arranging them with elaborate precision at his elbow. "Would you rather I waited outside?" she asked, managing to sound both innocent and derisive.

His irritation with her grew. "You may sit over there and keep your peace until I've done."

"You're sure you need no help with the words or the figures?" she asked him, inwardly pleased at the expression that flitted across his eyes.

He found his teeth clenching again. "I assure you, my schooling can at the very least match your own, Miss O'Hallion."

She looked the soul of innocence. "I've heard that English lords don't have to have any schooling. There are so many to take on all the tedious tasks for them."

KATHLEEN

"I am heir to a dukedom. It cannot be run by an incompetent."

"Oh?" He glared at her as she dutifully walked to a chair across the room and settled into it, smoothing her homespun skirt.

His eyes returned to the page.

She watched him work, watched him bend toward the sheets of the account book, writing furiously across the first page of foolscrap she had given him. A lock of thick dark hair spilled down across his forehead. MaryKate told herself he was unkempt. Not the picture of the gentry at all. He was an ungrateful boor and a menace to Lady Amelia's future and her happiness. His clothes looked as if he had simply grabbed them and thrown them on. He had none of the other one's polish. At least Lord Cumberland looked and acted the part of an English lord, even if he was a worse fop than this one.

Time stretched out across the room as the sun's rays stretched across the carpet, lengthening toward noon. And still he worked. MaryKate was fidgeting, unused to sitting idle for hours on end. She started to ask if he needed help and then stopped, wondering if he would think she was trying to distract him from some dastardly deed she'd done. And so she kept her silence a little longer.

Until the sounds of the girls spilling out of the schoolroom and heading toward the kitchens brought her out of her chair. He paid no attention. She moved restlessly toward the window, staring outside and then looking back toward the man who sat bent over the small desk, his size dwarfing the furniture he sat at.

"It's time for luncheon," MaryKate said finally.

He didn't reply. She walked toward the desk, standing in front of it and glaring down at him until he looked up.

"Your figures are accurate," he said grudgingly. "So far," he added.

"And how far back have you gone?" she asked.

"Through this past year and the year before," he told her.

"And are you intending to sit here until morning going over the rest, inch by inch?" she asked pointedly.

"I haven't decided," he told her. And then relented. He sat straighter, his shoulders aching. And then stood, flexing his back a little under the loose cotton shirt. "If you're hungry, you'd best find your lunch."

"Ah, but we Irish are used to going hungry," she told him.

His expression darkened. "Don't start on that. These people have obviously mismanaged if they've found a way to hurt one crop while all else is thriving. Let alone the utter lack of sense in holding to one crop in the first place."

"Lack of sense?!" She stared up into dark eyes that gave no hint of what lay behind them, his impatient tone goading her forward against all better judgment. "I'll not sit by while you slander people you know nothing of!" she told him. "You've never even *seen* this land you call *yours!* It's our sweat and blood that it's soaked with, not yours! You haven't the first idea of what you're even talking about!"

Stung, he found himself close to answering in kind. And then he turned away, silently furious. She watched him leave, watched the door close after him, and then threw herself back into one of the wingchairs that fronted the fragile rosewood desk. "Now you've gone and done it," she told herself, staring at the closed door.

"I want her fired," Harry told Amelia, his voice none too low, as he stood across the empty schoolroom. "And I want you out of the business of helping farm girls get above their station in life."

"I need her," Amelia said. "I'll not let her go until I'm gone myself."

Harry stared into his wife's mutinous eyes. The weight of what he had to do with this woman, of what the rest of his life would be like if she stayed on in London, crashed down upon him. "We don't even know each other," he said out loud.

"No," she agreed.

He hesitated and then left the room, MaryKate passing him on her way inside.

MaryKate didn't speak until she reached Amelia's side. "Are you all right, Your Ladyship?"

"All right?" Amelia almost laughed. "I think I may never be all right again."

Words wouldn't come to MaryKate. She watched the

woman who had befriended her, who had been such a bulwark of strength to the entire valley since she arrived. Sudden tears tried to well up in MaryKate's eyes, and she turned away, determined to keep her composure. "Reverend Grinstead has arrived," was all MaryKate said.

"Oh, dear lord, what will we do?" Amelia asked herself, and then reached for her Bible. "There has to be a way to avert his plans."

"Perhaps the reverend . . ." MaryKate said faintly, holding out little hope that the English minister would do much more than commiserate with them.

Amelia brightened at the thought, a fragile smile in place as she went to greet the cleric.

MaryKate watched her benefactor walk away. Pugs gave out a little sound, standing up on his hind legs once she turned his way. "Begging, is it?" MaryKate said softly, reaching to pet the small dog. And then she stood up, her eyes still on him. "Maybe you're right, Pugs. Maybe we both need a little fresh air."

She picked up her heavy skirts and walked outside toward the lychgate, Pugs at her heels. She opened the gate, starting down stone steps to the fields that stretched away toward the river. Pugs raced ahead once the gate was open, waiting at the bottom for his mistress, his tail awag.

Once on flat ground MaryKate lifted her skirts high and raced fast, as if devils were pursuing her, Pugs loping along ahead and beside.

The heather purpled away across the field, MaryKate's heart racing as madly as her feet. She fell to the ground along the riverbank, gasping for breath and letting Pugs jump into her lap. He licked at her chin and she laughed, hugging him close. "It'll be all right. The Good Lord won't let this happen, Pugs. I just know there's a plan in here somewhere. If only we can find it."

She sat in the sunlit spring afternoon, in the shade of river willows, plucking at the grasses that carpeted the bank beneath her. "There has to be a way."

The sounds of a man's deep-timbered laugh brought her to her feet. She looked behind her, seeing Leo coming down the stone steps ahead of Lady Amelia, holding her hand to ensure her safety as they negotiated the steps MaryKate and

KATHLEEN

Pugs had just left behind. The Reverend Mr. Grinstead descended more sedately, smiling at something Lady Amelia was saying.

MaryKate moved along the riverbank, away from them, as their eyes stayed on the slippery steps. By the time they reached the ground, she had circled around the nearest bend of the river, heading slowly back toward the Priory by way of the east gardens.

Letting herself in the far gate, she held the door open for Pugs and then latched it carefully, dragging out each movement that led back toward her duties. Telling herself she was being remiss and then gloomily asking herself what would it matter if he were going to close down the school in any event.

And then she saw him. He stood on the narrow ledge of a porch that ran the length of the side of the huge building. He was staring down toward the river. MaryKate stood where she was, hearing the distant sound of Lady Amelia's laughter floating up toward her husband.

She looked toward the soft carpet of heather that ended at the riverbank, seeing that the English minister had taken his leave, walking off in the opposite direction from the couple whose laughter carried up the hill toward the old stone buildings.

Far beyond them a white cloud stood above the mountain peaks. MaryKate stared at it uneasily. It had hung there, as dazzling in the sunlight as if made of whitest snow, for days on end. Around it the sky was crystal clear in every direction.

MaryKate turned to go inside. Harry caught a glimpse of movement and turned to stare into her surprised eyes. Pain was written large across his stiffening expression, anger replacing the pain as she kept staring back, unable to break their eye contact.

"Are you spying on me?" he demanded.

Stung, she spoke before she could stop herself. "That looks to be more your field than mine."

The shock of realizing he was being watched, the pain that had not gone away in over a decade, the irritation that this Irish wench provoked every time he saw her, tumbled over each other within him. No one in his life had ever been able

KATHLEEN

to goad him so easily, nor had less right to do so. "This situation is untenable," Harry told the girl.

"I agree," MaryKate replied. "It is also undignified and ungentlemanly."

He found himself still staring at her, incredulous. "Does your mouth never stop?" he demanded. And then he registered her words and said stiffly: "I was referring to your attitudes and your grossly disobedient tongue."

She watched the only English lord she had ever been near, a lifetime of bitter stories at her relatives' knees coloring everything he said. And did. And was. "Ah, it's I that's to blame, then."

Finally he realized he was still staring at her. Good manners decreed he break his gaze, but good manners meant nothing to this Irish heathen, who stared back, as bold as brass. "Are you trying to imply that there is some blame I should be shouldering?" Harry asked, his utter innocence obvious to his own eyes. Before he could stop himself he continued, "And to what undignified and ungentlemanly thing are you referring? Assuming, that is, that you understand the meaning of dignity. Let alone good manners or gentlemanly behavior."

"Well, now, begging your pardon, Your Great Lordship, but even here in the wilds of rebel Cork"—she saw his eyes flash at the words, saw his surprise that she used the epithet that London and Dublin both labeled the western lands with—"here, in rebel Cork," she repeated, "we are not cut off entirely from the English language. Or the English landlords, much as we'd like to be."

"Do you do this deliberately?" Harry asked. "Or is it just me that you are so totally brazen with?"

"Don't flatter yourself. My brothers will tell you I've a tongue inherited from my gram, who stood four feet eleven in her stocking feet and kept five strapping sons and two strapping grandsons in line until the day she died."

"And are all the other grandchildren such as yourself, hard-eyed and sharp-tongued females?"

Hard-eyed stopped her. He saw her reaction, hurt edging into the defiance of the green eyes that braved his wrath and all the English on earth and in hell. Quickly covered over, but he sensed he had hit a nerve. At least she reacted to something human.

"We are what we must be. And we do what we can," she said more quietly. "There are no grandchildren besides my brothers and I. Starvation doesn't breed large families."

"Starvation again! In a country this rich with food!"

"Yes," she agreed. "It's a crime, wouldn't you say?"

"I'd say more than that. It's utter stupidity," Harry replied.

She smiled. "We agree."

He stood watching her, aware that whatever she was saying it did not mean what he was saying. "No one has ever accused me of undignified behavior before. That is, I'm assuming you mean me."

"Is it dignified to force yourself upon a defenseless woman?" MaryKate met his eyes, fear rising within her but determined to do what she could for the woman who had befriended her.

His expression told her nothing. "And ungentlemanly?"

MaryKate tried another approach. "Can you not see how she would feel about all this?"

Harry's eyes hardened. "I have thought of little else since I was sent on this mission. Unfortunately my feelings are beside the point. As are hers. We are married."

"You make that sound like a judgment of doom," MaryKate said with some asperity.

"The best I can wish you is that you never find out," he told her.

"You've left her alone for ten years!" MaryKate burst out.

"Yes. I have," Harry replied. "I'm sorry." He drew himself up to his full height, towering over her, his voice going stone cold. "I'm not in the habit of discussing my life nor my decisions with the household help."

MaryKate reacted as if she'd been slapped, pulling sharply back as he turned on his heel, striding across the porch toward the stableyard. Pugs started to prance around the earl's feet, dancing after the tall man until MaryKate called the dog back to her side.

Reaching down to pick up her small charge, MaryKate told the animal, "He'd as soon kick you as look at you.

You'd best beware or he'll hurt you cruel. Mark my words, Pugs, me boy."

She stood up, still holding the small brown and white dog. As MaryKate walked toward the house, Harry swung up astride the huge black horse he'd ridden from Dublin.

Leo rounded the side of the house, alone, seeing Harry and coming forward. "Want company, old man?"

"No," Harry said curtly, wheeling the huge animal around and heading off down the winding road that led to the bottom of Priory Hill and the village of Beare at the sea's edge.

Leo looked back toward the disappearing figure of MaryKate as she entered a side door and firmly closed it behind. Leo turned back toward the house, striding after her with more alacrity than he usually possessed. He caught up with her in the main hall. "I say, MaryKate—"

She heard Lord Cumberland call out, irritation at his usage of her nickname welling up within her. She blamed it on her dislike of the English, Lady Amelia excepted, and tried to swallow it, turning around toward the man who stopped behind her, smiling. His gaze was too familiar, as if they shared some secret she would not want known, and she stared back at him, her green eyes shooting sparks of warning.

"The earl seemed upset," Leo spoke smoothly. "I was wondering if you might know why." He smiled ingratiatingly. "Or if you'd had some further trouble with him."

She held her temper in check for once in her short life and smiled back at the English fop. Too thin, too rich, and too effete, was her sudden judgment. "Not I, Your Lordship. But the earl did seem a bit upset, didn't he, now? I can't imagine why." She smiled again, her words and her eyes innocent. "He was asking me about household matters and watching the river and Her Ladyship." MaryKate held her laughter at the stricken expression that flitted across Leo's fashionably gaunt face.

"Was he . . ." Leo searched for the proper words. "Had he been there long? Looking at the scenery?"

"Why, I couldn't say, Your Lordship. Would you like me to be asking him?"

"Good grief, no!" Leo told her. "Dear girl, after all, even

out here in the wilds, you must have some idea of the ways of the world."

MaryKate's wide-eyed expression spoke volumes to the jaded Londoner. "I must have what, sir? I mean, Your Lordship?"

Leo inwardly groaned. "Nothing. Nothing at all. But, please, there is nothing to ask the earl. I was merely worried about my friend, you understand?"

"Oh, yes, Your Lordship. I understand."

MaryKate watched Leo move away, heading toward the stairs to change for the afternoon. In that moment she felt the first glimpse of fellow-feeling for the haughty man who had come to disrupt all their lives. The earl might be cold and hard and selfish, but he was not the fop she had first labeled him. Seen next to Leo, he was anything but. Of course, that did not make him likable, she told herself firmly. Merely less odious than the smarmy man whose eyes seemed to undress MaryKate merely by looking at her.

Later she admitted to herself that was not the first moment of sympathy for the big, angry foreigner. The look of pain his eyes had held on the porch was one MaryKate was well familiar with; it may have been for different reasons than her own, but it was not a foreign look. It made its wearer seem almost human.

8

THE MILD, DRY MORNING was followed by heavy afternoon rains, drenching Harry as he rode the black as hard as he could. Thunder and lightning played across the landscape, so out of place from the pleasant sunny hours just past. Harry, cantering into the small village, was chilled to the bone by his wet clothes and the cold air that blew across the narrow coach road.

A small village pub stood near the edge of town. Harry reined in and dismounted. A portly man dressed in cleric's robes squinted into the sudden winds and then came forward toward the stranger who was tethering his horse.

"And would you be from the Priory, then?" the cleric asked, startling Harry.

"What?" His English accent seemed even more clipped than usual. "Yes. Why?"

The portly priest smiled. "And His Lordship, Himself, is it then?"

Harry hesitated. "I am Earl Lismore."

"And I am Brian Ross, Your Lordship. Father Brian Ross to the poor benighted people hereabouts. We welcome you. And envy you such a saint of a wife."

KATHLEEN

Harry kept his opinion to himself, turning toward the pub, the wind whipping his jacket back away from protecting him.

Father Ross bent into the wind, walking along beside toward the pub door. "And what weather the good Lord's been sending lately, isn't it? Hot and cold as a shy maiden's promises." The priest saw the English earl's reaction and smiled a wide, Irish smile. "We have a saying in Ireland. If you don't like the weather, wait an hour, and it'll change."

"Like the people, I dare hope," Harry said caustically.

"Ah, well, now, the people. That's another matter." Father Ross reached the door first and opened it for the big man who ducked to clear the lintel and followed the priest into the snuggery.

Conversation at the rough-hewn bar came to a stop when the two men entered, the patrons and the barman all three looking toward the priest and the man beside him.

"And here's the lord of the manor, as it were," Father Ross told the others. "James-me-boy, a pint of bitters for our betters." Father Ross smiled at Harry, taking the edge off his words. Harry was uncomfortable in his wet clothes and still cold from the winds that continued to howl outside the wattle and daub walls of the pub and the tiny inn to which it was attached.

The men at the bar, still silent, made room for the priest and the newcomer. One had his eyes averted, but the other customer and the barman both stared openly at the English landlord as if seeing ghost or ghoul.

"And it's not taking offense you should be," Father Ross told Harry, "at my familiar speech, I mean. It's just that you've come in the nick of time, and we're that glad."

Harry took the pint of dark beer the barman held toward him, watching the man reach to pull another for the rotund priest. "It's the first I've heard any glad to see me," Harry told the priest truthfully.

"Never!" Father Ross told him roundly. "There's some that don't realize how much we need you here, but they'll come around. Never fear. What's right is right."

Harry stared at the man. "I beg your pardon?"

"Why, coming all the long way from London just to help those that depend upon you. It's a truly Christian and kind thing you do, as I'm sure the Reverend Grinstead has already told you." The priest watched Harry's perplexed expression. "You've come not a moment too soon," the Irishman continued. "And it's not only your tenants that we're hoping you'll be helping, but so many others as well."

Harry put his pint glass down on the rough oak bar. "I don't understand."

"It's this way, Your Lordship." Father Ross hesitated over his words, glancing toward the men at the bar and then motioning Harry toward the far corner of the little pub, where two small tables sat empty. "If you don't mind."

Harry hesitated before following the older man to the table. Once seated the priest came to the point. "There are those who aren't as filled with the milk of human kindness as yourself."

"I beg your pardon!" Harry said, astounded.

"Now, don't go denying it." Brian Ross waved his hand at Harry's dismay. "It's just between us I'm talking, and it's none other that will hear. But, speaking plainly, there are that many English landlords who are absentees, gone most of the time or never here at all, leaving their estates to the worst form of scum hell has ever invented—the estate agent. Not like your lovely countess, who has made her life's work the helping of those less fortunate than herself. A true saint she is." Father Ross lapsed into silence, his expression loving as he looked toward the man who had married such a woman. "And begging your pardon, you must be a saint yourself to let her take on so much so far from home. I can't imagine how you've gotten along without her until now."

Harry kept his silence.

"And you needn't be saying," Father Ross continued. "I can well understand all the duties and obligations you must have in foreign parts, as well as here. Truth be told, we didn't even know she was married. Not a word of complaint has she ever uttered."

Harry looked into the priest's kind eyes, realizing the man was sincere. Harry didn't know how to reply.

Father Ross sensed it and shook his head a little. "But I'll not bother the modest with making them uncomfortable. It's just that I want you to know there's many grateful ones around who will do all they can to help you help those less fortunate than themselves. In any way that they can, myself

KATHLEEN

included. You tell us what you need in the way of brawn or whatever we've got to offer, and it's yours and hers."

Harry downed the last of his bitters. "Help?"

"With the poor starvin' farmers and their babes. And anything else. The reverend, bless him even if he is trying to steal my little flock away, has been feeding three families himself, and the rest of us pitch in where we can. But we need direction and, of course, the wherewithal to be able to buy food to keep the poor alive and seed to get them back on their feet." Brian Ross smiled at Harry. "You've just no way of knowing how glad we are you've come!"

Harry stood up. "I should be getting back before the storm gets worse."

"Ah, and it won't. It'll be clear tonight and bright and sunny tomorrow. Just you wait and see."

Harry stared at the priest. "How can you possibly know that?"

Brian Ross shrugged. "Sure'n it's the blight weather, now, isn't it?"

Before Harry could respond, the door blew open, wind and rain accompanying a burly Irishman whose rain slicker dripped puddles onto the earthen floor of the snuggery. "Well, I'm back, the devil take the—" The man stopped, shaking himself out of the oilskin and seeing the tall man who stood beside the seated priest. Then the man came forward toward the table. "And Brian, who is it you're bringing to my pub?"

Father Ross glanced toward the standing Englishman, looking almost apologetic as he said: "Your Lordship, my brother, Tom Ross, the proprietor of this little inn."

Tom Ross gauged the man before him, looking up toward the tall man's dark eyes. "I've heard tell you met Johnny O'Hallion a mite earlier. He's behind me, seeing to the horses." The man's words seemed more warning to this fellow Irishmen than information, although his eyes never left the Englishman's face.

Harry grimaced. "I've met more than one O'Hallion."

"Ah, and little MaryKate works for you there at the Priory, doesn't she, now?" Brian Ross interjected.

"For the moment," Harry replied cryptically before the door was shoved open again, and Johnny O'Hallion walked

69

inside. He stopped in his tracks, staring at Harry across the length of the room. Then, deliberately ignoring the Englishman, Johnny walked to the bar.

The voices of the men at the bar were a low murmur in the background as Tom Ross still smiled at Harry. "I hope Your Worship comes as often as he likes to my poor establishment."

"Poor, is it?" His brother snorted. "Thomas, leave be. The earl has more important things to do than make you any richer."

Harry put his glass down. Father Ross hurriedly finished his own and stood up. "Anytime—" Tom said, walking them to the door. He reached to open it. "Come anytime at all." Tom beamed, his smile wide until they were gone. Turning back to the men at the bar, he heard Johnny O'Hallion's snigger, "Anytime, Your Worship, anytime at all. . . ."

"Give over, Johnny," Tom came forward. "One day you'll learn a frontal assault isn't the only way to fight."

Johnny's snigger turned into a scowl. "I'll not have it said I bowed down to the likes of them!"

"No, but you'll have it said you were hanged for your stupidity if you're not careful," Tom Ross told him. "You listen to me and the Peelers won't be hauling you off to jail just yet. Nor the rest of you." Tom's glance included the other three men at the bar.

Outside the winds had died down, a steady drizzle of rain graying over the spring afternoon, the sun hidden behind thick dark clouds. Brian Ross bent his head, soaked before they reached the stable overhang. Harry seemed not to notice the rain that beat down upon him, taking his mount from the stableman and swinging up into the saddle.

"Any can point you to the church," Father Ross told him, shivering under the small protection of the leaky stable roof. "Whatever I can do to help, you just let me know, and I'll be doing it."

Harry looked down at the portly little priest. "I'm not even sure I agree with what the countess has been doing to this point," he told the man honestly.

But Brian Ross merely smiled. "Oh, you will, Your Worship. The more you know, the prouder you'll be."

KATHLEEN

Holding his own opinions private, Harry pulled on the reins, leaving the puddled yard and the Romish priest behind, heading back toward the Priory and the troubled lands and people it contained. On the road he met Archie, who wisely kept his questions and his thoughts to himself.

They arrived back to find two carriages just leaving, their occupants hidden within their interiors, closed away from the storm.

"Who were they?" Harry asked Wallace as he walked inside, pulling off his drenched coat.

"Lady Ennis, Your Lordship, has just left. And the Reverend Grinstead."

Harry grimaced. "He's always underfoot. Who is she?"

"I believe her to be a friend of Her Ladyship's and a patron of the school."

Harry's expression clouded over. "The school." He went toward the stairs. "Inform my wife I shall want to talk to her directly I've changed."

But Lady Amelia was within the confines of the second carriage, MaryKate across from her. Beside Amelia, the Right Reverend Mr. Grinstead looked irritated, though he was trying to hide it. "I trust," he began, "you will let me apprise you of some of these issues in privacy, Your Ladyship."

Lady Amelia glanced toward MaryKate. "I'm not sure this is the right time—"

"It is vital. You must," he insisted.

MaryKate tried not to listen, embarrassed by the man's overfamiliarity with her mistress.

"It's raining quite heavily—" Amelia began and stopped. She looked toward the girl. "Please ask the driver to stop."

MaryKate did as she was bid, rapping on the roof of the carriage. The driver opened a small door above MaryKate's head, listening and stopping.

"Mary-Kathleen, if you would not mind sitting with the driver for a little way—"

"Of course, Your Ladyship." She looked up at the driver. "I'm coming up to join you." She closed the small trap door on the driver's surprised expression.

Rain poured down in torrents as MaryKate climbed out and up to join the driver, pulling her cloak over her head as the driver opened a large black umbrella and held it for her until she sat beside him.

"Thank you," MaryKate said, taking the umbrella and holding it over both of them as he reached for the reins, starting out at an easy trot.

"You don't have to hold it for me, miss."

"I'll not get drenched, and I'm certainly not going to hold it over my head while you get poured upon."

He shrugged. "I'm used to it. They want to be alone again, eh?"

MaryKate bristled at his tone. "There's nothing wrong between them!"

"Of course not," the man said.

"They are discussing charitable works!"

"Sure'n they must be."

But Amelia was speaking in low, urgent tones within the carriage, the rain thudding down upon its roof, making Hugh Grinstead lean in to hear her.

"This is a mistake!"

"I can't help it"—he drew her into his arms—"Dearest Amelia, I have to hold you—"

He pressed her close, kissing her lips, which slowly opened, her arms going around his waist as he leaned to kiss the decolletage that rose above the bodice of her yellow satin gown.

He reached for the ribbon that laced the front of her gown closed. "No, Hugh. We can't—"

"Just a little . . . just a few moments . . ." he spoke against the top of her breast, Amelia's eyes closing. She shuddered as he loosened her bodice, pushing her silk chemise aside to expose one pink nipple.

"If they open the trap, they'll see. We can't," Amelia whispered urgently as Hugh Grinstead's lips reached to cover the exposed nipple, pulling on it, teasing it as it hardened.

His hand went to her hemline, reaching beneath the yellow satin dress and the yellow silk of her chemise to the white silk of the lace-edge pantaloons beneath. Amelia's eyes went to the trap door as he reached between her thighs. She let him fondle her through the silk as his mouth exposed the

KATHLEEN

other nipple, teasing it in turn and moving to kiss between her breasts, to bite lightly at first one nipple and then the other.

"Bloody clothing." His voice came from low in his throat. He sat up, straightening his clothes. "We must meet alone!" he said. "You must get away from him for an hour."

Amelia's eyes opened as he moved. Slowly she sat up, reaching to pull her chemise over her breasts, reaching to tie the ribboned bodice closed. "But you've said it would be too dangerous now."

"Not if we're careful," Hugh urged. "Tonight."

"I can't tonight. There's no way—no excuse."

"Yes. You're right. But soon—promise me?"

She watched him. And then smiled. "I'll try, Hugh."

The Reverend Grinstead looked pleased. He reached to kiss her hand. "My dearest, thank you." When he straightened, he continued smoothly, "We'd best get the Irish girl back inside before we come near the Priory."

"Yes, I'm ready." She reached a hand to pat her hair as he tapped on the trap door.

The driver opened it, Hugh looking up at both the driver and MaryKate. "Her Ladyship wishes you to return," he told the girl.

MaryKate nodded as the driver closed the trap and pulled on the reins, stopping again.

"And now it's back to the Priory, right?" he said, grinning. "A nice day for a little outing."

MaryKate bit her lip. The driver held the black umbrella out for her as she climbed down and inside.

"Are you all right, Mary-Kathleen?" Lady Amelia asked.

MaryKate heard anxiousness in her mistress's voice and nodded, taking her seat across from the reverend and Her Ladyship.

At the Priory the reverend took his leave, and MaryKate accompanied Amelia to the countess's rooms. Amelia watched MaryKate in the mirror as MaryKate recombed Her Ladyship's hair, arranging it into tight curls. "Are you quite well?" Amelia asked.

"I'm fine, Your Ladyship," MaryKate said faintly.

"Perhaps it was too wet and cold for you."

"Perhaps."

"If you feel I should not have asked—"

"It's not that! Your Ladyship can ask anything of me, and I would do it. It's just that . . ." She trailed off, unsure how to continue.

"It's just what?" Amelia spoke sharply.

"I worry for you, Your Ladyship."

Amelia took a moment to digest the girl's words. "I don't understand," she replied finally.

"The driver thinks, I mean, people would think, he might talk to others."

Lady Amelia paled. "What did you see?" she demanded. When MaryKate hesitated, Amelia feared the worst and spoke quickly into the silence. "You must never tell anyone what you see!"

"I don't. I mean, I didn't see anything, Your Ladyship."

"Yes, that's what you must say, Mary-Kathleen. You see Hugh and I, the reverend and I, have a very special friendship, but that is no one else's business. *No one* else's. Do you understand me?"

Her heart sinking, MaryKate nodded. "Yes," she said quietly. "I think I do."

"You might see things, but I can rely upon you. Upon your discretion."

"Of course," MaryKate said unhappily.

"Good." Amelia looked relieved.

When Amelia came down to dinner, Harry looked up from his soup. "I fear we did not wait on you, Amelia."

Amelia glanced quickly at Leo and then sat where Robert pulled out her chair at the opposite end from Harry. She thanked him, looking toward her husband. "I want very little; I'm not feeling quite well."

"Still?" He stared down the length of the candle-laden table, his eyebrow raising slightly. "Are you always this unwell? Perhaps the climate here does not suit you."

Leo offered his wineglass to Robert for a refill. "The climate here could drive one mad. Hot and cold, dry and wet, from one moment to the next."

"Amelia?" Harry pursued his subject. "You didn't answer."

KATHLEEN

"I'm usually quite content here," she told him quietly. "Lady Ennis paid a visit today from Enniscomb. Our nearest neighbor," she explained. "She thinks we should host an evening to introduce you to the county."

"Is there anyone worth meeting in this godforsaken hinterland?" Leo smiled at Amelia as he asked.

She spoke quickly, "It would only be proper."

Harry said, "I have no wish to meet anyone, but I have nothing against the plan if you desire it."

Amelia examined Harry's face. "Do you mean it?" She sounded as if she were afraid to hope he did.

He shrugged. "I don't say things I do not mean. But I doubt you can arrange one before we leave."

"But I can! I mean, I would very much like to. When . . . when do you plan on leaving?"

"I don't," Harry told her, earning her startled look. "I plan on *our* leaving as soon as possible."

"Then you are saying I cannot arrange the party."

"I mean what I said. It's entirely up to you, if you're planning on doing it immediately."

She faltered. "It would take a few days' planning."

Wallace came into the dining room with the roast, supervising the carving as Robert and Archie did the duties of footmen with serving plates filled full of steaming potatoes, onions, and carrots.

Harry waited until Wallace had left before he spoke. "How did you spend your day, Leo?"

"I?" Leo took his time. "How can one spend a day in this backwater? I walked a bit and slept a bit and generally got bored with my own company."

Amelia was staring at her plate. She looked up to see Harry's eyes upon her. "I'm quite through. I think I'll retire."

"Of course," he replied mildly, standing up. Leo slowly got up, too, standing until Robert opened the door for Amelia to pass through. "I've told the staff to transfer whatever personal articles you see fit. You might like to advise them," Harry told her. She turned back toward him just before she went through the door.

"I don't understand," she said.

KATHLEEN

"From tonight," Harry replied, "you will share the duke's suite."

She stared at her husband. "Your suite?" she asked faintly.

"Our suite," he told her.

She left the room, Robert closing the door behind her.

Leo watched Harry. "Don't you think this might be a bit premature?"

"Premature? Are you serious?" Harry asked back. And watched his friend shrug and turn back to his port and cheese.

Upstairs Amelia called for MaryKate, twisting her handkerchief between her hands until MaryKate came through the doorway.

Amelia spoke quickly. "I'm to go to his rooms, to take my things."

MaryKate spoke without thought. "But you can't!"

"What choice do I have? I know him. He'll drag me there if need be! And then he'll make me leave Ireland."

"What will we do without you? The school will have to close!"

"Lady Ennis promised she would oversee financial matters, and you could run it. If he will let the Priory be used, at least I shall be remembered for the school."

"And what of the tenants? And the rents that are due? Your Ladyship, you know they cannot be paid until after this year's crop. And he has insisted on seeing them in the morning."

Amelia spoke faintly. "Perhaps he'll let me stay a little longer if he gets his way tonight."

MaryKate felt herself near to tears. "You can't sacrifice yourself for everyone else's benefit!"

"Reverend Grinstead said this afternoon I must do my duty. I am his wife, whether I wish to be or not."

"That's easy enough for him to say!" MaryKate told her employer.

"It's very practical," Amelia said faintly.

Unsmiling, MaryKate stepped nearer. "A little too practical if you ask me."

"There's nothing else he could say," Amelia said.

KATHLEEN

"This is so unfair!"

"We all have crosses to bear," Amelia replied softly.

"That sounds like something your English minister would say," MaryKate told her employer. Amelia searched MaryKate's face. "You do not like Hugh? The reverend?" Amelia amended quickly.

"No, Your Ladyship." MaryKate stared at the woman. "I'm sorry. But no. I don't."

In the ducal chambers later, MaryKate put the last of Amelia's fresh linens in a cedar-lined drawer, closing it and looking around the huge front bedroom.

The bed, on its raised pedestal, dominated the room. Massive, four-postered, and canopied, it was hung with dark red velvet curtains, which were pulled back and tied to the cornerposts. A coverlet of claret velvet lay atop lace-edged, cream-colored satin sheets, falling like spilt wine across a tablecloth.

MaryKate looked up from the bed to see the earl standing in the doorway, watching her. She bent her head, avoiding his eyes, and moved past him toward the hall beyond.

He didn't speak until she was past him. "Where is Lady Amelia?"

"In the changing chamber," MaryKate said faintly.

"Your Lordship." He said the words as she had done ever since he arrived. His exaggerated precision sounded derisive.

"Your Lordship," she repeated faintly, turning and walking swiftly away down the hall toward the stairs to the upper regions of the house.

After watching her go, Harry moved to close the hall door. He stared at the bed as MaryKate had done. Sounds of movement from the small dressing chamber beyond made him reach for his cravat, beginning to pull it off as the door opened and Amelia stepped into the bedroom.

She stopped, seeing her husband with his tie in his hands. She was dressed as a bride. In a pristine white robe and a gown heavy with crocheted lace. She watched his gaze travel down the floor-length robe and then back up to her amber eyes. Her pale blond hair framed her delicate features.

"I'd best undress," he told her, moving toward the dressing room, leaving her alone in the room while he closed the door between them.

A tap at the hall door brought Robert inside, stopping, awkward, to stumble over his words to Amelia. "Does His Lordship need me to help him retire, as usual? Or has he, uh . . ." Robert's words petered away.

"He's in his dressing room," Amelia told the young man, waiting until Robert crossed the room and knocked before she moved to the dressing table that sat between two huge front windows.

Harry's voice bellowed out "Enter!" as she sat down on the tapestried bench, staring at herself in the ornate mirror that hung above the dressing table.

9

The sounds of her long-absent husband and his valet came through the wall as she stared, bemused, at herself in the tall mirror. Out beyond the windows that flanked the mirror, the Irish night was dark and cold, a sliver of moon high up and far off in the inky firmament.

She heard a door close beyond the wall—Robert leaving by the back hall—and after an instant Harry opened the dressing room door, dressed for bed, his robe hanging open to both sides of his long cotton nightgown.

She watched him in the mirror as he came near. He stopped a few feet behind her, looking at her reflection in the mirror.

"Why did you not let me explain?" Her words came out all rushed together, pent up for years on end.

His eyes grew darker as they contemplated her face in the mirror. "What was there to say?"

"There were reasons," she began, only to be cut off.

"Of course there were reasons. There was one reason. You loved him."

"I *did* love him!" she burst out, shocked at herself and the tears that began to spill down her cheeks.

KATHLEEN

"Who was he?" Harry asked in spite of himself and the decade between. In spite of his determination not to bring up the subject, his determination that it was no longer important.

"It's hardly important now." She was trying to contain her tears. "Haven't I been punished long enough?"

"I wasn't aware you'd been punished at all," Harry replied quietly.

"Not punished!" Laughter rose from her throat, as unbidden as the tears. "Sent away in disgrace, never to take my rightful place, never to see any that I loved again!"

"You are about to take your rightful place," Harry told her. "I am unaware of whom you love, so I shall leave that be, but if memory serves, you were not sent away, you wished to be gone. You begged to be released from your marriage vows and allowed to pursue your lover to—where was it? France? Italy? One forgets."

"Am I in France?!" she demanded, her voice rising. "I was told I could retire here or be disinherited, divorced, and disowned by my entire family!"

Harry turned toward the huge, raised bed. Amelia watched him with growing agitation. Turning around on the bench, she faced his back as he disrobed, his ankles and feet bare beneath the edge of his white cotton gown. He carelessly threw his robe across a nearby chair. The silk robe slipped off the chair to the floor as she spoke.

"You could have defended me!" she told him.

"You did not ask for my defense," her husband told her. "You could not bear to look at me, if I remember, let alone ask me for help."

"You had no need to be so cruel!"

Harry stared at her. And then sat down on the bed, swallowing his anger and years-gone hurt. "There are those who would disagree, but in fact, I am not aware that I was."

"You made my family send me here!"

"I did not. I was not informed of where you'd gone until five years ago when my father apprised me that you had decided to seclude yourself and seek redemption."

"Decided!" Amelia laughed out loud, the sound eerie and bitter in the silence that surrounded them. There was nothing to be heard except the wind outside and their own voices, as if none else dwelt in the room upon room of the Priory. "As if I had a choice!"

Harry spoke softly, "And what would have been your choice?"

She stared at him, her eyes huge in the shadowed room. Candlelight from the dressing table behind her backlit her blond curls, firelight from the fireplace across the room flickered across them both, Harry's face half in shadows as he sat, half-turned from the fire, staring at his wife. Wife in name only, he reminded himself.

"You are not answering, Amelia," Harry told her.

"What do you want me to say?" she asked.

"The truth would be unexpected," he said.

She stood up, coming nearer, her voice rising. "You'll never believe me, never trust me, no matter what I say!" She stopped in front of him.

"Deeds are what trust is measured in. Not words."

"I've done nothing but good deeds since I arrived! I've helped the people, I've ministered to the poor, I've trained their wretched children, I've done everything possible to atone for . . ."

"Childhood folly?" he supplied.

She slapped him, the flat of her hand flying toward his left cheek, leaving a burning red welt when she withdrew it, tears falling in earnest. "There's nothing I can do that will ever make it right between us!" she cried. "Why did you come to torture me?"

He rubbed at his cheek, seeing her flinch as he raised his hand. "Words are not the issue between us. Although an apology might go a long way toward reconciling us," he told her.

"I'm *not* sorry!" She spit the words out at him before she could stop herself.

He stared at her, his eyes harder and colder. "I am well aware of that, Amelia."

"Then why are you here?!"

"To get an heir, as I informed you upon arrival," he replied flatly.

"Go to hell!"

He smiled a cold, hard smile, the sight chilling her. "I've already been there. Now we shall both do our duty."

KATHLEEN

"Now?!" Her voice rose higher. *"Never!"*

He stood up, reaching for her as she started to pull away. "I have no wish to make this any more unpleasant for you than it is for me. But I have given my word, and we both have obligations to the titles we bear. Therefore, the word *never"*—his voice hardened—"is beside the point. There is no time in the foreseeable future when we shall be reconciled. Others have overcome such situations and continued their line without incident. When our duty is done and a son and heir is procured, you may do as you wish. I shall not expect you to raise him. I shall not expect you to love him any more than you do me. He will be able to overcome that lack as others have done. But *have* him you shall!"

"Never!" she shrieked at him, his hands tightening around her upper arms. She tried to pull away, wrenching against his grip, screaming in earnest now, her words garbled into cries for help that rose louder and louder.

Harry heard the pounding at the door, ignoring it at first and then barking for whoever to enter.

MaryKate came through the open doorway, her face pale when she saw her mistress screaming and being held by the half-clad Englishman. "What are you doing to her?!" MaryKate hissed the words, coming forward to reach for Amelia.

Harry abruptly let go of his wife. Amelia fell, sobbing, into MaryKate's arms. "Get me away from him! Please, help me, help me get away from here!" Amelia cried against MaryKate, sobbing loudly.

MaryKate's look toward the earl was defiant, as if expecting him to attack her, too. He turned away from them both, reaching for a decanter of brandy on the nearby night table and pouring a large measure into a crystal glass that stood with a twin beside the decanter. Next to the decanter an early rose was wilting forward, its delicate pink petals drooping toward the tabletop.

He did not turn around as MaryKate led the hysterical Amelia back to the rooms she had occupied since she first arrived.

Neither did he see Archie appear in the open doorway, watching the earl's turned back for an instant and then moving away, his nightdress disheveled and half-buttoned.

KATHLEEN

MaryKate's bare feet made no sound on the thick carpeting as she ran back into the front bedroom. He turned more at the sense of someone's presence than at any noise.

The girl was glaring at him, her hands on her hips, her homespun nightgown clinging to breast and hips, flowing loosely over the rest of her slim frame from neckline to ankles. Small pink toes dug into the dark red carpeting beneath her feet as she faced the huge man towering above her. "What can be in your head?!" she asked, incensed at his brutality with her benefactor.

"I beg your pardon?" His icy words would have warned any of his own servants to have a care, but MaryKate stormed on, her eyes emerald in the firelight, her small mouth speaking to him as no one ever had.

"You should beg hers! How *dare* you assault someone as fine and good as she?!"

Harry considered slapping the insolence out of the chit, feeling his own cheek still smarting under Amelia's blow. He turned away from the small shrew whose verbal abuse seemed to know no bounds. Picking up the brandy decanter, he poured himself another healthy dose.

MaryKate watched him down it. "Is it the drink, then, is that the excuse you're hoping for?" she demanded.

"Excuse? Excuse!" He turned round to face her. "How dare you ask these questions?"

"Why? Are they that hard?" MaryKate asked back.

"What is it you bloody well *want?*" he bellowed at her.

MaryKate stood her ground, a bare foot away from the thunderously upset Englishman. "I want to know what *you* want from my mistress!"

The crystal glass he was holding dropped from his hand, spilling golden brandy across the dark-patterned Turkish carpet. MaryKate realized the glass was falling in the same moment that his hands reached out to grab her arms.

"*You* want to know!" he roared. "*This* is what I want!"

Harry pulled the chit toward him, pulling her almost off her feet. Only her toes still touched the carpet as he bent forward, bruising his lips against hers. He forced her closer, his tongue reaching out to force her lips apart. His touch was harsh, his lips, his tongue brutal.

MaryKate's shock at his sudden brutality permeated his

KATHLEEN

overwrought brain, his touch changing, hunger seeping through his pain and anger. MaryKate felt his touch change, something happening to the pit of her stomach, wrenching it, weakening her knees. In her twenty-six years she had never been kissed with such urgency. She had never felt the onrush of emotions that surged through her, bringing her arms to cling against him, feeling the hardness of his body.

"I say, I thought I heard—" Leo's voice from the open hall door pulled Harry toward his senses, his mouth leaving MaryKate's. Her arms felt bereft as his hands left her arms, his body no longer against hers. He turned toward his friend.

"What do you want?" Harry asked Leo sharply, his body at odds with his brain, the night distorted and out of control.

"Nothing, old boy." Leo looked from his old drinking and gambling partner to the serving wench, smiling. "Sorry I intruded."

"Come inside!" Harry commanded, his voice rising.

Leo hesitated and then came forward. "One never wants to be the fifth wheel, old son."

MaryKate saw the look in Leo's eyes, her face blazing crimson. Harry caught her eye, starting to reach for her and then letting his hand drop back to his side. "I must apologize," he said stiffly. "You asked a question. That was the answer."

Both men watched her flee the room, Leo turning back to grin good-naturedly. "I say, that must have been some question."

"The girl tries one past all endurance," Harry said in his own defense.

"Most assuredly," Leo answered smoothly. "But there was no need to send her away on my account."

Harry eyed his childhood friend. "I didn't."

Leo's brow rose, his quizzical expression turning Harry back toward the brandy decanter. Leo watched Harry lift the crystal piece. "It's this changeable weather," Leo was saying. "I don't know how anyone endures it. And the damnable storms that come out of nowhere. It could quite drive one mad."

Harry never poured more brandy. He raised his arm, smashing the glass decanter into the bricks of the fireplace, shards of cut crystal catching the firelight and scattering

KATHLEEN

across the hearth as the liquid puddled across the fireplace apron, runnels of it seeping into the Turkish carpet.

"So there you are," Archie said, coming in from the hall and closing the door. "Is it a party then, or what?"

Leo turned toward the now closed door. "I rather think not. And if I were you I'd beat a hasty retreat before you're the next object hurled into the fireplace."

Harry stood where he was, his eyes on the flames, while Archie motioned Leo on out, waiting until the door closed before he turned back to the tall man whose bleak eyes had not yet acknowledged Archie's presence.

"Well, then," Archie spoke calmly, seemingly unperturbed when Harry finally looked toward him, "should we talk about it or shall we find someone's skull to bash?"

10

Breakfast found a silent, sullen household, as if the strange white cloud that still hovered over the distant mountains had moved to hang over the Priory. The staff was somehow made aware of something amiss between master and mistress by the hidden intelligence system that permeates large establishments. Or more amiss, as Cook told the scullery maids, since nothing had been right between them since the earl arrived. Talk of screams in the night was whispered throughout the day, conversations quickly cut off when Wallace came near, his expression set into a repressive glare.

Lady Amelia breakfasted in her bed, looking fragile and ill, according to her lady's maid, and only nibbling at the dry toast and tea she ordered. Her guest, Lord Cumberland, decided a splitting headache and lack of sleep would keep him within the guest room he inhabited at the back of the second floor. Toast, eggs, kippers, rashers of bacon, strong tea, marmalade, and scones barely managed to keep him comfortable.

MaryKate did not take her breakfast in the kitchen at the long table with the schoolgirls as she usually did. Bridie told the others she had heard MaryKate pacing in the room above hers all night, or as much of the night as she was awake. And MaryKate had been up at dawn, slipping out early.

Archie told Robert to have a care and keep to the earl's rooms if he had any sense. Things had not gone well last night. Archie himself stood in the dining room, the only person to greet Harry when he walked in, bleary-eyed and short-tempered.

Archie served Harry breakfast, watching as the earl tried to eat and then pushed his food away, staring at the table for long moments before rising and striding out toward the stables.

In the shadow of Priory Hill, MaryKate walked the back road that wound past small farmhouses, their thatched roofs and whitewashed walls standing few and far between. A distant sun tried vainly to warm the winds that blew in from the sea toward the lonely figure who bent into the wind, her hands in her pockets, her dog, Pugs, at her side.

MaryKate's feet followed the familiar path, her thoughts all jumbled together and falling over each other. She told herself she was incensed with the brute of a man who had come to disrupt all their lives and force himself upon his unwilling wife.

She told herself she would do anything on earth to help her benefactress, that she owed all she was to Amelia, and none could ever make her disloyal to her obligations.

She told herself she was angry and upset, and all that she told herself was true. But behind the anger and the thoughts of righteous indignation and pious loyalty lurked the image of a tall man with dark hair and hazel eyes that looked black as night in a shadowed, lamplit room.

Her lips felt bruised from the force of his kiss. She could still feel his lips against her own, her breath caught in her throat. Forgetting to breathe with the pressure of his tongue touching her lips and then forcing them apart, the feeling welling back up over her as she walked through the cool spring morning.

She could feel his body straining against the length of her,

KATHLEEN

could feel the strength of his arms as they lifted her off her feet and to his mouth.

She stopped herself, blazing inwardly at the folly, the evil, dangerous folly, of her thoughts. She was no wanton to be carried away by an Englishman's passion. An enemy of her people and her land, a man she had no respect for, a man who would turn from frightening his wife with his passions and then vent them on her servant. MaryKate felt tears welling up behind her eyes. She despised him. She never wanted to see him again.

She would leave Amelia's employ and go back to her brothers' home as she should have done already. Johnny was right, the English aren't to be trusted; she had been a fool and a traitor to fight against what her brothers wanted for her.

Brother wanted for her, she corrected herself. Paddy, bless him, didn't count. He would do as Johnny bid and have nary a thought of his own about it. What Johnny thought was what Paddy thought and always had been.

Johnny, her big, tough Irish brother who knew what was right, wrong, and indifferent about everything. If he knew what the Englishman had done, he would waltz past all comers and grab Harry by the throat and wrestle him down and kill him dead for daring to put a hand on MaryKate.

Harry. Harry was a king's name. MaryKate kicked at a clod of turf beside the dirt path. A bad king, an English king who murdered wives and divorced them.

MaryKate stared at the O'Hallion cottage directly in front of her, surprised she'd reached it so soon. She hesitated, thinking of going in the gate and pouring out her anger and frustration for Sophie's sensible ears to hear.

MaryKate was angry her rebellious mind would do nothing but flit from thought to thought and always back to the giant who had lifted her from her feet and invaded her mouth so harshly she had almost cried out in fear and pain.

Until something had liquefied within her at his touch; his touch that had gentled and become more insistent all at the same time. Her thoughts skipped to Her Ladyship in those selfsame arms, kissed by those same lips, and she shuddered. Why would she not want to be held by him, how

KATHLEEN

could she have left him—Reverend Grinstead's image crowded into her thoughts.

She couldn't imagine him kissing someone. Lady Amelia hadn't said he did, but she had been upset at the driver's words, had sworn MaryKate to secrecy.

Stop it, stop it, stop it, she railed at herself, turning around on the path and beginning to run. Picking up her skirts, she flew as fast as bare feet would go down the narrow dirt path, running from the cottage and the Priory and her own evil, wanton body that would not let go of the man who had grabbed her close and turned her inside out.

Pugs barked behind her, caught unawares by her sudden race.

She ran until, out of breath, a stitch in her side bent her double. She reached to press in on the stitch with her two hands. She took deep breaths, refusing to think, refusing to think about anything or anybody. She willed her mind to go blank and stay that way until she had it under control again.

Movement caught the corner of her eye. She straightened to see the black horse streaking across a distant field of heather, its rider urging it faster. He didn't see her, didn't look to the right or left. Horse and rider flew toward distant, purpled hills and the strange white cloud that sparkled in the late spring sunlight.

Her heart rose to her throat and hammered at the inside of her skin, trying to get out. Sweet mother of God, she cried inwardly, sinking to her knees in the soft loam of the recently tilled field, her head bowing, her eyes closing tight. Don't let me feel this, take it away and give me back my sanity.

Pugs came near, licking at her tear-wet cheek.

It was a long time before she stood up, walking with resolute step back toward her duties and her obligation to the woman who had befriended her.

MaryKate got through the day and the next one after and the next, moving determinedly from schoolroom to Lady Amelia's chambers.

Her Ladyship took to eating all her meals in her own sitting room, going forward with the dinner party she and

KATHLEEN

Lady Ennis had agreed upon, issuing instructions for MaryKate to carry out.

Amelia asked MaryKate to eat with her on the second day and to set up a cot in the sitting room this time, to be near in the night.

MaryKate did as Amelia bid, staying with her all the hours MaryKate did not teach, using the back stairs, the servants' stairs, to run between the great hall and the upper floors.

She did not see the earl, and ran into Lord Cumberland only once. Her cheeks flamed as he sketched a bow in her direction. She had two of the schoolgirls with her, their arms full of sewing and lacework. When MaryKate snapped at them to hurry along, the girls looked shocked.

Bridie teased her. "Since when did the nobility bow to Irish girls?" But MaryKate's sharp retort caused the girl to stare openly at her teacher. "You don't have to bite my head off! I was only joking."

"The English aren't to be joked about!" MaryKate told Bridie, Siobhan watching wide-eyed.

"I thought you liked the English." Siobhan spoke softly, glancing down the hall they had turned into to make sure no English were about to hear her.

But MaryKate did not reply.

Archie seemed to hang in the back halls each day, MaryKate nearly stumbling over him day after day. She listened to whatever questions His Lordship sent via Archie to Her Ladyship, her replies forwarded back to His Lordship via Archie.

She told herself she was not avoiding him. Was not avoiding anyone. She was simply doing what she must, and life was going on as usual.

But the nights came all too soon. In her cot near the sitting room door, she could hear the sounds from the billiard room, could hear cues striking the ivory balls, and the distant sounds of male laughter.

She would fall asleep to the sounds of his laughter and an occasional word, too far away to be heard properly. Only the deep tone of his voice rising toward the second floor sitting room and MaryKate's ears. Unwilling ears, she told herself over and over. Unwilling to admit she strained to hear more. She avoided the sight of him, longed for the sound of him, and told herself she did neither.

The day of the party dawned stormy and dark, the winds rising early to blow about the huge stone walls, hurling themselves at the hundreds and hundreds of windows.

Two of the schoolgirls were called to the side parlor before breakfast, two sisters whose father had come to take them home. Lady Amelia stood with the farmer who twisted his cap in his hands as he tried to talk with the English swell.

His land was in County Clare, where the blight had hit again this spring, potatoes rotting in the fields. His wife had come down with a birthing fever and the girls were needed at home to help with the other three children and work in the fields. If they could get enough spuds out of the ground soon enough, they might be able to salvage some of their crop. The blight seemed to seep up from the very soil itself, rotting shoots that had been green and growing.

"What can be done?" Lady Amelia asked MaryKate after the man and his daughters left. "What can be done to help?"

MaryKate shook her head. "None know. And for some there'll be no help if the crops fail again. Thank God it seems we're to be spared this year."

Wallace interrupted them, the house alive with servants, all the students helping ready guest rooms for those who would come early and stay over, the distances too far and the weather too wet to attempt the night hours.

"Lord Cumberland wishes to know at what hour the guests will be arriving, Your Ladyship, so as to be ready."

Amelia glanced toward MaryKate. "It seems at least someone is concerned about propriety." There was an edge to her voice that unnerved MaryKate until Her Ladyship continued to Wallace, "Did the earl say when he would be back?"

"No, Your Ladyship."

"Or where he was off to so early?"

Wallace hesitated. "I believe his man Robert mentioned trout, Your Ladyship."

"Fishing." Amelia turned away, reaching for her keys. To MaryKate she said, "We'll check the guest linens next, I think." MaryKate followed Amelia out into the hall, Amelia silent until they had left Wallace behind on the lower floor. "I have impressed upon Lady Ennis how important it is that she and Lord Ennis help convince the earl that I am needed here." She lowered her voice: "He will grow tired of this situation, and being used to London society, he will not stay past a certain point. If he knows all expect me to stay and that I shall have nothing to do with him whatever he attempts, there will be no reason for him to stay. Our lives can then go on as they were."

"I hope so." MaryKate's words sounded like a prayer.

"He will not stay where he is not wanted. His pride is too great," Lady Amelia continued. "He has never stayed the course on any point of action before. Everything will work out if I can delay our departure until he grows tired of this charade."

Lamps and candles were lit early, the afternoon dark with rain and clouds but strangely humid. On its sentinel hill, the Priory stood tall, a lighted beacon in the gloom, awaiting its guests.

From stable to upper attic all was ready for the gentry who began arriving by midday, retiring to their guest rooms to rest and then ready themselves for the evening ahead.

Downstairs in the public rooms Leo acted the host to early arrivals who came looking for a drink or a quiet smoke before the ladies descended.

Musicians were setting up in the long gallery, the sounds of their tuning strings rising over the men's conversations and mixing with the smells of meat and fowl and vegetables being readied in the kitchens and laid on to huge serving tables in the main dining hall. Vast platters piled high with sugared pastries and desserts sat in the pantry, awaiting hands to carry them to the tables, skullery maids scurrying to ready more platters and plates.

In the kitchen Cook stood over the Sylvester Apparatus, Lady Amelia's newest acquisition. It was a huge intricate cooker with the bottom of the side oven open to the fire. Within it more meat was cooking, smoke rising from the grate toward Cook's perspiring brow.

An enormous brown-painted dresser held shelves and cup hooks and drawers and cupboards filled with the paraphernalia of cooking for the huge establishment. Pots, pans, lids, small mops, and jugs stood upon or hung from open wooden shelves that filled the recess made by the chimney breast.

A fat wooden towel rail held a roller towel above the sink. An iron gas chandelier hung above the large, scrubbed kitchen table that was filled with sauces, breads, condiments, and savories, awaiting their turn to be served.

And around all the equipment maids and footmen moved, following instructions from Cook and Wallace.

In the front of the house the doors between the long gallery and the dining hall were thrown wide open onto the ballroom, footmen moving between, readying glass and silverware, carrying in the punch.

Sconces ablaze with white candles lit the ballroom with showers of flickering lights, silver candelabrum branching out across the serving and side tables with more white tapers illuminating crystal and silver and porcelain serving dishes.

A festive atmosphere began to permeate the household, covering over the anxieties that had filled the staff since the earl had announced himself at the door and turned the household upside down.

The guest-filled rooms gave a warmth to the ancient building that was from more than all the fires in all the grates. Human conversation and laughter spilled out into the halls and down the huge stairwells, the house ringing with life and the sounds of enjoyment.

MaryKate escaped it all. Putting the sounds of the pouring rain and occasional thunder between herself and the party, she puttered about the annex's large main room, picking up the girls' Bibles and hornbooks, straightening papers and chairs, dusting off the shelves filled with ancient books and newer acquisitions.

Archie found her there finally, dripping as he came inside, shaking off his wet hair and jacket as a dog shakes his fur. "It's no wonder the Irish are such a moody people with weather like this to contend with."

His first words turned her toward him. Hands on hips, arms akimbo, she glared at the Welshman. "And just who are the likes of you to be talking, then?"

He paid no attention to her contentious tone, smiling back

as innocent as a babe in arms. "The countess is looking for you to get ready for the dinner dance."

MaryKate stared at the man. "What are you saying?"

Archie grinned at the girl. "Her Ladyship wants you to accompany her to the party."

"I?" MaryKate's disbelief showed. "I don't understand. I can't."

"And can you not do your duty?" Archie asked back.

"I'm not expected at the party."

"You'd best talk to your mistress, then, for she's planning on your being there."

"I haven't anything to wear."

Archie shrugged, more drips of water spilling to the stone floor beneath their feet. "She's looking high and low for you."

It wasn't until she had pulled her cape over her head and dashed across the side yard, wasn't until she was inside the Priory and heading up the back stairs for Her Ladyship's rooms, that she wondered how it was that Archie found her. Or why he would volunteer to even look.

Amelia, beside herself with nervousness, was uninterested in MaryKate's excuses. "There is nothing to be discussed. Surely you can see you must accompany me. If we are to keep the school open and if, God forbid, I must leave, then you are the only one to oversee it. They must see you, must know you are capable. Besides, I need you there. We are friends, aren't we?"

MaryKate swallowed, nodding mutely.

"Then as one friend to another—I need you there. This will be a trial for me at best, as only you can truly know. None else know how he forces himself upon me, or what our situation truly is. I must appear normal, and you must help me maintain appearances. Promise me you'll help me."

"There's no need to even ask," MaryKate replied quietly. "I would do anything I could for you."

"Then accompany me tonight."

"Your Ladyship, truly, I cannot appear as I am. And I have no finery. You would not want to be ashamed of me. It would be better if I kept to my rooms. I can meet whoever you feel I need to another time."

"What other time?" Amelia asked. "I have clothing I

never wear, finery, as you call it, that's been in closets since I arrived. Some of it will no longer fit me but should fit you." Amelia looked the girl up and down. "It's hard to tell in those clothes, but I think you to be as small as I once was. Call Betty to help us, and tell her to bring needle and thread. We shall see what can be done." Amelia sounded almost fretful. "I have tried to find you all afternoon so as not to leave this all so late. You must accompany me down. I shan't live through this alone."

All afternoon MaryKate stepped out of one gown and into another, Her Ladyship and Betty both deciding this one was too low cut, this one much too old-fashioned, this one the wrong cut, color, design, fabric.

And finally, in a pier glass in the middle of the countess's bedroom, MaryKate saw herself in emerald satin, full puffed sleeves narrowing at the elbow to slim ribbons of ruched ivory lace that descended to her wrists.

Ivory lace overlaid the bodice, and silk ribbons floated over the satin overskirts in the same emerald green hue.

"You look positively beautiful," Betty breathed, staring into the mirror beside MaryKate. "A princess in a story."

Lady Amelia looked MaryKate up and down. "Very nice," she pronounced. "Now there's nothing you can say about not being dressed."

"Ah," Betty interjected, "but her hair, Your Ladyship."

Amelia looked into the mirror, seeing MaryKate's reflection. "Yes. It should be up, at least."

"It's fine the way it is," MaryKate protested.

"It's not and well you know it," Betty told her roundly. "But it will be once I've put a curling iron to it."

"It'll take too long to heat," Lady Amelia told her maid.

"I've already put it over the coals," Betty replied, "in case you were needing it," she added at the countess's expression.

MaryKate accepted Betty's ministrations with bad grace, feeling out of place and foolish. A small knot of anticipation twisted within her stomach, a feeling she was hard put to explain to herself.

* * *

KATHLEEN

The sounds of guests descending to the main rooms, of music welling up from the long gallery, of laughter and noise and pleased greetings and friendly male argument filtered through the halls, faint as they reached up to the attic room where, finally alone for a moment, MaryKate stared at herself in the small looking glass that had been hung long years before MaryKate arrived.

The narrow bed she slept in stood along the wall nearest the window so that on kind nights she could look out and see the starry moonlit night before she fell asleep. She had pulled it round to where it was, pushing the much battered clothespress back against the far wall, with an old Regency tripod washbasin and ewer next to it. A chair and chamber pot were the only other accessories aside from the picture of the Holy Virgin MaryKate had tacked to the wall of this English Protestant household.

None ever came to her room, MaryKate doing her own cleaning, so none knew of her silent defection. One small oval rag rug covered the scrubbed wood floor near the bed, a calico curtain hung on rings across the solitary window, as clean as clean could make it. Her few clothes hung in the press, one small chest of drawers holding her underclothing and shawls.

In this stark chamber twenty-six-year-old MaryKate stared at herself in the cracked looking glass. The girl, who had been raised in a cottage with turf fires smoking the small main room, stared at the English finery, emerald-green satin falling from ivory Irish shoulders, the rest of the dress lost from view in the tiny, narrow looking glass.

She had never seen herself in such clothing, nor had she been to a ball. And he would be there. He would see her like this. The thought of him brought back all the emotions that had given her such unrest since the night he had kissed her. Ever since her dreams had been filled with the feeling of lips crushing hers. His lips crushing hers. Harry. Inwardly, she repeated his name, all the while feeling like a traitor to people, to country, and even to benefactor.

Harry's lips. She must never call out his name, and he must never know what he had made her feel. She was a servant in this household and she was Irish to boot. He was an Englishman, a lord at that, an earl, and one day to be an

English duke. Lord of all he surveyed and careful of nothing but himself and his own. He would take advantage of her, she would be ruined, and he would never suffer nor care.

Her brain worked feverishly to remind her of the reality of her situation, of the direness of her plight. She could not allow herself to feel anything for this man who was her mistress's enemy as well as her mistress's husband.

She did not feel anything. She would confess her sinfulness on Sunday next, and the Good Lord would absolve her of all this, would end her dreams and her misery.

But in the meantime, in her secret heart of hearts, she could dream a little. Her whole life had been built on dreams. Dreams she knew would never come true, could never come true. Dreams weren't for the likes of her.

In the cold morning light they always faded back into what they really were. Chimeras as distant as desert oases.

But in the wee dark hours they filled the bare attic room and warmed her heart.

11

THE PARTY WAS IN FULL SWING when MaryKate descended the stairs toward Amelia's rooms. Amelia was waiting impatiently for her companion and none too ready to hear her excuses for being late.

"I realize this is unlikely for you and that you are uncomfortable, but consider, please, myself, and your obligations. After all, I am doing all this for your people, not my own."

MaryKate heard the words, apologized, and followed the countess down the long, wide stairs to the public rooms below.

Leo was the first person MaryKate saw, walking toward her and smiling at the countess. He spoke of their late arrival and how well worth waiting for they were. His polite smile took on a tinge of familiarity when his eyes rested on MaryKate.

Lord and Lady Ennis were nearby, Leo already in Lord Ennis's good books, having proved himself at afternoon billiards.

"And where is this reclusive husband of yours that none have seen?" Lord Ennis asked good-naturedly.

KATHLEEN

"Isn't he down yet?" Amelia asked, smiling, determined to put on a good face.

"Not that we've seen," Leo responded affably.

"I'm sure he will be down momentarily," Amelia said, relaxing visibly as she walked forward, introducing MaryKate to the many English the Irish girl had never met. "My helper, MaryKate," Amelia told those who'd never before seen the girl.

Lady Ennis had met MaryKate before and was the first, and not the last, to gaze with surprised eyes at the Irish lass in the fancy green dress. "I've never seen you so pretty," Lady Ennis told MaryKate graciously, earning a small, uncertain smile from the young woman, who did not feel pretty. She felt out of place, a fish out of water, and unsure what was expected of her.

There was a stir behind them and suddenly the room was too small. He walked in behind her. MaryKate did not have to turn around to know he was there. She could have told without the curiosity that filled the room with undercurrents of eddying whispers, surrounding her with his name. She moved away from the small knot of English nobility at the door, feeling suffocated by his presence.

The conversations around her were full of crops and last year's failure and the peculiar weather that had descended upon the island nation.

"May I have the pleasure of this dance?" A familiar voice spoke from behind MaryKate. She turned, looking up into Leo's smiling countenance. Before she could speak he reached for her, pulling her toward the dancers in the middle of the floor.

"I don't know how," she told him, feeling awkward and unsure.

"Then I'll teach you," he replied, still smiling. He led her toward well-dressed women who moved with knowing precision to the music, their escorts effortlessly leading them across the floor.

MaryKate unwillingly let the Englishman lead her toward the dancers, who moved across the floor in strict cadences, MaryKate more and more unsure. When they were almost to the dance floor she stopped short.

"I can't." She sounded desperate.

KATHLEEN

"Of course you can," Leo told her. "There's nothing to it."

MaryKate looked up into the leering face of the English dandy who seemed to smile and belittle her all at the same time. She backed away from him, Leo following her from the floor. "I assure you, I can be the most sincere of lovers," Leo told her.

MaryKate stared at the Englishman, words fleeing from her grasp.

"Mary-Kathleen," Amelia spoke nearby, turning MaryKate away from the man whose eyes glowed with a knowledge he thought he shared with her. "I was telling Lady Ennis of our plans for an additional schoolroom." Amelia sounded desperate.

But Lady Ennis was turned toward Harry, smiling and insisting he must not waste his time talking to her when his wife awaited his pleasure.

Harry smiled politely, looking toward Amelia, who pretended not to hear. "Amelia, dear," Lady Ennis continued, "I know this husband of yours wants nothing more than to dance with you."

Harry bowed slightly toward his wife, Amelia shrinking back as if he would attack her. "I don't dance—I mean I can't—I haven't felt well." Amelia's gaze went from Harry to MaryKate. She pushed the girl toward Harry.

MaryKate's cheeks burned as she was thrust forward. "She doesn't dance, either, Amelia," Leo said, smiling. "What can you be teaching these poor dears if they don't even learn a simple dance step or two?"

Harry stared down at MaryKate, his expression unreadable. She saw his hand move to take her arm. She stepped backward involuntarily. Harry reached across the space between them to touch her arm. His fingers closed around her wrist. She stared into his eyes, letting him lead her toward the dance floor.

Behind them, Amelia looked relieved. Leo looked amused.

"I can't dance," MaryKate spoke over the lump that was filling her constricted throat.

"I, on the other hand, have ample experience and have

100

been told I am an adept. If the ladies have not lied, you should be able to follow me with ease."

"What?" MaryKate only half heard him, knowing something was terribly wrong inside her. Now her ears were near to bursting, something within her head roaring loud enough to make the sounds around her recede into the distance.

"Follow me," he said again. They were on the floor, and he reached for her other hand, turning her toward him and hesitating for one instant, his eyes not leaving hers.

He began to move, MaryKate lost beyond thought, frightened. Feeling ill and terribly visible, she waited to make a fool of herself, for the people surrounding her to laugh.

The music began to rise above the inner roar in her ears, his hands moving her surely across the dance floor, their bodies moving in unison to a beat that began to hammer within MaryKate's breast.

"I thought you gone." His voice sounded strangely choked.

"Gone?" she spoke the word and stopped.

"You had ample reason to leave my employ."

His hands directed her gently, surely, her body melting into the music as it had into his arms. She looked up at the lips that had crushed hers.

"What's wrong?" he asked. "You're trembling."

"I—I feel faint . . ."

His eyes bored into hers, asking questions his lips didn't echo. "Do you need some air?" was all he asked.

They were near wide terrace doors that opened onto the long side porch.

"I say, old man—are you going out?" Leo appeared at the edge of the dancers near the doors as Harry led MaryKate off the floor.

Harry's voice was neutral. "MaryKate felt faint."

"But she fibs about not dancing, does she not? She looks to have had practice, I'll warrant."

"Or I'm a very good teacher," Harry said mildly.

"Oh, we know you're that, don't we, old boy?" Leo smiled. "If you're still feeling faint, I can escort you, MaryKate—the countess is looking to introduce her husband to a late arrival. Imagine someone coming out in this beastly weather at this hour. They must really want to meet you, Harry, old chap."

"I'll be fine," MaryKate told them both as Harry looked deep into her eyes and then offered his arm to her, escorting her back to where Amelia and the Ennises still stood.

Leo walked along beside. "I must say you bring out the best as well as the worst in my poor friend, dear MaryKate. I can't remember when I've seen him this attentive, except perhaps to the queen herself."

MaryKate's cheeks burned, fires raging within her, coloring her pale skin in the soft candlelight. "Thank you," she managed to say when they at last stood beside the others. Leo moved closer, standing too close beside her.

Amelia glanced at MaryKate. "Are you quite well?"

"No, Your Ladyship. I think I'd best retire."

Amelia nodded, feeling more sure of herself now, surrounded by guests who would stay the night.

MaryKate moved to escape, Leo blocking her path. "Allow me to escort you, my dear."

"Leo," Harry called to Leo, turning his friend around, "if you please . . ."

With less than good grace, Leo turned toward Harry. MaryKate escaped the room, willing herself to walk sedately until she reached the green baise door to the back halls and then racing down the servants' halls and up the back stairs to the safety of her attic room.

In the ballroom Harry responded politely to questions and conversation, leaning in finally to speak privately with Leo. "I know you, Leo. Let her alone."

"Spoken-for property, old chap?" Leo's brow lifted.

"You've made a mistake about her. Entirely my fault. She's not what you think."

Leo's brow rose farther. "And this from Handsome Harry, the ladies' lament? Dear heart, since when did you bother to protect a lady's reputation from me? Let alone a serving wench's."

Harry's eyes bored into his friend's. "I am entirely serious. She does not deserve this conversation, and if your attitude continues I will be forced to apologize to her in your presence. A situation I would rather not be forced into."

"Good grief, leave off," Leo said. "She's pure as the

KATHLEEN

driven snow, all right?" Harry was already turning away when Leo added, "But she isn't a child, after all. I mean, she's not seventeen. Country girls grow up early." When Harry looked back, Leo grinned. "Has to do with milking the cows or something, I presume."

"Let her alone."

Leo watched Harry move away through the crowded room. Harry wasn't acting like himself at all. Leo looked around and then moved toward Amelia's side, insisting she feel better and give him a dance.

She looked about for Harry. Not seeing him, she allowed herself to be persuaded.

Upstairs, high above the continuing party, MaryKate pulled the English finery off, reaching to unpin her long hair, letting curls fall down across her neck and back. She stood with jug and cold water, bathing her burning face in the icy nightstand water, not even bothering to light the log in the tiny fireplace grate.

Her eyes closed, but sleep was not about to come easily. Long hours later she tossed and turned on her narrow bed, moonlight flooding the bare attic room with a cold white glow. Pugs, tired of her upsetting his sleep, jumped off the bed to the floor beneath it.

Wakeful long after the party sounds were gone, the others fast in their beds, MaryKate stood up, shivering, pulled her blanket around her shoulders as she went to the window to pull the curtain closed against the full moon.

She paced her room for what seemed like hours and then quickly dressed, determined to tire herself enough to sleep. Pugs opened sleepy eyes and then decided to ignore his mistress's aberrations, going back to sleep near the cold fireplace.

The house was silent as she slipped outside beyond the garden gate to the river below. The night was quiet, only small sounds of the river and field mice interrupting the silence surrounding her.

She followed the river past the sharp bends, walking alongside the riverbank toward the distant hills, her eyes on the ground, her hands stuffed deep into the pockets of her brother Patrick's old jacket.

KATHLEEN

Far across the heathered fields in front of her were the ruins of an ancient Druid fort. The little people were said still to dwell in the tiny, mostly underground rooms made from stones worn round by centuries of rain and sun.

It was in the ruins that she finally halted her pace. Tired, she sank to a stone mound.

"I see sleep eludes you too."

MaryKate looked up to see Harry standing in front of her. Her pounding heart stammered in her chest. "You frightened me!"

"I'm sorry."

"I thought you little folk!"

"Hardly that," the large man replied, smiling a little. The shadowy light played across them, winking between the branches of the ancient oaks that surrounded the ruins.

"Somehow I imagined nothing could ever frighten you." He hesitated and then began again. "Actually, I visited this place riding the other day." At his words she remembered his racing the black giant of a horse across the meadows the morning after—the morning after. She stopped the thought, looking away from him. "I saw you running as if pursued. And I was afraid you might have been."

"Pursued?" she asked quietly.

"Yes." He stood where he was, two feet away from her.

"Only by you," she told him.

"Yes. Well, then you're in no danger."

"Am I not?" she asked softly, staring up at him with frightened eyes.

He saw the fear in her eyes, frowning at the sight, coming closer. "Do you think that, truly? I am not a complete cad."

"No." MaryKate shook her head. "I know."

He hesitated. And then moved to sit across from the rock mound she occupied. "I have had a talk with Lord Cumberland. He has been put to rights about what he—thought—he saw . . . that night."

MaryKate felt her cheeks burning with sudden heat again. "Please. I don't want to talk about it."

"Of course. I merely wish to say that I have corrected his assumptions and that further you have nothing to fear from me. Nothing of the like will ever happen again. I assure you."

KATHLEEN

A strange sadness crept over her embarrassment. She looked toward him, her eyes unreadable in the shadows. He strained to see them better, looking into them as if trying to see into her soul. She found herself staring back at him, their gazes locking. Neither looked away. Both refused to think.

"I think we'd best be back," Harry told her quietly.

She nodded and then stood up, walking beside him back through purple heather. In nearby fields lush green stalks shot up out of the dark loam of the potato fields, healthy and thick with promise.

12

Morning brought a vast and terrible stillness, the air hanging heavy and warm over the countryside. There wasn't even a whisper of wind. As the sun rose higher the white cloud finally began to move away from the distant mountains. Lazily it spread out across the sky. It lost its form, dissipating into a dense white fog that spread wider and wider. Coming closer. In the distance the whitish vapor glistened in the sunlight. A fine rain of tiny whitish particles fell gently from it to coat the countryside beneath. And still the cloud moved forward, toward the Priory and the village beyond.

A heavy smell of decay washed down from the northern hills, brown spots spreading across the lush green stalks. From evening until morning brown swatches of decay shadowed rapidly over the fields, engulfing the tender shoots that slowly leaned over under the onslaught, blackening and dying.

By the time the sun woke the farmers, a sulfurous stench very like the smell of foul sewer water was gradually growing stronger. And yet there was no moisture with the strange white vapors, the stench leaving an arid feeling in the nostrils.

The Priory's tenant farmers collected in the main hall, waiting to plead their cases to the earl or the countess. Whispered words worried about God's curses and what they'd done to deserve yet another season of blight.

Harry was told of the Irishmen waiting below as he dressed. "The hall is full?" Harry asked Robert as the young servant held out Harry's jacket.

"Stuffed, Your Lordship."

In the upper hallway Harry met Amelia, heading toward breakfast with Lady Ennis and Lord Rossett. "I hear you have visitors below," the corpulent Lord Rossett told Harry. "They'll beg off on rents, mark my words. The Irish are wonderful at excuses, if nothing else." The older man's cynical appraisal turned Harry's expression grim.

"If they think me the fool"—Harry gazed directly at Amelia—"or soft-hearted, they'd best have a care. I fear the estate's affairs have not been handled in a businesslike fashion to date."

"Have you found any improprieties in the books?" Amelia demanded suddenly.

"No. But weak judgment is just as dangerous as thievery."

"A great deal more," Rossett said as they reached the top of the stairs. "Skullduggery you can fire or jail. But your own mistakes haunt you forevermore. A firm hand is what's needed with the Irish. They're children at heart, plain and simple. The only way to deal with them is as a strict parent. For their own good as well as ours."

The people below stared upward at the descending English nobility. Hats came off into hands, here and there a cap still firmly atop a sober and careworn visage.

Harry stopped at the foot of the wide stairs, waiting while his wife and her guests proceeded across the hall to the dining room. The shuffling of peasant shoes was the only sound that accompanied their own footsteps across the floor.

Wallace stood at the green baise door, a muscular young footman beside him, there to ensure that peace would reign. Harry called to Wallace, telling him to show the guests into the ballroom.

KATHLEEN

Wallace moved toward the double doors, the footman opening one side as Wallace did the other. Harry stepped down the last step, leading the way through the ballroom doors, twenty-three Irishmen following him into the huge, bare room.

"It's not begging that we are, Your Lordship." Davey Muldoon had been elected spokesman as the oldest tenant, his grandfather's father first owning and then working the land the English had confiscated from him. "It's just plain and simple facts we have to lay before ye. The blight's struck some of us already, and all of us before. We'll not have the crops to pay you your rent this quarter."

Harry looked from one closed face to another, the eyes before him unreadable. "Nor last quarter. This will make half a year's debt in arrears, three-quarters of a year due next quarter. Have any of you the crops to pay that amount of debt?"

None spoke, until Davey Muldoon glanced toward the others. "Well, now, the man's asking a necessary question, lads. I mean, His Lordship's asking, begging your pardon, Your Lordship." Davey turned back to face Harry. "It's like this. None of us could come up with all that in one payment, like, but we figured, if you were to let us settle this half-year's debt over four payments, starting with next quarter—why, in a year you'd have this paid back, and we'd be out of debt."

"It's cutting it tight," another farmer told them both. "For my part, we'll be without chickens or pig—and you all know what that means."

"Debt's got to be paid," Davey Muldoon told them philosophically.

"On land that's rightfully ours in the first place!" One of the men whose cap was still on his head spoke from the rear of the group, his defiance loud behind his words.

"And it's not His Lordship here that's responsible for that, now, is it?"

"It's his kind," another voice said mutinously.

"I won't have this kind of talk under my own roof," Harry told them all. There was a murmur of resentment through the room and then dead silence. Harry stared at each one in

108

turn as he spoke, trying to assess which were the troublemakers who had spoken from behind the others' silent backs. "If I agreed to hold the rents in abeyance, if I further agreed to partial payments, all this agreement would be predicated on the assumption that there would be no more crop failures. What if there are?"

"What did he say?" a voice asked.

Davey Muldoon answered: "He said if he says yes, how does he know the blight won't strike the next crops, too."

"Why didn't he say so?"

"Why doesn't he just ask the Almighty Himself, then, and then he can tell us." Harry saw the thin face that spoke. It was O'Hallion.

Harry ignored the sarcastic comments. "I can't believe you're unable to salvage your crops. Everywhere I've ridden, everywhere I've looked, food is green and growing."

"Have you been out, then, this morning?" Davey Muldoon asked. When Harry did not reply: "Last night, when Barney here went to bed, he had four full fields of green shoots. This morning two of them are blighted and the others threatened. We spent the wee hours pulling up all that we could from the bad fields. It comes up somehow through the soil and strikes without warning. One will be black, the next one as green as grass, and there's no telling which will be which or why."

"Overnight?" Harry's disbelief showed in his tone. "You must have missed the warning signs."

"And what are they, then?" O'Hallion challenged. "What are these warning signs?"

"It's your crop. Surely you must know," Harry told him.

O'Hallion barked out a short, hard laugh, none of the others laughing with him. "You'll be praised higher than Saint Patrick and the Great O'Connell himself if you can find any signs of the blight coming before it's hit and broken our backs! It's best not to speak of what you do not know."

MaryKate's voice came from the open doorway behind them all. "And isn't that a fact, Johnny O'Hallion? Perhaps you should listen to your own words, then."

The men moved to make a path for her through the throng, Harry watching her as they did. She moved through the rough-looking men, a slim figure shorter than any who surrounded her, and somehow commanding their attention.

"I'm sorry, Your Lordship," MaryKate told him. "Sorry for my brother's bad manners when he's here as all others are—looking for help. They've not the money to buy seed for another crop, let alone for their rents, and I'll not have it said that a pigheaded O'Hallion turned you against helping people who need your help badly."

All the eyes in the room turned toward the earl, who didn't speak right away. When he did he spoke to the men before him. "I cannot give you the answer you want." He waited while the murmur that met his words quieted. "I want to see for myself exactly what is happening on my land and what can be done about it. There must be something that can avoid this plague in the future."

"And don't we all hope you're right, Your Lordship," Davey Muldoon began diplomatically. "But I for one would also like to know what's to happen to us."

Harry hesitated. "I want to see what can be done."

Davey watched the earl's eyes. "You've only just arrived, that we know. We're sorry it's to such a state of affairs."

"It's none of our fault!" another farmer said.

"Fault's not the issue," Harry spoke crisply. "A cure for the blight is the issue. And assurance that this state of affairs won't continue."

One of the men at the back moved toward the open doorway, Davey spotting him. "Barney?"

Barney turned back reluctantly, to face Davey and the English lord beside him. And the diminutive girl who stood between. "While all else is decided, I've still got fields with potato shoots that have to be protected if I can. And young potatoes I can save if I get them out of the ground soon enough. I'm going back to my fields. When His Lordship decides what he's to do with us, he knows where to find me. Meantime, I want to save what I can and all this talk's doing is wasting time."

Two men followed Barney out, and Davey apologized to the earl. Harry shook his head. "I agree with him. There's more you can do for yourselves out there this morning than there is in here."

MaryKate watched her brother walk out, the others

around and behind him, Davey the last to go, the only one to pay his respects to His Lordship before leaving.

Harry was left standing in the middle of the huge, empty ballroom, the tables from the party stripped clean and bare in the night hours between. MaryKate started toward the doors. "Your brother does not like your interference," Harry told her.

MaryKate stopped, looking back. "He's not alone."

Harry watched the girl. "I've never met a tongue like yours. Except perhaps in the woman who raised me."

"Your mother would have needed a sharp tongue raising the likes of you." She saw his expression darken.

"My mother had no part in raising me," Harry said coldly. He turned away himself, walking toward the terrace doors to the long narrow stone porch.

MaryKate's nephew Johnny raced in from the main hall, calling out his aunt's name, the child's voice high-pitched and frightened.

Harry stopped in the terrace doorway, watching the gawky young boy skid to a stop beside his aunt. "Where's my da?! Ma says he's got to come quick, it's come and it's spreading, and we have to get the spuds up. She said to tell you to come, too, if you can—any who can help, or we'll be ruined! It's just growing and growing across the fields!"

MaryKate grabbed the boy's shoulders, gently shaking him. "Hush, now, Johnny! Didn't you see your father? He just left."

"There were a bunch of men on the drive, but not my da. They said when he left he'd be going on with Jamie Boyle to old Tom's."

"He's already left. We'll fetch him at the pub before we go back."

"Ma said come quick!" Johnny nearly danced as he spoke, his aunt's hands still holding him down.

"As quick as we can," MaryKate told him.

Harry spoke from beside them, the boy freezing when he saw the Englishman, who had come back toward them. "Send one of the footmen. I'll have Bess saddled." MaryKate stared at him. Harry continued, "I want to see the blight for myself, and a horse is quicker than foot."

"But you—I mean, Your Lordship, there's no need—"

111

KATHLEEN

"Yes, there is!" Johnny burst out of his trance, tugging at his aunt. "Ma says they're dying by the minute!"

MaryKate moved beside man and boy, the young boy dancing ahead with relief as Harry strode out toward the stableyard. The stench was just beginning to permeate the air around them as Harry called for Black Bess to be saddled.

Harry sent the stableboy on the chestnut mare to fetch Johnny O'Hallion at Tom Ross's pub, the boy taking off as Harry placed MaryKate aboard Bess and swung Johnny up onto a young roan. "Can you ride?" Harry asked Johnny as Harry himself mounted Bess behind MaryKate.

"No, sir," Johnny said, his usual torrent of words stuffed back inside by his awe.

"Hold on tight, then." Harry grabbed the roan's reins and started out of the stableyard.

"I should ride with him," MaryKate said into the wind that was whipping her hair back against his cheek as they loped down the path.

"Can you ride?"

"I can learn," MaryKate told him tartly. Her breath was taken from her as they rode faster, Bess hitting stride. The roan followed along beside, reaching its legs to keep up with the older horse, stretching out with the sheer pleasure of a free run across open fields of heather.

The lush green fields to both sides of the heather were still covered with purple blossoms rising above the green stalks and the dark loam of the ground beneath.

All looked as it had, the branches of the potato stalks matted as thick as a carpet in the hollows that led up from the riverbank.

And then he saw it.

Tiny brown spots appeared on the leaves, spreading before his eyes like an incoming tide over a flat, sandy shore. It spread in all directions at once, patterning across the healthy plants, green stalks turning brown and wilting, drooping toward the ground, their purple blossoms resting in the dirt.

KATHLEEN

"Jesus, Mary, and Joseph!" MaryKate's words were swallowed back in her throat, the stench filling her nostrils.

As they rode through the countryside, young Johnny clutched at the roan horse, his eyes wide with fright. The cloud deepened above, and all around them the sound of wailing began to rise from the cabins they passed as the sun was completely blotted out.

13

Johnny O'Hallion's cottage sat along a lane that wound gently upward into the northern hills. To the west and the south the coastline curved around a little promontory, the land dipping downward toward the Atlantic Ocean and all the western worlds beyond Ireland's rock-strewn, emerald shores.

The thatched-roof cottage was a large one, two bedrooms and an attic loft beside the main room, where all gathered around the fireplace to eat and talk and live out their lives. It was made of stone and built many lifetimes ago, two centuries of sunlight mellowing its colors.

On normal days the smell of peat mixed with the ocean air and all the roses Sophie had planted near the doorway. But today the smell of decay permeated everything, a frightening smell that depressed the spirit. With the baby in her arms, Sophie paced back and forth across the yard, where her chickens should be scratching in the dirt. They huddled together in the chicken coop, the flocks of crows and starlings from yesterday vanished overnight. Sophie turned at the sound of pounding hooves to stare in amazement at son

KATHLEEN

and sister-in-law. And the great brute of a black horse that had nearly killed her upon the earl's arrival.

The sight of the earl himself seemed hardly less miraculous than if the Virgin Mary had entered the yard and begun to speak. "We are here to help," he said, his deep voice sounding nothing at all like the Virgin's would.

Sophie stared up at him. MaryKate slid down from Bess's back, the earl reaching to help a reluctant Johnny down from the roan.

"Ma, did you see me riding?" Johnny asked, his eyes still round with wonder.

"What can we do?" MaryKate asked.

Sophie stared at the English lord. "We?"

"Little Johnny and I. Sophie, what's wrong? We sent someone for Johnny, and he'll be here as soon as they find him. Where are the girls?"

"In the north field. MaryKate, the girls run too slow. I told them to keep working, I had to bring the baby back, I was afraid he'd catch whatever it was, lying on the ground there where it's spreading."

"Take the baby inside. We'll go help the girls."

"And him?" Sophie asked in spite of herself.

Harry spoke for himself. "Show me where the field is."

MaryKate, Little Johnny, and the earl started across the lane and up the road, Sophie staring after them. She took the baby inside and sat down on a narrow wooden rocker, rocking back and forth, the babe in her arms. "What are we to do?" she whispered over and over to the sleeping child. "Sweet Mother of God, what are we to do?"

The smell that had hovered at the back of Harry's consciousness since first stepping outside this morning rose in his throat, his nostrils clogging with it. The sulfurous smell rose thicker as they crossed into the O'Hallion potato fields.

The potato plants were sown in wide rigs, wide ridges, with a furrow at each side. Along the rigs, four young girls, the oldest just turned twelve, the youngest nearly four, were pulling at the potato shoots, young, half-grown potatoes coming up into their hands.

"It's too soon," MaryKate said almost under her breath, moving fast to join the girls and reaching along beside them to pull at the crop, lifting it from the stench-filled field.

KATHLEEN

Johnny started toward the farthest row and stopped, staring at the brown-spotted stems surrounding him. Beyond him were stalks totally blackened by the blight. They looked deadly.

Harry saw the boy's fear and moved past him, reaching down with leather-gloved hands to wrench the spotted stalks up out of the ground. When he had some in his hands he turned toward the boy. "What do I do with it?"

Johnny swallowed and then showed him, pulling the half-grown potatoes from their stems and tossing them into the nearest rough-woven basket. Harry stripped off his gloves, handing them to the boy.

Johnny took them, holding them until he saw Harry reach with his bare hands to pull more stalks out of the ground. The boy pulled on the gloves, seeing his sister Betsy's eyes on him. He looked at her bare hands and bit his lip.

But he kept the gloves on as he reached toward the blackening stalks.

MaryKate talked to the girls, urging them on as if it were a game of who could get the most potatoes pulled quickest.

But young Sally stared up at the huge Englishman. "He'll win," she told her aunt.

"I always win," Harry told the little girl.

MaryKate looked up at him and then snorted, reaching to work faster. "And are you going to let that big lug talk you out of your prize, my girls? Or are you going to show him it's wrong to boast so soon after starting something? He'll be lying in the ditch, panting for air and out of breath from all the work while we're still going strong!"

The girls giggled, looking toward Harry and imagining him lying in the ditch.

Harry gave MaryKate a look, most of his attention on the potatoes. "We'll see," he told her and the others.

"I'll win!" Johnny yelled.

"You don't count. You've got gloves on, so your hands won't hurt," Sally told him, earning a dark look from Johnny.

"Where did you get those gloves?" MaryKate asked, seeing them for the first time.

"Let him alone about the gloves," Harry told her flatly,

his tone brooking no argument. She stared at him, surprised. "I gave them to him," Harry added.

The cloud still tumbled down the far mountainsides like a soft, silent avalanche, whitish vapors twisting forward and rolling forward across the valley, smothering the distances in white.

Harry straightened up, suddenly chilly. Wind came up, coming from the north and cold, the temperature dropping as they worked. "The weather's changing again."

She looked up. "It came like this last year," she told him, her teeth chattering. She looked toward the children, who huddled over their work, their bare arms and legs goose-fleshed. "Betsy! Johnny! Why didn't you say anything? Sally, Kate, Meg, come along now. It's inside you go."

"But we've not won!"

"We'll count up at the cottage. Come along, I'll not have you freezing to death."

Harry picked up the largest bushel basket, Johnny and Betsy carrying one each, the younger three helping Mary-Kate back to the cottage, stumbling in their hurry to get to the yard and count what they'd done. "How will we know, MaryKate?" little Meg asked. "Our spuds are in with yours!"

"Mine are in with his," Sally said. Her young voice was shy, her eyes drifting toward the large stranger, but never meeting his.

"We'll each win if we've more than they do," Harry told her.

"But mine were done alone!" Johnny wailed.

"And mine," Betsy put in.

Harry looked back toward them as they crossed the narrow lane. "Then we must have twice as many and one more than the most that either of you have, or you win and we lose."

MaryKate's eyes met his. "If you could come up with an equally good plan for the farmers, you would have even my awe," she murmured.

He downright stared at her and then reached for the gate. Sophie came to the open cottage door, her shawl around her shoulder. "Johnny's not gotten here!" she told them all, focusing on MaryKate. "Are you sure he got the message?"

KATHLEEN

"If he was where they said, he got it," MaryKate told her sister-in-law. "There's more to be done, but we need heavier clothes—the children are freezing."

Sophie didn't hear MaryKate's words right away. She was staring at the earl's dirty hands and the dark earth that now encrusted the knees of his riding breeches and his boots. She looked up to see his eyes on her and veered away, finding MaryKate's and then not speaking of it. "Come inside, then." She hesitated. "All of you that wants."

"Where do we put the potatoes?" Harry asked.

"Inside!" came Sally's instant reply. "We have to count and see if we won!"

"Won?" Her mother stepped back inside the large main room, letting the others come forward. Sally tugged on the earl's coatsleeve, almost shoving him forward, into the house with the basket of potatoes.

Sophie found her children pulling at the potatoes, making separate piles as MaryKate looked toward the earl. An uneasiness MaryKate would have denied was shyness suddenly enveloped her here in the room she had grown up in. "My great-grandfather Patrick O'Hallion built our house." She heard her own tentative words, amazed at how strangled they sounded. "We've all grown up here. Except Sophie, of course, who came when she married my brother."

Harry eyed Sophie. "You're Johnny O'Hallion's wife, then."

Sophie met his eyes. "I am. And these are his children."

"And the brother?"

MaryKate answered, "You mean Patrick? He grew up here, too. Still lives here."

"I see," the English earl said. "But you've lived at the Priory for . . . ?"

Something inside MaryKate flared, taking offense. "Half my life, almost. Since I was fourteen. And it's better quarters I had here at home," she added defensively.

"You dislike your rooms?" Harry asked, surprised.

"Rooms?" Sophie asked. "Do you then have more than one, MaryKate?"

"Of course not!"

"MaryKate, you must come count!" Johnny yelled toward her, turning Harry toward the children.

KATHLEEN

"Haven't you learned counting in school?" Harry asked.

"Bless me, what school would it be for my poor ones?" Sophie asked, almost laughing at the thought.

Harry looked puzzled. "There's no school?"

"Aye, there's the Protestant school, but it's not for the likes of us."

MaryKate explained, "There are fees." She moved to hunker down next to the children.

Harry stood where he was and then, motioned forward by Sophie, stood in front of the fireplace. A three-legged stool sat there and after a bit he moved it nearer, sitting down and pushing at the peat fire to stir its embers.

The smoky peat smell filled the cabin, covering over the smell of decay. Harry reached to put more peat on the hearth, trying to drown out the sulfurous smell. Beside him the baby stirred in its crib and absentmindedly he reached out to rock the tiny wooden rocker.

MaryKate saw Harry's unthinking action, bending her head to count the potatoes along with the exuberant children, each adding their two cents to the discussion of what they should win if they won. "They'll not be silent, Your Lordship," MaryKate said, the children belying her words and going quiet at the sound of two of her words: *Your Lordship*.

Harry looked toward them. "I beg your pardon?"

MaryKate found herself smiling at the big man whose hand was still on the crib. As she smiled he must have realized what he was doing, for he stopped, the child lulled back to sleep and silent under its quilt. MaryKate continued: "Everyone has different ideas about what the prize should be for the winner."

Harry looked from one child's upturned and innocent face to the next. They looked impossibly young, fresh-faced, with cheeks glowing red with the cold that was slowly leaving their bodies in the comfort of the cottage.

"What do we win?" Johnny asked him, looking with high hopes toward the tall man on the three-legged stool.

"Something fitting," MaryKate put in.

"What's this talk of winnings?" Sophie asked.

Harry answered young Johnny, "Something that's fitting should be your fondest desire."

"Good grief," MaryKate responded.

"Don't go giving them ideas, Your Lordship," Sophie put in. "You've no idea what their fondest desires could be."

"What could they be?" Harry asked.

"Impossible to come by, for one thing," Sophie said, sounding for a moment almost as spirited as MaryKate. "Each must remember his place in this world, and fondest desires are just that. Fond and desires. Not real things in this mortal world."

Harry watched the children's crestfallen faces. And then looked at MaryKate's disappointed face. "And your objection?" he asked her.

MaryKate glanced toward the fireplace. Then back to stare into his dark eyes. "You had me thinking there for a while, you had answers to a lot of things. Maybe even to our real dilemma."

Harry's heart constricted in his chest, seeing the hope in her eyes. And the distrust that crowded in to cover it over. He took his time answering, glancing toward Sophie, who was cutting slices of soda bread at the large, rough-hewn table that dominated the room.

"I don't know if there is an answer to the real dilemma," Harry replied quietly. "As for the winner's reward"—he saw the children's eyes light up—"to that we might find a solution." He looked toward young Johnny. "What would your fondest desire be, Johnny?"

"A horse!" Johnny's words tumbled out, the sound of his sisters' indrawn breaths matching his mother's own.

"You see what we mean," MaryKate said.

"A horse is not an impossible desire," Harry replied.

"For you," MaryKate answered.

Harry shrugged. "If they win, it means we lost. Correct? A gentleman always pays his debts." He looked toward Sally. "What is your name?"

Sally blushed. "Me, my name is Sally."

"Your Lordship," MaryKate prompted.

"Your Lordship," Sally repeated dutifully, her voice lowering to a whisper.

Harry smiled at the child. MaryKate had never seen him smile, had never seen the soft look that brought Sally's

KATHLEEN

spirits back up as he spoke: "Let's not worry about titles right now, shall we?"

Sally smiled shyly. "You talk funny."

"Sally O'Hallion!" her mother scolded from across the room.

"I should like . . ." Sally started and then, seeing her mother's eyes on her, trailed off. She looked up to see Harry still watching her.

"She wants a horse, too," Johnny put in hopefully.

"I do not!" his sister shot back. "I want a shawl of pure silk! Blue!" she added defiantly, earning loud sounds of derision from her brother.

"And you?" Harry asked the oldest girl.

"I'm Betsy, sir."

Harry smiled. "That's usually short for Elizabeth," he told her.

"Yes, sir. Your Lordship, I mean. It is."

Harry looked toward MaryKate. "A strange name for an Irish girl."

"It was my mother's name," MaryKate told him. "And hers before her."

"You are a strange family, you O'Hallions." He found his eyes would not leave hers.

"That we are," MaryKate replied, entangled in his gaze and unable to break free of it.

Betsy took Harry's eyes away, speaking into the silence as aunt and landlord stared at each other. "I should like to read like Aunt Kate. And have a book," she added.

Harry took a minute to reply. "Aunt Kate?"

"The children call her Kate, Your Lordship," Sophie told him. "MaryKate's given name is Kathleen, as her mother's was Elizabeth. Mary-Elizabeth." Sophie did not notice Harry's English surprise at the juxtapositioning of the two names. "All called her mother Mary, and since she had only the one girl, she was called Mary's Kate, when she was little. And her brothers, and all, still do."

"You look amused," MaryKate told him. "At Mary and Elizabeth being joined. There are stranger things, you know. Mary is a common enough name in Ireland, even if Elizabeth isn't."

121

KATHLEEN

Harry replied, "Have you read Irish and English history?" he asked.

"There's not been the time, no," MaryKate told him. "Nor, in truth, the inclination, what with chores and all the major learning to do."

"Major learning?"

"Reading, writing, arithmetic, and the Scriptures."

"The Douay or the Saint James?" Harry asked, a smile lurking behind his eyes. "Scriptures," he added.

"Are there more than one?" she asked, surprised.

"Yes. The Catholic is the Douay. The Protestant, or at least the Church of England, is the Saint James."

"Now, would you believe that!" Sophie put in. "And are they that different, then? Different stories and all?"

Harry hesitated. "I'm no authority. But I believe there's not too much dissimilarity. They are in most part the same."

"And isn't that a relief! I mean, how could the Protestants have the face to lie about the Lord's own words?" Finishing speaking, Sophie realized who she was addressing, her eyes going wide with alarm.

"I doubt any lie, intentionally, about the words of Christ," Harry replied mildly.

"Of course! I meant no disrespect," she said quickly.

The cabin door was opening, Johnny O'Hallion coming inside to hear her words, his brother behind him. "Whose horses are tethered at—" He stopped in midsentence, his eyes fastened on Harry, who stood up by the fireside. MaryKate jumped up between the two large men. Harry was larger, but Johnny had a reputation for decking men who stood in his disfavor.

Sophie came toward her husband and her brother-in-law. "You'll not believe it, Johnny. His Lordship's helped the children bring in the crop. As much as they could before the chill took over. Where were you? We sent for you!"

Johnny paid no attention to his wife. He came forward, Patrick one step behind, both of them facing the man at Johnny's own hearth.

"What is it you're wanting?" Johnny asked belligerently.

"And that's a fine way to greet a man who's spent the day trying to help your own kith and kin!" MaryKate excoriated her brother. "His Lordship sent a man to find you when

KATHLEEN

Young Johnny came running that you were needed, and he brought us here on horseback to help the girls bring in the potatoes and stayed to help himself! Just look at him! It's thanks you're after at this point, John Joseph O'Hallion!"

Dead silence met her words.

"Hardly," Harry said into it stiffly. "I intended this morning to look into the blight further at close range."

"Hardly by picking potatoes," MaryKate told him tartly, seeing her oldest brother turn to stare at her.

"A 'man,' is it, who's been helping?" Johnny asked his only sister. " 'He,' is it? Speaking to him as you do to me, with all the pepper that tongue can muster—just what is the meaning of your own attitude, MaryKate?"

"I pity you if she speaks to you as she does to me," Harry told her brother, earning the Irishman's eyes glaring into his own. "From the moment I arrived in Cork, this young woman has acted the harridan and harpy. Demanding I leave when first we met."

Johnny's disbelieving look brought Sophie into the conversation. "And that's the truth, for I was there to hear it." At MaryKate's withering look Sophie appended: "Not that he didn't deserve it." She stopped, realizing who she was talking about. And that he was standing there. "Your Lordship," she added, earning a small wry smile from the English earl.

"We're not used to dealing with the nobility," Patrick said.

His brother cut off his words: "There's no need to apologize for who we are. Or explain what we mean." Johnny stared at the Englishman. "The likes of you aren't around the likes of us enough for us to learn your ways. Or you ours. And there's no need for either." He glowered toward his sister. "At least, there wouldn't be if each kept to her own place!"

"My place is where I say it is!" MaryKate flared.

Harry looked across the room at the children, who stared wide-eyed at the exchange between the stranger who had promised them a winner's reward and their father who was obviously upset the man was even there.

"Who won?" Harry asked MaryKate.

She stood up, brushing at her skirts. "It's not important."

"We did!" Sally burst out to the Englishman, quick tears filling her blue eyes.

"It was close!" Johnny hollered at his sister.

"What are you two arguing about now?" their father asked, silencing them both.

Sullen faces looked toward the floor, Sophie's heart going out toward her children as the English earl took three long strides, reaching the door and opening it. "Thank you for your hospitality, Mrs. O'Hallion, but I must be gone."

She was flustered: "I was just about to offer tea and the soda bread I've just made."

"He don't need your soda bread," her husband told her.

"I should have enjoyed it," Harry told the woman gallantly. The strain of her poverty and the life she led showed about her eyes, the rest of her face and body still young and blooming.

Johnny turned on his sister. "And are you staying? Or are you going back with him?"

MaryKate moved away from the children. "You make it sound like a choice. Or an ultimatum."

"Isn't it, then?" Johnny asked her back, standing his ground.

MaryKate glared at her brother. "No, it's not! But then, everything is an ultimatum with you, isn't it?" She moved toward the door.

Harry held it open for her, closing it behind them. They left Johnny O'Hallion to glare at his brother and then turn toward his wife, asking what exactly had happened there that day.

Outside, a bleak twilight greeted MaryKate and Harry as they walked out the tiny gate, untethering the horses.

She didn't speak until they had the horses free. "Do you hear anything?" she asked him.

He shook his head, seeing her shivering. He pulled at his coat, taking it off to hand it toward her. "Here. You'll need it on the ride back." At her hesitation he grinned. "You'll not look any worse in it than you did in that one you had on last night."

"Paddy's?" She stared up at him. "Did I look so bad, then?"

"You never look bad." Lost in her green eyes, he remembered the feeling of those lips pressed against his. Heat rose within him against his will. He pulled back within himself, determined to stop the feelings that were hardening his flesh.

"You said you heard something?" was all he said.

"Nothing."

"What?" He stared at her in spite of himself.

"I hear nothing. Do you?"

He stopped, listening. The countryside was silent, shrouded in whitish fog. "This isn't healthy," he said finally, reaching to help her up onto Bess.

"The other horse—" she began and stopped.

"You're not a rider. Yet," he told her, his arm around her tiny waist, his hands putting her up atop the huge black beast. He reached for the roan's bridle, leading it beside them as he stepped up into the saddle, seating himself behind MaryKate.

As he turned the horses around, heading back down the lane, he saw Patrick O'Hallion at the cottage door, watching them. Somewhere in the distance a dog began to howl.

His arms closed around her at the sound. She was so small, his own large frame surrounded her. He could feel the warmth of her body against his chest. He rode the horse hard, his face set into displeased lines.

14

The birds came back the next day, after the winds cleared the last pockets of the sickly white fog from the ground. A light frost of something like powdery snow clung to the blackened potato stalks, the sewerlike smell growing stronger across the valley and the village.

The sounds of despair rose from the thatched roofs of the tenant cottages, no anger, no power, not even an appeal for mercy in the wailing of the women whose anguish was so utterly devastating that nothing could help. Children clung to their mothers' skirts, eyes wide and frightened at the change in the world around them.

Wives, sons, and daughters wore frightened expressions as they worked alongside the men to pull up the stalks that withered at their touches, stalks snapping like rotten wood. But the potatoes under the stalks were whole. "Pull! Pull!" they urged each other on, working feverishly to save what they could.

Women cleared the decayed stalks and the weeds from the ridges, making the digging easier for the men, whose spades pulled up the plants by the roots, staring at the little cluster of half-grown potatoes and tipping them into little heaps with their spades as they continued to dig out what was left of the crop.

People were digging potatoes all over the valley, the rasping sounds of spades hitting stones sounding out over the countryside now and again, curlews back on the wing overhead, calling out above the lowing cattle. All would have seemed normal if not for the smell. And the urgency with which the people dug.

Then the rains began again. The ground became so sodden that water splashed from under the tenants' feet as they ran from one stricken plant to the next, working against time and nature to salvage what they could.

The Priory was silent, the girls sent home to help their families, the servants worried for friends and relatives, many of them disappearing into the nearby fields to help.

Only the cook, MaryKate, and the English servants kept to the house. The English walked silent and apprehensive through the ancient corridors, the changeable Irish weather depressing them, the smell of rot making them edgy and superstitious about what was happening and what harm could come to them from even smelling the foul air.

MaryKate came to the back parlor Harry used as an office and stood silent in the doorway until he looked up.

"You sent for me."

"Yes," Harry replied. "I want to ride the entire estate. You know the land. And the people. Will you come?"

She hesitated. "It would take days to ride the entire estate."

"Then it will take days. I want to inventory where the blight has most affected the potato crop. And I want to check the rest of the crops. Will you come?" he asked again.

"Of course."

He hesitated then. "This is not in your normal duties. I realize I have castigated you for becoming involved in the land management. But since you are the only one here who has been involved with the tenants and the rents, it will be easier if you are there to apprise me as to which tenant is which."

MaryKate replied quietly, "I already said I would."

"How soon can you be ready to start?" He spoke in a crisp, businesslike tone.

"The sooner the better."

Amelia was at the doorway. "The sooner the better what?" she asked.

Harry's explanation brought her further into the room.

"I shall come, too."

"There is no need," Harry began stiffly.

"I wish to do so," Amelia replied. "I shall change and be ready within the quarter hour."

Amelia turned and left the room, Harry's eyes finding MaryKate's and then turning away. "Please see to it that four horses are saddled."

"Four?"

"Archie will come with us in case of need."

"Do I get to ride my own horse, then?" Mary-Kathleen asked softly.

Harry did not look toward her. "You had better," he said cryptically. There was nothing she could name about his tone of voice that made her heart thump at the sound of his words.

She turned away first, her heart pounding, her brain unsure what was the matter with her.

Harry stared at the London papers on his desk that told of the crop failure in Ireland. He did not look up as she left.

"I say, old man." Leo stood in the doorway. "We really must talk about leaving. After all, one doesn't know how all this muck is affecting one. It could be unhealthful."

"I can hardly leave with my father's estates in turmoil," Harry told his friend.

"All the same, I'd feel much safer in Dublin at the very least. I mean, how long do you plan on staying in this godforsaken backland? You had said we would barely be here."

"I had not planned on any of what has happened," Harry said.

Leo watched him. "You could always bring her to Dublin." At Harry's look he continued, "Or even to London for that matter, old chap."

"Bring whom to London?" Harry asked, his voice distant and cold. Very cold.

KATHLEEN

"Well, good grief, whosoever you want." Leo backed off at the look in Harry's eyes.

Standing up, Harry rounded the desk to stand in front of his lifelong friend. "Obviously my wife will accompany us when we leave."

Leo didn't speak right away. "Obviously," he repeated finally. Watching Harry walk toward the door, he spoke again. "I must warn you I shall not stay much longer, Harry. I really cannot."

"Do as you wish," Harry said as he walked out of the room. Leo sighed, walking toward a small cherrywood cabinet and opening its door to reach for a decanter of sherry.

Taking decanter and glass Leo settled down in a wingback chair by the fireplace, fortifying himself against yet another dull afternoon.

Harry and MaryKate led the way, Amelia and Archie just behind them on the narrow country lane that traversed the Priory lands. Harry had the bridle for MaryKate's horse, holding it loosely in his hands.

"I shall never learn to ride if never given the chance," MaryKate told him.

"You are learning your seat right now. This weather has made the horses as nervous as it has those dogs that keep howling out in the night. I don't intend to waste time racing after you if that animal is spooked by a moving weed and decides to take off toward Dublin with you."

"This is the McCarthys'," MaryKate answered, diplomatically avoiding the subject.

"Did you say the McCarthys'?" Amelia asked from behind.

MaryKate looked around. "Yes, Your Ladyship. Millie's family it is."

"Millie?" Harry queried.

"One of the students," MaryKate told him.

"I want to stop and see how she's getting on," the countess said, prepared to argue with her husband. But Harry voiced no opposition.

At the door of the tiny cottage a small naked child sucked its thumb, staring at them as they approached. When they reached the gate to the postage-stamp-sized yard, the little girl turned and ran into the gloomy depths behind her, calling out for her mother.

"Looks like we scared the tyke," Archie said. He held the reins of Lady Amelia's horse as she dismounted, then took Harry's and MaryKate's, too. "Best I stay here. 'Twas probably me she ran scared of."

"They're just not used to visitors on horseback," MaryKate told the Welshman.

There were no sounds from inside the cottage as they approached the open doorway. Not even the child could be heard. Lady Amelia knocked on the doorframe. No one answered.

After a moment MaryKate came forward. She looked inside, past the countess, peering into the gloom, and then stepped across the threshold, calling out for Millie McCarthy. "Are you there then, Millie?"

There was one door that led from the small main room and it was closed. The fireplace was stone cold, the room chill and bleak. Amelia frowned, looking from the solitary table to the two three-legged stools that sat beside the cold fireplace. "Millie? Are you here?" Amelia called out.

The door across the room opened a little, the tiny naked child peering out at them, her eyes rounded and wide in the interior darkness. Amelia moved slowly toward the girl, who stood her ground until Amelia was a few feet away. She then ran back inside the inner room.

Harry and MaryKate came behind Amelia as she opened the door wide. Inside was a bare, disheveled bed that held two women, one of them looking far older than her forty years, the other, younger one looking impossibly thin. The little girl had grabbed the older woman's hand, the woman making an effort to open her eyes and shush the child.

"Good Lord!" Amelia cried out at the sight, coming near the bed and reaching to feel the woman's fevered brow. "Millie? Is that Millie?" Amelia demanded, MaryKate coming around the bed to brush back the thin girl's hair.

"Oh, Millie—what's happened to you?" MaryKate whispered the words the unconscious girl could not hear.

"No—food." Millie's mother managed to force the words out.

"Where is your husband?" Harry asked, frowning.

KATHLEEN

"The works . . ." The woman could manage no more words. At Harry's questioning of what she meant, it was MaryKate who replied to him, "The government's invented jobs for some. Building roads that go nowhere."

"I beg your pardon?" Harry stared at her, incredulous.

"The English government said some could be employed, but none in Ireland were to benefit from being on the dole. So the roads they build could not go anywhere. They just start and stop anywhere. At a hill or in a bog."

"You can't possibly be serious," Harry replied.

Amelia meanwhile was checking out Mrs. McCarthy and reaching to touch Millie's forehead. "The girl is burning up. Send Archie for the doctor, Harry."

Harry turned on his heel, yelling for Archie. The little girl shrank back against the bed at the sound of his raised voice. MaryKate came around the bed to reach for the little girl. "You need clothes on, little one. It's cold in here."

The girl still shrank back against her mother. MaryKate looked about and moved to the one chest in the tiny room, opening a drawer and finding a tattered shawl. She looked for more clothing, finding a folded man's shirt and pulling it out, taking it to the child.

Slowly, soothing the child's fears, MaryKate managed to slip the shirt onto the tiny body, rolling up the rough-sewn sleeves and buttoning the soft flannel so that it hung down around the girl in huge folds. It grazed the floor and her grubby bare feet.

15

Leo, Lord Cumberland, took his afternoon constitutional around four o'clock each day of his life. He would do a turn about the inner yard of whatever country estate he was visiting—or once around the square if in his London townhouse—and then promptly go in for tea and biscuits, fortifying himself for his nap before the dinner hour's pressing engagements.

On this warm summer afternoon, in the west of Ireland, with the faint odor of malignancy in the air, Lord Cumberland was stopped by the sight of horses and riders, of peasant carts carrying prone persons, arriving at the Priory.

Mercifully they stopped at the annex, disgorging supplies and people, while Leo beat a hasty retreat to the Priory itself and coaxed Robert to have a look-see and report back who these minions were who were invading the grounds with the look of those who intended to stay.

Harry was nowhere to be found, still gone about his rounds, and strangers were ensconcing themselves on the premises.

"I am quite inept at handling arguments," Leo told Robert flatly. "If he is to blame me, then I shall have to insist he

KATHLEEN

reconsider. I could hardly hold off an army of Irishmen with naught but words."

Robert stared at the man who was at the moment peering from behind a curtained window at the incoming flux. "Her Ladyship invited them, Your Lordship."

Leo took a moment to digest this intelligence. "I beg your pardon?"

"Her Ladyship has brought them to be nursed."

"Are you possibly talking about Amelia? The countess?"

Robert nodded his head.

Leo stared at the man. "Impossible," he stated flatly. And then turned back to look in the direction of the annex, where at that very moment Amelia herself was dismounting, Harry close behind. When Leo saw Archie and MaryKate accompanying them, he let the draperies fall back into place. "Robert, I wish my things packed posthaste."

"I'll find Archie, Your Lordship—"

"There's not far to look. He's outside with the Irish."

Robert hesitated. "I'll fetch him."

Leo turned away, heading toward the stairs and his rooms as Robert bounded toward the front door, his step slowing as he neared the carts where obviously ill people were being unloaded and carried inside the school annex.

Harry came into tea quiet, saddened by the sights of the afternoon. Leo was pouring himself a healthy portion of Madeira. He looked toward his old friend and poured another out, handing it across as Harry came forward.

"I say, we have to talk," Leo told him.

Harry took the proffered glass. "You should see them, Leo."

Leo shuddered, only half in jest. "Perish the thought. Which brings me to my point." He waited until he was sure he had Harry's attention. "You know I am yours forever, but I'm leaving for Dublin at first light."

Harry stared at his friend. "I beg your pardon?"

"Well, now that you mention it, yes, you should. But I am above casting recriminations. Suffice it to say that I have done my duty. I have come to this godforsaken island, and I have stood by you through the worst kind of evil weather and god-knows-what-all dangers to our health. But now you

KATHLEEN

have trespassed beyond the pale. You have brought disease and infliction into our living quarters, and with that I cannot put up." Leo saw the lack of comprehension on Harry's face. "You certainly know that your wife has brought these miserable Irish peasants onto the property by the drove."

"They are sick," Harry replied.

"Precisely," Leo told his friend. "That is precisely my point!"

"I can't believe you're saying this," Harry told him.

"I can't believe you are allowing this," Leo replied.

"*Allowing* it?! These people are my dependents!"

"My dear Harry, we're not in medieval times. And face it, you've nothing owed here. You've never even met these people!"

Harry's face was set in stubborn lines. "I have now."

"Yes. And you've met the Irish wench."

Harry came to his feet, his fists balled at his sides. Leo took an instinctive step backward and then stopped, standing his ground. Harry's voice came out hard and loud. "I have given you my word as a gentleman that what you are saying is untrue. If you disbelieve me, there is nothing left to say."

Leo stared at his schoolhood friend. "My God, you sound totally sincere." The two men stood a few feet apart, gauging each other—Harry's eyes cold, Leo's confused.

"Harry—are you serious?"

"She is beyond reproach!" Harry replied.

"She is a serving wench!" Leo told his friend. "Any can have a serving wench! I can have her myself if the price is right."

Harry took one step forward and then stopped himself, his eyes as hard as pebbles in the stream that ran beneath Priory Hill. "You are wrong."

Leo watched Harry. "And you are possibly infatuated. How would you like to wager that I am right and you are wrong?"

"I have no interest in wagering on that score," Harry said.

"Or are afraid to?" Leo asked.

Harry delayed his response, watching the man who had

been his closest friend since childhood with new, harder, eyes. "I am afraid of nothing," Harry replied.

"Then you will let me prove my point," Leo responded.

"I didn't say that."

"Either you believe in what you're saying or you don't. If you have such trust in an Irish chit's morals, then you'll wager on them. You've wagered much money on much less, my friend. Do I have to remind you?"

Harry hesitated. "I haven't the right to endanger her," he told Leo.

"Nor will you. If you are right, she can't be endangered. Correct?"

"Anyone can be entrapped."

"I assure you, as a gentleman to a gentleman, I shall act with total propriety. I shall assume you are correct and treat the serving wench as a lady." Leo watched Harry. "The question then becomes do you trust her reactions to be those of a lady?"

Harry looked out toward the darkening twilight beyond the study windows. "She is like no one you have ever met. She is not a lady."

Leo smiled. "Then there is nothing to talk about."

Harry turned back to face Leo. "I'm not saying that. I said what I meant. She is nothing like you know, nothing like what passes in polite society as a lady. Still in all, she is more of a lady than any I've ever known."

"So you accept my wager?"

"I do not want her hurt," Harry told Leo flatly.

Leo shrugged. "I have no intention of hurting anyone. Let us say that you will either see her react as you think impossible—or you will not. In either event I shall take no liberties with your servant. At least until you see that she does, truly, wish them. Agreed?"

The two men stared at each other.

"Harry—don't tell me after all these years you've grown soft in the head. Or are infatuated."

"Hardly," Harry said coldly.

"Capital!" Leo responded, smiling. "Then I shall have a pleasant few hours seducing a maid before I leave for home."

* * *

KATHLEEN

In the annex MaryKate was helping Amelia set up pallet beds for five patients, three women, one man, and one girl-child. The tiniest McCarthy, still dressed in her father's flannel shirt, huddled beside her sleeping mother for warmth.

Amelia had the fires raised in the two fireplaces that flanked each other across the huge rectory room, MaryKate bringing in supplies and medicines the parish priest and the village doctor had procured for them.

Reverend Grinstead arrived as they were setting up the dispensary. He nodded civilly to Father Ross, who smiled an insincere smile and continued to bring medicines in from a cart near the doorway.

The English minister went to Lady Amelia as she ministered to Millie McCarthy, wiping the girl's fevered brow with a damp cloth, talking softly all the while.

"Your Ladyship, you are truly an example of Christian virtue."

Lady Amelia glanced up toward him as he reached for one of the narrow wooden chairs that were lined up along the sides of the refectory table just as the students had left them. "Hardly that, Reverend."

The minister brought the chair near hers, sitting down beside the narrow pallet where Millie tossed and turned in an uneasy sleep. "I think of you always as such." His words carried across the large room to where Father Ross and MaryKate sorted out the medical supplies Dr. Kilgallen had brought with him.

Brian Ross nodded toward the pair of them. "Is he always like that, then?"

"Always like what?" MaryKate asked.

"So cozy with Her Ladyship."

MaryKate glanced toward Amelia and the reverend, then turned back to her work. "I don't know what you mean."

Dr. Kilgallen called out for help with blankets, MaryKate moving to find some as more people appeared at the door.

A young farmer stopped her as she tried to pass by. "They said in the village the Priory is taking in the hungry and sick. Is it true, then, MaryKate?"

"James Dugan, you have eyes in your head. Look around

KATHLEEN

you and stop asking foolish questions," MaryKate told him tartly. "I've work to do!"

Jamie Dugan watched her stride quickly toward the house as he hesitated by the annex door. Then he pulled at his cap, pale red hair falling straight across his freckled forehead as he stepped over the threshold and stood just inside.

Father Ross came toward him. "Now, Jamie, and what are you doing here?"

Jamie twisted his cap tight, his mouth tight from the effort it took to beg. "Me mother and the young ones. She's got a terrible fever and the little ones are going thinner and thinner."

Brian Ross sighed. "Sure'n it was your wife the fever took off last year, Jamie, and now your mother's ill with it. Come along, then; we'll tell Her Ladyship about it."

Jamie Dugan followed his parish priest toward the English lady all called good-hearted for all her being English. As his mother had said when Her Ladyship sent food last year, we don't pick where we're born and that's a fact. She couldn't help being English.

Inside the huge house MaryKate ran up the wide stairs and down the length of the hall toward the linen room. Leo stepped out of his rooms, looking surprised and pleased to see her.

"MaryKate, you're out of breath."

She didn't bother to answer, speeding on beyond him. He started to follow and then changed his mind, turning toward the stairs.

MaryKate piled blankets from the servants' supplies into a heap, gathering them up and flying back toward the annex.

When she got there Leo was standing near Amelia and the Protestant reverend. He came toward her, looking concerned and taking the pile of blankets. "I had no idea," he told her.

MaryKate studied his sober expression.

"Mary-Kathleen," Amelia called to her, and MaryKate moved around the English lord.

"Yes, Your Ladyship?"

"Please take a list of the items the doctor says he will

137

need. Lord Cumberland has agreed to send for another load of supplies. Would you please see to whatever he needs?"

MaryKate spoke as Leo smiled at her, his eyes lingering on her mouth. "Yes, Your Ladyship."

Leo gestured toward the doctor across the room, waiting for MaryKate to pass him. She went around the other side of the pallet to avoid coming near him.

Amelia looked around the large room which was already overfilled with pallets. "We may have to move the school table out. There's so little room left already."

Hugh Grinstead glanced at the table. "What of your school needs?"

"There is little school left with most of the students going home to help their families. I'll worry about the school after the current emergency is over."

"The current emergency seems to be endemic in this land. The Irish are forever having famines."

Amelia's brow furrowed. "Please speak more quietly."

"I'm sorry."

"If you have any wish, any hope, of converting these people, you have to first at least try to understand them. Even if you never truly liked them."

"I didn't say I do not like them."

Amelia spoke in low tones: "You did not need to."

"They are converting already," Hugh said complacently. "My church superiors are well pleased."

"I wonder why," Amelia said.

"With my progress," Hugh reported.

"Yours? Or hunger's?" she asked.

"That's not kind," Hugh told her. And then he spoke in louder tones, his voice carrying beyond them, "You should protect your own strength, Your Ladyship. I really must insist or you shall never be able to continue helping our poor unfortunate Romish charges. I shall have to take you away from all this for a few hours or you shall know no rest."

Amelia stood undecided for a moment and then nodded toward the reverend. After telling the doctor she would soon return, she left MaryKate and Leo to sort out the doctor's needs and allowed the reverend to escort her outside into the square of lawn that edged the annex building.

Across the lawn and the gravel drive beyond it, the Priory

rose dark and forbidding before their eyes. Amelia turned away, heading toward the side gardens and the gate to the riverside.

As she moved she spoke softly, "I feel as if that house now has a thousand eyes."

The reverend glanced toward it but did not speak until he had opened the roofed gateway that led to stone steps and the river below. When he did speak it was in a different tone. "With Harry at every one of them."

"You mustn't call him Harry," she told him.

He shrugged slightly as they descended the wide, shallow, stone steps. "None can hear."

"You're liable to slip sometime, and then where shall we be?"

"I shan't slip. Besides, where are we now? He's determined to cart you back to London, and I've just been posted here. It could be months again before I could put in for a change."

"You have me confused," she told the minister.

"Dearest Amelia—why?" he asked.

"You say we must be discreet and then you undress me in the carriage and demand we meet."

"I can't help wanting you, dear heart," he said smoothly. "Or urging you to meet me for an hour."

"You've been telling me you would follow me to London rather than chance things here."

"In truth it would be much easier to meet in London."

"But we'd be apart for months!" she told him.

"Which would be torture," he agreed easily.

"I must find a way to stay as long as possible."

"I fail to see what you can do, dear heart."

"If I do find a way, we can't meet in carriages!"

"You can still pay calls at the rectory. If we're very careful. We can't afford gossip about us."

"Bother the gossip!" she burst out before she thought to lower her voice.

"Shhh . . ." Grinstead looked up toward the Priory. "You know how voices can carry on these winds, Amelia."

She stared out across the valley, past the river to the mountains purpling in the distance. "It's so very pretty here, isn't it? One would never think that blight has struck again. It seems such a gentle country."

Hugh kept to his point. "I could never marry a divorced woman without leaving the church. More to the point, you were not raised to be a pauper. Even if my position somehow survived, you'd never be able to subsist on the pittance I make from the church. I am not an earl and an heir to a dukedom, after all. I am a mere third son, in line for nothing but others' leavings. And we both know your husband would not be generous with you."

Amelia glanced at the man beside her, something arch in her gaze. "We're both benefiting from my marriage, it would seem. At least monetarily."

He stopped walking. "That's not funny."

"Actually, it is, when you come to think about it. I'm sure Harry would think it was," Amelia replied.

"Before or after he challenged me to a duel?"

Amelia laughed. "There's no dueling in this day and age!" Amelia smiled impishly. "But would you die to be with me?"

"I'd rather live. And be with you as much as possible," the Reverend Grinstead replied.

Amelia sighed. "Men have no poetry in their souls."

"How can you sat that! There's Shakespeare, Byron, on and on—"

She dismissed his words with a wave of her gloved hand. "That's in words. I mean in life. Men talk a fine prattle, but they never really mean it."

"I'm wounded."

"No, you're not. But you would be if you dueled with Harry, most likely. He's probably good at that sort of thing."

"Lots of practice?"

"I rather think he has practice at all sorts of things," she said sourly. "I'm sure he hasn't sat at home for a decade and pined for me." She scowled. "He despises me for leaving him."

"Surely you can understand that."

"Pride," Amelia pronounced. "What men have in lieu of true sensibilities."

"And I?" Hugh asked.

KATHLEEN

Amelia turned her heart-shaped face up toward him, her eyes meltingly sweet. "You, I wish I could kiss. Here and now." She heard his groan.

"You promised last week you'd find a way to get away."

Her smile was almost evil. "We had a few moments in the carriage . . . alone. . . ."

"It wasn't enough!" he told her sharply, turning to stop her, facing her squarely. "I need more!"

"Oh?" Amelia sounded the soul of innocence. "I rather thought you were manipulating me that rainy afternoon—"

"Amelia!" Hugh looked and sounded totally wounded.

She relented, reaching to touch his bearded cheek. "I'm sorry—forgive me . . . I'll find a way."

"You'll get away?" Hugh asked, grabbing her hand away from his cheek, his gaze barely glancing toward the Priory high above them.

"I'll get away, at least for a little. I'll just follow your lead from earlier. I'm very tired and need the respite of a few hours away to rejuvenate my spirits."

"Wonderful!"

"But now we'd best get back before someone comes looking for me," Amelia told him.

They retraced their steps along the river path, heading back toward Priory Hill. The Reverend Grinstead paced along beside the countess, his hands clasped behind his back. From a distance they looked the souls of propriety.

Before they got to the steps, he said, "Why are you doing all this? I mean setting up hospital. Surely you didn't do this last year, did you?"

"No. But anything that can be used as an excuse to keep me here is of benefit to us. Isn't it? Besides, these people really do need help. How some are to survive another year of famine, I can't imagine."

They started up the steps. "And what of us?" Hugh asked.

She saw his somber expression. "Perhaps the Lord will allow us our pleasure in each other if I continue my good works. And you continue yours."

"I rather doubt He can be bribed," Hugh told her.

"You rather doubt He exists," Amelia told him back.

"Ah, well. That's another story. You would be amazed at

the number of priests, reverends, and preachers who believe in nothing more than themselves."

"I wonder," Amelia replied as they came near the closed gate. "I wonder if I would be surprised at anything, anymore."

Later that afternoon, tired beyond measure, MaryKate walked with a slow step, crossing from the annex toward the Priory itself.

A small sound intruded into her secret thoughts. She looked to her right and saw a black-cloaked figure loom beside her. For one brief second her heart raced, leaping at the thought of Harry standing there.

When she recognized Leo, her pent-up breath expelled in a long sigh.

"Did I frighten you?" Leo asked, coming closer.

"No," MaryKate replied. She started past him, only to find herself stopped by his arm.

"I have the feeling you've been avoiding me," Lord Cumberland said.

"I have no idea what you're talking about, Your Lordship."

"No?" Leo risked a glimpse back behind himself at the draped library windows. Then he grabbed MaryKate closer.

Harry dropped the curtain he held, staring at his own hand for a long moment. Then he turned, taking long strides out of the library and onto the terrace that surrounded the back half of the Priory.

As he walked outside, directly in front of him, Leo held MaryKate in his embrace. Harry stopped in midstride. His heart twisted within his chest, churning the pit of his stomach. Part of Harry thought of his mother's perfidy. And of Amelia's long years ago. He hesitated, afraid MaryKate would be untrustworthy like all the women he'd ever known. And still he found himself wanting to smash Leo's face and rip him away from her.

As he watched, MayKate fought back against Leo's avalanche, freeing herself. She reared back, the flat of her palm striking the side of his cheek. The blow resounded in the quiet afternoon hours. "Of all the insufferable, unmitigated, boorish *boors* alive in this land, you, sir, are the worst! How *dare* you?!"

Harry's laugh interrupted the scene. MaryKate's face flamed red, Leo quickly reaching for her hands to forestall another blow. "I'll make it worth your while," he whispered hoarsely. "*Very* worth your while."

MaryKate's eyes flew back toward where Harry stood. He was gone. She stared at the empty space, shaken that he could see this scene, could laugh, and then just leave.

"You name it," Leo urged her. "Just name it and it shall be yours."

MaryKate turned back to face Leo. "I should name something," she said.

"Yes!" Leo replied, impatience in his every movement.

Beyond them Harry stood in the shadows of giant potted trees that stood sentinel at each end of the length of the terrace, the sun slowly sinking from sight.

His fingers were curled into a fist, his mind resisting his body's urge to step forward and smash those fists into the soft pulp of Leo's effete belly.

In one small part of Harry's heart, he hoped MaryKate would disappoint him. Hoped she would succumb to Leo's blandishments and his bribes and therefore free Harry from whatever this compulsion was that kept drawing him against all reason toward MaryKate.

"Name it!" Leo urged. "Name anything!"

"What I want," MaryKate told him plainly, "is for you to unhand me." Her voice was stone cold. She waited for him to let go of her. "And that you never inform the earl of your actions today."

"I never shall!" Leo agreed.

Harry, hearing the exchange, felt his heart grow cold within him, innate distrust welling up at her words. He waited, silent and unseen, for the words that would brand her forever.

"Good," MaryKate said. "I should hate for His Lordship to find he had given friendship to a low-grade lout who forces his attentions on servants, making them the unwilling victims of his unwanted advances!"

MaryKate swept past Leo, on through the side parlor door.

KATHLEEN

After the door slammed shut, Leo heard Harry's deep-throated laughter in the shadows beyond. He walked toward it. "Don't be so sure of yourself," Leo said sourly. "We both heard you. She was playing to your benefit."

"You were wrong about her. Admit it," Harry said.

"Even if I am wrong about her, I still may have the last laugh, old boy."

Harry's brow creased, his eyes clouding. "What are you saying?"

Leo smiled. "Possibly nothing, old man . . . then again . . . possibly everything. . . ."

Leo walked away, leaving Harry to stare after him.

16

Harry called MaryKate to the library after dinner. She found him there, pacing the floor. He stopped when he heard her enter, turning around to face her.

"Please—sit."

She watched him. "I'd rather stand, Your Lordship."

An uneasy tension colored the air between them, each of them aware of it, neither of them willing to name it. "Yes. Well," he said finally and then fell silent, staring down at his own boots. Rousing himself, he moved toward the fire. "Tell me about Ireland."

There was no answer. He looked toward her, seeing her confused expression.

"I don't understand," she was saying.

"I want to understand what is happening here. Why people continue to live on potatoes and nothing else when the crop keeps failing year after year. Why they choose to starve."

"Choose!" She found her voice, coming forward to glare at him, the firelight mirrored in her eyes. "How dare you, an *Englishman,* say that?! Do you not know what you've done to us?! You stole our land. The people own none but the smallest, rockiest patches. The patches you English did not think good enough to grab and call your own! We work as your tenants, all the grains belonging to you for rents. The land that's left won't grow enough wheat or barley to feed a family! The potato will grow in the cracks of the rocks, that's why we live on it! We live on it because you've made it so!"

His eyes bored into hers. "Do you hate us, then?"

She stood her ground. "Should we not?" But her voice lowered. "And doesn't the Bible preach charity? We've seen none coming to us. Except Her Ladyship's. When you create a mess, the least you could do is help clean it up."

"Yet you work for us."

"There's none else who can pay," MaryKate told him.

He watched her still, his words quiet. "Do you hate me?"

Her breath caught in her throat. She looked in his eyes, seeing what seemed to be deep within them. Something hurting and unsure. "I . . . I hate none." She faltered over the words.

Harry didn't seem able to pull his eyes away from hers. "I've sent round to the local officials. They'll meet with me to discuss what can be done. And I've sent to my father to forward funds to buy enough grain to sustain our people through this."

"Our people?"

He did turn away then. "My tenants." The fire sputtered up in the grate. Harry reached for an iron, prodding a log over so that it burned more evenly.

MaryKate watched his broad neck as he turned away, watched the curve of his neck as he leaned to reach toward the wood. "Thank you," she almost whispered the words.

"I'm not doing it for your thanks." His words came out sounding rough and hard. "Nor any else's. My family is responsible for these people, and I do not like what I find here."

He turned back to find her eyes lowered, the glisten of a tear on one cheek. His heart wrenched over and he found himself moving without thought, letting the iron drop and reaching for her. He tipped her face up toward his own, seeing the sparkle of unspilt tears filling the emerald eyes that looked huge in the firelight. Everything around him was pale and insipid next to the eyes that stared back into his own.

They stood as if in tableau, neither of them pulling back, caught in time and afraid to move.

The sound of steps in the hall beyond startled them, Harry dropping his hands to his sides. The door opened, Leo looking inside. Harry stood bare inches away from MaryKate. "Am I interrupting?" Leo asked languidly.

"Yes," Harry spoke harshly. "We have been discussing the fate of Ireland."

"Oh, really? Such a weighty topic for this time of night, don't you think?" Leo looked back behind him. "Amelia, where did you get to?"

Amelia came through the doorway, looking from MaryKate to her husband.

"Excuse me," MaryKate said. "But if you've no further need of me—" She spoke to the earl, who hesitated and then nodded. She turned toward the door, speeding out into the hall and away from them all.

"Harry and MaryKate were discussing Ireland," Leo told Amelia.

Amelia moved toward a seat by the fire. "I didn't know you were interested in the topic," she told Harry.

"I am now." Harry paced the room as Leo plopped into a chair.

"Oh, do stop. You tire me out just watching you," Leo told his old friend.

"Is something bothering you?" Amelia asked her husband, watching him turn round to stare at her.

"Is something bothering me? Isn't something bothering you?" He stared at her in disbelief as she replied:

"I am quite content."

"Content! Content to leave these wretched people to grow ill and starve? Or content to stay and watch them die before your eyes?"

Amelia spoke complacently. "I am doing all that one can to help."

"You are doing no such thing! You are doling out charity. What they need is a plan of action to end this miserable cycle of blights and famines!"

KATHLEEN

"That's the Good Lord's work. Not mine," Amelia told her husband firmly.

"I hardly think he's doing the job properly," Harry told her.

"Harry!" Amelia stared up at him.

He stared back. And then turned away, striding out of the room. Leo smiled over at Harry's wife.

"One of his moods. That's all. Soon over," Leo ended.

Outside, Harry marched toward the stables, the night sky inky black with clouds that seemed to hover over the valley closer and closer each night. The smell of putrefaction was faint on the breezes now, ocean salts and fishy brine rolling in on the landward winds, covering over the smell of the ailing earth that held corruption and disease within its loamy black depths.

The stables were empty of all save the horses in their stalls, the stableboy long gone to his bed. Harry lit a lamp and then just stood in the middle of the straw-strewn barn, hardly noticing the freshening winds that whistled in around him, turning colder by the minute and losing the smell of the ocean to the crisp clean smell of icy cold.

Harry walked past the first stalls, seeing the black he had bought in Dublin. He spoke to the stallion, calming its uneasy movements within its stall, the winds carrying a message of danger to the animals that humans did not seem able to grasp.

The Earl of Lismore let himself into the stall, reaching a hand toward the black's mane, rubbing its nose and reaching for a currying comb, brushing the stallion's sides.

Archie found him there an hour later. "I thought you might be needing this." Archie handed over a thick wool cape. "In case you hadn't noticed, it's colder than a witches' tit about now."

Harry straightened up, putting the brush down. "Thanks."

Archie shrugged. And just stood at the mouth of the horse stall, eyeing the man before him. "You want to talk about it?"

Harry scowled. "About what?"

KATHLEEN

"I've known Your Gracious Lordshipness since you were little, Master Harry, and already getting into more trouble than any three monkeys put together could. Asking me 'about what' "—Archie mimicked Harry's cold tone—"or trying to put me off with that scowl you've copied from your old da isn't going to work."

When Harry spoke he wasn't looking at Archie. "There's nothing to talk about."

"For starters, there's how long we're staying here," Archie told him.

"I can't leave while all is in disarray," Harry said flatly.

"Then there's what you're to do with a wife who wants no part of you."

"Don't be impertinent," Harry said.

"I'm being practical. Which is more than I can say for the old duke or you, yourself. How do you get a child by someone who wants you as little as you want her?"

"Others have done," Harry replied grimly.

"Aye. But the kind of man that does that isn't you by half, Mister Harry."

Harry examined Archie's expression. "You still treat me as a child."

"Do I?" Archie thought about it. "Maybe that's soon to change." Archie studied the dark eyes that searched his own. "Maybe your old da was right after all in sending you over here. Right for the wrong reasons, but still right."

"I don't know what you mean," Harry said.

Archie stretched, yawning wide before turning away. "Maybe I don't know, either. I'll tell Lord Leo you've decided to stay awhile longer."

"And have I?" Harry asked to Archie's back.

"Haven't you?" Archie never turned around.

Harry watched him until he was out of sight.

As Archie walked inside, MaryKate slipped out of the house. Bundling her old cloak around herself, she walked swiftly through the chilly side gardens, rounding toward the stable.

Her head bent against the incoming ocean winds, she did not see Harry reach the doorway just ahead of her, coming out as she started in.

KATHLEEN

Harry saw MaryKate in the same moment that she saw his feet bare inches ahead of her. She stopped, startled.

"Oh!"

"What's wrong now?" Harry asked, seeing the look in her eyes.

She shook her head. "Nothing."

"Where are you off to?"

"I—I've been spending the nights at my brother's, helping Sophie out."

Harry stepped back inside the stable, letting her enter. "Are they all right?"

She answered slowly, "As well as any."

"And the children?"

MaryKate's expression softened. "Thank you, they're fine so far."

"I want to send them their rewards."

She looked troubled. "I don't know if that would be wise."

"Your brother?"

She nodded.

Harry reached for the roan. "Can you handle a horse on your own?"

"I've been taking the black." She saw him turn to stare at her. "He's quicker," she explained. Seeing his slow smile, she returned it. "And he seemed to know me," she added.

MaryKate watched the English earl saddle the black stallion for her, bringing him out of the stall.

She spoke shyly: "You do that as if you've had plenty of practice."

He looked at the horse. "I've probably spent more of my life around horses than around people." Thinking of what he had just said, he felt suddenly self-conscious. He stiffened his posture, his eyes turning opaque—until he saw her trusting expression. Then something within him softened. "I'll help you up."

She felt the warmth of his flesh as he reached to hand her into the saddle, her body melting against his touch.

Harry's hands felt the change within her, her body softening under his hands. He held her tighter, bringing her back against his chest, her breath as short as his.

He turned her around to face him, his heart trip-hammer-

KATHLEEN

ing as he watched her face. Her eyes melting into his, her lips slightly parted, her breath stopped as if waiting for whatever he would do next.

He leaned forward, slowly, covering her mouth with his own. She surged toward him. His arms tightened around her, and she clung within his grasp, drinking him in.

He let her go finally, wrenching himself back away from her. Staring at her with eyes filled with longing and pain.

"My behavior is inexcusable." His words were as sharp and flat as stones flung at her. "I don't know what came over me."

MaryKate reached for his arm, feeling him flinch under her touch. "Let me help."

Harry stared at her, his voice self-protected and far away, "I don't know what you mean."

Her hand left his arm, doubts shadowing the eyes that never left his own. Her skin was the palest pink in the lamplight, a faint shadowing of freckles across the bridge of her tiny nose. Her lips were soft, his gaze caught by them, his own lips longing to crush her to him again.

She saw the war within him, but did not understand it. "How can I help?" she asked softly.

He wrenched his gaze away from her lips, his eyes skipping across her and then away toward the door to the outside world. "No one can help."

She watched him stride away, her heart going out to him. A storm of unwanted feelings raged within her. She could still feel his lips on hers and she wanted his arms back around her, his strength flooding through her. She was frightened and unsure of his moodiness and the sudden coldness that thrust her aside with stiff words and strode away without a backward glance.

She wanted to comfort him. She wanted to run away from him as he had from her.

She leaned against the stallion's side, feeling its warmth. Then she straightened, leading it out of the stall and toward a low wooden box. Standing on the box she could reach the stirrup, pulling herself up into the saddle.

Harry stood by the river wall, staring outward at the stormy night skies. When he heard the horse's hooves, he turned, watching MaryKate disappear down the hilly road.

17

Sophie O'Hallion stood near the fire, the sound of her children's light snoring filling the tiny cottage with their presence.

Tired beyond measure, she sank to the three-legged stool beside the hearth, reaching for more peat. She watched it catch, the soft, smoky light it gave off patterning the whitewashed walls, drifting upward toward the thatched roof.

The baby, Brian, moved in his wooden crib beside his mother, one tiny arm flung outside his quilt, the hand balled into a fist. To the other side of the fireplace, little Meg slept fitfully, coughing every now and then with the phlegm that was building in her nose and throat.

Sophie heard the sound of the horse outside, not looking round when MaryKate came through the door. Her eyes on the tiny sputtering flames, Sophie spoke in a soft tone that would not wake her sleeping children. "Meg's cold is worsening."

MaryKate went to the child, feeling her fevered brow, and then coming to sink to the floor beside her sister-in-law. "Are you sure you don't want to bring her to the Priory? The doctor's set up an infirmary in the annex."

KATHLEEN

"And wouldn't your brother kill us both, then? He'll not hear of the English at all these last days." Sophie sighed, her shoulders rounded with tiredness.

"Why don't you lay down? I'll put some tea on and wait up for Paddy and that unforgiving husband of yours."

Sophie heard but didn't answer right away. She stared into the fireglow as if answers could be found there. "Is it a curse, do you think, MaryKate? Is God that angry with us, are we that bad that he would do this to us again?"

"Nonsense!" MaryKate said stoutly. The baby stirred, and she lowered her voice, reaching to grasp Sophie's hands. "We're no worse than anyone else and much better than some that have no famines at all. This isn't God's punishment. It's man's own."

Sophie turned to look at her sister-in-law. "What are you saying, then?"

"We've put all our eggs in one basket, Sophie. A basket of potatoes! We should have planted the swedes and whatever else we could and learned to do with other things besides. We should never have let the English steal our land, and we should be taking it back."

Sophie's eyes widened. "MaryKate, they'll arrest you for saying things like that!"

"I don't mean we should steal as they do. I mean we should fight in courts and Parliament and in England itself— we should send men there who can stand up and speak against the landlords."

Sophie shook her head, then looked back into the fire. "Those that have things never give them up easily, Mary-Kate. It's not the way of the world. They'll take, but they'll never give back. Not without a fight. And how can poor Ireland fight England? Sure'n they own the world! Even the heathens in India and Africa do what they say and let them take their lands away. If they can do all that a thousand thousand miles away, what all can't they do to us, sitting here next door, as it were?"

"There has to be a way," MaryKate said.

"Aye, there's a way. And all you hot-tempered O'Hallions are after knowing it. But it's a fighting way and there aren't enough of us and that's a fact. All we'll do is break our hearts and kill off our men with talk like that."

"So we're just to submit?!" MaryKate demanded.

Sophie looked back at her. "That's not a word you'd be after knowing about, Mary-Kathleen O'Hallion, now would it? Your mother died too young and your brothers raised you too wild. Sure'n you're more the youngest boy in the family than the youngest girl. Someday you may find out the meaning of the word. It's a woman's lot to submit, Mary-Kate."

MaryKate's eyes darkened. She looked away, staring into the flames, feeling her cheeks flaming with color at Sophie's words. The feeling that melted her against the earl, that weakened her knees when he simply looked at her, came washing back over her.

"What's this now?" Sophie was asking. "What's wrong?"

"Nothing." MaryKate's voice was low and soft.

"Nothing, is it? Or have you finally figured out what you've been put on this earth for, Mary-Kathleen?" Sophie teased the younger woman, watching MaryKate's cheeks flame again at her words. "You're as red as my best petticoat."

"I'm not!"

"You are, and it's not the fire's reflection, so don't go saying it. What have you been up to?" Sophie smiled, her eyes happier at the thought. "Tell me right now, before your brothers get home and put their noses where they don't belong."

MaryKate almost answered. Almost poured her heart out. She wanted to empty it of all the confused feelings Harry caused within her. Wanted to ask what she should do and how to stop herself before it was too late. For she had a presentiment that one day soon it would be too late. She would cross a bridge that could never be crossed back.

But she couldn't care about an English earl. Or any Englishman. She couldn't look at Lady Amelia's husband and want to throw herself into his arms.

"MaryKate?" Sophie questioned her.

MaryKate hesitated. "I don't know what you're talking about," she said finally. How could she tell her brother's wife she was a wicked and spiteful harlot who wanted nothing in this world more than to be held in the arms of her benefactor's husband. An Englishman to boot. He wasn't even Catholic.

"I'm probably a little feverish myself," MaryKate said after another small silence.

Sophie still watched her, concern showing on her brow now, deepening the fine lines that were beginning to crease her milky skin. "It's nothing to do with that big Englishman, is it?"

MaryKate's head snapped up. "What?"

"The English earl, or the other one. Tell me it's not, MaryKate."

"Don't be ridiculous!" MaryKate's true dislike of Leo came through her words. "If you think some English fop could possibly be someone I'd look twice at, you've gone crazy."

Sophie relaxed a little. She sighed, letting out a long, slow breath. "Mother Mary, I must be tired to the bone to have such thoughts. Of course you'd never let one of those ne'er-do-wells touch a finger to you. Forgive me, MaryKate."

MaryKate felt guilty at Sophie's words. And a little defensive. "You can't call Lady Amelia's husband a ne'er-do-well. He did well enough right here for you and your children, remember."

Sophie shivered. "What a sight. An English earl in my home. And Johnny coming home to see it. I thought he'd kill him then and there."

"The earl's done nothing to us."

"MaryKate, how can you say that? He's English!"

Before MaryKate could answer, the door opened, Paddy coming in first, Johnny close behind. Both of them were muddy and tired.

"Don't go tracking those boots across me clean floor!" Sophie stood up, and Paddy stopped where he was. Putting one foot behind the other, he pulled his feet free of the dripping boots.

Johnny walked to a stool and sat down, Sophie reaching to help her husband. "Just look at the two of you!" she scolded as she pulled his boots off.

"Leave off, Sophie." Johnny stared across the room at MaryKate. "You're spending a lot of time down with the likes of us these days."

"I want to spell Sophie when I can."

"We don't need charity. Yours or the English."

MaryKate bristled. She stood up, her arms akimbo, hands on her hips as she glared at her oldest brother. "Leave off, yourself, Johnny O'Hallion."

"MaryKate, Johnny, don't be starting or you'll wake the children."

MaryKate swallowed her words, still glaring at Johnny as he eyed her and then looked away. "As long as you're here, make yourself useful and fetch our tea and some bread."

After a moment of rebellion MaryKate did as she was told, Sophie sighing again, this time with relief. "And how is it?" Sophie asked the two men.

Paddy rubbed the back of his own neck, twisting his back a little before sinking to the stool beside the fire and the two sleeping children. "We got what we could out of the ground. Half-grown, but we filled the pit and brought some home." He reached into his pockets, pulling out the small potatoes and dumping them into a little heap in an empty pot beside the fire.

"There's half that's no good," Johnny reminded his brother.

"Aye, but half a crop's better than none at all," Paddy replied. "Old John Sweeney asked if we could be after helping him at sunup. I said I'd go over—he's having a terrible time of it, trying to bring his crop in with the boys gone on the government service."

"Government dole you mean! What good is it to build roads that go nowhere? I ask you the sense of it. It's better to stay home."

"It's coins in their pockets," Paddy replied. "I've been thinking of doing it meself."

"You'll do no such thing," Johnny told him.

MaryKate saw Paddy's expression. They caught each other's eye as Johnny leaned to his cup of tea. MaryKate handed Paddy a cup, smiling a little when she turned toward him.

"And where's the bread, then?" Johnny was demanding.

"I'll get it," Sophie said, but MaryKate stopped her.

"I already have it," MaryKate told her brother. "There's

KATHLEEN

even a smidge of butter with it, although why I bother with the likes of you, I surely don't know, Johnny O'Hallion."

"You fetch and carry for the English, you can do it for your brother," he told her.

She bit her lip, putting the bread on the table with the pot of butter. Johnny reached across for his knife, cutting into the loaf and throwing a piece toward Paddy.

Sophie was looking toward the baby.

"He's doing fine," MaryKate told her. "Sleeping like a dream. You go on and lay down now. Let me look after these two lummoxes."

"The children—"

"I'll keep an eye and call you if Meg's cough worsens. I'll climb up to the loft in a minute and check on Little John and the other girls. Go on, now."

Sophie smiled wearily. "If you're sure—"

"Go on with you!" MaryKate told her.

"Might as well," Johnny agreed. "If she's here and planning on staying the night."

"Or most of it," MaryKate told her brother. Sophie opened the door to the small bedroom she shared with her husband and the two smallest children.

"I'll carry the wee ones in when I come," Johnny said as his wife left the room.

"If you work up at the Priory by day and here for Sophie at night, when do you sleep, MaryKate?" Paddy asked.

MaryKate shrugged. "I get plenty of sleep. The work's not hard either place, and I'm young."

"You're getting no younger, and that's a fact," Johnny said. "Sophie and me was married and on to having Little John and Betsy and Sally by your age now, Mary-Kathleen O'Hallion."

"At least I have no big lummox like you telling me what to do!" she told him pertly.

"No, you've got an English lord doing it," her brother shot back.

But he didn't see her expression as she quickly turned away, her cheeks flaming again. When she turned back, Johnny was cutting into more bread. But Paddy was staring at her, questions in his eyes.

"He lets you use the horse, then," Paddy said into the

silence when Johnny went to the bedroom, carrying the baby to his crib.

"Yes." MaryKate didn't look up.

Johnny came back, reaching to pick up little Kate, who coughed in her sleep. He carried the restless child away. MaryKate watched Johnny's back, her worry plain in her eyes.

"She'll be all right," Paddy said.

"I hope so," MaryKate replied. "We have medicines up at the Priory."

"Sure'n they've got everything in the world they want up at the Priory, MaryKate," Paddy told her, "but it might as well be on the moon, now, don't you know that? It's got nothing to do with the likes of us."

"Lady Amelia's taking in tenants and even villagers who are ill and helping them get better."

Paddy frowned. "Don't be saying that in front of your brother, then. Johnny hears you, and there'll be hell to pay and well you should know it. He'll be thinking you want him to ask for English charity for one of his own, and he'll blow sky high."

"If he'd listened to me about the turnips—"

"What about the swedes?" Johnny was in the open bedroom doorway, his nightshirt hanging to his bare ankles. He didn't look pleased.

"Nothing," Paddy answered for her. "MaryKate was telling me a story about one of the villagers."

"Not an honest day's work between them." Johnny turned back into the bedroom and closed the door.

MaryKate finished her work, putting the potatoes and water at the edge of the fire where the water would heat and cook them through by morning light. "I'd best get back," she told Paddy.

He stood up and walked her to the door. Scratching at his chest through his flannel work shirt, he watched her go to the large black horse. Leaning against the door, his head against his hand, he waited until she was mounted before he called out, "Be careful."

She looked back at him. "I'm all right."

"I don't mean of the horse, MaryKate," Paddy told her.

158

KATHLEEN

MaryKate stared at her brother. "I'm all right," she said again, this time with much less conviction.

Small drops of moisture fell from the sky, the rain beginning again, slowly at first, the river rising toward its banks as MaryKate rode the horse slowly, carefully, up the Priory hill.

18

By dawn the rain was pouring down savagely, lashing showers of hail mixing in when the temperature dropped.

It was a perishing rain that didn't stop for days on end. The farmers continued trying to pull their wilting crops out of the sodden, blackened ground, coming down with colds that brought fever and then wracking pain to them and soon to all who surrounded them.

Johnny O'Hallion ran back and forth between his cottage and his tiny barn, a sack over his head and shoulders. He shouted out curses to the sky above, Sophie hearing him from the doorway and crossing herself, frightened that God would hear her husband and punish them further.

Sophie looked toward the dark and lowering sky, frightened by the sight. Behind her the children were strangely silent, only the baby crying softly, as if aware of danger and crying out for help.

In the distance the mountains seemed to be coming nearer. Swollen by more and more rain, turbulent streams of falling water flowed down the mountainside, the sounds of roaring rain never ended.

Sophie stood in the doorway, her children behind her, her

KATHLEEN

husband running through the pounding rain, cursing the heavens above. Tears filled her eyes. "Jesus, Mary, and Joseph, what can we do to end this misery?"

No one answered her prayer.

Day after day the rain continued, villagers, tenants, and farmers staying inside, away from the freezing cold of the hail showers, eyeing nature's revolt from under their dripping roofs. The river rose above its banks, overflowing into the nearby fields, the swirling waters covering the potato patches.

The Priory stood sentinel on its hill, its dark gray walls blending with the dark gray days and the gray, lowering skies.

Within its walls the rains dampened the rooms, coloring the spirits of those who dwelt within. Leo kept Archie busy packing his trunks for the first two days of the rain. The next two days Leo paced his rooms and then the lower reaches of the house, testy and uninterested in any topics other than the weather and when he could make his departure.

Amelia was among the missing for hours on end in the days, staying the nights in the annex with the patients MaryKate watched by day. Toward morning MaryKate would come relieve her, dozing for a little before the next day began in earnest.

Leo searched out Harry, finding him once in the billiard room, savagely hitting the small hard balls into their pockets, finding him more and more in the library, pouring over ancient history books of Ireland.

Bored beyond endurance, Leo slept away his afternoons, preparing for departure the instant the weather lifted.

And still it rained, a deluge of water pouring from the sky as if it would never end.

On the fifth day Dr. Kilgallen and Father Ross arrived on foot, soaking wet. The doctor's carriage caught in a deep, muddy rut, his horse lamed and left there until they could get help.

Robert found a change of clothing for the doctor, who changed and then went immediately to work with the annex patients. While he worked, Father Ross went back with

KATHLEEN

Harry, Archie, and the stableboy to see to the horse and buggy.

"Your Lordship needn't bother," Brian Ross began when he realized Harry intended to accompany him.

Harry cut the priest off with a wave of his hand. Leo watched the small group take off in the pelting rain and then retired to the comfort of the library until teatime when an exhausted Dr. Kilgallen walked in, sinking to a chair.

"A glass of port, Doctor?" Leo offered, reaching to refill his own glass.

"Thank you, yes." The man sighed, his eyes closing for a moment. "Forgive me, I've had precious little sleep all week."

"I can well imagine. How have Lady Amelia's patients fared without you?"

"As well as can be expected."

Leo heard a tinge of hopelessness in the words. "What is this fever that's felling so many?"

"They call it Blight Fever. It accompanies the worst blights. But it's the typhus that concerns me."

Leo stared at the man. "Typhus?" He didn't want to believe his ears. "Are you telling me there's the possibility of typhus here?"

"Possibility?" The doctor shook his head. "Hardly a possibility. The young McGonigal has it already. We've got to move the rest of the patients away from him and pray it hasn't already spread."

Leo was on his feet. "Are you saying we are all exposed to the typhus?"

"I warned Her Ladyship of the dangers before she began this project; by rights she could have left for Dublin or London and saved herself this grief and work."

"Could have? Should have!" Leo barked. "She is not only endangering herself, she is endangering the rest of us! Why, even you could be carrying the germs to infect me on the spot!" Leo put his glass down, backing away from the man.

"I have no symptoms, Lord Cumberland," the doctor replied wearily.

"None yet. I am sorry, Doctor, but I see no reason to place myself in further danger than I already am because of a foolish notion of coming along to help out a friend! This is asking too much of mere friendship!"

Leo strode out of the room, leaving the door to the hall wide open. A cold draft spread across the fire-warmed room. The doctor stood up and closed the door, then poured himself another glass of port. The sounds of the rain pouring down outside the heavily draped windows drowned out the sounds of the household help going about their work.

The doctor moved to the bookshelves, fingering a volume here, pulling one from a shelf there, until he saw the small pile of books on the desk near the windows.

He was glancing at a history of Irish parliament when the door opened and Harry walked inside.

"Sorry," the doctor said. "I didn't mean to startle you."

Harry eyed the book in the other man's hand. "Your horse should be all right. It looks to be only a sprain."

"Thank our Gracious Lord. I didn't know where I was to get another."

"Your carriage is another matter. It will require a great deal more work than it's worth to repair it."

"Ah, now, that's another matter. I have patients who pay in services for that which they've no money. I'll be able to have it patched together well enough for it to serve a few more years. That's about all I'm good for myself."

Harry threw himself into a fireside chair, running his hands back through his wet hair.

The doctor watched him. "There was no need for you to go yourself, Your Lordship—"

"It did me good. These past days have been enough to drive one mad. How are the patients?" Harry asked.

The doctor hesitated. "I'm afraid they are more than Her Ladyship bargained for. And Lord Cumberland seems very upset by their proximity."

"I beg your pardon?"

"It's understandable," the doctor continued. "There is surely no reason for any of you to be exposing yourselves to fever and typhus."

Harry stared at the man. "Typhus?"

"It was inevitable. I told Her Ladyship, but she would not listen to me." The doctor watched the earl's troubled expression. "She has done everything possible, I assure you. I could not have done more had I been here."

"She has been sleeping in the annex along with the ill, as has her assistant."

"MaryKate? Ah, and isn't she something, then? Nary a complaint about hours or tiredness or whatall. Going from dawn to dawn right along beside Her Ladyship. A real gem you have there, if you don't mind my saying so, Your Lordship."

Harry stood up. "I don't want them spending the nights there."

"Yes, I agree. Overtired and rundown they'll be no help to the poor and in danger themselves. I've said as much to both of them. But MaryKate will stay as long as Her Ladyship asks. And begging your pardon, Your Lordship, but it's more than I can do to change Her Ladyship's mind about anything once she's set herself upon something."

Harry looked grim. "I shall insist."

The doctor nodded. "That's a wise decision. I hope she'll listen."

"She will listen," Harry replied, reaching to ring for Wallace.

It was a quarter of an hour before Amelia appeared in the library, impatiently asking what he needed. She saw the doctor across the room near the fireplace. "If this is about removing my patients, I won't discuss it."

"Your patients?" Harry asked.

"Our tenants," Amelia replied. "They are, most of them, our tenants, and they need our help."

"Have I said they do not?"

She paused. "What is it you wish?"

"I do not wish. I insist." He said the words quietly but there was no mistaking how emphatically he meant them. "You will find help for the evening hours. There will be no more dawn to dawn hours spent in the annex."

"There is no way—"

"You will *find* a way," Harry told her.

Amelia saw his determination. "It will do you no good," she said plainly. The doctor looked away, trying not to hear their intimate conversation.

KATHLEEN

"It will do me the good of not having you contract typhus," Harry told her baldly.

She hesitated. And then clasped her hands together. "If you are so determined, I suppose there is nothing left for me to do. I shall find someone to help Mary-Kathleen."

"MaryKate will not stay overnight, either," Harry said flatly.

"These people are sick; they can't be left alone all night!"

"Do you intend for MaryKate to work with you during the daylight hours?"

"Of course! How can I handle it all myself?"

Harry looked grim. "Then she shall not spend her nights there. Find someone to sit with them. The doctor will be here until the rain lets up; if there is anything amiss, they will send for you. But I will not tolerate your exposing yourself, or MaryKate, to excessive danger."

Amelia heard the change in his voice when he pronounced MaryKate's name. Turning away, she walked out into the hall. Leo came around the corner from the main hall and saw her.

"Amelia, I'd sent to the annex for you. We need to talk."

"I have to get back."

"*Not* until we've talked," Leo insisted. He took her arm, drawing her toward the library door.

She stopped him. "The doctor and Harry are in there. I do not wish to see them."

Leo turned toward the side parlor. "Neither do I."

"Well?" Amelia asked when they were inside.

"You have to leave here immediately."

"What are you talking about?" Amelia replied.

"I am saying that you are in danger. And in danger in more ways than one." He looked into her uncomprehending eyes. "Typhus is deadly, Amelia. You are endangering not only yourself, but all the rest of us."

"I can't leave."

"You can and you should." He reached for her hands. "Come to Dublin with me. Make Harry come!"

She almost laughed. "Make Harry? How does one make Harry do *any*thing?"

"Do you realize what is going on here? *You* may be staying

to help these benighted people, but *he's* staying because of her!''

"Her?"

"Don't tell me you don't know. Can't you see what's going on under your very nose?!"

Amelia watched her husband's friend. "Are you saying there is something between MaryKate and my husband?"

"Yes."

It took her a moment to digest his simple reply. Then she shocked him, smiling suddenly. "I wondered why he was no longer demanding my bedroom. Hopefully that will mean he'll not demand I leave."

"My god, you don't care!"

"About a man I was married to against my wishes? Whom I ran from at first chance? I lived in Harry's house for six weeks and had not seen him in ten years before his father decreed that he should walk in this door." She paused. "Oh, yes, I care, Leo. I care very much. But not in the way you think. Now, if you will let me pass, I shall get back to my good works."

Leo stared at her. "That sounds positively sarcastic."

"Does it?" Amelia thought about his words. When she spoke again she sounded totally sincere. "Perhaps I am uncomfortable with all this talk about my good works. One does what one can."

Leo watched her, gauging her. "Some would say one does too much. I have to tell you that I have no intention of staying in this godforsaken, plague-ridden country."

Amelia hesitated. "You must do what you feel best. Have you told Harry your feelings?"

"I shall at first opportunity," Leo said.

"Good. Perhaps he'll leave, too."

"And take MaryKate with him?" Leo asked sarcastically.

"I hardly think she'd go," Amelia said, unperturbed.

Leo tried to read Amelia's expression. "And you, yourself, have no intention of leaving."

"No. But I sincerely hope that you convince Harry to accompany you back to England."

"I don't think he will leave without you," Leo told her.

"I pity us all if you're right," Amelia said.

Leo watched her. "What is happening here?" he asked, seeing her eyes cloud over at his question.

"A great mistake." Amelia turned away, leaving Leo to stare after her. Then he moved toward the library, grim determination in every step.

Within the library, the doctor was telling Harry it was time for him to get back to his patients. Leo opened the door to find the doctor ready to come through it. Leo stepped back, letting the man pass, and then confronting Harry. "I am packed for Dublin."

"The roads are impassable," Harry replied.

"Nevertheless, I am prepared, and I will leave at first opportunity." Leo spoke with great force, as if expecting an argument.

"I can understand your decision," Harry told him.

Leo hesitated. "And you should insist that Amelia accompany us."

"Amelia is determined to stay, and for once I agree with her. And I myself shan't leave until our dependents are out of danger."

"This land could kill you! And the people would like nothing better!"

Harry shrugged. "That's neither here nor there. My duty is to see that they are taken care of."

"Even if it kills you?" Leo asked sarcastically. "What good will you do them then?"

"If I do not help, at least I shall not continue to harm them."

Harry's words brought an impatient gesture from Leo. "I fail to see how you have ever harmed these people. You'd never even seen them before this benighted trip your father insisted upon!"

"Precisely. And thousands of others like us have contributed to this wretched state of affairs by abdicating responsibility to land agents and bailiffs."

"Irish land agents and Irish bailiffs."

"Irish and Anglo-Irish. There's no patent on stupidity and greed."

"Oh, lord, Harry. You are beginning to become tiresome. Even boring. I like you much better gambling at Crockford's and seducing the ladies." Leo hesitated. "If you're so

KATHLEEN

inclined, why don't you bring the girl as well? At least as far as Dublin. Surely this infatuation will have worn off by then."

"What infatuation?!" Harry demanded sharply.

"Come off it, old man. You got me off the point last week, but you shan't do so again. It's as plain as the nose on your face. And her calf-eyed expression when she looks at you would tell a wall-eyed fool what's going on."

"Nothing is 'going on,'" Harry said ominously.

Leo yawned. "Look, old boy, it doesn't matter one whit to me. Except for the fact that it's keeping you hanging around this godforsaken backwoods much too long for your own good. Not to mention my safety. I shan't have it, I tell you. I shall return, and I shall tell your father all, if he berates me for coming back without you. I swear it. I shall tell all."

"There is nothing to tell!" Harry boomed out, guilt making his anger loud. "Don't be a bloody bad loser, Leo!"

"Loser?! Are you talking about the little Irish baggage? Harry, old boy, left alone, far from here and prying eyes, I could get that little milkmaid to do my bidding on any part of my anatomy I chose."

"Leo, leave it alone."

"Oh, I shall, old boy, never fear." Leo smiled wide, his eyes cold. "If you'll excuse me, however, I have more important things to worry about than an Irish . . . servant."

The door closed between them. Harry stared at it, his eyes tortured. The training of an entire lifetime told him to go after Leo and make amends. He stood up, and hesitated, unable to go after the man who held her in so little esteem. Anxious, upset, berating himself and Leo, too, he paced the room, looking from the door to the bookshelves that lined the room to the fire in the grate.

His hand tightened around the glass he was holding, his fingers closing tighter and tighter. Until he noticed what he was doing and stared down at the half empty glass in his hand. The blood red port pooled within the small cut-crystal glass.

Anger at himself, at his own helplessness, grew within him, rising higher and wider until he thought he would burst with it. He raised the arm that held the glass and smashed it as hard as he could into the fireplace.

Shards of glass caught fire sparks as the crystal shattered, glistening as the prismed glass bits fell all around and into the logs.

He told himself he was going completely insane. He told himself Leo was a total fool. He told himself he wanted nothing more than to be free of this house, this land, these feelings, and the wife in name only who had brought him here. The young snip of an Irish girl did not enter the equation.

She meant absolutely nothing to him.

Nothing at all.

~ 19 ~

THE MORNING THE RAIN STOPPED, farmers all over the valley rushed to their sodden fields, surveying the damage to their crops.

Johnny and Paddy were out at first light, spades in hand, staring at the blackened, dead stalks that lay across the wet ground. Johnny shivered, more at the sight than at the cold morning air. A deep pit of fear opened up in his stomach, sucking all hope away.

"It's not as bad as some." Paddy spoke the words softly, petitioning God that it would be so. He used the spade as a brace, leaning on it, his eyes going toward the potato pit. Then, as if reading Paddy's mind, Johnny grabbed his spade and raced toward the potatoes they had salvaged before the rains began in earnest.

Johnny was already digging, laying bare the covering of wet ferns as Paddy reached his spade to help.

"Johnny—they're rotten, too . . ." Paddy reached to pick up a handful of the decaying ferns.

Johnny O'Hallion stared down into a mass of corruption. A sound came from deep in his throat as he sank to his knees on the damp earth, plunging his arms into the mass of rotten ferns and potatoes, as if his hands could find what the spade could not.

His arms were up to the elbows in the rotting heap of potatoes, his hands groping in the slimy mass, trying to find some, find any, that had not already turned.

"Johnny . . . give over . . . " Anguish brought Paddy to his knees beside his brother. "God in Heaven, what are we to do?"

Johnny pulled his arms out of the mess, holding them out toward his brother as if in supplication. The slimy black corruption dripped from his skin. "We're to die. That's what we're to do. Unless we steal back what's ours. And fight."

"Fight?" The only fights Paddy knew were fist against fist in the pub, rowdy men venting frustrations and having a good time.

"The bloody bastard English have brought all this upon us. Stealing our land, stealing away our crops with their marks on them so we've nothing left in a land of plenty but these stinking rocky bits that'll grow naught but potatoes. There's corn and barley to be had all over this island. And more besides. That English earl is right. Up at the Priory there's food enough for all. What he doesn't say is that we're not allowed to eat it. He's stolen all of it!"

"He's just come, Johnny—"

"He and his kind!" Johnny got to his feet heavily, anger hardening the weathered planes of his face. "They're always just coming, on and on until they've stolen us blind! Our land for the English lords, our food for English bellies, our women for English pleasures! By God, it stops here!"

Paddy got to his feet, picking up Johnny's spade as Johnny strode away across the muddy field. "Where are you going?"

Grimly, Johnny said, "I'm going to remind the others of the Fian!"

"The Fian?" Paddy trailed behind, carrying the two spades. "But the Fian are gone."

"Aye, they've been gone for hundreds of years. But they'll be gone no longer! They were warriors who knew

KATHLEEN

how to handle tyrants and thieves. They expelled the marauders from our shores and the monsters and beasties from the land, and fed the whole of Ireland for an entire year when the plague first came upon the land."

"But they're fairy tales, Johnny."

Johnny stopped, turning to look back at his brother, his expression unreadable. "Are they?" he asked. "You go home and tell Sophie I'll not be back tonight."

"Where will you be?"

"Wherever I have to be," Johnny replied, not answering.

Paddy watched him turn toward the village. "It's not smart, taking on the Peelers—the law's the law!" he yelled, but his brother did not stop, did not turn round again. Johnny was to the edge of the lane when Paddy shouted after him again, "Where can I meet up with you?"

Johnny shouted back: "At Old Tom's! But stop Sophie from sending to look for me, first. And don't be telling her where we'll be!"

Paddy didn't have to say a word when he let himself in the cottage. Sophie sat by the fire, the babe in her arms. She stared up at him with haunted eyes, seeing what she feared.

"Johnny's gone away." Her words were flat, no inflection, no question.

"Only for a bit, Sophie. . . ." Paddy looked uncomfortable. "I'm going to meet him later."

A little hope came to her eyes. "Then he's just gone to drown his sorrows, is it?"

"I didn't say that! I didn't say where he was going!"

"What's wrong?" Sophie asked her brother-in-law.

"Nothing." Paddy turned away.

"Patrick, did you save any?" Sophie watched his back slump.

"There's no lumpeys. They're all rotted."

Sophie hugged the baby closer. "We've got through it before, we'll get by now."

"Sure'n we will." Across the room Meg coughed in her sleep. Paddy turned toward the sound, seeing the other children huddled in the far corner. They were silent, staring up at the two adults with fear in their eyes. He tried to smile down at them and felt his heart breaking. "I'd best get to

172

KATHLEEN

the village." He walked outside, away from the children's fear-filled eyes.

MaryKate was in the Priory annex, turning from a sickbed to see Harry in the doorway, glaring at her.

"I said you were to have some rest!" He barked the words out.

"There's so much to do."

"Archie told me you spent the night here. Again."

"Your Lordship, these people need help."

"Come with me." His voice was cold. He turned away, striding out.

MaryKate thought about staying where she was. She turned and saw the eyes of an old woman watching her every movement.

"If we're to be turned out . . ." the woman said out loud and then let the rest of her thought trail off into silence.

"He'll not turn you out," MaryKate told the old woman.

"Why not?" The woman's voice cracked with weakness, a fit of coughing bringing MaryKate to her side, to lift her a little on her pillow. As she did, Harry walked back inside.

"MaryKate!"

"I'm coming!" she told him tartly. "Can't you see I'm busy?"

He saw the old woman staring at him and turned away, waiting in the doorway until MaryKate came forward and followed him outside into the dreary afternoon.

MaryKate looked up toward the gray expanse above them. "Do you think it's over?"

He glanced at her and then at the sky above them. "It had better be." He spoke as if Mother Nature herself would bend to his will.

"I have to get back to my patients," MaryKate told him.

"They're not your patients, they're the doctor's patients."

MaryKate's hurt sharpened her tongue. "Thank you for reminding me of my place."

He stopped walking, turning toward her, stopping her with his hand. "I didn't mean that."

"Then what did you mean?" she demanded, defiantly glaring up into his dark eyes.

KATHLEEN

Harry hesitated and then turned away. "Follow me. This is no place to talk."

She followed him inside the main house, down the main hall and into the library. Harry held the library door for her and then closed it behind them as she walked through.

"I must get back," she told him.

He reached for her arms, startling her. "Listen to me."

She struggled against his grasp, Harry tightening it against her efforts. She looked up into his eyes and saw them change. His hardened expression frightened her. "Let me go!" She struggled harder.

He pulled her closer, staring at her upturned face. At her mouth. And then he reached for it, leaning to kiss her as she fought against his grasp.

As his lips touched hers, began to search hers, she felt his need and responded to it without choice. She sank against him, letting his arms and his need envelop her, opening up to his demands.

They clung to each other, forbidden feelings rushing at them, carrying them past reason and thought. Into a space only wide enough for two. They clung there, suspended in time and space, drinking each other in.

When his lips left hers she felt bereft. Her eyes opened, staring up at the being who had somehow invaded her, whose arms left her limp and needy.

"Why are you looking at me like that?" he asked.

"I"—she swallowed, her eyes never leaving his—"I can't help it."

"Oh, god." He stared down at her and then reached to pull her close again. "Stop me or I'll kiss you again."

Her voice was as soft as early morning spring sunlight. "Please—please. Kiss me again."

He did. Over and over. MaryKate felt her knees buckling, felt herself sinking toward the floor as Harry kissed her harder, his arms straining around her, his body hard, strong, and pulsing.

They sank together toward the Oriental carpet, all thought lost, all other considerations swept away in the midst of their need and their response to each other.

"MaryKate—" His voice was strained.

"Harry—" She breathed the forbidden name, saying it

KATHLEEN

into his lips, his ear, his hair, over and over, feeling his flesh react as she did. Feeling him strain closer. "Oh, God, Harry ... Harry ..."

"I can't stop." His words were desperate, his hands grabbing her hair, cradling her head, tasting her lips as if all the nectar in the world was within them.

She reached up toward him. Pulling him closer to feel the weight of his body pressing down upon her, the reality of him, of his strength, filling her heart as he pressed against her flesh.

He was here. And he wanted her. He wanted her as much as she wanted him. She reveled in it, her unschooled hands reaching to pull him closer, her arms, her body, reaching out toward something she'd never before felt.

Sounds of the household around them brought them to their senses. A maid's trilling laugh as she passed by in the hall beyond. The sound of someone moving heavy trunks down the stairs. Horses neighing in the yard beyond the tall draped windows.

He groaned, pulling back a little and then a bit farther, staring down at her, her red hair splayed out across the dark purple Turkish carpeting.

He had used women for his own pleasure his entire life. Used and discarded them. Paying them well in one way or another. With favors, money, or compliments, depending upon whether they were ladies of the evening or jaded socialites.

But he had never abused his position. Had never taken advantage of a servant, feeling it beneath his dignity and without honor. For that matter he had never taken advantage of any woman who was anything less than completely willing.

Now there was this Irish girl, a servant in his house, a thorn in his side, and more than willing. Staring up at him with wide, questioning eyes. Innocent, guileless eyes.

He couldn't hurt her. There was too much danger for her in any of this. And so he pulled away, unsatisfied, raging to be nearer, his body screaming at his head as he stood up, moving far away from her. He could feel her confusion, could hear her behind him as she got to her feet.

"What's wrong?" she asked.

"Nothing. Everything." He turned back to see her standing across the room. If she took one step nearer he knew he would take her. Here and now, without preamble and without thought. But her eyes, soft and loving as a baby lamb's, looked too vulnerable to be hurt.

"I don't know how to apologize," he began. "I seem to behave inexcusably around you—"

"Why are you apologizing?" she asked.

"Because I had no right to take advantage of you. Of the situation."

Her eyes were steady, searching his opaque ones. "Is that what you were doing?"

His voice was strained. "I don't know what I was doing."

He looked into emerald green eyes and in that moment was closer to her than he had ever felt to anyone in his entire life. He felt himself closing off the feeling. Part of him wanting to keep the closeness, but part of him frightened, almost angered by it. It was as if she were attacking him in some way he didn't want to even acknowledge.

He turned away, striding purposefully to the library door and opening it before he could think about it twice. Then he stopped: "My point is that I do not want you overworked to the point of exhaustion and illness. You will do as I say, and what I say is that you shall not work through the nights."

"If that's what you want," she said meekly.

"I won't discuss it further, you shall simply obey what I—what?" He stared at her. "What did you say?"

"I said yes."

Harry watched her. "You sound as if you mean it."

"I do."

"Why?" he asked her.

MaryKate hesitated. "Because you asked it. Because it's important to you."

Harry stared across the length of the room, stared into her eyes. "Do you mean that?" he asked her.

She took a moment before answering. Thinking about it, and all that had happened since she had first laid eyes on him. "Yes," she told him. "I do."

His eyes melted. She saw him let all his defenses down, saw warmth in his eyes. And in that moment she knew she loved him.

KATHLEEN

Harry saw the change in her expression, saw it soften, and then saw love shining out at him. He took one step toward her and stopped himself. "We can't," he told her in a strangled voice. And after another moment: "I don't want you hurt. Ever."

Archie knocked on the open door, his expression innocent. "His Lordship Leo wants your attendance, if you please. I think he might be leaving." Archie glanced at MaryKate.

"Leaving?" Harry repeated.

"Aye," Archie replied. "He doesn't like the weather."

"And what about you?" Harry asked Archie.

"Me, then? I've been thinking about staying on."

Harry stared at the man. "Staying on without Leo?"

"If you've no objection." Archie waited.

MaryKate moved past them.

"And where are you going?" Archie asked, as if it were his own business. MaryKate looked toward Harry, who said nothing.

"I must get back to my duties."

Archie watched her go, then turned back toward Harry. "Do you have any objections? To my staying on, I mean? I've got a strong back and a weak mind. Which seems to suit me well to Ireland."

Harry laughed, surprising himself at the sound.

The two men gauged each other. And then both smiled, Archie looking pleased with himself.

"If the truth be known, you always were my favorite," Archie told the young earl.

20

IN THE VILLAGE the Protestant rectory had a long queue of people standing at the side gate. Lady Amelia's carriage pulled up at the front, around the corner from the throng of waiting farmers.

"Should I wait, Your Ladyship?" Archie asked as he put the steps down for her.

She descended from the coupe, glancing toward the high shrubbery that lined the side of the old stone rectory. "What were your instructions?" she asked him baldly.

"I beg your pardon?"

"Do you?" She gave him a haughty stare. "Timothy has been my driver since I arrived. Now His Lordship requests that you ferry me about. He must have his reasons."

Archie spoke slowly. "I'm sure I wouldn't know, Your Ladyship."

She watched the Welshman. "Perhaps you wouldn't. If I have the choice, I would prefer you return within the hour. I'm not sure how long I shall be."

"Very well, Your Ladyship."

Archie escorted Amelia to the rectory door, knocked for

her, and then stood back as a maid opened the door, curtsying swiftly and waiting for Amelia to pass by.

Hugh was in the library. The maid closed the door behind Amelia, then scurried to the kitchens to help Cook feed the men who stood waiting.

"What's happened?" Hugh asked when they were alone.

"Nothing," Amelia said, smiling. "Although Leo suspects Harry of carrying on with my maidservant."

"Is he?"

Amelia shrugged. "It would be too much to pray for, I suppose."

"Amelia! God will not become a partner in adultery!"

"Theirs? Or ours?"

"We are not the same! We are on a higher plane. The things that drew us"—he saw her expression—"I mean, draw us, to each other, are of a higher order than mere fleshly revels."

"I always felt so," Amelia replied. "You said the earthly part was due to your only too mortal flesh."

Hugh closed the Bible in front of him, putting his quill pen down. "Yes." He stared at the pages he had been writing.

"Have I interrupted your work?" she asked, seeing his gaze return to the ink-spattered pages.

"My sermon," he said. "For Sunday."

"I'm sorry. Do you wish me to withdraw?"

He stood up, smiling unctuously. "Never. You are my inspiration. You know that."

"I hope that. You know how much I want to be a part of the good you do. Of how hard I've worked to do good."

"Everyone knows that," Hugh Grinstead said.

There was a moment of silence, when their eyes met. Finally Amelia said, "There are a great many people outside."

"Yes. Our food program is going well." He leaned back in his chair.

"I had no idea the church was so beneficent." She watched the man for whom she risked so much. "Especially to Roman Catholics."

"This is a God-given way to make these people see the error of their ways."

KATHLEEN

"Surely you're not saying change your religion and you'll be fed." Amelia spoke the words lightly.

"That sounds terrible. It's not what it is at all." He saw her watching him. "Well, I mean, that's what it is, but it is for a greater good."

"I see."

"You sound as if you disapprove," Hugh told her.

"It's not up to me to approve or disapprove. Nor would I presume to do so when you tell me it is the right thing to do." She hesitated. "I can understand the logic of it."

Bringing the conversation back to themselves, Hugh asked, "Then your husband does not suspect us?"

Amelia shrugged once again, Hugh reaching for her shoulders, watching her carefully. "I hardly think he cares," Amelia replied.

"Then why is he here?" Hugh asked.

Amelia sighed. "When you marry into a titled family, there are obligations that go beyond what you might want for yourself. Or even for each other."

Hugh brought her into his arms. "Do you care about him, then?"

"I do not. Nor have I ever." She relaxed against him. "He is too wild, too undisciplined, not like you at all."

"Your husband could be a very violent man." Hugh spoke softly, his gaze going to the closed door.

"Perhaps our answer is to find a way to get him so involved with Mary-Kathleen that he has no interest in what we do."

"Amelia, I cannot conspire for another's immorality. You must see that," Hugh told her. "And, after all, he is your husband."

Amelia replied quietly, "He has always been my husband, Hugh." She reached to touch his cheek.

"He was not here before."

"Does that make him any less my husband? The fact that he was across the sea?"

"Amelia, this is too dangerous now. Don't you see?"

"No!" Amelia burst out. "Don't say it!" She reached for his hands. "Don't say we must stop! What would I do without you?"

"Amelia, I'm only saying we must be most discreet. For

KATHLEEN

both our sakes. We can't afford the kind of notoriety this would engender."

She turned away, fingering the top of a carved mahogany clock that sat on Hugh's desk. "Then what are we to do?" she asked.

He hesitated, coming toward her, reaching for her hands. "Amelia—dearest—this is very difficult, I know." He waited for a response. None came. "You are, after all, his wife."

"Yes. You keep reminding me. So long as he's here, I should do as he asks. Is that what you're saying?"

"I'm only thinking of keeping him from suspecting us."

"And if he wishes me to go back to England with him, then of course, I must." She watched his familiar face relax, his slight nod turning something to stone within her. "If he should go, and allow me to stay, however, we could of course continue as we had before his arrival."

Hugh smiled. "I should, of course, like nothing better, my dear."

"Yes. Of course."

He watched her. "You do understand, don't you?"

"I understand only too well," Amelia told him. She moved away from him, Hugh reaching for her arm.

"Amelia—"

She looked down at his hand on her arm. He had long hands, his fingers delicately tapered. The skin soft and smooth. "I must get back to the Priory. To my patients. And my husband, of course."

Hugh dropped his hand. "We must be brave."

"You be brave, Hugh. Be very brave. And feed your new converts." Amelia opened the door, walking purposefully out into the narrow hall, her head held high.

The Right Reverend started to follow her and then stopped in the doorway, watching her move to the front door without a backward glance.

When it closed behind her, he turned back toward his desk, reaching for his Bible.

Amelia stood on the rectory porch for long moments, watching villagers and farmers pass by the gate toward the kitchen door. Caps in their hands, their eyes downcast,

181

KATHLEEN

something about the bend to their backs making them seem defeated.

She lifted the front edge of her skirts and walked down the steps to the path. Unlatching the gate, she stepped into the lane, looking for Archie and her coach.

He wasn't there.

"Lady Amelia?" She looked behind her, seeing Father Ross's buggy, the rotund little priest bringing his horse to a stop. "I hope you don't take it amiss, but I should dearly love to speak with you for a few moments."

She nodded, coming forward. "Of course."

He reached to help her into the buggy, speaking as she settled herself beside him. "I'm on my way to the Priory. If it's not presuming upon your kindness, we could talk on the way."

"It's your kindness, Father Ross, not mine. I expected to be longer and sent my carriage home. You will be doing me the favor."

He snapped the reins, his old horse taking off at a slow clip-clop through the village street. A villager here and there looked up toward the buggy, calling out a greeting to their priest. The words choked off when they saw the regal lady who rode beside him in the humble buggy.

Father Ross smiled a little. "I fear we shall be the talk of the village by evening."

Amelia smiled faintly. "I daresay."

"You were at the rectory then," Father Ross said by way of starting.

"Yes."

"And you saw the kitchen."

"Yes, Father Ross. I did. And I must tell you that as I think about it, I do not approve."

The old man sighed. "You can't fault people for wanting to eat. And I can't fault your minister for wanting to feed them. But it's bribery that's taking my flock and turning them into heathens. Begging your pardon, Your Ladyship."

"There is no goodness in bribery, Father. And there is no true conversion. Only trouble will come from this practice."

"I'm glad to hear you say it, Your Ladyship. I was hoping I could convince you to talk to the reverend about it."

KATHLEEN

"It will do no good," she told the Catholic priest.

He took his time answering, trying to find the right words. "It's just that your wishes carry much weight with many of us. Especially, I should say, with your own minister. He might listen to you where he wouldn't listen to another. And stop this tempting poor souls into mortal sin."

"I shall speak to him at first opportunity," Amelia said.

"Oh, Your Ladyship, thank you! It's a lot to ask, it being your own church and all—"

"The God I believe in does not accept bribes, Father Ross. Nor condone bribery. I say again, however, I doubt it will do much good my speaking to him."

"Anything you can do will be a blessing, Your Ladyship. There's even talk he's telling them he can feed their children if they'll put them in Protestant homes to be raised as enemies of the holy faith—begging your pardon."

"We shan't agree on religion, Father. Especially as to which faith is holy and which is not. I daresay God has large enough ears to hear any who petition Him. And I also daresay He will not look kindly upon bribery in His Name's sake."

After that they rode up the Priory Hill in silence. Father Ross glanced at his companion, ready to make conversation, but something in her set expression stopped him. He left her to her own thoughts until they pulled up outside the annex, a stableboy running to help her down from the buggy.

Archie came behind the stableboy. "I was just ready to return, Your Ladyship. You said an hour—"

"Yes, yes, I know. Father Ross here was kind enough to drive me back." She turned back toward the little man in the long black cassock.

"Is there anything else I can do?"

"I was hoping I might be of some help to you, Your Ladyship."

"Thank you. I shall change and then be down to relieve MaryKate. Will you please tell her?"

"Of course." The old priest watched her go. Turning, he saw Archie watching him. "Faith, but I've never seen the likes of her. She's a saint and nothing but."

'That's one way to look at it," Archie said mildly.

* * *

KATHLEEN

In the library Harry was facing a disbelieving Leo.

"You can't be serious," Leo told his old friend. "You want me to arrange for the sale of Exeter House? You can't!"

"I can, and I shall. Since you are determined to leave, you can be of help if you will see to the details," Harry told him.

"And what of your father?" Leo asked.

"The duke does not own Exeter House. It is mine to do with as I see fit."

"And you see fit to sell it and to use the proceeds to help these wretched heretics." Leo stared at Harry. "You have gone mad. This detestable weather has driven you around the bend."

"Will you do it?" Harry asked impatiently.

"I'll have no part of it. And I warn you, I shall tell the duke the moment I set foot in England that you have lost your mind."

Harry smiled grimly. "Tell him what you wish. He sent me here."

"Well, he's getting more than he bargained for!"

"I daresay," Harry replied.

"And less," Leo added pointedly, watching Harry's face. "You were to get an heir by your wife. Not by a servant girl." He took an involuntary step backward as Harry started toward him. "You can beat me to a pulp, but it won't change the truth."

Harry stopped where he was, anger darkening his eyes. "It is not the truth. I am responsible for these people."

"Including MaryKate."

"Yes," Harry said sharply. "Including MaryKate."

"It's not that I have anything against the wench. Or even that I wouldn't do the same myself. Lord knows, we've both done our bit through London over the years and we even bet on my being able to do so here, with her—".

"Don't talk about her like that!" Harry nearly roared at this friend.

Leo stopped, shocked. Harry turned away. His hands clenched behind his back, he moved toward the window, staring out at the dreary gray afternoon. "Don't speak about

KATHLEEN

her in that tone of voice," Harry said, quietly now. "She doesn't deserve it."

"Lord, Harry, you really have gone round the bend, haven't you? I mean, you actually care about her?"

"If I do, there's no comfort and no peace in it." His back was still turned. "And nothing to be done about it. She deserves better than anything I can offer her."

"Come home to England with me," Leo said. "There's nothing for you here. Amelia wants you as little as you want her."

"I will come home as soon as this crisis is over."

"And Amelia?"

"Amelia will do as she pleases. Stay or come. But if she comes, she shall have to produce an heir."

"And if she stays?"

"I shall try to explain to my father why the line will pass to my cousins."

Leo watched his friend. "Others have divorced."

Harry grimaced. "I have done much harm to Amelia by allowing my father to insist we marry. I can't do her more by divorcing her."

"And if she wishes it?"

Harry turned around then, staring at Leo. "Why would she?"

"Perhaps she's tired of the farce, too."

"No woman wishes to be branded a divorcée."

"But if she does?" Leo persisted.

Harry stared at Leo. "Then I should be free."

"To remarry as you please," Leo added.

Harry's eyes clouded. "As I pleased." He shook his head. "Hardly that. As I must, if I am to please the duke."

"A lusty Irish wench would make lots of healthy babies," Leo told Harry. And watched Harry's expression change. A glimmer of hope rose and then faded in his eyes.

"It could never work," Harry told Leo.

"It would not be easy," Leo conceded, "but others have married beneath them and survived to tell about it. A little schooling in the social graces, a deaf ear to the spiteful calumnies of society, a healthy heir to show the old duke, and you're home free."

"Home free," Harry repeated. He told himself he did not

wish anything of the kind. Told himself Leo was crazed, and he himself was crazed to even consider the possibility. He did not love the girl. Did not want to spend his life with her. She was nothing more than . . . than . . . His thoughts stopped.

Wallace knocked at the open door, informing Leo that his carriage awaited.

Leo nodded, then turned back toward his friend and walked across the room to grasp his hand. "If you truly want Exeter House sold, I'd best handle it. Or these Irish land agents will surely bilk you dry."

Harry tightened his grip on Leo's hand. "Thank you."

Leo shrugged. "I shall still tell your father I think you've gone native. And pray that you and Amelia come to your senses. Otherwise, I may be the only polite society that will visit you in the future."

"Polite society!" Harry scoffed. "The two words are totally incompatible."

They walked out together, Harry beside his oldest friend, his emotions so mixed he did not understand them himself.

It left him with a peculiar feeling he did not much like. As if he no longer knew himself as well as he had thought.

Amelia came down the stairs in time to say good-bye to Leo. Standing with Harry in the courtyard as the coach and four drove away down the steep hillside road, Amelia turned to her husband. "Harry, we must talk."

"About what?" Harry asked as the coach was lost from view.

She hesitated. "You sound so distant."

Harry turned to stare at her. "Madam, I thought my distance was what you wished."

"It has been," she replied calmly.

Harry watched her carefully. "Am I to assume this has changed?"

"Perhaps."

"Why?"

"Why?" she asked back. "I don't understand."

"Neither do I," Harry replied.

"It's possible we might get on together."

KATHLEEN

He outright stared at her. "Is it?"

"It's what you want, isn't it? What you came here for."

"It's—what I came here for. Yes."

She nodded a little. "I must see to my patients. Our tenants," she added. She started for the annex and then turned back to see his eyes. "We can discuss this after dinner."

His eyes were cloudy. "If you wish," he replied. He watched her go, confused feelings welling up inside his breast.

Dinner was an almost silent affair, MaryKate excusing herself and eating in her room, Leo hours gone. Three servants brought course after course to the earl and his countess, removing course after course half-eaten.

Desultory attempts at conversation broke off before hardly begun. The staff gossiped in the kitchen about the state of affairs in the dining room while Harry stared down the length of the table at his wife. "You said earlier you wished to discuss our situation."

Amelia poured herself more wine. "Did I?"

"Yes. Are you saying you don't remember?"

She looked up to find his eyes still on her. "I had thought, perhaps, we could get on a little better."

"I assume you are offering to make good our obligation to create an heir," Harry said plainly.

"No!" Amelia burst out. She added, "That is, I understand my duties."

"I'm glad to hear it," Harry said dryly.

She glared at him. "I felt we might find a way to ensure an heir by someone else."

Harry's eyes glittered. "I don't understand," he told her.

"Don't you?" Her voice was faint. "I had rather thought you would."

"The heir to a dukedom must needs be legitimate, madam. In case you have forgotten," Harry said coldly.

"How could I forget?! I'm telling you, he would be! I would say he was mine! Ours. Don't you see? None else would ever know!"

Harry stared at the woman, the wife, he barely knew. "And what of the real mother?"

"She would be amply rewarded!" Amelia warmed to her subject. "She could even stay on if you prefer. Be the child's nurse, if she liked."

Amelia did not know Harry well enough to hear the ominous tones in his quiet tone. "And if the child were a girl? Would we then throw it away and keep trying?"

"Don't be vulgar," Amelia said.

"I? I?!" He roared the word, standing up so quickly his chair crashed backward to the floor. "Madam, it would seem you could teach us all about vulgarity!"

Archie came through the pantry door in time to see Harry striding from the room.

Lady Amelia told Archie he wasn't needed. Pleading a raging headache, she retired to her rooms as Harry strode into the billiard room, stopping in midstride. He stared at the cues, at the table, and thought of Leo, halfway to Dublin by now.

And, unwillingly, his thoughts raced to the attic room that enclosed MaryKate.

Harry strode out of the billiard room to the library and a healthy portion of port. He picked up a book and then threw it down, unable to concentrate. Irritation followed his unrest, irritation at himself. At Amelia. At MaryKate. At Ireland itself and his father for sending him here. At God for allowing things to go so far astray that all was mixed up and unreal.

Her eyes were as green as the moss that climbed the sides of the old stone Priory. Her skin was like alabaster flecked with tiny freckles. Those self-same freckles probably lightly dappled her chest, edging down toward cream-colored breasts—his eyes closed as if in the closing he could stop the thought.

He thought of Amelia. Classic blond beauty, rounded and soft. Amelia was by far the more classically beautiful of the two. But his thoughts kept coming back to MaryKate. To her green eyes and freckles. Her hands roughened with work, her body thin but somehow more sturdy, more human.

Her breasts were smaller than Amelia's but somehow more appealingly made. He had touched them, briefly, in this very room. He stared toward the dark Turkish carpet where they had lain for so brief a time.

He had never denied himself before. Never felt the longing

KATHLEEN

that now coursed through him, disrupting his calm, making him question himself. His actions. His needs.

MaryKate had made him face the fact that he had never looked deeply inside. That he did not know himself half as well as he had thought.

When he strode toward his rooms, his expression was so full of irritation that the servants gave him a wide berth. He was already in his rooms when a tap at the door made him bark, "Enter!"

"You look surprised," Archie said. "I told you I wanted to stay."

"Yes—but where's Robert to undress me?"

"He left with Lord Leo," Archie replied.

Harry took a moment to digest the information. "He did what?"

Archie shrugged. "He wanted to go in the worst way. And Lord Leo was that upset I wasn't about to leave you—leave yet." Archie corrected himself quickly. "It was only right that Robert should go with him. You know as well as I do Lord Leo can't do without help."

"He never said a word," Harry replied.

"Lord Leo?"

"Robert." Harry stopped. "It's not important," he finished.

A soft tap at the door startled them both. Harry stared at the closed door, feeling his heart thud within his breast. He reached toward Archie, grabbing his arm. "What you may see or hear is not to be discussed. With anyone." Harry's voice was urgent.

"And when have I ever?" Archie asked back.

Harry took two long strides to the door, wrenching it open. Staring down at Amelia. His heart calmed, his expression clouding over. "Yes?"

Large blue eyes stared up at him. "May I come in?"

Harry hesitated. Amelia moved past him and then stopped. Archie avoided her eyes. Picking up Harry's discarded clothing, he moved toward the door, his eyes still downcast.

"If there's nothing else, Your Lordship—"

"There's nothing else. For the moment," Harry replied.

189

KATHLEEN

Archie closed the door behind himself, seeing Harry and Amelia eye each other across the large room.

Archie carried His Lordship's shirt and underclothes to the laundry room down below, leaving them to be dealt with later. Reaching for a cigar he walked outside into the quadrangle beside the huge house.

Moonlight filtered through the cloudy dark skies, softly lighting the distant countryside in shades of dark gray mixed with the blackness of night.

Archie paced the quadrangle, pulling on his cigar and taking in the cold evening breezes. The moon came out from behind clouds, lighting his path as he moved slowly around the quadrangle.

A figure stood alone and silent, on the wide stone porch that lined the back of the house. Archie slowed, stopping before she noticed he was there. MaryKate, leaning on the stone balustrade, was staring out toward the sea. Archie looked toward where her eyes searched and saw nothing but fog and darkness.

He thought about retreating, and in that moment she turned, seeing him. When she did, he smiled, pulling the cigar out of his mouth and coming up the steps toward where she stood on the stone parapet.

"It's a grim evening, this one," Archie said.

"Is it?" MaryKate looked bemused. "It seemed rather gentle, to me."

"God's truth?" Archie watched her. "Maybe that's the difference between us Welsh and you Irish."

"Is there, then, so much difference?" MaryKate asked lightly.

"How are we ever to tell?" Archie asked back. He watched her. "I take it you were as restless as I."

"I couldn't sleep," she admitted.

"Aye and I know that feeling. Many's the night I've waited up for Their Lordships and worried about where they were."

"That has nothing to do with me!" MaryKate told Archie sharply.

"Of course not. Did I say it did?" Archie asked her. "I

was merely saying I know the feeling. Not being able to sleep," Archie added, looking innocent.

MaryKate looked glum. "I guess we all do, one time or another."

"Aye," Archie agreed. "And things will soon be better around here, mark my words."

MaryKate turned to see his eyes. "What do you mean?"

"I'm an expert on the subject of my Lord Harry, if I say so myself, and I've seen with my own eyes the impossible happen tonight." He smiled at her. "Lady Amelia came to his rooms, and they sent me away."

MaryKate stared at the Welshman. "I don't understand."

"Neither did I," Archie told her. "But I guess Her Ladyship came to her senses and realized what she's got in my Harry. Or what she could have. They never got along. Lord love them, they never lived together long enough *to* get along—but maybe things will work out now." His tone was innocent, his eyes opaque as he watched MaryKate's reactions.

MaryKate looked off toward the far hills. "Maybe things will work out now," she repeated. "For them," she added. And turned to find Archie watching her. "Any who care about them couldn't ask for more. He's her husband and she's a saint; she should have everything she wants."

"A saint," Archie repeated. "Everyone seems to say so."

"She's been a saint to our people," Mary-Kathleen said stoutly. "None has ever done more for us and asked less of us."

Archie watched the young Irish woman. "You feel beholden to her."

"Don't we all?" MaryKate replied. "I'd best get in. I must be up early."

"You're all right, then?" Archie asked as she left.

MaryKate looked back toward him. "All right? Why wouldn't I be?"

Archie watched her. And then, finally, shrugged. "I didn't know but what you had a—special feeling—for His Lordship."

191

KATHLEEN

She watched the Welshman. "And if I did? I would wish him the same, wouldn't I? I would wish him to be happy. And to live out his life as he pleased. With love surrounding him and—" Her words stopped, her head bending quickly to hide her tears.

She was gone before Archie could say more.

~ 21 ~

Upstairs, Harry watched Amelia as she came forward, looking tentative and out of place.

"This must seem like an extreme reversal," Amelia told him.

"I am at a loss, I admit," Harry told her.

"It's just that I—that I've been thinking about what you asked. About why you came. And about my obligations."

"Your obligations?" Harry questioned.

"Yes. I mean, after all, I did marry into your family, into the dukedom. There are certain things I must live up to."

"Suddenly," was all Harry said.

Amelia riveted him with her gaze, trying to see beneath his opaque expression. "I admit it has taken me a while to see my duty."

"Over a decade," Harry said dryly.

"Be that as it may"—Amelia brushed the ten years and more aside—"I am your wife, and I am prepared to do my duty."

Harry stared at her. "I am overwhelmed. To say the least."

"And happy, I hope," she added.

Harry took his time. "Perhaps incredulous would be a more apt adjective. Why?"

"I beg your pardon?"

Harry stared her down. "I asked why. Why this sudden reversal? Why this sudden desire to conform?"

"I don't understand."

"Neither do I," he replied.

They stared at each other across the room. "You won't consider—my proposal—so I must consider yours. After all, that's why you're here. You'll not leave until you have an heir. Correct?"

"My father sent me here for that express purpose," Harry told her harshly.

She took a step toward her husband. "If we do our duty, we can then go our separate ways. Therefore—I am here."

"For my use," he supplied, seeing her expression stiffen and then, purposefully, relax.

"I would hardly put it that way. I am your wife."

"As of when, madam?" Harry asked her sharply.

She stared at him. "If you do not wish my presence, you have merely to say so."

"I do not wish your presence," he told her.

Amelia's breath caught in her throat, the words hitting her hard. "Are you saying you refuse?!"

"Madam, I am telling you plainly that I am not even sure I could perform under such circumstances."

They stared at each other, each of them gauging the other. Amelia broke the silence: "Then it's true."

"What's true?" he replied sharply.

"That you're interested in my serving girl."

"Who told you that?!" he demanded.

Amelia watched the husband she'd never known. "Are you denying it?"

"Denying what?" he barked.

"You very well know what," she told him.

Harry stared at her. He then turned away, his fists clenched. "If you are wise, you will leave my presence. Now. Before I tell you what I really think. About you. And your precious minister. And all else." He turned back to watch her. "There are many things that are better left unsaid. Unacknowledged. To say them is to have to deal with them." He watched her. "Don't drive us to that point, for it is a point of no return."

Amelia hesitated. "I don't know what you're talking about. I am your wife, and I am here. And I am willing to get you an heir. Under some conditions."

"Such as?" he asked.

"Such as, once I have, our 'connubial' affiliation will be at an end. I shall have done my duty and shall be left alone to pursue my own path."

"Which is?"

Amelia hesitated. "I'm not sure. But I shall let you know as soon as I am."

"Thank you," he told her sarcastically.

"And you, of course, shall have your own freedom."

"I shall?" Harry asked.

"As long as you are discreet, I shall raise no objections."

He studied her. "I believe you are sincere."

"Oh, I am!" she told him. "I am. It is no concern of mine what you do beyond ourselves. As long as you are discreet."

Harry turned away. His hand was on the doorknob when next she spoke. "Did you hear what all I have offered?"

"Yes," he told her. He looked back, briefly, before he opened the door. "I heard you very clearly." And with that he was out the door, Amelia watching the heavy oak slab start to close between them.

She moved swiftly, catching his hand. Startled, he found Amelia against his chest, her lips reaching toward his own.

"Amelia—"

"Shhh . . . Harry, we've never given it a chance." Desperation colored her words as she strained nearer him. "I didn't mean to sound so cold about it—perhaps we could get on together." She punctuated her words with kisses to his cheek, his ear, his mouth.

He wrenched away from her, holding her elbows, keeping her at arm's length. "Amelia, don't do this."

"I can make you want me," she told him. He let go of her, her hand pressing against his chest, and then trailing down toward his waist.

He stood in the doorway, feeling the movement of her hand, watching her eyes. She looked determined, almost frantic. He took a step back, her hand falling to her side.

KATHLEEN

"She can't give you an heir unless I agree to it!" Amelia spit the words out.

"Whatever you think of me, Amelia, I am not an animal. Nor am I a fool. You want me even less than I want you. Why are you doing this?"

"Because I want you to leave!" Her voice rose with angry frustration, stripping away all pretense.

"And leave you and the child behind?"

"I'll give you an heir any way you want, then we both can be free! You can go back to England and when it's born you can send for it!"

"You will give it up to me?" Harry asked.

"Yes! Just let me live on here alone, that's all I ask!"

Harry studied her. "Then what you really want is divorce, if I would grant it."

"No!" Her vehemence surprised him.

"Amelia, you want no part of me or of my child. What possible reason do you have for wanting to continue as my wife?"

"I must continue as your wife. I would have no social standing, no place in church or society."

"And your friend will not jeopardize his position by associating with a divorced woman."

Amelia stared at her husband. "He cannot," she replied honestly.

"At least we now have honesty between us," Harry said.

"Do we? What about your friend?"

"I have no friend," Harry told her.

"Then you have every reason to agree to my plan," Amelia said.

Harry's heart felt leaden within him. "Perhaps I do." He hesitated and then turned away.

"Where are you going?" she asked quickly.

"I'm not sure."

"Will you be back?" Amelia asked.

"I'm not sure. I have to think." Harry walked away, his booted feet resounding against the steps as he moved slowly, heavily, down them.

Amelia sank to the edge of his bed, her shoulders hunched forward, her mind racing with possibilities.

* * *

KATHLEEN

Upstairs, the attic rooms whistled with the night winds that buffeted the sides of the old stone building, pushing to get in and then running along the sides to roar off down the countryside.

In MaryKate's room the soft moonlight silhouetted her slender frame as she undressed, her heart leaden within her breast.

Archie's words reverberated within her, visions of Lady Amelia and Harry following them, giving her no peace. He had kissed her that afternoon, had held her in his arms, and now he held Amelia. His wife.

She started to take off her shift and then stopped, letting it fall back around her. She reached for a heavy coat, pulling it on over her shift and slipping her feet into her shoes.

Too upset to lay down, she let herself out into the attic hall.

Sedge cotton lined the hollow Harry rode through, the moonlight outlining its downy white heads as they waved in the ocean breezes.

The river wandered nearby, a thick copse of overhanging trees ahead of him. He reined the black in, dismounting under the trees, holding the reins loosely as he paced forward, the horse beside him.

He had given the black his head, racing across meadows and fields still muddy from the rains, dying potato stalks all around. It had been an hour since he left Amelia and still he fled their conversation and the decisions he would have to make.

A semicircle of great, pale-gray boulders lay protected in the middle of the copse, mosses growing over and around them. Something in the shadows moved. Harry stopped, the horse impatient at his side, its hooves digging into the dirt.

Moonlight drifted through the tree branches, outlining MaryKate as she walked through the center of the stones and stopped in her tracks, seeing Harry loom up ahead.

"Oh!" Her eyes widened, her breath caught in her throat.

He felt his heart begin to thud within his chest, his body hardening as he stared down at her. "We seem to keep meeting here." His voice sounded strange to his own ears, loud in the silent night.

"I—I couldn't sleep."

Harry watched her. "Nor could I." He glanced at the ancient, rounded stones, his voice softening. "At least this time you didn't think me one of the wee folk."

"I thought you were—" MaryKate began and then cut her words off.

"I was what?" he asked.

"Nothing." She looked away. "I must be getting back."

"You thought I was what?" Harry persisted.

Her voice was so soft he barely heard her. "I thought you were with her."

Harry grimaced. "The walls have ears and wagging tongues, too."

"I'm glad you're not." She breathed the words, afraid of what he might reply.

He looked down at her. "Are you?" He hesitated, then: "She thinks we've been having an affair."

MaryKate hesitated. "Have we? Are we?"

He heard the groan that escaped his own lips as if it came from another. MaryKate watched him drop the reins, saw his hands move toward her as he groaned again, the sound singing through her veins, melting her limbs.

He reached for her, bringing her close, lowering his lips until they touched hers, emotions exploding through them both as they clung together under the overhanging trees.

They kissed without stopping, kissed until her lips felt raw with his searching, and still she clung to him, desperate to keep him close.

The ground was damp beside the huge stones, the moss deep and springy beneath them as he lay her back in the stone shadows and reached for the large buttons that held her coat closed.

His hands were large and square, like the rest of him, their movements quick with desire. She moved to help him, her hands gentle against his.

She felt him surge toward her when his hand slipped inside her coat, finding only the thin cotton shift covering her breast. His lips explored her body, followed his hand. MaryKate rose toward his touch, liquid fire flowing through her veins as his lips searched through the thin fabric, finding her nipple.

Her arms tightened around him, her breath coming faster. Small little moans escaped her lips, exciting him further, his lips moving from one softly rounded breast to the other. MaryKate bent her head, kissing his ear, her breath sharp within his ear, sending shivers down his spine and hardening his flesh.

He rose above her, his elbows straight, his eyes dark as they searched her moonlit face. Her lips were curved into a gentle smile, a softness in her eyes he had never seen before. It warmed his heart even as the heat in his loins pressed him down against her.

His eyes closed. He moved against the length of her body, all reason gone. Nothing existed beyond the small plot of mossy ground that held the two of them—he above her, groaning a little as he moved, she making soft little moaning noises when his body pressed harder against her.

He reached to tear away their clothes, reached to bring her closer, a shudder coursing through her body when their naked flesh met. Her hands reached to touch his chest, curving the curly dark hair around her fingers.

"Harry." She breathed his name against his cheek.

"MaryKate . . . I don't want to hurt you," he whispered into her ear. He cradled her close, feeling her tense when he moved against her legs. His hand reached down to her belly, pressing his palm between her legs, feeling her tense again and then, slowly, slowly, relax.

When she began to move with him, responding to his touch, he reached to kiss each breast, his legs between hers.

"Oh!" The word was an expended breath, the pressure of his body melting her against him. She reached upward, to draw him closer, moving with him.

He entered her, the intensity of their coming together shocking through each of them. He felt her sudden pain, moving more slowly, trying to be gentle with her unschooled body, aching to pour out all his need but holding back, afraid to harm her.

Pleasure overcame the pain, MaryKate arching up toward the source of all this beauty. The sensations his body brought to her rippled across nerve endings, the feeling shimmering through her, blending them together.

Their movements became more rhythmic, Harry slowly more insistent. She reacted to his every movement, reacting to the change in his breathing, the sounds that escaped his lips as he spoke into her hair. He called her name over and over until suddenly their movements crescendoed into an intensity that stole her breath away.

"Too soon"—Harry's voice was ragged—"Oh, God, I want you so much." His body poured forth within her as she cried out.

They clung together, their bodies melded as one, a peaceful languor invading them. Their arms entwined, they held each other, content just to be close.

"I wish time could stop right now and leave us here forever," MaryKate whispered the words, feeling him squeeze her a little in reply. "I don't want this to end," she told him.

"Everything ends," Harry said quietly. Slowly he pulled away and sat up. Moonlight drifted down between the tree branches to design patterns across them that kept changing as the branches moved in the cold night air.

"It's cold," he said, suddenly realizing it and reaching to draw her coat around her.

"I never felt it," she told him quietly, watching his drawn expression. "Are you sorry, then?"

"What?" He stared at her.

"What's wrong?" she asked him, reaching for his hand. He watched her kiss it, his heart welling up within him.

"Everything's wrong, MaryKate. You don't have to ask." He reached to brush a tendril of her hair back from her forehead. "I don't want to hurt you."

She spoke softly, "Then don't hurt me."

"Oh, god, MaryKate, I don't want to!"

"I love you," MaryKate told him.

He searched her eyes in the moonlight that filtered through the trees. "You do?" was all he said.

"I have from the beginning," she told him.

"The beginning." A small smile hovered around his eyes. "When you wouldn't get out of my hair?"

"Even then," she replied. "I just didn't know it."

KATHLEEN

MaryKate buttoned Paddy's coat closed over her thin shift. She watched Harry button his clothing, watched him try to smooth out his rumpled shirt as he tucked it in. "Are you sorry, then?" she asked softly.

"I don't know," he told her honestly. "Amelia is determined to force an arrangement between us." He hesitated. "Between you and me."

MaryKate's eyes widened. "Between . . . I don't understand."

"She figures to get an heir by you and me. Adopt the child. And all this farce to end."

MaryKate felt the blood rushing to her face. "I—I don't believe—how can she think, how could she suppose— Does she know you are here? With me?" Dread filled MaryKate's tone.

"Who knows?" Harry replied as MaryKate stared at him.

"Did you agree, then?" she asked.

"Agree?!" He stared at her, shocked. "How could you think that?!"

"You are here," she said simply.

"You think that I—" He pulled away, standing up. "We must get back."

"Harry?"

He heard the questions in her voice. His eyes closed. And then he opened them, turning resolutely to face her, his face a mask. "I have no excuses for what I have just done. I have behaved badly with you from the beginning. Now I've taken advantage of you."

"Harry, don't shut me out. Not now."

"I don't know what you mean," he said stiffly.

"Tell me why you came to the ruins tonight."

His eyes glanced at hers and then avoided her gaze. "I don't know." The words were wrenched out of him. "That's not true. I hoped you would be here—that's the truth."

"Thank you, for the truth." MaryKate's eyes shone in the moonlight. He reached to lift her to the stallion's back.

"We should not go back together. Someone might see us."

"I'm not in the habit of skulking about," he told her flatly. "I don't intend to start at this late date." He handed her up before pulling himself up behind her.

KATHLEEN

She leaned back against him, content just to feel the warmth of his flesh, afraid to ask more questions. Some wisdom deep within told her to just let it be. Let it all just be.

When they arrived back, the stableboy Tim came out, sleepy-eyed, to take the black from Harry. The boy hardly seemed to notice that MaryKate was with the earl. As Tim led the horse toward its stall, Harry paced beside MaryKate toward the great stone house.

In the downstairs hall MaryKate silently told herself it had all been real, that he had wanted her. Not just the heir they sought for the dukedom, but her. His arms had held her close, his body reaching out with love and need. She could still feel him within her, filling her up; her lips were still bruised and swollen with his kisses.

And yet he strode, silently, beside her.

On the stairs Harry waited for her, avoiding her eyes, walking beside her to the floor above. Then walking past his own rooms, accompanying her down the hall to the door that led to the back stairs and the attic beyond.

At the door she reached for the knob. And then found his hand over hers, on the knob. She looked up into his dark eyes and saw pain. He pressed her hand, and then released it, watching as she moved away from him, climbing the stairs toward her attic room.

He watched her until she was out of sight. Then, slowly, heavily, he retraced his steps down the wide hall to his own suite of rooms.

Archie looked up from a chair by the fire. "Well, then, you finally decided to come back, did you?"

When Harry didn't reply, Archie stood up, following him toward the dressing room. "And don't you look a proper mess. What have you been doing, rolling around in—" Archie bit off his words, falling as silent as the man he served.

Upstairs in her attic room, MaryKate reached for Pugs and brought him to lay beside her on the narrow bed.

Tears dampened her pillow for long hours as she lay in the moonlight, unable to sleep, caught between pain and bliss.

22

Morning dawned silently, the few birds that had come back after the rains already silenced by hungry hunters. Hill slopes that had been dotted with nibbling sheep, fields that had held herds of lowing cattle were emptier as food became more and more scarce.

The carcasses of diseased cattle were now eaten along with joints from starving horses put out of their misery by their owners. Young Johnny O'Hallion told his mother people were whispering that in some cottages rats were being trapped out of sight of the children and being added to soup pots that held little else but grass or gruel.

Sophie reached to bathe Meg's feverish brow, scoffing at the tales of people eating rats and sending the children on about their chores. But she kept her gaze on the window, watching for the first signs of Johnny and Paddy coming home.

They'd not been back for nights on end.

At the Priory MaryKate stared at the slanted ceiling in her tiny attic room until dawn flooded light in upon her, Pugs still at her side.

KATHLEEN

Jumbled feelings over what had happened last night kept her wakeful through the long dark hours. Her face wreathed in soft smiles, she relived the moments in Harry's arms. Then tears spilled out when she remembered his words. She forced herself to open her eyes, facing the reality of the day ahead.

She had betrayed her benefactor. Had willingly walked into Harry's arms, had wanted him to come to her. Hot tears slid down her cheeks. She would do it again. She would do it forever, if he would let her.

Yet there was no future in it for her except one of pain and loss. She would have to leave here. Leave the only home she'd known these last years. And the woman who had befriended her. Hot shame coursed through her. And then the thought of him again.

Never to see him again. She turned on her side, pulling her pillow close and sobbing into it at the thought. She would never see him, never be close to him.

He would not let that happen. He would come for her, he would find her. He would—she felt her heart breaking inside her. He would do none of it. He could do none of it. He was an earl, a peer of the realm, and English. He could not turn out his wife and marry an Irish serving girl.

Marry. She had never considered marriage. None had ever come so close to her heart that she would consider spending her life with them. She thought of Sophie's pushing her to talk to this farmer or that villager. To Tom Sweeney, who had acreage near Sophie's parents. To any available bachelor; for every woman should be married. To be barren was to be half-alive, Sophie told MaryKate over and over.

MaryKate lay back, her tears subsiding, her body still alive with his touch. If she closed her eyes she could still feel his arms closing around her, his body weight pressing down upon her, reaching inside her. Her body turned liquid with the feelings, replete, filled-up, and yet still hungry for him.

To finally find love and have to give it up in the same instant seemed more cruel than she could bear. She wanted him in her arms. She wanted to give him everything in the world, to make him happy and bring him peace. And children. Even the heir he sought.

KATHLEEN

The thought shocked her. Would she do that if he asked? He said even Amelia wanted it. Was it true? Could it be true? Her Ladyship wanted no part of Harry, that was plain. She never had. She found comfort with the English reverend; could she possibly—MaryKate stopped the thought. It was impossible. Her Ladyship could not possibly be involved with the reverend. Not that way. And even if she were, what difference would that make? Harry was still English. Was still married. Was still Protestant and a peer of the realm. She had no place in his life, nor he in hers. He was an enemy of her people.

MaryKate closed her eyes, and prayed to God. She prayed for strength, for help. She prayed for Harry, God forgive her. Let him be happy. Give him what he wants and needs. And let me learn to live with it. Listlessly, she sat up, staring with hollow eyes at the bare floor, telling herself that she must get up. She must face Lady Amelia and their famine patients and all else. Including him.

Harry tossed and turned in his own bed, rising at first light irritable and determined to thrash all of it out, to end this farce and get on with his life.

He dressed hurriedly, not calling for Archie's help, going over and over what he would say to Amelia. She must understand that the situation was untenable. She must be made to understand that he did not wish to bring another child into this world that was unwanted by its mother. That nothing good could come to such a child. As he knew better than any.

Thoughts of his dying father rose to confuse him. And then the thought of MaryKate. His body hardening. Wanting her. Wanting her now. Under any terms. He told himself he was being unfair. Selfish.

Ending the farce with Amelia did not mean he could have MaryKate. They would be ostracized by all society, he and MaryKate, both in England and Ireland. He cared not one whit for himself, but for her it would be impossible.

He told himself others had married beneath their stations in life. Some had even been able to keep their loves close at least, while marrying where they must.

But MaryKate would never survive as a light of love, and

he knew it deep within his heart. She was too honest. Too direct and headstrong. She deserved better than his leavings. Or anyone else's leavings. He felt the love surging within him, felt the heat of wanting her and beyond the wanting, the softness that she brought out in him. He wanted to protect her from everything, including himself.

He strode purposefully out into the hall, heading for the door to Amelia's rooms, unsure what to do. The situation had to be faced—first with Amelia, then with MaryKate.

It was MaryKate who stopped him.

"She's not feeling well," MaryKate told him at Amelia's door.

He looked determined. "This has to be settled. I cannot leave matters as they are."

MaryKate touched his sleeve, each of them reacting to the touch. She hurriedly withdrew her hand, blushing when she looked up into his questioning eyes. "Please," she said softly, "she's truly not well. There's no need—not just this minute. Perhaps later—"

Harry watched her. "Why don't you want me to speak to her?"

"It's not that. It's just—" MaryKate bit her lip. "I should like to be able to speak to her. To tell her myself," MaryKate added finally.

"Tell her what?" he demanded.

"That I love you," MaryKate said simply, melting his heart and seeing her reflection in his dark eyes. "I doubt she'll talk to me afterward," MaryKate continued softly.

"What is happening between Amelia and myself would have happened regardless, MaryKate. It started long before you and I."

"She's been so good to me," MaryKate pleaded with him. "I have to say something to her myself—but not now. She truly is feeling ill. This afternoon, or tomorrow, isn't that soon enough?"

"I don't deal well with deception," he told her.

"Nor do I, and well you know it," she replied.

Harry hesitated. Glancing toward Amelia's door, he felt an emptiness he'd never before known.

As if she sensed it she touched his hand, and he grabbed hers, bringing it to his lips to kiss her palm. When they

KATHLEEN

looked into each other's eyes they were as close as when their bodies blended into one being.

"I must go. I must see to the patients downstairs." He nodded and watched MaryKate move toward the stairs. He still stood by the door to Amelia's rooms, pain and love mixing within his chest, hurtful emotions welling up to fill him with unease. He felt hamstrung by circumstances he could not control, could not change. For the first time in his life he felt completely thwarted. And he hated the feeling.

Confused and worried, Harry stared at Amelia's door. Then he turned away, thinking of MaryKate's request: not yet. Not just yet.

Harry headed toward the stairs. Taking them two at a time, he went in search of Archie and physical activity. Anything to take his thoughts away from MaryKate.

Amelia's ennui was not better the next day. She kept to her rooms, MaryKate moving between Amelia's sickroom and the annex below, Father Ross sending his housekeeper to help spell her as the week wore on.

The doctor visited Amelia on his rounds, then came long-faced to Harry in his study. "We have to talk."

Harry looked up from his paperwork, shoving it aside. "Is it about Amelia?"

"Yes." The doctor came forward, putting his black bag on the edge of Harry's desk, then let himself sink to a wingchair nearby. "Her Ladyship's fever is still high and she cannot seem to keep any food in her stomach."

Alarmed, Harry leaned forward. "Are you saying she has the typhus?!"

"No!" the doctor spoke hastily. "No, not that. At least not yet. But she is weak and ill and must not be allowed near the annex and her patients until she is fully well. A relapse could bring on something worse."

"I see," Harry said. "It is somewhat difficult to keep Her Ladyship from doing anything she wishes to do."

"I full well know it," her doctor told him. "But her life is what we are speaking about. Her impulses to help must be kept in check. If such a thing is possible, she is too good. Too Christian. She has made herself ill caring for these Catholic peasants."

207

KATHLEEN

"I shall do what I can," Harry told the man.

The doctor stood up, reaching for his bag as Harry continued, "Have you checked on MaryKate? I mean, Mary-Kathleen O'Hallion, my wife's assistant?" At the doctor's look Harry's expression hardened. "She has been with the ill as much or more than my wife. And is still caring for Her Ladyship."

"Oh." The doctor nodded. "I see. Of course, I shall take a look at her if she will permit it."

"Tell her I insist," Harry said.

But MaryKate told the doctor she felt perfectly well. There was no need to take his time up with the likes of her when so many were truly ill.

He continued on his rounds without protesting. MaryKate and Father Ross continued to wrap bandages in the large annex room across from the rows of beds that kept multiplying with more and more patients.

MaryKate looked toward the beds. "What will we do when there's no more room?"

"Faith and I don't know, Mary-Kathleen. God is surely troubled with us as it is."

MaryKate stared at the old man. "Do you believe that?"

"What else are we to think?" Father Ross replied. He shook his head. "Surely, we must be the worst of his children to deserve this."

"I don't believe that!" MaryKate burst out, guilt rising within her. "You can't tell me of all the people on earth, we are so terrible!"

"Then what do you think this is if not a curse on our wickedness?"

"Perhaps it's a curse on our stubbornness," she said. "Or maybe it's a challenge for us to learn to grow other things, to stand up for ourselves. If something keeps happening and happening, then surely you must learn from it!"

"You're young, but not that young. You know it's never been this bad. Not in all my long years has it ever been this bad," Father Ross told her. He put a roll of bandages in the basket between them, watching MaryKate's troubled expression. "Is something else the matter?" he asked.

Startled, she looked up into his kind eyes. "What?"

KATHLEEN

"You're not yourself these days, Mary-Kathleen. . . . I've known you since you were born. Is there something troubling you?"

"No!" She spoke too quickly.

"You haven't been to confession in weeks."

She stood up, moving away from him, her movements jerky. "I have to see to the new medicine the doctor brought."

He watched her leave, his gaze meeting that of his own housekeeper's, who sat beside one of the beds across the room.

Father Ross stood up, moving nearer his housekeeper. "Well, then, and what do you make of all that?"

His housekeeper shrugged. "Sure'n it's none of my business, but mark my words, there's a man in it someplace."

Father Ross shook his head. "You think a man's at the bottom of everything."

"And isn't he, then?"

"The root of all evil's supposed to be money, Delia."

"Sure'n whoever thinks that has never had sex rear its ugly head."

"Delia! I'm surprised at you! Talking like that. And to a priest, after all."

Delia shrugged. "Truth's truth."

"And what would you be knowing about matters of sex?" Father Ross teased.

"And wouldn't you be surprised to find out! Make yourself useful and hand me that pan of water," she told him.

He did as she ordered, then moved among the beds, speaking to one and another, praying with those who asked.

The problems began to multiply as the week dragged on. Word came from across the valley that tenants of Lord Ennis were being evicted for nonpayment of their rents. And then Lord Cameron's.

Among them were the Sullivans, Old Sean's great-great-grandfather, the first Sullivan to till the acreage they then called theirs—before the laws changed and Catholics were disallowed the vote, their estates dismembered and taken from them.

Now they were tenants on their own land and being

KATHLEEN

evicted. Old Sean's wife could not believe it was happening. She ran wildly to and fro, trying to stop the estate agents from taking her spinning wheel and heaving it into the lane.

Her daughters, her granddaughters, and their children all lived with her, and the children began to scream with fright at the sounds of their mothers wailing as the roof and portions of the cottage walls were thrown down.

"We have naught to go! We'll be in the lane! God have mercy, what are you doing to us?! This is our land!" Old Sean's wife struck out at one of the bailiffs. He turned quickly, defending himself, his arm raised and hitting the old woman across the side of the head.

Her grandchildren clustered around her, crying. One of the estate agents called to the others, yelling at the one who struck the old woman.

"I didn't mean to!" the man replied, more scared than he wanted to admit.

They rode off to report to Lord Cameron's bailiff, leaving the women and children of the Sullivan family in the lane, without home or food.

Old Sean, his one son, and two sons-in-law were off on the public works, Old Sean lying his age to make a few pennies to send home so that his children's children could be fed. They were lucky to get on the public works. Over two million people depended upon the lowly potato in Ireland, depended on it for survival as well as sustenance. There were less than one hundred fifty thousand public works jobs in the whole of the nation, and only room for another hundred thousand in the workhouses all across the island.

At Tom Ross's pub in the village more and more able-bodied and unemployed men filled the large room, their voices loud with outrage and frustration as the problems increased.

"They won't let us work!"

"They've got food here, in depots, and they won't release it!" another voice rose above the others.

"Depots! What about our *own* food! The dirty English are shipping out enough food to feed us all for the entire year!" Johnny O'Hallion's voice rang out, bitterly.

"And what are we to do, then?" someone asked.

KATHLEEN

Johnny took his time. He gauged the faces of the men around him. "I say—we take it back."

Silence met his words.

Slowly the murmur of other voices rose again around the bar, Tom pouring freely as the men ranted and raved.

Paddy leaned in toward Johnny. "Isn't it time, then, to be going home?"

"You've been home, have you not? And all's well."

"Aye, but Sophie's that worried, Johnny. You'd best be letting her know all's right with you."

Johnny smiled at his brother, handing over his mug for more beer. "Not yet, Paddy . . . wait a bit, and she'll know all's right with us and everyone else." Johnny turned, seeing Young Tim from the Priory stable and rumpling his fair hair.

"Well, then, and are you with us, too, then? Or are you spying for the English landlord?"

"I?!" Young Tim took the words seriously, staring up at the older man, stung to the quick. "How could you think that?!"

"And I don't, then, Young Tim—we're glad to see you. You could be a real help."

Tim looked eager. "How? I want to help, but how?"

"Why, by telling of anything you hear about what the English are doing. Your Lordship will be told by the others, I'll warrant. And you can tell us."

"Sure'n he doesn't come to the stable to discuss what the English are doing. Why don't you ask your sister?" Young Tim asked innocently.

Johnny was turning away toward the men. He stopped, looking back at the boy. "What? What did you say?"

"MaryKate isn't with Her Ladyship all the time, even now that she's ill. His Lordship sometimes takes MaryKate for rides."

Johnny pulled the boy to the corner of the room, as away from the others as he could get. When people crowded in around them, he reached for the door to the kitchen, bringing Young Tim with him into the smoky room.

Tim was confused, looking around himself at Tom Ross's wife, who worked at the fire, cooking up stew across the room.

KATHLEEN

"What did you mean in there?" Johnny asked the boy. "What rides with the Englishman?"

"What?" Tim pulled a little away. "I didn't say nothing."

Johnny's grim visage frightened the boy. "You said MaryKate went riding with the Englishman. When?"

"Lots of times."

"Collecting rents?" Johnny asked.

"I guess so . . ."

"And?" Johnny persisted.

"I don't know!" Tim replied. "I guess they just like to ride."

"When did they last ride?"

"Just last week or so," Tim told her brother.

"And they visit tenants."

"Well, I guess so. I mean, sometimes."

Johnny towered over the boy. "And *some*times—what?"

"Well, sometimes, I mean, it's so late, I don't suppose there's many up when—"

"Not many up." Johnny spoke the words slowly, distinctly, making sure he had heard correctly.

"I don't know."

"How late?" Johnny asked.

"I don't know!" Tim spoke quickly, his voice rising and then falling again. "I didn't see them leave. I only saw them return late, that's all."

"How late?" Johnny repeated, Tim watching the large man's mean eyes.

"Honest, I just don't know. I was in bed when I heard them."

"What time did you go to bed?"

Tim hesitated. "Around about ten or so."

Johnny shoved the boy away. "Say no more about it. To *any*. Do you hear me?"

"I hear you."

"I'll handle my sister," Johnny said. He looked grim.

Tim watched Johnny O'Hallion walk back into the front room of the pub, scared by Johnny's reactions. And curious now about what MaryKate was doing with the earl in the middle of the night. Alone.

23

The weather was turning colder, winter already in the air. At the Priory Lady Amelia was better, eating a light breakfast and coming down to the annex to check on her patients.

MaryKate found her there when she arrived from the kitchens with a huge pot of breakfast gruel.

"Your Ladyship, you're not to be here!"

"Nonsense." Amelia dismissed the issue, moving among the narrow cots, straightening bedding and reaching to help dish out the gruel MaryKate brought.

MaryKate fell silent, following Her Ladyship from bed to bed until the food was ladled out.

Amelia stopped MaryKate as she headed back out with the empty pot. "How are you feeling these days, Mary-Kathleen?"

MaryKate turned back, startled. "What? I'm fine, Your Ladyship."

Amelia watched the Irish girl. "You've had no symptoms?"

"None, Your Ladyship."

"You are quite well, then? You look peaked."

KATHLEEN

MaryKate bit her lip. "I've not slept much lately," she admitted.

"You should not work so hard," Amelia replied lightly.

MaryKate faltered. "Yes, Your Ladyship."

"Have you seen my husband?"

"What?" MaryKate stared into Amelia's bland expression.

"This morning. Have you seen the earl about?"

"No." MaryKate's reply was almost inaudible.

"You'd best see to fresh linens for these beds."

"Yes, Your Ladyship." MaryKate escaped the sickroom, Amelia watching the girl's retreating back.

Archie found MaryKate in the laundry a little later. "You've got a visitor in the kitchen," he told her.

MaryKate folded the bedding she was holding, putting it atop a pile already folded. "Who is it, then?"

"I'm not sure, but she's in a rare state."

In the kitchen Sophie turned from talking to Cook, wringing her hands on her apron. "Oh, MaryKate, and what have you been doing?!"

MaryKate stopped in her tracks. "What are you talking about?" she demanded.

Sophie started to speak and then looked toward Archie and Cook, behind MaryKate, watching their exchange.

"We must talk in private," Sophie told her sister-in-law.

MaryKate hesitated, looking back toward the others, and then nodded, putting the bedding on the huge wood table to one side of the kitchen. "Archie, could you see these get to the annex?"

Archie came forward, MaryKate taking Sophie toward the back stairs and up to her attic room.

"Well?" MaryKate demanded.

Sophie looked around the bare little room. "Everyone's saying you're seeing the earl."

"What?"

"That you and the Englishman are spending time together. Alone. At night."

MaryKate felt her cheeks begin to burn. "Who said that?"

"Sure'n the whole countryside is talking! And they talked

KATHLEEN

to your brother! Johnny came home in a fair state, I'll tell you, gone two days and hollering his head off about the English and all. You've got to talk to him! You've got to tell him it's not true."

"I'll not do that," MaryKate said.

Sophie could not believe her ears. "Are you saying it's true?!" She looked horrified.

"I'm not saying it's true or it's false. I'm saying my life is my own and my business is my own. None others'. Not even my brother's."

"But he's the head of the family!"

"That may be. But I've lived this long without another's interference, and I don't need it now."

Sophie watched the younger woman. "It's true, then, isn't it?" She sounded tired suddenly. "Oh, Lord, MaryKate, what have you done?"

"I've done nothing that concerns any but myself."

Sophie shook her head. "No one's life is their own these days, MaryKate. Not when you mix English and Irish together. None will approve, not his people nor your own. I just hope Johnny doesn't take it into his own hands."

"You tell my brother—" MaryKate stopped. "Never mind, he'll not listen to you. I'll tell him myself."

"Tell him it's a lie," Sophie told her firmly. "I don't care what else, tell him it's a lie. Unless you want more trouble for your Englishman. And jail for your brother."

MaryKate opened the door. "I've got to get back to my work."

Sophie came out past MaryKate, turning on the landing to search the younger woman's face. "No matter what the truth is, tell him it's a dirty lie. And make him believe it." MaryKate heard a firmness in Sophie's voice she had never heard before.

"What of Meg?" MaryKate asked as Sophie turned away.

Sophie hesitated. "She's not well yet."

"Bring her here, please. It's her life we're talking about!"

Sophie hesitated. "It's the Lord's will that will be done no matter what."

"Stuff and nonsense!" MaryKate burst out. "I've lived

215

KATHLEEN

long enough to know the Lord helps those who help themselves!"

Her sister-in-law crossed herself. "MaryKate, these heathen English are teaching you to blaspheme!"

"Sophie, please."

"No. Johnny wouldn't like it. He wouldn't like me here now. I must go." MaryKate watched Sophie cut across the back kitchen garden toward the river before, with dragging step, she herself started back into the annex.

While MaryKate and Amelia worked in the annex with the famine patients, Harry escorted men into the large south parlor. Lord Ennis, Lord Rossett, and the rest of the landowners from across the valley filed into the Priory, their carriages waiting outside.

The Englishmen were not happy to be here, were here because their duties, their responsibilities, their honor, had been called into question by Henry, Earl of Lismore, Baron Lichfield.

"I'd like to know by what right you've called this meeting," Lord Endicott said, his huge mustache twitching as he spoke.

"If you felt there was no need to attend, surely you wouldn't be here," Harry countered, the others settling down to a murmur as he spoke. "There is a dire problem here in Ireland and we English are responsible for its resolution."

"Why?" Lord Ennis asked, his tone bemused. "After all, it's their island, their nation, their problem."

"Is it?" Harry moved toward Lord Ennis. "Who rules it? Whose soldiers police it? Whose laws have stripped it of all its wealth?"

"Wealth?!" Lord Ennis scoffed. "What wealth?"

"Count the food that is leaving here shipload after shipload, while the Irish starve. Go to Dublin harbor and ask what wealth the Irish have. Or had before we confiscated all that was theirs."

"Theirs!" Lord Endicott nearly shouted at the earl. "How dare you! Where would they be without us?!"

"Perhaps they would be fed," Harry replied. "We talk of the power of England. Her navy, her gold, her resources . . .

oh yes, and her enlightened statesmen and leaders. While the plain fact is England cannot keep the children of her bosom fed. Perhaps those dissident voices are correct. Perhaps the Irish aren't worthy of the dignity of belonging to the great family of the empire. Perhaps they should be regarded as aliens, as the London papers have suggested; even so, the queen, at her coronation, swore to protect and defend her subjects, *all* her subjects! There was no exception in the case of Ireland recorded, was there? Was there?! So how is it that while there is a shilling left in the treasury, or even one jewel in the Crown of England, that patient, suffering, subjects of that crown are allowed to perish with hunger?! You who go to bed fat of belly at night, you tell me what should be done!"

"It's not our fault!" Lord Innisfree called out.

"And whose fault is it?" Harry demanded. "Have we allowed these people enough land to keep themselves from starvation? Have we rescinded the laws that make it impossible for them to grow more crops? To get out of the poverty they face? The people are calling out 'bread or blood!'—people who are half-clothed, if that. People whose pallid visages already show the ravages of famine. Imagine if they were your *own*, and then tell me it's none of our concern!"

"Word's out that you're selling off your Dublin house to feed the Irish poor." Lord Ennis spoke softly, the others turning to watch Harry as he answered.

"And if I am? Is it less than any of us should do?" Harry countered.

Lord Ennis turned to the others. "You see? The earl is at best too sensitive to deal with issues here in Ireland. They call for a strong hand, not giveaway programs that will make the entire countryside reliant upon government funds, government relief. At worst he is an apologist for those who would give away all that England holds dear to people who merely want to drain her dry."

"What does she hold dear?!" Harry nearly yelled at the others. "Is not honor, is not compassion, part of our heritage? We have helped *cause* these problems! Have we no responsibility to put them right?! Here's a letter about Ireland sent to the Duke of Wellington by one of his justices of the peace . . ." Harry motioned toward Archie, who handed a paper forward. Harry bent over it, reading slowly, "In one hovel six famished and ghostly skeletons, to all appearances dead, were huddled in a corner on filthy straw, their sole covering a ragged horsecloth, their wretched legs hanging about, naked above the knees. Approaching in horror I found by a low moaning they were alive and in fever, four children, a woman, and what had once been a man." Harry looked about the room. "Children! A woman. And what had *once* been a man! How are we to shirk our responsibility to these people when the food necessary to feed them is being carted off their land and shipped out their ports by British bottoms every day of the week!"

"That grain is ours!" a voice called out. "We own it!"

"By what right?! The right of might?!" Harry shouted back. "Do we owe *nothing* to people whose land we've stripped from them?!"

"Gentlemen—gentlemen—" A voice rose from the center of the room. A portly man, well built and rather conceited-looking, spoke. "There's nothing to be gained by shouting and recriminations." The man walked toward Harry. "I'm sure you agree."

"I agree we should be calm," Harry spoke through almost clenched teeth. "But we *must* also act!"

The man smiled. "Let's talk about it." The man bowed slightly. "I am Arthur. Prince of Connact. I believe we are cousins, by the by."

Harry stared at the shorter man. "Can you help?"

Arthur shrugged. "Can any? I mean, after all, we're dealing with people who do not want to be helped . . . aren't we?"

That night Amelia took her dinner in her rooms, calling MaryKate to her side after her tray was finished.

MaryKate found Amelia sitting pensively beside the tiny fireplace in her sitting room, a half-finished needlepoint pillow cover lying discarded in her lap, her needles and threads lying sorted out on the small cherrywood table beside her.

"You wanted me, Your Ladyship?"

"Yes," Amelia spoke slowly. "You'd best sit."

MaryKate did as she was bid.

KATHLEEN

Amelia took her time. "I understand there is talk about you and my husband." MaryKate looked stricken. "Is it true?" Amelia persisted.

"I—I don't know what the talk is, Your Ladyship. But I have wanted to talk to you about—about what is the truth."

"Please stop!" Amelia watched MaryKate. "I have a proposition to end this situation."

"I beg your pardon?" MaryKate looked stricken.

"I said I have a proposition for you both," Amelia repeated. "My husband and I have no wish to be together, as I'm sure you full well realize. But he has a duty to produce an heir. When he has accomplished that duty, both he and I can be allowed to continue our separate lives." Amelia paused, gauging MaryKate. "If, however, he is attracted to you, you could do us all a great deal of good."

"Your Ladyship, please . . ."

"Hear me out. Harry and I will not have to deal with each other in an intimate fashion, which neither of us wants. The dukedom shall have its heir. And you shall be well paid and looked after."

MaryKate began: "You can't mean—"

"But I do mean. After all, it would not be your child. It would be mine," Amelia told her calmly. "You will stay here with me, and I shall legally adopt the child as mine. In England none need ever know it was anything other than a normal birth."

"You would take our child?" MaryKate said faintly, Harry's own words echoing within her memory.

"He would be heir to a dukedom. You certainly could not begrudge that birthright to a child of your womb." Amelia gave MaryKate a moment to consider what had just been said. "Harry will want to raise the child in England, and I shall stay here. There is even the possibility, if you are discreet, that you could accompany him to England as the child's nanny."

MaryKate stared at the countess.

"You look shocked," Amelia told the girl. "It seems to be the only practical thing to do. Unless you are unwilling. It could of course be done with someone else, but if he is

KATHLEEN

attracted to you, and you are willing, we would make it well worth your while."

MaryKate stood up. "Please, stop! You must excuse me. I . . . I can't talk about this!" She turned and ran out of the room, tears welling up and streaming down her face.

She ran past Harry, who reached out to grab her. "What's happened?" He looked toward Amelia's open door. "Did Amelia say something? Do something to you?"

MaryKate shook her head, her body shaking with her sobs. He pulled her close. She buried her head in his smoking jacket, his heart thudding steadily against her ear.

"Harry?" Amelia spoke from her doorway. "I see that Mary-Kathleen's spoken to you."

"She's said nothing." His voice was hard. "What did you do to her?"

"I don't think this should be discussed in the halls." She disappeared back inside.

MaryKate stepped back from Harry. "Someone will see us."

"Damn and blast them, who cares?!" Harry reached for her. "What's happened?"

She stared up at him. "She asked me to have your child."

Harry took a moment to digest MaryKate's words. His expression hardening, he turned toward Amelia's rooms.

MaryKate turned toward the back stairs, unable to face any of it.

In Amelia's rooms Harry stared at the wife he barely knew. "Have you gone mad?" he barked at her.

"Harry, we've already discussed this."

"You remain countess and remain in Ireland while I return to England with an heir and a mistress?"

"Precisely," Amelia replied. "If the child has the misfortune to be born a girl, you can entail the estate to her sons. Don't look so shocked, Harry. Surely you'll not say you've never had a mistress." She watched him. "My maid tells me you've already had MaryKate. Perhaps your heir is already on the way."

Harry watched Amelia. "You're enjoying this, aren't you?"

"Yes. I am." She smiled. "I can see an end to our troubles."

"You are very unlike what they all think of you. They think you a saint. Not a manipulator."

She smiled again. "Perhaps I am both."

He left her there. Smiling.

Harry followed the back stairs to the attic rooms above, unsure which was MaryKate's. He opened three, finding a frightened scullery maid, a surprised cook, and an empty room before he opened the fourth and saw MaryKate look up at him. She sat on the bed, still dressed, tears drying on her face.

"You shouldn't be here; someone will see."

"All have already," he told her. He reached for her. "I don't want you hurt. By anything. Or anyone." She was limp in his arms. "If you want to leave, I'll see that you're provided for."

She leaned against him. "I don't want to leave."

His arms tightened around her. "God knows I don't want you to leave."

"I have nowhere to go."

He heard her sadness and tipped her head to look into her eyes, studying her. "Is that the reason you want to stay?"

"No." She felt the tears welling up. "But it's the truth. My brothers, the villagers, even the church, they all say I have no right to feel what I feel for you."

"There's no such thing as the right to a feeling, Mary-Kathleen. You don't choose to have them."

"But you can choose not to act upon them."

"Yes," he replied, "yes, you can."

"I've dreamt about you since you first arrived," she told him quietly.

He smiled, a sad, lopsided smile. "You had a strange way of showing it. Biting my head off all the time, waging war over all things English."

They stood quietly, holding each other.

"Everything feels rights when I'm in your arms." MaryKate spoke softly. "Nothing else matters." She reached to kiss his cheek. "Nothing."

Her touch was as gentle as a snowflake against the rough

stubble of his growing beard. He turned his head to kiss her lips, getting lost in the feelings that welled up at her touch. He felt his body responding, surging out toward her, stiff and hard.

She felt him harden, her hand reaching down to touch him, to feel the strength. He groaned, surprised at her touch, drawing her closer, wanting the feeling to continue.

"We have to stop," he told her. "You have to move away from me."

"What do you want me to do?" she asked him. "Tell me what to do."

"MaryKate." He called her name out, over and over, bringing her past the narrow bed to the scrubbed floor beside it, laying her down, finding her mouth with his own.

"I want to please you," she told him, feeling him react, his mouth finding her eyelids, her cheek, her ear. His breath was ragged, shivering through her, his teeth finding her neck and tracing it to her shoulder.

Suddenly Archie came clamoring up the stairs toward the attic and rapped on MaryKate's door.

"Not now!" Harry hollered, MaryKate sitting up as Archie opened the door and slipped inside.

Harry yelled at the man as he pulled away from MaryKate, but Archie pretended to see nothing. "Sorry, Your Lordship. Mary-Kathleen. But it's the troops. There's been trouble in the village, and they've taken into charge some of your people. And her brother."

"Trouble? What kind of trouble?" Harry asked.

"They've broken into the government food store and gotten one of the guards."

"Is he hurt?" MaryKate asked, forgetting all else.

Archie answered to Harry: "No. But the constable wants to talk to you about it all. And he's got English troops with him. It seems some of them got away."

"And my brother?" MaryKate came toward Archie.

He glanced at her and then back at the earl. "One got away. But the other one didn't. The younger brother is in custody and being charged."

"Paddy?!" MaryKate protested. "Paddy's never done anything to hurt anyone in his life!"

"I'll be down directly," Harry said.

KATHLEEN

"I'll wait," Archie said pointedly.

Harry stared him down. "Then you'll wait downstairs."

Archie turned toward the door. "I'll wait outside."

"You don't work for me. And at this rate, you never will."

Archie smiled. "Aren't I lucky."

"You're here on my sufferance," Harry told him.

"A piece of left luggage, left by Lord Leo. I know. And such a holiday I'm having *not* working for you around here." Archie closed the door.

Harry looked toward MaryKate. "I'll see what can be done."

"Please help Paddy. Harry, he's never done anything wrong, never."

Harry looked grim. "Can you say as much for your other brother?"

She reached for his hand. "Whatever else, Johnny's still my brother."

"How I wish he weren't!" The words were wrenched out of the Earl of Lismore. His voice softened as he looked down at her, saying, "There must be something good in him if you and he have the same blood flowing through you."

"I won't have soldiers all over my property!" Harry roared at the constable.

The man looked uncomfortable, but held his ground. "It's the law, your lordship."

"There's no law in the realm that says you can come onto my property with troops! Not without orders from the queen herself!"

Harry strode outside, calling for his greatcoat, blistering the ears of the sergeant outside.

"He's right, sir," the sergeant told the constable. "You'd not said it was an earl's land we were on."

"But they fled here!"

"If they're here," Harry told the constable, "I shall have them questioned. And brought in if necessary."

"If necessary!" the constable began and then stopped, seeing the soldiers already leaving. "We'll just see about this!" The man took to his horse, glaring back at the earl.

"Get horses saddled; we'll ride in and get her brother released."

223

KATHLEEN

"And the others?" Archie questioned.

"And the others," Harry said grimly. "If they're our people, they have no need of uprisings. They have food here."

"For now," Archie said.

"For however long it takes," Harry told him.

24

The hungry were becoming desperate. And more and more were going hungry. Without money, credit, or anything left to sell or pawn, farm laborers whose wages were paid in food had to be laid off, their employers no longer able to feed even themselves.

Village tradesfolk, tailors, carpenters, shoemakers, and all the rest who accepted poultry, eggs, and milk as payment now had no employment. And no food.

Harry and Archie rode through the evening shadows into a scene of rioting people. A force of police, with bayonets fixed to their carbines, were drawn up in front of the door to the government storehouse, an angry mob of villagers shaking their fists at the uniformed men.

The district inspector stood next to the head constable and all the sergeants in the garrison, a drawn sword in the inspector's hand. "Halt!" the inspector called out to the surging crowd. "Halt, I say!"

Johnny O'Hallion came out of the crowd toward the district inspector.

"There he is!" the head constable yelled. "Get the troublemaker!"

"We've had enough of your threats, you hired murderers!" Johnny spit the words at the inspector and the head constable. "No one's going to stop these poor people from demanding justice. And *food!*" He roared out the words: "Food! Come on, men, rush them and feed your children! God save Ireland!"

The inspector took an involuntary step backward at the ferociousness of the crowd, which began to move forward toward him. "I forbid this!" the inspector yelled, finding his voice.

"Stop!" Father Ross came up behind Johnny O'Hallion, his arms raised, pleading with the crowd. "Don't cause more trouble here!"

"We're not causing it!" a voice called out.

"My youngest is in the ground, my wife nearly gone, too!" another voice yelled. "There's *food* in there!"

"Get out of here, Father," Johnny O'Hallion said.

Father Ross turned toward Johnny. "Can't you see this won't help?"

"Food will keep us from starving long enough to kill the bloody bastards who've caused all this!"

"This district is proclaimed!" the inspector called out, his guards close about him. "All assemblies liable to lead to a breach of the peace are forbidden! You are all criminals!"

"Criminals?" Father Ross stared at the man in shock. "Is it criminal now to want to feed your loved ones?!"

"Careful, Father, or you shall be in contempt, too," the inspector told him.

"There's no breach of the peace here!"

"Mr. Ross informed us there would be a raid on his shop," the inspector said.

Johnny O'Hallion looked surprised, and Father Ross shook his head. "My brother would not say that, for it's a lie! These people are only asking for help! They want the food depot opened so they can feed their little ones!"

"Then they must go through their proper representatives on the Relief Committee!"

"We'll starve!" a voice called out.

"This crowd must disperse at once or take the consequences." The inspector's words carried more weight as a detachment of troops moved to block the crowd from behind

KATHLEEN

as well as ahead, Harry and Archie now caught in the midst of the angry mob.

"Inspector!" Harry called out, his English accent carrying a note of authority. The crowd barely parted for the black horse and its rider, Archie trying to stay close beside amidst the angry murmurs.

"Inspector," Harry continued, coming closer, "if relief food is inside there, what is the point in keeping it from those it's meant to feed?"

The inspector looked up toward the mounted earl. "That's the Relief Committee's business. My business is to keep the peace."

"Who is in charge of the Relief Committee?"

"Reverend Grinstead and Tom Ross," the answer came back, a ripple of surprise running through the men who crowded close around, the answer being repeated for those at the back of the mob.

"Tom Ross?!" Johnny O'Hallion stared at the policeman.

"Let me get him here," Father Ross said.

"This crowd must disperse first," the inspector began.

"Not bloody likely!" Johnny called out, others joining him.

"Inspector—you're outnumbered," Harry told the man, then looked toward Johnny. "And you, O'Hallion, you may be able to rush them, but how many of your men are you willing to lose? You have no weapons but the rocks and spades in your hands. Look again at those bayonets and carbines."

"Better to die fighting than to starve!" Johnny called to the crowd, other voices agreeing.

Harry turned toward the crowd. "And who will feed your families once you're dead?!"

Sullen faces stared up at the tall man on the black horse. Harry looked from one face to the next in the unfriendly crowd. "I give you my word, I shall see that this depot is opened to you by the morning! And all of you who wish can come back with me to the Priory. Bring something to put it in, and I shall give out grain to each of you to see you through until it is."

"Don't listen to him!" Johnny O'Hallion said. "Do you want to go on living on English doles?! It is *our land and our*

227

grain! Not the bloody English thieves' who've stolen it all and put their boots on our necks!"

The crowd was slowly pulling away from Johnny, only a few angry men still near him. As the crowd pulled back, the policemen came closer.

Johnny fell back a little, into the crowd, seeing the troops at the rear as well as the policemen coming toward him.

The head constable called out to the others around Johnny. "Let the police pass. That man is wanted for the uprising in Colleycomb earlier."

Johnny started to break for the lane behind the storehouse as police came after him at a run. Troops from behind angled through the dispersing crowd to cut him off.

Harry urged the horse forward, calling to Archie to follow. They were between the troops and Johnny before the troops could close in, Johnny O'Hallion and two others sprinting away around the side of the building, the police in foot pursuit.

"What do you think you're doing?!" The head constable was furious, glaring across the lane at Harry.

"Trying to help catch your criminal," Harry said blandly.

"You helped him escape!" the constable accused.

"I?" Harry looked the soul of innocence. "I was trying to cut him off."

The troopers were angling around Harry and Archie, pushing past the horses and following the police around the side of the building.

"You'd best stay out of it, if you know what's good for you!" the constable said angrily.

Harry turned his full attention on the man. "Are you threatening a peer of the realm?" His voice was ominously low.

"I'm carrying out my duty!" the man blustered, his anger collapsing into concern for his own skin.

"Then do so," Harry told him crisply. "And while you're at it, I'm here to post bond for Patrick O'Hallion."

"You can't do it here; he's in Colleycomb Jail."

Harry watched the constable. And then turned toward his man. "Archie, came along." The earl turned the black toward the parsonage. Troopers stood in his way, their carbines in their hands. Harry stared at the man in front of him. The trooper stared back. And then stepped back, motioning to the others.

A narrow path was made for Harry's horse, Archie coming behind, away from Father Ross and the crowd he was urging to disperse.

Archie came alongside Harry as they moved up the lane toward the Protestant parsonage. "That Johnny O'Hallion will get his neck in a noose sooner or later."

"Hot-tempered," Harry agreed. "It must run in the family."

Archie gave Harry a sidelong look. "It seems you've got your hands full of O'Hallions these days."

Harry didn't reply.

There were people, mostly women and children, still standing in line at the side of the Protestant rectory long after the dinner hour. Harry glanced their way as he dismounted. "If he feeds them here, why is he unwilling to open the food stores?"

Archie took the black's reins. "It's his way of getting converts." He saw Harry's expression. "It's one way to change Catholics to Protestants."

Harry shook his head. "Ridiculous." He started toward the narrow front gate and then stopped. "Isn't that ours?"

Archie looked toward the carriage parked just past the gate. "Looks to be."

Harry hesitated. "Stay here until the driver gets back. If it's ours, send him home."

"But," Archie began, saw Harry's expression, and stopped. "Yes, Your Lordship."

Harry's eyes flickered when Archie used his title. And then turned away, striding toward the gate and the narrow stone house beyond.

He reached his hand up to rap on the door and then thought better of it, taking the doorknob instead.

The narrow hall inside was empty. Harry walked in, double doors to a front parlor standing open in front of him. No one was there. He looked down the hall. A green baise door was at the end, two closed doors between Harry and the green baise.

Sounds came from beyond the green baise, people talking,

women's voices. Harry moved toward it, stopping at the first closed door. It opened to an empty dining room, dark and gloomy with heavy drawn drapes.

Harry hesitated, looking back toward the front door and then up toward the green baise. The only other closed door was across the narrow hall.

He reached for it, opening the door that led to the Right Reverend Hugh Grinstead's study. The couple embracing on the velvet couch in front of the fire pulled apart at the sound of the opening door. Hugh and Amelia stared up toward Harry's towering figure.

"Harry!" Amelia pulled away from the parson.

Harry took his time. "I see you are fully recovered," he said mildly.

Hugh Grinstead stood up. "Your Lordship—"

"I should have knocked," Harry told them both. "But I must admit that my curiosity propelled me forward. I rather knew what I would find."

"How long have you been spying on me?!" Amelia demanded.

"Please, there is an explanation . . ." Hugh Grinstead began.

Harry raised his hand. "I'm sure there is. Part of which has to do with why my wife has wished to stay on here alone."

"You already know why!" Amelia snapped.

"Amelia, please," Hugh protested. "Nothing is to be gained by anger. A reasonable discussion—"

"A reasonable discussion!" Amelia looked at him as if he were demented. "Don't be absurd!"

"I quite agree with you," Harry told the minister. "A reasonable discussion is quite in order. And it can be brief. I shall see that my wife's belongings are brought here before the morning."

"Her belongings!" Hugh looked aghast. "But you can't!" Hugh stared into Harry's mild expression. "It would ruin me! And your wife's reputation!"

"Harry's right," Amelia said unexpectedly. "Hugh, I'm tired of all the deception. Harry and I have no wish to be together."

KATHLEEN

"What about my career?!" Hugh asked her, agitatedly looking from Amelia to Harry and back to Amelia.

Amelia turned to face Hugh squarely. "What about it?" She stared him down. "We have thought of little else so far. I think it's time to consider ourselves for a change."

Hugh looked past Amelia, seeing Harry's expression change at her words. Uncomfortable, Hugh reached out for Amelia's hand. "My dear, my career is all that I have. You could not live destitute. Nor even on a minister's salary."

"I have money in my own right," Amelia said. "If Harry will not petition against me." She looked toward her husband.

"I can't marry a divorced woman!" Hugh burst out. "Lord Lismore! Surely you see that!"

Harry almost laughed. "I wasn't aware you were so devout, Grinstead."

Hugh turned toward Amelia, taking her by the shoulders and nearly shaking her. "Amelia, dearest, surely you can see this cannot work—you cannot expect this of me!"

Amelia watched Hugh. "I expect much more than this of you, Hugh. Much more."

Harry walked out of the study, his booted feet slapping against the hall carpet, the sound receding as he reached the front door.

The sound of it slamming behind him punctuated the quiet in the study as Hugh and Amelia faced each other in silence.

Outside, Archie came toward Harry, handing over the horse. The carriage was gone.

"It was Young Tim. He said Her Ladyship had said to wait, as usual." Archie spoke with no inflection to his tone.

"Her Ladyship won't be needing the carriage," Harry told the Welshman. He mounted the horse, turning it back toward the village and the Priory Road beyond.

Archie mounted, following swiftly, and coming alongside the earl. "Should I have it sent back, then, later? It's getting late."

"No."

"Well, pardon me for asking, but what's to happen now?" Archie asked with some asperity.

"An end to hypocrisy," was Harry's reply.

231

KATHLEEN

"If you ask me, it's the beginning of a proper mess, is what this all is. Not the end of anything."

On the Priory Road, climbing toward the house, Archie spoke again: "You can't just leave her there."

"She's been there all along."

Archie looked toward the man he'd helped raise. "I don't understand."

"Don't you?" Harry asked.

They reached the stableyard, the carriage still hooked up outside. Young Tim stood clutching a lantern. He came toward them, taking the reins as the earl dismounted. "Should I be going back, then, Your Lordship? To the vicarage?"

"No," Harry told the boy. "Not yet. You will go later and deliver to Her Ladyship some things she will need."

The boy's eyes grew round. Harry was already moving toward the house. The boy looked toward Archie, who shrugged, and then thought better of it, reaching out a hand to chuck the boy's shoulder. "Keep out of it, my boyo. Just do as you're told."

Young Tim watched the wiry Welshman walk into the Priory. Then he turned back toward the horses. He didn't see the men hiding in the stable until one of them grabbed him, a hand covering his mouth before he could scream.

Inside the Priory Harry took the stairs two at a time to MaryKate's attic room. She wasn't there. Harry hesitated and then went back down the stairs, searching the huge house. He found Wallace, telling him to find Amelia's maid and have her things sent to the vicarage.

"This evening, Your Lordship?" Wallace asked, his face a mask.

"As soon as possible. Have you seen Mary-Kathleen?" Harry asked the butler.

"I believe she's with Her Ladyship's patients, Your Lordship."

He found her in the annex, ministering to the famine patients. He stopped in the doorway, surprised at the number of pallets and cots that now filled the large room, making it seem crowded.

She was soaking a cloth, wringing it out and placing it

KATHLEEN

across an old woman's forehead. Harry watched her, seeing the moment when she felt his gaze and turned toward him.

Her eyes lit up when she saw him. The sight made his heart lighten, his own eyes soften as she stood and came toward him.

"Are you all right?" she asked. "They said you left with the police."

"I'm fine, but your brother is in Colleycomb Jail still. I shall go there in the morning."

"Paddy?" she asked.

Harry nodded.

"And what of Johnny?"

"I don't know, Mary-Kathleen." Harry hesitated. "He was fleeing the authorities when last I saw him."

MaryKate bit her lower lip. Starting to reach for Harry's hand, she thought of the patients behind her and glanced back at the cots that filled the large room. "I must go to Sophie."

Harry nodded. "Tell me what to do, and I shall see these people are attended to."

MaryKate looked up at him in surprise. "You?! You can't!"

"And why not?" Harry demanded.

MaryKate hesitated. Her smile, when it came, was soft, her hands gentle as she reached for him and pulled him out onto the narrow porch, away from the prying eyes of those who were awake inside.

"Because you were not born to be a nurse. You have no knowledge of what they need, no patience for what has to be done. It would sicken you to do the homely things these people need."

Harry watched her carefully. "How do you know?"

MaryKate started to reply and then stopped, watching Harry's face. "I just know. You were born to be served. Not to serve. Especially not to serve Irish peasants."

"And who, now, is the bigot?" he asked her.

Earning a small smile. "I'm no bigot. Merely a realist. You would not know what to do with bedpans." His expression made her smile grow. "You see I'm right," she told him, going onto her toes to kiss his cheek, "but I dearly love you for volunteering."

233

KATHLEEN

He grabbed her hands. "And only for that, then?"

"There's more I could mention," she told him saucily.

He brought her closer. "I want you with me."

She went toward him. And then realized where they were, pushing a little against his chest, trying to keep her distance. "Harry, there are people about."

"Hang them all."

She smiled sadly. "I hope it doesn't come to that."

He watched her. "If there were a way we could be together, would you be happy?"

She stared at him. "Would you?"

He still watched her. And then, slowly, smiled. "I think I might be."

She smiled back. "Don't go getting too enthusiastic, then, Your High and Mighty Lordship."

He pulled her closer, kissing her soundly, stopping all conversation.

Across the stableyard Johnny O'Hallion stood hidden in the stable shadows, staring out at his sister and the English lord, seeing the man bring MaryKate near and bend to kiss her lips.

Johnny's mouth set into a thin, uncompromising line, the man behind him coming close.

"What are we to do now, Johnny?" the man asked.

"Stand back!" Johnny's whisper was harsh. The man jumped back. "We wait," Johnny whispered. "And then we strike."

"Something's happened, something else, hasn't it?" MaryKate asked Harry.

Harry hesitated. "I found Amelia with the parson."

"I don't understand."

Harry walked toward the back gardens, his arm around MaryKate. "She's known him well, MaryKate. And I must tell you something else. If my father wishes, he can disinherit me. It will mean I will have very little. Possibly nothing. If you and I should marry, he may very well do so."

"Marry?" Her voice was hushed. "What are you saying? How could we marry?"

"There may be no legal way. In my church or yours, since

yours does not even acknowledge divorce in the first place. Therefore we would be branded for life. Or, in reality, you would be branded. But I shall divorce Amelia in any event. We've never been truly married, MaryKate, as I'm sure you can attest."

She turned toward him. "Are you saying you'll do this? Are you saying you truly want to marry me?"

He looked down into eyes as green as the sea beyond the nearby hills. "I'm saying I want to be with you. No matter what happens to either one of us. But I'm not being practical, and you must make your own judgment."

MaryKate laughed, the sound ringing out against the old stone walls, warming his heart. "My judgment?! My judgment is to never let you go."

Harry scooped her up within his arms, lifting her off her feet. He heard her giggle, felt her laughter against his chest as he held her close, his own lips curving into a smile. "We're daft, you know. This can't work."

"And who's to say not?!" she asked him, kissing his neck as he held her off the ground.

Harry bent toward her auburn hair, burying his face within it, drinking in the scent of her fresh-washed hair. "All common sense says not."

They clung together, content to hold each other close. Never looking toward the hundred windows that glared in the pallid late afternoon sunlight, staring down upon them.

"I'll ride to Colleycomb and bring your brother back," Harry spoke into her ear. "Then I'll send for our Dublin solicitor and find out what has to be done to straighten things out."

MaryKate started to question if anything could, but she kept her doubts to herself, content to have him hold her close and pretend all would be well.

"Are you all right?" he asked, turning her face up to see her eyes. His hand stayed under her chin, his touch gentle. "Do you want me to stop by your sister-in-law's on my way to Colleycomb?"

"I'd best go to her myself."

Harry nodded. "I'll bring Paddy there as soon as I can free him."

"I'll get Dorie from the kitchen to sit with the ill until

Father Ross and his housekeeper arrive in the morning." Then, searching his familiar face, she said, "Thank you."

"Why are you thanking me?" he asked her.

"For trying to help my poor brothers. It can't be easy for you. I know you don't think much of Johnny."

"I think he's a hothead and part of the entire problem. Not part of the solution." His voice softened: "But he's your brother, after all, so there must be some good in him."

"There is. And he means well."

Harry grimaced. "The road to hell is paved with good intentions. You go on to your sister-in-law. I'll find the maid and tell her to spend the night in the annex."

"And you?" she asked him shyly.

"I'll see to Amelia's things and give Archie a few hours sleep before I haul him up. We'll be in Colleycomb by first light." Her smile warmed his heart. He leaned toward her. "Tell your sister-in-law the sacrifice I made this night—letting you go."

"I'll do no such thing!" she told him stoutly. "Sacrifice is good for the soul."

He grabbed for her but she danced away, laughing a little and then sobering quickly. "Oh, Harry, how can I be so happy when all about us are so unhappy? It's not right!"

"Don't say that. And don't even ask. Never question the fates."

She looked out across the stone walls, across the back gardens toward the river far below. "I'd best get down to Sophie."

"Have Tim saddle up the mare," Harry told her.

As she started away he called out after her, making her turn round. "I'll see you first thing. As soon as I can free him."

She smiled a little. "I'll tell Sophie."

"And if you see your other brother, for God's sake, tell him to quiet down before he goes too far and none can help him."

MaryKate nodded again. "I'll try. But Johnny O'Hallion doesn't listen to anyone. Let alone me." Harry watched MaryKate head toward the stables and then turned to face the Priory and the task ahead.

* * *

KATHLEEN

MaryKate walked into the shadowy stable, calling out for Young Tim. No answer came back. She looked for a lamp, walking toward the first stall, still calling out Tim's name.

A hand clamped across her mouth. She tried to pull away, elbowing backward at her assailant.

"Stop it, MaryKate," Johnny whispered. He felt her relax a little, and then punch out at him.

"You frightened me!" she told him when he lifted his hand from her mouth.

"I have to talk to you."

MaryKate hesitated. "Well, speak quickly. I'm on my way to Sophie."

"Good," Johnny told her. "We'll both go."

Something in his tone of voice made her look up at him through the darkness. "You sound strange."

"You would too with half the county looking for you."

"Is it safe for you to go home? Won't they watch the cottage?"

"We'll soon find out, won't we?" Johnny said. He sounded careless, as if it didn't matter.

MaryKate didn't like the sound. "I need Tim to help me saddle a horse."

"I can help you," Johnny said.

She stood back as her brother reached for the mare. "I'll find a lamp—"

"No!" Johnny said sharply. He brought the horse out of the stall, a little moonlight filtering in through the open barn door. In the light of the moon, Johnny worked quickly, saddling the horse and reaching to lift MaryKate up upon it before he swung up behind her.

25

THE FIRST SNOW of the season fell during the night. The morning sun shone brilliantly across fields, stone fences, and narrow, winding roads. The countryside looked milky pure in the early dawn.

The mountains that rimmed the northern edge of the valley rose blindingly bright ahead of Harry, Archie, and a riderless horse as they rode through the cold. The horses' steel-shod hooves left deep tracks in the drifting whiteness.

The magistrate was not yet in when they arrived in Colleycomb. They waited at a nearby tavern, where Harry ordered them each a glass of hot ale. Archie stared glumly at the tavernman as he drew the ale and then pushed a hot poker into each mug before handing them over.

They took the ale to a rough table near the front window. The magistrate's office was across the road, next to the military barracks just off the main street.

"Would you look at them all," Archie said, nodding toward the mass of hungry vagabonds they'd just come through. Somber men slouched or sat huddled near the government offices, looking toward the officials who came and went with beseeching eyes. Now and again one tried to stop an official, a uniformed policeman coming near to pull the man away. None of them noticed the beauty of the brilliant sunshine. Here in the town the snow sank into pavement foul with refuse, scores of men making their beds on the cold pavement, waiting for word of work or food for their families.

Harry picked up a newspaper, scanned it quickly and then looked at Archie. "Peel's done it. He's brought in the Labor Rate Act. Public works are to be started in Ireland, the money lent to the Irish by the treasury at five percent. But there is to be no industry established, in case it might interfere with English industries. There are to be government inspectors to ensure none of the activity is either useful or productive! They can even build roads as long as they go nowhere! I didn't believe it when she first told me!"

"I beg your pardon?" Archie said.

"Aye, you heard me. They're to start from no other road and go to a mountainside or whatever, but *not* to another road. Or God forbid a town! They must be useless!"

"What sense is there in that?" Archie asked.

Harry threw down the paper. "What sense is there in any of this?!" He stood up. "Let's scare up this magistrate and get out of here before I tell them what I think of them!"

"The Irish? Or the English?" Archie asked the earl.

"Both!" Harry snapped. He was already heading out the door. Archie downed the last of his ale and followed.

They tracked the magistrate down to an estate just outside Colleycomb. The magistrate, the sheriff, and a small group of constabulary stood with a group of Irishmen who looked ashamed, crowbars in their hands.

"All right, now," the sheriff was saying as they rode up. "You are the landlord's lawful agent, are you, now?"

"You know I am," a thin man with a high, wide forehead told the sheriff. "I've called you here, haven't I? Now, get on with it!"

"This, then, is given over to your possession. Officer— call out the names!"

A relieving officer began to call out people's names, walking toward the closed door of a tiny cottage, and then walking down the lane to the next and the next, calling out names.

KATHLEEN

A wail came from inside the cottages, becoming more insistent as the constables knocked down each door, dragging women and children, kicking and screaming, out into the snow-covered lane.

The women ran back inside, grabbing kettles and spinning wheels, whatever they could—protesting all the while. An old woman and her daughter dragged out a bed from one of the far cottages, another trying to help her children with an old chest.

The women's voices rose in prayers and entreaties, threats and reproaches, as the impatient agent hollered out to the Irishmen who stood by with crowbars to get a move on.

A middle-aged woman spit at them as they came near her cottage, her children half-naked and clinging to her aprons. "They couldn't do it without you Irish destructives!" She spit at them again. "May God find a special place in hell for you all!"

One of the men stared at her with bleak eyes, stopping as he passed her. "He already has. Three of my four children are dead of starvation, my wife along with them. They've evicted me already, but my son will eat tonight if I help them."

"What about *my* sons?!" she sobbed.

"Thank God you still have them," he told her. He passed by her, starting for her cabin as next door the women beat their breasts, keening louder. One of the women fell to her knees in front of the agent's horse, telling them to kill her then and there.

Another carried her youngest on her hip as she tried to climb into the sheriff's carriage to plead with him as the thatch from her roof was torn down.

"Get on with it, boys! Get *on* with it!" the agent told the Irishmen.

Two of the men jumped up on the roof of the next cottage, finding the supporting beam that extended from one gable to another. Fastening a rope around it, they passed the rope through the door of the house to the workers below. A saw was handed up, weakening the beam and then the crowbars began to dismantle the wall plates at the gables' angles.

A stout pull on the rope broke the back of the roof,

bringing it down in a cloud of dust, into the walled-in area that had sheltered the family who lived inside until today.

Harry stared at the scene. Women with long, dark hair, bare legs and feet, all of them wearing tattered petticoats, their bodices patched and repatched, reached for crying children, crying themselves. The elderly ones crouched together along the road bank, watching with haunted eyes as the able-bodied men completed their work.

Archie brought the magistrate near Harry's horse.

"Begging your pardon, Your Lordship," the magistrate said, "what with all the confusion, I didn't see you."

"You've been busy," Harry said dryly.

"Yes, and that's a fact. Your man said one of your people's being held in Colleycomb."

"I need him to work."

"Of course, Your Lordship. I'll come along directly." The magistrate called out to the sheriff, readying his horse.

Harry's eyes went back to the cottages that were being torn to the ground. "How many of them are there?"

"Here? Just eight. Not much at all today."

Harry turned his horse around, waiting for the official. "How long will it take to level them?"

"Three hours or less—depends on how hard the men work. We're getting it down to a science, as you can see." The man seemed proud.

A child's sudden wail rose above the other sounds. Harry looked back, stopping his horse. The little girl, half-clad, was trying to climb the flattened, fallen roof of her cabin.

"She's gone, wee one, let it be." The child's mother ran after the girl. "The cat's dead."

"No! Tabby, Tabby!"

An old woman came forward to stop the child, holding her back, consoling her.

Harry turned his horse back toward the cabin.

"Where's he going, then?" The magistrate turned toward Archie.

"With His Lordship, you never know," Archie said.

Harry rode into the yard, past a crowd of women and children who began to yell and spit at him. On the back of the stallion, Harry leaned into the corner of the collapsed thatch, rooting around with his arm up to the elbow in the smoke-blackened thatch.

A tiny squeal came from inside and then his hand brought out a dusty kitten, twisting to get free of him. Harry reached down to deposit the kitten in the little girl's outstretched arms.

"Oh, bless you, bless you, sir!" the little girl cried.

"Don't be daft and bless a bloody Englishman! They're the ones who've taken the roof from over your head!" an older woman called out, her voice bitter.

The little girl put the kitten down, sinking to her knees besides it in the muddy lane. As Harry rode away the young cat began to groom herself.

The magistrate stared at the English lord as he came near. "Your land is near Beare, then?" he asked.

"Yes," Harry replied.

"I didn't catch your title, Your Lordship."

"I didn't throw it," Harry replied.

"I beg your pardon?" the man asked.

Harry saw Archie's look. "I'm Henry, the Earl of Lismore."

The magistrate was impressed. "Oh, and I'm honored to be of assistance, I assure you!"

"Good," Harry said crisply.

Paddy O'Hallion blinked when they let him out of the dark cell into the sunlight. He saw Archie first and then stopped in his tracks, seeing the earl.

"What's this, then?" he asked, scowling.

Archie spoke softly, glancing toward the front of the building where the magistrate was coming toward them. "It's your way out of jail, if you keep your mouth shut long enough to get away from here."

Paddy looked past the small Welshman toward the magistrate, who stopped in front of the duke.

"He's free to go, Your Lordship. Under your jurisdiction, of course."

Harry nodded. He looked toward Paddy. "Your family is waiting for you."

"Johnny?" Paddy looked surprised. "Have you seen Johnny?"

KATHLEEN

"I've seen him all right," Harry replied grimly. "We'll talk on the way back."

Paddy sat rigid, his face set as he held the reins tightly and urged the horse forward. Harry kept Paddy between himself and Archie.

"Am I in your custody, then?" Paddy asked.

"Officially, yes. Unofficially, I would appreciate your word not to do anything to invoke more official notice. I doubt they'll listen next time."

Paddy looked at the man beside him. "You want my word?"

"I would appreciate it."

"You'll accept my word?" Paddy repeated.

Harry glanced at the man. "Is there any reason I shouldn't?"

"You're English, and I'm Irish. Isn't that reason enough?"

"It's beside the point," Harry said.

"Is it?" Paddy asked as they rode on. Harry did not reply. After a few moments Paddy spoke again, "You've got my word, I'll do nothing you do not know about first. That's as far as I can go."

Harry hesitated. "Accepted."

"And what about his brother, then?" Archie asked beside them.

"I doubt Johnny O'Hallion is going to listen to reason. Or to me," Harry said, earning a grim laugh from Paddy.

While Harry rode toward Beare, Johnny O'Hallion paced the front room of his cottage, MaryKate and Sophie sitting on three-legged stools near the fire.

"Come sit, then, Johnny, have a wee bite," Sophie said.

"Of what? I'll have no more of that Englishman's charity!"

MaryKate's irritation showed. "Well, you'd best eat enough to have the strength to rant and rave about him!"

"I saw you! Do you hear me? I *saw* you! With my own eyes. God help us all." He looked heavenward. "We're doomed."

"I haven't doomed us!" MaryKate flared. "And if you had more sense, you'd see he's not the one to fight!"

243

KATHLEEN

"How often has he had his way with you?" Johnny came toward her, his anger lighting his eyes. "Tell me that, then. Tell me how much shame you've brought us!"

"Does the number of times count?" she asked him angrily. "Is it better if it be once, worse if it's a hundred times a hundred?"

"God save us! Listen to the tramp!" he yelled, scaring the children. The baby began to cry, Sophie scooping him up and looking reproachfully toward her husband.

"Yes! There's a difference!" Johnny shouted, turning on his sister. "If he forced you once, I can kill him for it. If you've let him have his way with you, I have to kill you both!"

"Johnny!" Sophie was terrified.

"He'll not be killing me, nor none other," MaryKate told Sophie. She stood up, her hands on her narrow hips. Johnny towered above her. "You listen to me, John O'Hallion; I'll not have you scaring your wife and children and ranting and raving at me any longer! I've stood enough. You're doing nothing but raising your own gall!"

"Yes? Yes?!" he menaced her.

"Yes!" She spit the word at him. "My life is my own to do with what I want!"

"I'm the head of this family!" he shouted.

"Then I'll be no part of it!" she shouted back.

"I wish to God you weren't!" her brother told her. "Shaming us before God and the neighbors."

"I've shamed no one!"

"Did he force you, then?!" Johnny demanded

"No!" she shouted at her brother. And then lowered her voice when she saw the looks on the children's faces. "No one's ever been able to force me to do anything since the day I was out of diapers, as well you know! And that includes you, you big bully!" She drew an uneven breath. "I know you're trying to do what you think you must," MaryKate told him. "But you'll not listen to reason. He loves me and I love him, and that's no one's business but our own!"

"What about his wife?" Johnny shot back. "Or isn't it her business, either?"

MaryKate fell silent. "I can't explain," she told him.

KATHLEEN

"Nor could any other. You've gone mad, is what you've done. A fallen woman, it's driven you mad!"

MaryKate looked from her brother to her sister-in-law. Sophie averted her eyes. Young Sarah stared up, meeting MaryKate's eyes with wide, dark ones of her own.

"He's a good man," MaryKate said softly.

"He's a swine and a blackguard and an Englishman! He thinks he can do as he pleases with our women and throw them back when he's through using them!"

MaryKate started for the door.

"Where do you think you're going?" Johnny asked her, reaching her in one long stride and grabbing her arm.

"Back where I'm needed!" MaryKate told her brother.

"Oh, no, you're not! There'll be no more talk about *my* sister!"

MaryKate stared up at him. "Do you not care about me at all, then, Johnny?" The sadness in her eyes and voice stopped him.

"Not care?! Of course I care!"

"Not about me, though. About yourself. About your precious reputation. About *your* sister not getting into trouble. But not about me. What I want. What I need."

"You need to do as I say!" Johnny told her.

She started toward the door, Johnny grabbing hold of her arm and pulling her back, hard.

"Stop it! You're hurting me!"

"I'll do more than hold your arm!" Johnny warned her.

"What do you think you can do?" she asked him harshly. "Lock me up somewhere and throw away the key?"

"If I have to, I will," he told her grimly. "You'll not disgrace us further."

"And when he brings Paddy home?" MaryKate asked.

"If he brings Paddy back, then I'll thank him before I kill him."

"And how are you to kill him?" MaryKate asked, for the first time beginning to fear her brother.

"With my bare hands if necessary. Or with this." He reached into a carpet bag, bringing out an ancient revolver.

"Johnny!" Sophie stared at the huge gun. "What do you think you're doing with that?!"

"Getting my country back," Johnny said grimly. He felt

245

KATHLEEN

MaryKate sink a little toward him and then push herself away from him. Stumbling, she reached for the door. "I don't want to hurt you, Mary-Kathleen. Don't make me hurt you."

"You're not just hurting me, Johnny," Mary-Kathleen told him sadly. "You're hurting all of us. Yourself, Sophie, your children, Paddy. Most of all your children and your country."

"I'm a patriot! I'll die for my country!"

"And kill for it."

"And kill for it!" he shouted at her.

"Wouldn't it be better to try to put an end to the troubles?" MaryKate asked her brother.

"There won't be an end until there's not an Englishman left in Ireland!"

The dog barked and Johnny pulled MaryKate back from the doorway, thrusting her toward Sophie. He reached for the gun. MaryKate screamed out, attempting to alert the visitors.

The door opened to reveal Sophie's mother and brother. Behind them three small children and her sister-in-law waited in the tiny yard.

Brian Flaherty stopped in his tracks. "Sure'n what is that, Johnny?"

Johnny put the gun down. "I thought you were the bloody English."

"Not I, but I'm with you if you're ready to get rid of a few."

"Brian Flaherty!" his mother said crisply. "You'll not talk so in front of the wee ones. Sophie, me darling, how are you then, mavourneen?"

Sophie came toward her mother, hugging her close. "Mama, there's nothing to you but bones." Sophie pulled back, horrified.

"Aye, my clothes hang a little, don't they?" Her mother smiled a tired smile.

"We've not been eating in a while," Brian told Johnny. "I didn't want to come, but me mother insisted."

"Of course you should come!" Sophie said. "And where else would you go? We'll find you food to take home with you."

246

KATHLEEN

"And there's no home to go to." Brian's quiet wife spoke up into the silence that greeted Sophie's words.

"No home?" Sophie sank to a stool. "Don't tell me they've kicked you off the land."

"Kicked off, turned out, and torn down. The house is gone, Johnny. You can't know how I prayed yours would still be up."

"It's up so far," Johnny said grimly.

"It will never be brought down!" MaryKate burst out. "And well you know it!"

"You've saved your crops, then? You can pay your quarterly rents?"

"No," Johnny said. "What my sister is saying is that she's the English landlord's whore and so we'll not be turned out."

The room went silent. MaryKate stared at the clean-swept dirt floor. And then raised her head, her tiny chin jutting out. "I'm no whore, nor will I ever be."

The sounds of horses outside registered on those inside the cottage. Sophie's mother cringed. "It's the authorities!"

"Johnny, hide!" Sophie said quickly.

"I'll not hide," Johnny told his wife. He reached for the gun.

MaryKate ran toward the door, wrenching it open to see Harry, Archie, and Paddy between them, stopping just outside the garden gate.

26

MaryKate ran toward Harry. "Stay away, stay away!"

Her shouts stopped the three men in their tracks. Johnny burst through the cottage doorway, pushing past MaryKate. The gun was in his hand, leveled at the three men near the gate.

Paddy stepped in front of the earl, MaryKate hitting Johnny's back, trying to get past him. "Stop this! Stop this now!"

"Johnny"—Paddy stayed between the earl and his brother—"what are you thinking of, then?"

"Get out of the way, Paddy," Johnny replied.

"There's no need for a gun, Johnny," Paddy told his older brother.

"And isn't there, now?" Johnny's words were loud, his hand tightening around the large pistol. "Stand away from the man who made our sister a strumpet!"

Paddy spoke quietly. "Let it be, Johnny."

MaryKate got around Paddy, racing to Harry's side. Harry pushed her back, his angry eyes raking across the

KATHLEEN

man who held a gun pointed at his stomach. "If I were you, I'd put down that gun."

"Yes, well, and you're not, now, are you?" Johnny yelled across the yard. "And if you were, you'd not be putting it down until it had blown a wide hole in the bastard who used your sister! Unless you're even less of a man than I think you are!"

"You'll just be making more trouble for yourself, using a thing like that," Archie said.

Johnny laughed, the sound bitter. "What the hell would a bloody Englishman know about trouble?!"

"I'm Welsh!" Archie said. "Don't you go calling me English!" He saw Harry out of the corner of his eye. "The Welsh have fought for every bloody thing they ever got from the English or any else!"

Archie saw Harry grimace. "Traitor," was all Harry said.

"What did he say?" Johnny demanded.

"He said I was a traitor," Archie answered truthfully.

"Johnny, put the gun down," Paddy said. "There's no need for it."

"He calls you a traitor, does he?" Johnny ignored his brother, looking past him to the Welshman. "Then you join a special fraternity—those who've felt the English heel and rebelled against it!"

"Johnny," Paddy began again, taking a step forward.

Harry stepped forward, standing beside Paddy. Mary-Kathleen pushed past her brother and Harry before they could stop her, standing in front of her oldest brother. A few feet away the muzzle of the pistol loomed round and dangerous. MaryKate's hands went to her hips, her anger flaring out at Johnny.

"And so it's a coward you are, after all, Johnny O'Hallion! Taking on the defenseless and a woman who's your own sister besides!"

"A coward!" The gun wavered. MaryKate saw his indecision and ran toward him.

Johnny saw her headlong rush, his finger tightening around the trigger, the hammer falling into place.

The sound of the gunshot was loud in the quiet country lane, the report resounding off nearby trees and cottages.

Even as the sound still reverberated, Harry sank, slowly,

to his knees. His doeskin britches muddied as they sank into the narrow path between gate and cottage door.

People were coming to the doors of their cottages, looking out toward the shouting.

"Harry!" MaryKate called out, turning back toward him. "Oh, Harry, what has he done to you?!" She sank to the ground at his side.

"Johnny?" Sophie came to the door.

"Get back!" he shouted to his wife. "Keep the children inside!" Johnny glared at his only sister. "You see?" He turned toward Paddy. "You see?! She calls him by his name! Does that not convince you of what's between the two of them?!" MaryKate tried to staunch the blood from Harry's wound with cotton torn from her own petticoat. She paid no attention to the others, all her concentration on stopping the blood that flowed from Harry's side.

"You *hear* her?!"

Paddy moved another step closer to Johnny. "I hear her." Paddy took another step and reached for the pistol. Johnny was staring at MaryKate. He turned on his brother when Paddy's hand touched the gun. "What the bloody hell do you think you're doing?!" he demanded.

"Saving you from a hanging," Paddy replied.

Sophie's brother Brian stared insolently at the English lord. "Don't let the bastard get away with it, Johnny."

"Brian Flaherty, you stay out of it!" Sophie yelled at her brother from the doorway.

Brian ignored his sister. "I'm with you, Johnny." He stood shoulder to shoulder with his brother-in-law, his fingers balled up into tight fists.

Brian's wife came to the open doorway, one small girl child clinging to her tattered petticoat. When she spoke her voice had the tired ring of someone who was used to not being listened to: "What is it, Brian—what's wrong now?"

"Get back inside," Brian Flaherty told his wife.

"Ally, you look ill." Sophie moved toward her sister-in-law.

"Ally, you get back inside!" her husband said again. "Do as I tell you or you'll wish you had!"

"Threatening women, now, are we?" Archie said as Ally turned away. "There's a couple of brave men."

KATHLEEN

"Why, you—" Brian's words were cut off by his mother calling out his name. She came up behind Sophie and Ally in the doorway.

MaryKate was on her knees beside Harry, helping Archie lift Harry to his feet.

"Saints preserve us!" Old Mrs. Flaherty said. She walked straight toward the downed Englishman. "Is he alive, then?"

"I'm alive," Harry said through gritted teeth. His voice was weak with pain.

"You'd best get him home," Old Mrs. Flaherty told them. Turning back toward the others, she stopped in front of Johnny and reached for the gun. He jerked back away from her. "Are you going to shoot a hole in me, too, then, Johnny O'Hallion?"

Johnny pushed past the old woman and Paddy. Brian pushed past them, too. "Stay out of it," Brian told his mother as Paddy tried to control Johnny.

"Johnny—what are you going to do now?" Paddy asked.

"Johnny!" Sophie called out, her arms still around the shaking Ally, who began to cry silent tears as her husband took off.

Johnny stumbled over Archie's foot, swearing at the wiry little man and hurtling himself out the gate. Brian Flaherty followed close behind.

Paddy took off after them, racing across the blackened field as Sophie yelled for them all to come back.

"It's no use," Ally said. "They never listen." She moved back inside the large cottage, picking up her little girl as she moved and hugging her close.

Archie and MaryKate had Harry to the horses. Sophie moved to help them. Harry's teeth gritted as he helped haul himself up onto the black stallion. Sophie pulled MaryKate back from the two men. "MaryKate, he didn't mean to do it!"

"Oh, yes he did!" MaryKate snapped. Tears sprang to Sophie's eyes and MaryKate relented, reaching to squeeze her sister-in-law's arm. "If you need anything, come up to the Priory. And Sophie, you've got to bring Meg to the infirmary."

"I can't!" Sophie said through her tears. "MaryKate,

251

he'd kill me for sure. Please don't you go back with that man, either—for all our sakes!"

"That man has rescinded all the rents; he's fed every person who's come asking and is still taking care of every sick one who asks to stay!" MaryKate moved toward the horse Paddy had ridden.

"You're coming, then?" Archie asked her.

"Are you saying I shouldn't?" she demanded, reaching for the reins.

"There's no time for discussions," Archie told her crisply. He helped her up, then mounted his own mare and came alongside Harry, leaning to help.

"I'll make it," Harry said through gritted teeth. His face was set into harsh planes as the horse moved, jouncing him forward down the dirt lane.

MaryKate came alongside Harry's right, taking the reins from his limp hands. "You can do it," she told him. "We must get you home." She looked across to Archie. "You'd be better off riding ahead and keeping the doctor there. Or finding him."

Archie hesitated. "If his horse bolts, you'll not be able to hold him."

"His horse isn't going to bolt," she replied grimly, holding the reins even tighter.

Archie eyed Harry and then took off, galloping hard toward Priory Hill.

"We'll make it," MaryKate told Harry again.

He was too weak to reply. It took every ounce of strength he had to stay in the saddle.

In the stableyard the last thing Harry saw was Archie's face coming near before he slumped forward, falling toward the ground. He was unconscious before he landed in Tim and Archie's arms.

Three days later Harry was still unconscious.

MaryKate was beside his bed, changing the dressings on his wound, when Wallace came to inform her Lord Ennis and a group of English gentlemen were in the front parlor, demanding to see the earl.

"I'll come down," she told the butler, finishing her work

KATHLEEN

and looking over toward the doctor. "Will you stay with him until I return?"

The doctor sat down again. "The fever's still bad," he told her.

She nodded, her eyes dark hollows from lack of sleep. "I'll be back directly."

Downstairs in the large front parlor Lord Ennis glanced up when MaryKate opened the door and then dismissed her presence, turning back toward the other men.

"Gentlemen," MaryKate said, "His Lordship is not receiving visitors today. May I take a message to him?"

Ennis turned around as she spoke, appraising her coldly. "We'll wait until we *do* see him."

MaryKate smiled. "Then I'd best ask Wallace to fix five bedrooms."

"Just because he's seen fit to dally with you, don't go giving yourself airs and graces," Ennis told her.

She saw the leers, the knowing gazes. Her chin came up. "His Lordship is ill and cannot be disturbed. *Will not* be disturbed."

"He's keeping to his bed, is he?" one of the men said, the others laughing.

"With you around, I might keep to mine!" another of the nobles told her.

"You wouldn't have the chance," she told the oily-looking Englishman. "Or the invitation." She raked each of them with an appraising look.

"Edgar, he's determined not to see us," one of the others said to Lord Ennis.

Ennis hesitated, gauging the Irish wench. "You'd best give him a message, if you know what's good for you as well as for him. Tell him what he's been doing has got to stop. Fomenting trouble, aiding and abetting rebels *and* their families," he continued pointedly, *"hiding* rebels, bailing them out of jail, and consorting with their women—we want it to stop. We'll be forced to take our grievances to the queen if he doesn't. He's betraying his own people!"

"He's betrayed no one!" MaryKate told them sharply.

"He's betrayed his wife for one," Ennis said. "She's had to seek rescue with a churchman."

KATHLEEN

MaryKate's cheeks flamed. "He's betrayed no one," she said again. "He's tried to help ill, starving people."

"He's rescinded his rents! He'll ruin us all!"

"Is this what it's all about, then? More English greed?"

"Have a care unless you want to end up in jail," Lord Ennis told her.

"For telling the truth?" MaryKate challenged.

"You can't talk to the Irish, Ennis, you should know that by now," one of the men said. "I'm leaving. If he doesn't want to see us, fine. We'll take it to Her Majesty." As he passed MaryKate he stared down at her. "Frankly, I hope you're worth what he'll have to pay to keep you. Losing a title is a high price."

Lord Ennis was the last to leave. At the door he turned back toward MaryKate. "Losing his title means he'll lose his lands, too. How long will you stay with him once he's poor?" She said nothing, and he left.

She stood alone in the room for an instant, forcing tears back. Then she moved swiftly toward the stairs and Harry's bedside.

"I tell you, I *must!*" Reverend Grinstead's voice barked out from behind MaryKate.

She looked back to see Hugh Grinstead in the doorway, Wallace blocking his entrance. "What is it now?" MaryKate asked tiredly.

Wallace looked up toward her. "His Lordship left strict instructions that this gentleman was not to be allowed to enter."

Hugh looked past the butler toward the girl on the stairs. "They said the doctor was here. He's not in the annex." His voice was shaky. "I brought her back; she's ill."

"Good Lord," MaryKate breathed the words.

"She's in the annex, she's got the fever. I can't keep her in my house, or we'll all get it!" Hugh said. "Tell him she's here!" And with that he turned away, heading for his waiting carriage. Lord Ennis saw him and leaned from his own carriage to ask questions.

MaryKate realized Wallace was still staring up at her. "I'll send the doctor down directly." She sped up the rest of the stairs and out of sight.

* * *

KATHLEEN

In Harry's chambers Archie stood near the bed, the doctor packing up his kit. "Doctor, Her Ladyship has come down with the fever."

The doctor groaned. "I warned her of this! I've done all I can here. I'll go to Her Ladyship at once," the doctor said.

"She's not in her rooms," MaryKate said, stopping him. "She's in the annex with the other patients."

The doctor looked disconcerted.

When he had gone, Archie came around the bed. "I don't think it will help things to mention her being away."

MaryKate's tired eyes closed for a moment. When she opened them, she nodded. "I understand."

"The less said about your brother, the better, too. I told the doctor we were riding when he got shot. I don't see any reason to say more. Do you?"

MaryKate shook her head. "Thank you."

Archie shrugged. "Your sister-in-law and those little tykes deserve better."

MaryKate pulled a narrow chair near the bed and sat down, leaning to bathe Harry's forehead with a fresh, cool cloth. Archie watched her for several long moments before speaking again.

"You care about him, don't you?"

MaryKate looked up, then went back to her work. "If he dies, I'll die, too," she told the man simply.

Archie sighed. "It's a right proper mess, is what this is. I don't know what's to become of us."

"Us?" she asked.

"Well, you don't think I've traipsed all the way over here just for the bloody hell of it, now, do you? That boyo means more to me than—" Archie choked off his own words. "Anyway," he continued, "I've burnt my bridges behind me, staying on with him, so I've got to see him through."

"He'll be all right."

"Of course he will," Archie replied. He stood there for a moment, awkward and shy. And then he turned and walked out, unwilling for her to see his worry.

MaryKate looked down at Harry's fevered brow, at his chiseled nose and lips. "Harry, can you hear me, mavourneen?" She spoke softly. "You are my mavourneen, my

255

KATHLEEN

darling, you are. Everything will be all right, if you'll just get well. Nothing else matters, mavourneen, nothing else at all."

She reached to hold his hand, leaning forward to bend over his head, kissing his forehead. "I'll be here until you wake up."

When Archie looked in later, he found her still in the chair, her head and arms curled around Harry's pillow, her hand still in his. Archie listened to their quiet breathing and then closed the door, leaving them as they were.

27

THE HOUSE WAS SILENT. The servants who were well, who were still working, slipped through the halls as if they were wraiths, silent and quickly gone.

In the large front rooms that housed the lord of the manor, the English earl lay unconscious and feverish. Stories of his slow dying were whispered from the kitchens to the stables and on beyond to the village.

More whispers followed. About Her Ladyship, ill to death from catching the plague from her patients. And other whispers, softer-voiced, about how Mary-Kate had truly poisoned them both, her sympathies with her rebel brothers.

MaryKate herself heard none of it. Sleeping on a straw pallet in Harry's room, she rose to oversee Lady Amelia's care, to go back and forth between the two sickrooms and the annex full of patients below, ignoring the doctor's warnings.

"You'll end up in one of these beds," he told her darkly. "You look as if you belong in one now."

"I'm fine," she told him. He watched her walk out of the annex, a pile of dirty linens in her arms. Shaking his head, he went back to his patients, reaching for the pale, thin wrist

KATHLEEN

of an elderly woman and feeling for her pulse. Beyond the woman others groaned and coughed.

MaryKate's footsteps dragged with tiredness as she carried the heavy laundry toward the back washrooms. Dumping the pile on the stone floor, she stared at the piles already there.

The laundress had fled the houseful of illness, carrying tales of evil curses and the wrath of God being visited on those that neared any English.

MaryKate shoved a lank lock of auburn hair back from her forehead and reached for one of the large wooden buckets, hauling it with her toward the fireplace.

Four vast iron pots hung above the huge fire. She was surprised to see water already heating within them. She put the wooden bucket down, hearing steps behind her and turned to see Wallace walking into the laundry room. His sleeves rolled up to his elbows, a fine sheen of perspiration was beading across his reddened face.

She stared at the normally immaculate butler. "What are you doing?"

He shrugged, as he brought in two more buckets and dropped them near the caldrons of hot water. MaryKate watched him reach for the closest iron pot, tipping its beakered edge toward one of the buckets. Scalding hot water poured into the iron-banded wooden bucket. "Archie's scouring the floors in His Lordship's rooms. I think he's figuring on burning the blight out." Wallace paused, seeing MaryKate's expression deepen into one of dread. "Not that His Lordship's caught it," Wallace said quickly. "Archie's simply determined to make sure it doesn't get to him while he's laid so low."

MaryKate nodded wearily. "The doctor said the crisis for his fever would be about seventy-two hours. The wound wasn't clean." She looked back toward the water. "He can't be planning on using all this much water." Her words came slowly, her tiredness showing. "I'll need a lot of it for the sheets and bandages and all."

"I'll see to the laundry," Wallace told her. "You've done enough. More than anyone should. Or any would have thought you would. I'll not stand here and watch you work and do nothing to help."

KATHLEEN

A faint smile came into her eyes. "There's a definite Irish lilt coming into your speech, Wallace."

"No, there's not," the English butler said rather stiffly. "Or, if there is, it will sound peculiar with my accent."

"Peculiar it is," she told him, the tired smile warming him. "But rather nice."

He smiled back. "You've got a trace of Englishness coming into your own speech, Mary-Kathleen."

"Do I? Well, maybe we'll all learn something from each other."

"I certainly hope so," he said, seriousness returning. "It's a proper mess the way it is."

"Isn't it just?" MaryKate agreed. "Thank you for the water. And the help."

A shy look crossed his face, his voice gruff when he replied: "I'd best get this upstairs." In the doorway he looked back. "Archie says he's always heard of the Irish washerwoman. He never thought he'd be a Welsh washman."

He earned a wide smile before he left.

MaryKate looked around the small stone-walled and stone-floored laundry room, imagining what it was like to spend one's life working in this narrow cubicle. And what it was like for an aloof English butler to enter it, roll up his shirtsleeves, and pitch in to help.

She wished Johnny were here. She wished there were some way to make him see that the divisions between people are much less apparent than the similarities. A different accent, a different way of presenting oneself to the world, a different way of describing how one sought after God. People assumed real differences where there were truly none that counted.

Everyone felt the same fears and the same hurts, even if for different reasons. Everyone searched for meaning to his life. Everyone spilt red blood when he was wounded.

The thought of wounds and blood brought all her worry over Harry flooding back to crowd out all else, her heart terror-struck and aching.

She nearly ran up the stairs toward his chambers, racing

to make sure he was all right, a fear clutching at her heart that knew no reason.

Bursting into the bedroom she ran almost head-on into Archie, who reached out to stop her headlong rush. "And what's this, now?" Archie asked her. "You look ready to fall over and you're running races?"

"How is he?"

Archie squeezed her shoulders before he let them go. "He's no worse."

Her eyes hurt, her fear staring out at the Welshman. "Which means he's no better."

"He's no worse, girl. Thank God for small favors, and let it be."

"I can't. I can't!"

"You can, and you will," he told her coldly. He saw the shock in her eyes and then a bit of anger flare. "Good. Now you might even be a help again."

MaryKate wilted against the small Welshman, her head drooping to his shoulder. "Thank you." Her words were whispered.

"It's the rest of us who should be thanking you," Archie told her tartly. "And don't you go forgetting it once these two get well."

These two. The words reverberated within her. "I didn't even ask," MaryKate told him. "I didn't even ask about her."

"Girl, you have a lot on your mind."

"I didn't even ask," she repeated, consternation growing. "I owe her so much, and I didn't even *ask!*"

"You've spent every waking hour between her and those down below that meant so much to her. You've slipped in here for a moment here and there and taken all the day with her and them." He watched her. "So you sleep in here. You have to sleep somewhere, girl. It's best to be near the one you love."

"Archie—"

"He's better for having you near," Archie told her flatly.

She hesitated. "I wish—"

"You don't have to wish. It's the truth. Now go tell him you're here, and you'll be back, and then get out of my way so I can swab this rig down."

KATHLEEN

She straightened up. "He doesn't know I'm here."

"How can you tell?" Archie asked.

"He can't hear me," she told him.

"How do you know?" he asked her.

MaryKate turned down the bed where Harry lay. Archie watched her gaze change, watched the love creep into her eyes when she looked toward Harry. He turned and left the room, letting her walk toward the bed alone.

MaryKate stopped near the foot of the bed, reaching for the heavy blanket that lay folded there. She pulled it back, taking the weight off his feet that stretched to the very bottom of the old carved bed.

The ducal coronet crowning the Exeter crest was carved into the footboard. She rubbed her hand across the ridges of the crest, reminding herself of who he was.

There was no hope in caring about him. And yet her heart yearned in ways she'd never before felt.

She stared down at his sleeping face, so vulnerable, with his eyes closed, his skin pale with illness. If he were ill and old and halt and lame, she would love him.

She smoothed the covers on his bed, reaching to feel his forehead, feeling the heat pour onto her palm.

The narrow chair beside his bed was where she had left it. She sank onto it, telling herself she had no time, in the middle of the day, to sit and stare at the man she loved. Gently she pushed his dark hair back from his forehead. He stirred a little under her hand and her heart leapt.

"Harry," she whispered his name, leaning forward to watch his closed eyes.

Slowly his eyes opened, staring up at her as if through a heavy haze. A moment of recognition flickered within them before they closed again, the effort too much.

She leaned to kiss his forehead before leaving, tears spilling from her eyes to his cheek as she straightened up. She left the room, closing the door gently. Wiping the tears away, she walked toward Lady Amelia's room.

In Amelia's room MaryKate reached to wet a fresh rag in the cold water basin on the nightstand. She pressed it against Amelia's pale forehead, leaving it in place as Amelia stirred.

"Water . . ." Amelia's voice was frail.

KATHLEEN

MaryKate reached for a cup and the carafe of water beside it. She poured a little, helping Amelia lift her head to drink.

"You didn't eat any of the soup," MaryKate told her. "Do you think you could try a little now?"

"No, please."

"You have to eat something."

"Talk—"

"You want to talk?" MaryKate leaned closer, trying to understand.

"Hugh."

"Hugh?" MaryKate watched Amelia try to nod. "The reverend? I'll send for him."

"Soon." Amelia grabbed MaryKate's hand.

MaryKate stood up. "I'll send for him now." She watched the countess lean back against the pillows, her face relaxing a little as MaryKate left the room.

At the foot of the stairs Wallace stood looking up toward MaryKate, his uniform the worse for water stains. "Your sister-in-law is in the kitchen."

"What's wrong?"

"She didn't say."

MaryKate started past him and then turned back. "Send for Reverend Grinstead, Wallace. Her Ladyship wishes to see him."

Wallace kept his thoughts to himself as MaryKate hurried toward the green baise door that led to the kitchens.

Sophie was pacing between the long center table and the ancient black iron stove, rushing toward MaryKate. "Oh, MaryKate, MaryKate."

"What's happened?! Has something happened to Johnny?"

"Sure to God, he'll die!" Sophie was crying again, her already red eyes swollen. "Oh, MaryKate, they say he's causing rebellion! Troops came looking for him and said he'd stolen something. They were going to fetch him to jail!"

"He stole something?"

"I don't know!" Sophie wailed. "Oh, MaryKate, I thought they were coming because His Lordship had died!"

"Don't say that!" MaryKate spoke sharply.

"I don't know what to do!"

262

"There's nothing you can do. Paddy's with him, he'll keep him out of trouble."

"Johnny's never listened to Paddy about anything." Sophie was still crying.

"Johnny's never listened to *anyone* about anything. That's his problem," MaryKate told his wife. Then she put her arm around Sophie's rounded shoulders. "I'm sure he'll be all right. You have to take care of the children. And wait."

"Oh, MaryKate, I'm so tired of waiting!"

"I know. Do you want to bring the children here?"

Sophie hesitated. When she shook her head no, she straightened up a little. "He'd hate my coming here."

MaryKate bit back the quick words that nearly came out. Instead she turned away. "I'll find Cook and have her put some things together for you to take back with you."

"Thank you" was all Sophie replied.

She was still standing in the same place, feeling alien and out of place in the large kitchen, when MaryKate walked back in, the cook behind her carrying two bags. "Is your family still with you?"

"All except Brian. We're that worried about him, too."

"If you need me, send young Johnny."

"I will," Sophie promised.

When she left, MaryKate sank to a chair beside the rough-hewn table. The cook placed a bowl of porridge in front of her. Listlessly, MaryKate shook her head. "I'm not hungry."

"Yes, well, you should be. And you're not leaving this kitchen until you've got something in your belly, and that's a fact." Hands on her ample hips, the cook stood in front of MaryKate and handed her a spoon. "Sure'n I don't know what we'd do if you come down with it, too!"

Wearily, MaryKate took the spoon and tried to eat a little.

The afternoon rounds lengthened into evening, the darkening sky barely lit by a narrow sliver of a moon. The valley was smothered in darkness, the narrow trails that led up into the northern hills unpassable for any but the native Irish men who knew every nook and cranny of the rock-strewn

KATHLEEN

paths. Men who could climb silently up the precipitous rocky defiles. Men who knew the way to the deep glacial trough.

Up above the glacial trough, a ravine lay hidden by the hills that surrounded it. In the ravine a narrow little lake bubbled up from under the earth's crust, the forested hills around it almost completely cleared of the nuts and herbs and flowers that had covered the ground for centuries.

At the edge of the lake the men who were gathering to Johnny's war cry were hunkered down for the night, huddled in their clothes, a tiny fire the only light to be seen.

"Are you sure the fire's safe?" one of the men asked, others looking up the steep cliffs that ringed the narrow ravine.

"It's safe enough," Johnny said.

Paddy stared at the gaunt men who had followed them into hiding, their eyes wide and hollow already, most of them too weak to stand a real fight. Coarse frieze coats with missing buttons and frayed pockets hung open over tattered shirts and grimy breeches as they tried to sleep.

"Johnny," his brother spoke low, "what is it you think can be done with the likes of these?"

"We can get food, and kill Englishmen," Johnny said.

"How can we fight? Look around you, Johnny."

"They'll fight, all right. When your children are starving, there's a lot you'll do."

"And what about you, then? Why are you fighting?"

"Do you think my children won't be next? Do you think I want my children growing up to have this happen to them? By God, it's better to be dead than to live with the bloody English boot on your throat!"

Men still awake around them heard Johnny's defiant words, grunting agreement, their angry grumbles flowing across the narrow space and echoing up into the empty trees, the birds all caught or flown far away from the plague-filled island.

"We need food," Paddy said quietly.

Johnny stood up. "I'm about to go after it."

"Where?"

"At some fat pig of an Englishman's—where else?"

KATHLEEN

Paddy watched Johnny start off alone. "Wait there," Paddy called out, Brian waking with the noise.

"What is it? What's happened?" Brian asked, sitting up.

"Nothing," Paddy told him. "It's no good, Johnny. You've got to face it," Paddy told his brother. "These men can't fight. You'll only get us all killed."

"If you're scared, go home!"

"Of course I'm scared! If you had any sense, you'd be scared, too!"

"Then I have no sense!" Johnny said harshly. "The Irish Fianna saved this island before, and we'll do it now!"

"The Fianna were stories from times before time itself began, Johnny. They're only stories."

"The Fianna are what the Fenians are descended from, and it's Fenians we are. It's us that will rid this island of all its oppressors, just like before." Johnny ducked his head, looking at his younger brother from beneath hooded eyes, as if afraid Paddy would laugh at him. He watched Paddy's concerned expression and then turned away, looking toward Brian and raising his voice. "Hey! Brian, boyo, you up for getting us some fresh meat?"

Brian turned over, yawning wide, and then stretched and sat up. He got to his feet. "Well, what are we waiting for?"

"You want me to come?" Paddy asked finally.

Johnny stared at his brother. "No. Stay here. Or go home to the women. You have too many scruples for this work."

Paddy watched as they left the encampment, climbing to the mouth of the narrow defile, disappearing from view.

When Paddy turned back toward the fire, he could feel the eyes upon him.

28

It was coming near dawn when Brian and Johnny crept near the edge of the flock of sheep.

The herd had moved restlessly all night, their neck bells tinkling, waking the herders again and again as the night wore on. Now the sheep herders hired by Lord Dunstable lay snoring, their rifles beside them.

Johnny and Brian communicated by hand movements when a single sheep came near where they hid, nuzzling the almost barren ground. Johnny moved quickly, grasping the sheep and slitting its throat as he silenced the bell with the hand he held around the animal's neck. He moved quickly toward where Brian still hid, ready for trouble if any came.

It came from behind him. "Thieves! Thieves!" The man's cry awoke the others as bells rang out amongst the herd. Rifles came up, as Brian shoved back the shouting man who ran toward them.

"Stop where you are!"

A shot rang out, missing Johnny narrowly. Brian took a rifle from the herder and shot back at the three men who were running forward, stopping them in their tracks.

"They've got guns!" one of the herders yelled out.

Brian fell in behind Johnny, ducking through the brush and slipping into the mantrap hole they'd discovered hours before.

Johnny was ahead of him, Brian pulling loose brush over them both. They huddled close as their pursuers came nearer.

"Where are they? Did they get away?!"

"Look in the trap!"

"We'd have heard them!" another voice said, but a lantern came closer, shining down into the deep pit. Its light patterned across the brush at the bottom.

"It's empty."

"Jesus, Mary, and Joseph, it'll be our necks in a noose if His Lordship finds out they got away!"

The sounds went farther and farther away. Finally Brian shoved the brush off and got to his feet, helping Johnny with the sheep.

Brian stood on the pile of stones, his feet slipping a little, but getting enough purchase to grab for the length of rope they'd tied to a nearby tree and hidden in the dirt.

Not quite long enough, it dangled near the top of the hole. It took him three tries before he could hold on to it and haul himself up.

He tied the rope around his waist quickly, using sailor's knots to keep it firm, and then leaned as far back into the hole as he could get.

Johnny reached the sheep up toward Brian, who grabbed it by the front hooves and hauled it out, both of them now spattered with blood and reeking of it.

Brian leaned down again, letting Johnny use his hands for grips as he scaled the dirt wall of the man-trap and vaulted out onto the damp ground.

Grabbing the sheep, they ran back through the forest, away from the sounds of the herders.

Johnny leaned close to Brian's ear. "It's a pity to be wasting those untended sheep."

"Enough's enough!" Brian hissed back. "They'll have left a guard."

"Then it'll be two to one. Unless you're as squeamish as my brother."

"I'm not squeamish, and you know it! But if we're to

strike a blow tomorrow, we need sleep. And the men need food. It's almost light.''

Johnny stopped running, looking back toward the herd. Undecided, he watched Brian continue off toward the camp.

As the sun rose higher Lord Dunstable was informed of the theft, his reaction swift.

First he had his herders flogged, then he sent for the constable, issuing an order of arrest for theft and treason against John O'Hallion and anyone found associating with him.

"Your men identified him, then?" the policeman asked the elderly English lord.

Nearly stamping his foot in his frustration, Dunstable answered none too honestly: "Of course! In any event, there are no others around who call for revolt and harbor wanted felons and malcontents! This was a safe and honest county until that O'Hallion got them agitated!"

The constable's expression was inscrutable as he returned the noble's glare. "I think the famine might have something to do with it, too."

"Nonsense!" Lord Dunstable snapped. "There is famine here as surely as there is rain, the Irish being what they are. They're children, unable to plan ahead and make provision for tomorrow. Why else do they need our protection?! There always has been famine and there always will be!"

"A sobering thought," the constable said, bowing low and leaving His Lordship's presence.

While Lord Dunstable was berating the constable, MaryKate was standing in the Protestant rectory, staring down the Right Reverend Hugh Grinstead.

"She's still waiting, since yesterday afternoon!"

Reverend Grinstead spoke smoothly, calmly. "There are many of my parishioners who need me at this time. And many of the newly converted, such as I hope one day you shall be—who have left their pagan ways and need constant guidance so as to—"

"Will you stop?!" MaryKate burst out, shocking him into silence. She stood her ground: "I know. Do you understand? I *know* about you and her—and as God is my witness, the entire countryside shall know. Your superiors shall know. Everyone in Christendom shall know if you do not come to her *now!*"

Fear squeezed the minister's heart, making it pump faster; his fear showing out from his eyes. "What do you want?" His voice was strained.

MaryKate's voice was harsh: "I want you to come with me now, and I want you to say whatever she wants to hear. She is ill unto death, and she needs you there!"

"I can't." His voice filled with despair. "Please, I can't."

"You must," MaryKate told him relentlessly.

"What if she lives?" Hugh whispered the words.

"What if she dies?" MaryKate replied.

There was a long, silent moment in which Hugh stared at MaryKate; she looked remorseless.

"I must finish my sermon," he said finally.

"I'll wait," she told him.

He still stood staring at her. And then turned toward his desk and the half-finished notations.

Within the half hour they were both on their way back to the Priory.

Amelia lay struggling for breath, calling over and over for Hugh. Archie tried to calm her, running between her sickroom and Harry's while the doctor slaved over a dying patient in the annex.

When MaryKate entered the room, Archie was ready to kiss her. "Thank God you're back!"

"What's wrong?" she asked.

"I don't know how you've been doing it, day after day," Archie told her. "I'm going back to Harry." Archie gave Hugh a sideways look as he left the room.

Hugh saw the look and turned away, becoming his most official self, pacing toward the bed, prayer book in hand.

"Your Ladyship," he began

Amelia's eyes fluttered open. When they focused, she reached for his hand. "You're here."

Hugh looked uncomfortable. His eyes slid toward MaryKate, who gave him one last, long look and then left, closing the door, leaving the two of them alone.

Turning toward Harry's room, MaryKate saw Archie at the doorway.

"What's going on?" he asked.

She shook her head. "I don't know." She came toward Archie. "I only hope he doesn't disappoint her."

Archie watched her. "Don't men always disappoint their women?"

MaryKate stared at the little Welshman, her heart turning over at his words. "Do they? Always?"

Archie shrugged. "What do I know? I've never married."

"Or loved?"

"Oh, aye—I've loved."

"And?" MaryKate asked.

"You're looking at me as if I should tell you something."

MaryKate shook her head. "I don't mean to ask what you don't want to tell."

Archie grinned. "Yes, you do. And that's all right. But it's a long story for a cold winter's night. Not for now."

MaryKate smiled a little. "Do you promise to tell me on a cold winter's night?"

"If we survive all this, the very first winter's night we've the time."

She smiled wider. "It's a deal."

"You know, you're not so very bad," Archie told her.

"For an Irishman?" she asked.

"For a girl," he replied.

They both grinned before her eyes strayed toward the closed door to Harry's room. "Is he all right?"

"He's the same. The doctor said it would be anytime now. One way or the other." Archie hesitated. "He contracted a fever. The famine fever maybe."

"With his wound." MaryKate breathed the words, afraid to think about them. "He can't die," she told his manservant.

"He *won't* die," Archie told her firmly. "Not Harry. He's too ornery, and he's nowhere near ready to meet his maker."

"Does that count?" MaryKate asked, her eyes misting over.

"Everything helps," Archie told her practically.

Wallace came up the stairs toward them. "MaryKate . . ." He looked uncomfortable. "I mean—I don't know what to call you." He stopped staring at her helplessly.

KATHLEEN

"You call me by my name," she told him. "What else?"

Wallace hesitated. "It seems wrong."

"And what would be right?" she asked.

"I don't know," Wallace answered honestly. "You're running the estate. It's not right to be so familiar."

"Maybe not for the English," MaryKate replied. "But for us Irish, we don't stand much on being so formal."

"What's right is right," Wallace replied.

"Did you have something to tell me?" MaryKate asked.

"A visitor has arrived who wishes an interview with the earl. She'll talk to none else."

"She?"

"Aye," Wallace said, his distaste showing. "She."

Archie looked from the English butler to the Irish serving girl. "There are many women who might call on His Lordship."

Wallace drew himself to his full height. "The lady in question is of a certain age."

Archie grimaced. "That never stopped him, either."

"What are you two talking about?" Neither answered. MaryKate continued: "Where is she?"

"In the small front parlor," Wallace told her.

"I'll be there directly."

Wallace hesitated and then nodded slightly. Archie watched MaryKate. "You want me to deal with the lady?"

Her brow arched: "You think I can't?"

"I think you can do just about anything. But I don't think you necessarily want to." Archie watched her.

MaryKate hesitated. Then, "I'll see to the visitor. You see to Har—to His Lordship."

Archie watched her start down the wide stairwell, her slim body looking even more slight against the huge mahogany steps and the stone walls that rose three stories around her.

In the small front parlor a diminutive woman paced from the tall front windows to the narrow oak door. She was halfway between them when MaryKate entered.

The woman looked regal. Her gray hair was swept off her forehead and piled high upon her head, her skin the color of rich pearl, her eyes as blue as the sea. Her gown was of softest pearl gray, a sapphire broach fastened to her long pearl necklace.

"You are the countess?" the woman asked, her amazement showing.

"No," MaryKate replied. "You wish to see the earl?"

"Yes. And who are you?"

"I am in His Lordship's employ. If you will state your business, I shall forward your request."

The woman watched her carefully. "It is not something I wish to discuss with hired help."

"There is no alternative," MaryKate told her.

The woman bridled. "And who are you to tell me that?!"

"Who are you to ask?" MaryKate asked baldly.

"I am Elizabeth," she said, as if that explained all.

"Elizabeth," MaryKate repeated, still staring at the older woman.

Elizabeth realized MaryKate had no idea who she was. "I am his mother."

"Harry's?! I mean, His Lordship's?"

Harry's mother watched the girl. "You mean Harry," Elizabeth replied. "And the answer is yes. Now. Where is he?"

"He's ill—wounded." MaryKate saw Elizabeth's expression change. "You must come up and try to wake him. He'll want to see you."

"No. He won't," his mother replied. Seeing the girl's surprise, she looked toward the tall windows that overlooked the park. "If he's not well, it's best I wait."

"But you're his mother!" MaryKate said.

Elizabeth turned back to search the girl's eyes. "What is your name, girl?"

"MaryKate."

Elizabeth watched her. "And you are Irish, are you not?"

"I am," MaryKate said proudly.

"Yet you call my son Harry." She saw MaryKate's eyes flicker. But not flinch. "It's all right, girl. It's surely none of my business; I've not seen him since he was a child. And he may have no wish to see me yet."

"But you said you were his mother!" MaryKate repeated, confused by the woman's attitude.

"Yes." Elizabeth spoke softly. "Were it that simple."

272

KATHLEEN

MaryKate hesitated. "I'll have Wallace see to your rooms."

Elizabeth watched the girl walk toward the door. "And the countess?"

MaryKate looked back. "The Countess is gravely ill. Her confessor is with her even as we speak."

"Her confessor? Is she Catholic?" Elizabeth asked.

"No. Don't Protestants ever need to confess anything?" MaryKate asked.

Elizabeth smiled. "Of course we do. But we're never so honest about it. Nor do we proclaim it to the world. Usually we hide our sins in the darkest corners of our lives and pretend they don't exist."

MaryKate searched the older woman's eyes. "So do the rest of us," she said.

Elizabeth moved toward Mary-Kathleen. "I like you," she said. "If my son likes you, as he must if you are on such familiar terms, then he has grown up better than I feared."

"Feared?"

Elizabeth hesitated. "You know none of it?"

"None of what?" MaryKate asked.

"Oh, dear, there's such a long story attached." Elizabeth hesitated. "And you know none of it?" When MaryKate didn't answer, "I would like to have a chance to rest a bit. And decide what I should do."

MaryKate turned toward the door. "Let me show you to a room."

As they left the small parlor, MaryKate spoke again, "You're sure you don't want to see him first?"

"It won't help him recover," his mother told MaryKate. But she didn't elaborate.

In the wide, echoing, front hall MaryKate preceded Harry's mother toward the stairwell. Hugh Grinstead was coming down the stairs as fast as his legs would carry him. MaryKate stood in his way.

"What's happened?" she asked.

"Nothing," he told her. He looked toward the older woman, a professional smile in place. "I must visit other parishioners."

"What's happened?" MaryKate asked again, her distrust palpable. "What have you done to her?"

"I've done nothing to her!" Hugh nearly shouted his words.

MaryKate swept past him. "If you have, you'll answer not only to God, but to the authorities as well!"

"As God is my witness."

"Watch what you say, Reverend," Elizabeth told the tall, thin man in the clerical collar.

Hugh stopped, staring at the newcomer as if he thought she possessed some special knowledge. Then he pushed past her, down the stairs, and out into the stableyard.

Elizabeth watched him go and then turned back to the obviously angry MaryKate. "This seems quite an interesting household."

Elizabeth followed MaryKate up the stairs. "You seemed none too friendly to the parson."

"If he said one thing to upset Lady Amelia, I shall see him drawn and quartered."

The ring of truth came through MaryKate's simple words. "You feel very strongly for Harry's wife, then."

"She has been kind to me," MaryKate told the earl's mother.

There was an edge to MaryKate's words Elizabeth could hear but could not define. Slowly the older woman climbed the great staircase, heading toward MaryKate and the upper floors.

At the O'Hallion cottage, Sophie was boiling a barley soup from ingredients the Priory cook had sent down, her mother and inlaws clustered around the fire, her children leaning in toward their grandmother.

They all heard the footsteps outside, a dozen pair of eyes turning toward the cottage door as Paddy walked in and stopped, staring toward his sister-in-law.

Sophie left her cooking, moving across her front room toward Paddy, her eyes wide and fearful. "Is he all right?"

Paddy nodded. "The last I knew. How's Meggie doing?"

"A little better I think. Come sit," Sophie said.

Her mother watched Paddy come closer. "You left them out there, then. Alone?"

"Johnny sent me back," Paddy replied honestly.

"Why?" the old woman asked.

"I don't want to kill anyone," Paddy replied.

The room went silent. Sophie moved back to the fire. "Supper's almost ready," she said into the silence.

Supper was almost ready to be served at the Priory for those who were still on their feet. The doctor finished his examination of Lady Amelia. Elizabeth changed in the large guest apartment MaryKate had opened and aired for her. MaryKate herself was hovering near Harry's bed, watching him toss and turn in his sleep. She looked with silent dread toward Archie, who looked away and then looked back.

"You've got to pray, girl."

"I doubt God will listen to such a sinner," MaryKate said softly.

"There's nothing else to be done," Archie told her.

MaryKate sank to her knees beside Harry's bed, her hands reaching for one of his and clasping it tight. She leaned her forehead against their clasped hands, her eyes closing.

He can't die. Her one thought was that he could not die. There was no way for her to go on breathing if he died. Whatever else, no matter how far apart they must be, at least he could be alive. She could know he was alive and happy and content, robust and argumentative and in his prime. Healthy and full of life.

Please, God, full of life. Her head came up, her eyes wide with fear as she stared at his drawn features. His closed eyes.

Her head sank to meet their clasped hands, her prayers all jumbled together and dwelling on one thing: he must live.

While in the countess's suite, Amelia lay slowly dying.

29

MaryKate did not go down to dinner. Wallace silently served a subdued Elizabeth, who afterward asked to be shown to her son's rooms. Archie was called to escort her.

She saw the hardness in Archie's eyes, meeting his gaze squarely. A little defiantly. "We have never met."

"No, Your Ladyship, You were already gone when I first knew young Harry—His Lordship."

"Are all the help on such intimate terms with my son?" she asked stiffly.

"Not so's you could notice—Your Ladyship," he added belatedly.

"I'd like to see my son," she told the Welshman.

He bowed formally, and showed her the way.

MaryKate stood up when the door opened, standing back from Harry's bed. Elizabeth hesitated in the hall and then swept inside, her jaw set, her head held high.

She did not look down at her son until she stood directly beside the bed. And then she sank to the chair MaryKate had used, staring, helplessly, at his pale, gaunt face.

"My God, he has to live," she whispered the words.

KATHLEEN

"Of course he'll live!" MaryKate said sharply. She came closer. Longing to reach out and touch him, she stood nearby, trying to will her own life-force into his brain and heart.

"Is this the famine fever?" Elizabeth asked.

There was an awkward silence before anyone replied. Archie looked toward MaryKate, but said nothing.

"No," MaryKate finally replied. "He was shot, Your Ladyship."

"Shot!" Elizabeth reached for his hand. "By one of your heathen Irishmen, no doubt!"

MaryKate bit her lip. "By my brother," MaryKate told the Englishwoman.

Elizabeth stared at her in horror. "What are you doing attending to him or any in this house?"

Archie stepped forward. "It wasn't any of MaryKate's doing," he began to defend her.

"I want her out of here!" Elizabeth said.

"No." The word, tired and just barely audible, came from the bed behind her.

Elizabeth whirled around as MaryKate dropped to her knees beside the bed, clutching Harry's hand. Archie stepped closer, seeing Harry's eyes open, his hand grasping MaryKate's. "Mavourneen." MaryKate was oblivious to all else in the room. "Mavourneen, it's all right. Everything is all right. You don't have to speak. We're here." Tears were spilling down her cheeks. "We're here."

She watched his eyes close again.

Archie watched Elizabeth. When she looked toward him, he stared at her openly. "If I were you, after all these years, I'd keep my bloody nose out of it. After all, Your Ladyship didn't make much of a success of your own career as a wife and mother."

Her face hardened. She hesitated for only an instant and then swept by him, leaving the room.

After she was gone, Archie came nearer the bed, staring down at Harry and then touching MaryKate's shoulder. "Get off your knees, girl, he'll be all right. He's coming around."

MaryKate let Archie help her to her feet. But she wouldn't leave the room. He pulled her straw pallet nearer the fire-

KATHLEEN

place and stoked the smoldering embers before he left. MaryKate's exhausted head bent to her bed.

In the morning Harry was awake when Archie tiptoed in at dawn, checking on them both.

"How long has it been?" Harry asked, his voice scratchy with disuse.

Archie moved past MaryKate, speaking softly, pouring Harry a glass of water. "It's been the better part of a week." He helped Harry drink from the glass. "From the sound of you, you need something stronger than water."

MaryKate awoke, sitting up still half-asleep, her eyes wide with fright. "What's happened?! What's wrong?"

"Nothing, girl," Archie told her.

Rubbing sleep from her eyes, she realized Harry was sitting up in bed. Looking toward her, his eyes were soft with love.

She sat up, suddenly aware she'd slept in her dress. One of her hands went to her hair, pushing stray tendrils back from her face. She reached to pin them tighter, shy now as she stood across his bedroom, watching him watch her.

"I must look a sight," she said faintly.

"I'll see to some breakfast," Archie said. As he started out he looked back toward MaryKate. "You'd best tell him the news."

"What news?" Harry asked, his brow furrowing. "Has something happened to the estate?"

"No," Archie and MaryKate answered almost at the same moment.

Harry's expression darkened. "Has it to do with my wife?"

Archie looked toward MaryKate. And then answered himself. "That's part of it. Grinstead brought her back."

"I want them out of here!" Harry's voice came out stronger.

"She's ill with the fever," Archie told him. "And Grinstead's already gone."

"Fever." Harry registered the words.

"MaryKate will tell you the rest," Archie said, leaving.

Harry looked toward the girl. "What rest?"

She came toward his bed. "You have a visitor."

KATHLEEN

"A visitor?" Harry stared at her. "Don't tell me Leo's come back."

"No."

"Well, out with it, girl. Who is it?"

"Your mother."

Harry stared at her, uncomprehending. "My mother," he repeated, as if the words were some foreign tongue that made no sense. Then the expression in his eyes slowly changed. "I dreamt she was here."

"It was no dream," MaryKate said.

Harry took his time digesting all the information they had given him. "I shall go to Amelia first. Then I shall see my father's wife and find out what she wants."

"You can't!" MaryKate came toward him, grabbing his hand. "You're not strong enough to go near the fever!"

"I can, and I must," he told her. But when he tried to swing his legs off the bed and sit up straight, pain wracked through his chest, sending him back against the pillows, panting.

MaryKate leaned over him. "You can't," she said again, softly this time. "It would do no good."

He couldn't speak for long moments. "Why is she here?" he asked finally.

MaryKate hesitated, unsure whether he meant his wife or his mother. "Your mother?" she ventured, seeing his weary, pain-filled gaze on her. "I don't know."

"Tell her to come."

"Are you sure you're well enough?" MaryKate asked. "Maybe a little later."

He tried to smile, trying to reassure her. "MaryKate, now." The smile left his face. "I want to get it over with."

As MaryKate left the room, Harry closed his eyes, summoning what little strength he had.

A few minutes later Elizabeth walked into her son's room, the two of them staring at each other across a gulf of almost thirty years.

She came forward slowly, stopping two feet away from the bed.

His gaze was cold. "I would hope there was an urgent

KATHLEEN

reason for your visit," he told her, his words as cold as his eyes.

She looked away from him, glancing toward the heavy drapes that covered the windows. "It is quite nice out, actually. For Ireland. Would you like me to open the drapes?"

"I'd like you to state the purpose of your coming and then leave," he told her flatly.

"You need my help," she told him, facing him finally. She came closer to the bed.

"If I ever did, I surely do not at this late date." Hurt and anger underscored the words he tried to keep emotionless.

"I'm not talking about the past," she told him.

"I am," he replied.

"The past is no one's business but my own!" she flared. "It has nothing to do with you!"

"Or my father?" he asked.

"Someday you may be ready to hear my side of the story. But at the moment it will do us no good to discuss the past."

"I know your side of the story," he said bitterly. "It hardly varies from woman to woman."

His mother spoke slowly. "I am truly sorry if your own situation has been anything like your father's and mine. But the important thing now is to appease the queen."

It took him a moment. "What are you saying?"

"Her Majesty is displeased with the rumors of your activities out here. Your friend, young Cumberland, did not help with his eyewitness accounts."

"Of what?" Harry asked.

"He seems to feel it's all a rich joke and that you have gone native, as it were. And that it is destroying your marriage," Elizabeth told her son pointedly. "Not to mention your relationships with your peers. Most of whom say you are creating an atmosphere geared for open rebellion. Please believe me, the queen, your cousin, does not find it amusing in the slightest."

"It's a pack of lies!" Harry said.

"I'm sure it is," Elizabeth said calmly.

Harry's gaze was sharp enough to cut as he raked her with it. "Why?" he demanded. "Why are you, of all people, sure they lie, and I do not? You do not know me."

KATHLEEN

"You are your father's son," she told him simply. "I can imagine you committing all kinds of indiscretions, but I cannot imagine you lying about a point of honor. Or of neglecting your duty to your title and your queen. Especially now."

He stiffened. "What are you saying? Why especially now?"

"Your father sent me here, Henry. Or I would never have come."

"Thank you," he told her coldly.

"I'm not being mean, Henry. I simply knew you would not welcome me, and it is not in my nature to go where I am not welcomed. I promised your father, however, I would come and tell you myself."

"Tell me what?"

She spoke slowly. "On his deathbed he asked for me. And he asked me to come and tell you myself."

Harry forced himself to sit up. "His death bed?!"

MaryKate hovered near the partially open door. Elizabeth was turned away from the doorway, the room silent. Harry was staring at his mother. Slowly he sank back against the pillows. When Elizabeth saw realization dawning in his eyes, she spoke softly, "You are now the Duke of Exeter. And as such have responsibility for the entire dukedom. Here and in England."

MaryKate pulled back from the doorway, out of their line of vision. A coldness gripped her heart. She stood motionless, listening to the conversation in the room beyond.

"Duke." His voice came faintly from beyond the partially closed door.

"You have very great responsibilities to live up to now, Henry," his mother told him. "There are many things that must change."

"Change?" He was still digesting the fact of his father's death. "I didn't want to leave him while he was ill."

"He knew that. Now you must go home. To England. To London. The bulk of your responsibilities are there, Henry. And only you can shoulder them. People need you."

"Why did my father send for you?" Harry asked finally.

"I'm not sure you want to know," she replied.

"I asked," Harry told the woman he could barely remember.

"He sent for me to apologize."

"And did you?" Harry asked.

"I beg your pardon?" his mother replied.

"On his deathbed—did you apologize to him?"

"It wasn't I who had to apologize, Henry. Your father wanted to apologize to me."

"You ran off!"

"There are sometimes two sides to a story, Henry," Elizabeth spoke quietly.

"How could—" He stopped. His voice strangled when he continued, "We expect our parents to be above reproach."

"And above temptation?" Elizabeth supplied. She watched the son she barely knew. "Are any of us?"

In the hall outside tears welled up in MaryKate's eyes. She turned away from the door and started blindly back down the hall.

The doctor came out of Lady Amelia's room. "Mary-Kate—" He saw her condition. "Girl, how did you know?"

She shook her head, pushing back away from the man.

He spoke kindly. "I know how much she meant to you. But she's going fast. Do you want to tell him, or should I?"

MaryKate turned away from the doctor, fleeing headlong down the corridor toward the back stairs and her attic room.

The doctor watched her go. And then turned toward the earl's rooms, walking with measured step.

The door to the sitting room stood open, the door to his inner bedroom ajar. The doctor knocked, waiting until a woman's voice called for him to enter.

He walked in, seeing the older, gray-haired woman beside the earl's bed. "Your Lordship, I have sorry news."

"Your Grace," Elizabeth corrected the doctor, who stared at her, uncomprehending. "His Grace, the new duke of Exeter," Elizabeth explained. "I am the dowager duchess of Exeter."

The doctor bowed toward them. "Your Graces. I am sorry to inform you that Her Ladyship, Amelia, is very near death."

Harry forced his legs off the bed. Elizabeth reached to

stop her son. "You should not go near the body!" she told him sharply.

"In your condition, Your Lordsh—Your Grace, the dowager duchess is quite right," the doctor put in.

But Harry stood up, swaying a little. "Take me to Amelia," he told the doctor. He took a step, the doctor coming quickly near to help him before he fell.

The dowager duchess of Exeter watched her determined son limp toward the sitting room and the hall beyond, aided by the burly English doctor.

MaryKate stood at the tiny attic window across from her own narrow bed. She felt suddenly ill. The enormity of who Harry really was swept through her, chilling her soul. She turned toward the bed, feeling dizzy, and buried her head in the thin pillow that had been hers for years, trying to stop the tears that rained down her cheeks.

She did not hear the tap at her door until the third time it came. She got up, brushing her hair back as she reached for the door.

She looked into the eyes of a man who looked vaguely familiar.

"MaryKate, I'm Dennis Kelly. Your brother says to come quick."

MaryKate stared at the man through swollen, red-rimmed eyes. "What's happened?" she asked.

"He says to tell you Paddy's ill, and he needs you now. There's not a moment to waste."

"I'll get my things."

"He said *now*," Dennis Kelly repeated. "Quickly, before any can stop you."

MaryKate started to protest and then thought of Paddy down with the fever or wounded. And Harry, with his mother downstairs. He was a duke now. He would have to go back to England. Reality came pouring in on her. She would be more alone than ever. And Paddy was family.

MaryKate grabbed her cloak, telling Pugs to stay before following Dennis Kelly down the back stairs. Kelly put his finger to his lips when she started to speak, shaking his head.

A light drizzle misted the night-darkened Priory courtyard

as they crossed the empty kitchen and slipped out toward the back gate and the river far below.

MaryKate pulled her cloak tighter, pulling its hood up over her auburn hair as she followed her brother's friend to the gate.

As she stepped through she reached to relatch it, looking back toward the huge bulk of the Priory's stone walls, rising square and dark against the night sky. A lone light shined from Harry's windows on the second floor, a bit of brightness in the dark.

She closed the gate, turning toward the stone steps that led past the kitchen gardens and down to the riverside far below. Dennis Kelly had stopped a few steps below, watching her. When he saw her turn toward him, he continued down the steps.

Upstairs in the huge house, Harry sat down on a small chair next to Amelia's bed.

He watched her closed eyes, her labored breath. "I've sat beside too many sickbeds this past year." Harry spoke softly, his words more to himself than to her.

Amelia stirred, her eyes slowly opening. Staring at him. Feverish. He reached for the bowl of cool water and the stack of cloths beside it, soaking a cloth and wringing it out before he awkwardly dabbed it at her forehead.

"Forgive me—must—forgive—" Amelia was saying.

"I?" Harry looked down at her. "I dreamt of you asking that. For years I dreamt of it. Then I gave up on it and on the idea that dreams can come true."

"Please, I know you hate me. You've not come near. But please—"

Harry reached for the cloth in the icy water. His voice, weakened by illness, cracked. "I've been ill, Amelia. Not angry. I have no right to be angry. Nor to forgive. You've done nothing I have not done myself."

"I lied."

"And so have I. Even to myself." Harry spoke softly. "Amelia, I never understood, until now, what drove you to do what you did."

"Until Mary-Kathleen," Amelia said faintly.

KATHLEEN

"I'm sorry." He spoke softly. "I never before knew what love felt like. What it could do to one."

"Hugh" was all Amelia replied.

Harry held back his anger. He took a moment to control his voice and then said, "What about Hugh?"

"He had to marry his bishop's daughter."

"Grinstead is married?" Harry stared at his ill wife.

"No." Her eyes closed. "No, widowed. She died too late for us."

Harry stared at his wife. "I don't understand."

Amelia turned to look at his eyes. "You don't understand?"

"No."

"You really don't. It was Hugh, Hugh and me . . ."

Harry digested Amelia's words. "It was Hugh." He stared at her, his eyes slowly hardening. "Are you saying it was Grinstead all along? That's what you're saying? He was the one you ran off with."

"Hugh." Her eyes closed again. She leaned back against the pillows. "We were apart for years. Met when we could . . ." She roused herself, grabbing at Harry's sleeve, desperate. "Everything I've done has been to petition God—to petition him to release Hugh from his vows. Every good deed. I've done years of good deeds! He thought I had money of my own . . . had to part when I didn't . . . hold me . . . Hold me! Don't let me be alone!"

Harry bent to hold Amelia close. "You're not alone!" As he said the words his heart wrenched within him. He told himself he didn't mean them. But out loud he told her what she needed to hear: Hugh Grinstead truly loved her—and had all along.

Harry told his wife that her lover was coming back, coming to be with her.

"It's all right, then?" Her voice was weak.

"Yes."

"We'll be together?"

"Yes," he agreed. "He'll be here soon."

"Everything's all right," were the last words she said.

The breath went out of her as Harry watched. Hot liquid filled his eyes before he realized he was crying.

* * *

KATHLEEN

For over an hour he sat beside her bed, staring at her lifeless face. Frustration and anger built as he stared at the woman he had been forced to marry—who had been forced to marry him. He thought of the blackguard she had chosen to love, if anyone ever truly chooses to love. His eyes closed, afraid of the subject. His brain insisted there were always choices, but his heart told him sometimes people were simply caught in love's snares, unaware of the dangers until the trap was sprung.

He opened his eyes, his expression grim. The right reverend had never been caught, had never been fair to the woman who had lost almost all because of him.

Down the hall Archie was polishing boots. He looked up when he heard Harry's heavy tread on the stairs. He came out of the duke's rooms to see Harry moving slowly, his hand grasping the rail tightly.

"And where do you think you're going?" Archie demanded.

"To pay a debt," Harry replied from the hall below.

"You're not well enough to go out!" When Archie saw Harry wasn't stopping, he dropped the boot and hurried down the steps after him.

"If you're determined to go, I'll hitch up a carriage for us," Archie said.

"Just do it," Harry said through gritted teeth, taking deep breaths and waiting for the pain to subside.

The pain still gnawed at him when they arrived in the village. "This is not a good idea!" Archie was telling Harry when they reined in at the rectory.

Lord Ennis stood with Rossett and Dunstable in the rectory doorway. Reverend Grinstead was looking out his gate, surprised and obviously unhappy to see Harry.

"Did someone tell Lismore we were meeting?" Ennis asked the others.

"Hardly," Rossett said.

Harry was climbing out of the carriage, coming toward them.

"Lismore—we tried to see you earlier in the week," Ennis began.

"It can wait," Harry said tersely.

"I must say your attitude leaves a lot to be desired, old man." Lord Rossett smiled insincerely. "I mean, we should be pulling together at this point."

"Amelia's dead," Harry told Grinstead baldly. As the others began to give their condolences, Harry continued: "Before she died, she told me all."

"I'm—I don't understand," Hugh Grinstead faltered.

"Oh, yes you do."

"I don't know what you mean."

Harry's fists were clenched at his sides. "I bring you a message."

"This should be in private, we can go into—"

Before Grinstead could finish his sentence, Harry's fist connected with the minister's jaw. Grinstead fell at Lord Ennis's feet, the others shocked.

"What the bloody hell are you about, Lismore?!" Dunstable roared at Harry.

"Stay out of it," Harry snapped. "And if I were each of you"—his eyes raked across their astonished faces—"I'd seek better company." Harry turned on his heel, reaching the carriage and starting to climb inside before his strength failed him.

Archie caught the duke, steadying him as Rossett watched Ennis and Dunstable aid the English reverend to his feet.

"What is going on between you?" Ennis asked Grinstead.

"I'd rather not say."

"You'd better say something, Grinstead." Rossett watched the pale man who swayed in front of him, unsteady on his feet. Grinstead's jaw was already swelling.

"If you must know, it's about the O'Hallions," Hugh Grinstead lied. "His wife was against his aiding them and had come to seek my counsel."

"Aiding rebels?!" Dunstable thundered. "That's torn it! I thought she came to you only because of the Irish maid."

Ennis said, "I've stayed out of much of it until now. But, by God, adultery *and* treason—I want the queen to know of this now! His lands had better be confiscated by the Crown before we end up with open rebellion out here!"

"Aiding rebels . . ." Rossett shook his head.

"Don't you believe me?" Hugh Grinstead asked sharply.

"My dear man—is there any reason I should not?"

Hugh took a deep breath. "No reason at all."

When he turned toward the door his maid flew back down the hall, slipping into the kitchen before he saw her.

"You'll never guess what's just happened!" she said to the cook.

Cook looked up from wiping the dinner dishes, her face impassive. "There's not much I've not seen already in this household."

She went back to her work as the maid excitedly poured out the story.

30

It was the next morning before Harry realized Mary-Kate had gone.

Early fingers of dawn glowed in the eastern skies, backlighting the heavy cloud cover. Archie gazed out of Harry's bedroom window, moving his weary body from its position on the window seat. He looked down at the empty carafe of port beside his feet and then sourly toward the newest duke of Exeter.

Harry sat, his chin on his chest, staring into the dead embers of last night's fire. The fireplace was cold.

"You should have gone to bed when I said," Archie said over a wide yawn.

"What?" Harry's head did not rise.

"At least I would have gotten a decent night's sleep," Archie said.

Harry roused himself enough to look toward Archie. "Go to bed."

"Now? Don't be daft."

"Why do I feel sad?" Harry asked the dead fire. "I hardly knew her. She wanted no part of me. Why do I feel sadness at her passing?"

Archie shrugged. "She was a human being. She couldn't help where her feelings lay."

Harry looked toward the man who sat on the window seat. "Can anyone?"

"You're as good a judge as any," Archie said.

Harry hoisted himself onto his feet, pushing away Archie's support as the Welshman came near. "I'm all right." Harry sounded testy.

"You're not all right. You're wobbly from the wound, and now you're wobbly from a night full of fighting and drinking. You're going to lie down and tell me what you want."

Harry let Archie force him onto the bed. "I'd like to see MaryKate."

Archie grimaced. "Now, why couldn't I figure that for myself?" He started for the door. "You stay put, your Graceful Pain in the Posterior, or I'll give you the same whatfor I gave you when you were ten, dukedom or no dukedom."

Harry's eyes closed, letting the tiredness seep through his alcohol-fogged brain. The wine had deadened the pain of his wound a little.

It did nothing for his peace of mind.

He dozed, waking with a start a few minutes later. Archie had not returned. "Archie," he called. Then he yelled for the man, louder, and heard footsteps running near.

Elizabeth came through the bedroom door first, hurrying to Harry's side. "What is it, what's wrong?"

"Archie!" Harry called out again.

Archie came through the door.

"What is it?" his mother asked again.

"Where is she?" Harry asked Archie, ignoring his mother.

"She must have gone for a walk."

Harry stared at the man. "A walk?"

"She's not in the house or on the grounds. She must have gone for a walk."

"At dawn?" Harry demanded.

"Who are you talking about?" Elizabeth asked.

Harry was already trying to get to his feet.

"You can't go looking for her," Archie said. "There's no way to know where she's gone."

"I know where she is," Harry replied.

His mother reached out her arm. "You have more pressing concerns, Harry."

Harry moved away from his mother. Archie caught up with him in the hall. "Where do you think you're going?"

"To bring her back."

"She's just gone for a walk!" Archie said.

"She's left," Harry said. "She's left, and I'm going to bring her back."

Archie stared at the man who was grabbing the stair rail for support as he moved down the wide steps. "And what are you going to do with her once you've got her back here?" Archie yelled, starting after him.

"I don't know." Harry didn't look back.

Elizabeth watched from the top of the stairwell as Archie reached her son's side, thrusting a coat toward the duke and heading with him out the door. Wallace stood below, looking up at her as the door opened to the cold morning mist and then slammed shut. Elizabeth paced slowly, back to the rooms MaryKate had readied for her.

At the O'Hallion cottage Harry dismounted unsteadily, as Archie reached the door ahead of him. At first Archie did not recognize the woman who opened it.

Sophie was far thinner, her eyes haunted when she stared out at the two men. "He's not here," she said in a hoarse whisper. "Please, we have the fever. He's not here."

"Where's MaryKate?" Archie said.

"Johnny's not here," Sophie said again.

"Where is MaryKate?" It was Harry who asked this time.

Sophie stared at him, uncomprehending. "At the Priory."

"You've not seen her?" Archie asked the woman.

Sophie shook her head tiredly. "Has something happened to her, too?"

Harry turned away. Archie quickly followed. "You believe her?"

"Yes," Harry said.

"Let's go back to the Priory. She's probably there already."

"She's not there."

"Where are we going, then?" Archie said.

Harry did not answer, expending all his energy pulling

himself up into the saddle. His chest throbbed, the pain in his side radiating up to his shoulder. He reached for the bridle, starting down the path, the horse's every hoofbeat causing him agony.

In the village, Paddy was just coming out of the pub, the men within asking questions he could not answer about his brother. Father Ross stopped his dilapidated horse-drawn trap beside the man. "Paddy—?"

Paddy walked toward the startled priest. "Father, you look as if you're seeing a ghost."

"But you're ill!" the priest told him.

It was Paddy's turn to look startled. "What are you talking about?"

"Dennis Kelly told the Priory cook you were ill. He said he had to take MaryKate to you."

Both men stared at each other. Paddy's expression hardened. "Then Johnny's got something up his sleeve."

Father Ross looked troubled. "There's more. The duke came to the Protestant minister last night and punched him."

"*Punched* him?"

"Grinstead said it was because of your brother, of the duke helping him."

"You must be daft!"

"That's what I thought," Father Ross replied. "His cook came to tell me there's more reason than that."

Paddy turned away.

"Where are you going?" the priest called out after him.

"To find my sister."

Father Ross sat watching Johnny O'Hallion's younger brother cut across the field beyond the pub. Then the rotund little priest turned the buggy round and headed in the opposite direction, toward Priory Hill.

The priest was on the Priory road when Harry reached the village. Archie was arguing all the way, "They'll tell you nothing. It's best to think this out."

"If I have to search every cottage between here and Dublin, I'll find her," Harry said grimly.

"Why?" Archie asked. "What have you got to offer her?"

KATHLEEN

Harry didn't dismount. He stared at his retainer, the words spinning around in his brain.

"Are you going to stay here? Are you going to take her with you to London? What are you going to do with her once you've found her? And will it be any good for her?"

Harry stared at the man. "I want to make sure she's safe."

"Will she be if she's with you?" Archie persisted.

An Irishman walked out of the pub, followed by another. They stopped when they saw the English lord. Harry stared down into closed faces. As they turned away he looked hard at Archie.

"Let's go home" was all Harry said.

Archie sighed. "The first sense you've shown all morning. You must be sobering up."

Harry didn't reply.

Upon reaching the Priory, Harry and Archie saw Father Ross talking to Young Tim. When Tim saw the duke he ran toward him. "Your Lordship—something's happened to MaryKate."

Harry steeled himself. "Is she hurt?"

"No. I mean, I don't know."

Father Ross came nearer. "I'm not sure what's happened, but I think there's a problem. I thought I'd best come tell you." The rotund priest looked up toward Harry's drawn face.

MaryKate climbed the narrow defile, Dennis Kelly following her, effectively cutting off any escape if she'd thought about it.

But her thoughts were divided between worry over her brother and pain over losing Harry. Forcing herself to face the fact that they could never be together, she felt the tears well up again. Thrusting the thought away, she told herself she was a fool, stumbling on the rocky incline.

"Are you all right, then?" Dennis asked, steadying her.

"Let's just get to Paddy," she replied.

"We're almost there," the man told her.

293

KATHLEEN

A lookout called to Johnny, bringing him toward the mouth of the defile. MaryKate saw him and ran forward.

"Where is he? What's happened?"

"Come along, and I'll explain," Johnny O'Hallion told his sister.

She followed him without question toward a small cave in the ravine wall.

While MaryKate followed her brother, Harry was questioning the Catholic priest:

"I'm telling you I don't know!" Father Ross nearly yelled at the new duke of Exeter. "I don't know where Johnny O'Hallion is holed up!" The stress made him considerably less than formal with the angry Englishman, who stood in front of him, fists clenched and ready for a fight. "If I knew I'd be telling you!"

Harry saw Archie's frown. He looked past Archie, toward the distant hills that lay purpled and still in the distance. "She's in danger." Harry spoke to himself but the words came out loud.

Father Ross looked troubled. "Aye, and I fear you may be right. Although I'd never think Johnny O'Hallion capable of hurting his very own flesh and blood. But it sounds as wrong to me as it did to Paddy." His troubled face creased into even more worried lines. "That's why I came—I'm that worried."

Harry watched the shorter man. "So worried you'd come to an Englishman for help." Harry watched surprise, worry, and even a little fear chase each other across the priest's face. "Which way did Paddy go?"

Father Ross hesitated. "Toward the Kerry Road." He spoke as if he wished he hadn't.

Harry saw what it cost the old man. "Thank you, Father."

The small priest looked up into the eyes of the tall Englishman. "I hope I've done right."

"You have," Harry told him before turning away. "I'll find her," he said grimly.

"You'll find not only her, then. You'll find them all. You cannot go unarmed," Father Ross said, watching them remount.

"He's right," Archie put in quickly.

KATHLEEN

"I'll never get near her armed," Harry told them both.

"He's already shot you once!" Archie's worry sounded like anger.

Harry hesitated. "Who would know where Johnny O'Hallion would hide?" he asked Tim, who stared up at him, wide-eyed and dumbstruck. "It could be MaryKate's life we're talking about," Harry added.

Young Tim swallowed. "Old Man Murphy . . ." the boy started and then trailed off, beginning again a moment later: "Old Man Murphy used to be the one that knew all the hidey-holes against the—"

"Which way?" Harry interrupted.

"I'll show you," Father Ross said. "I've brought this about. I'd best see it through."

Tim watched the three of them ride away, Father Ross maneuvering his decrepit old buggy ahead of Archie and Harry's horses.

When Tim turned back he saw the duke's mother in an upstairs window, staring down the steep, narrow road.

Miles away from the Murphy cabin and hidden deep in the glacial ravine, MaryKate stood, with her hands on her hips, glaring at her older brother.

"And you dare to stand there and tell me that Paddy's not ill?!"

Johnny shrugged, lifting a jug of poteen brought all the way from Old Tom's pub. He sat it back on his knee and wiped his mouth with the back of his hand, smiling at her. "What I'm saying is that I'd not be knowing whether it's well he is or not, since it was me who sent him packing."

MaryKate's eyes blazed. "What's all this about, then?!" she demanded of her brother. "Why am I here?"

They were in front of a small campfire, the men Johnny had gathered watching brother and sister as Johnny drank and MaryKate stamped her foot against the mossy ground. Her exasperation gave off more heat than the dying embers of the open fires.

"It's about killing the bloody English," Johnny told her.

"What's that to do with me?!" she demanded.

"One at a time," her brother told her.

Fear clutched at her heart. She stared in horror at the man

she'd grown up admiring. Respecting. With all their arguments, he had been the closest thing to a father she had ever known. "Johnny—you can't mean it."

She saw his face harden. "I can mean it, girl," he told her. "Killing your English lover means one less English boot against our necks! He'll come after you, and I'll do it right this time!"

MaryKate took one step nearer her brother. "Johnny O'Hallion, I've loved you and I've *respected* you my whole life long! Don't make me regret it. It does no good to hurt innocent people!"

Her brother was beyond reason. "Innocent?! There's no innocent English! There'll be one less, *that's* what good it does!"

MaryKate stared at him. Slowly she backed away. Her foot hit the leg of one of the men. The man moved his leg, allowing her to move away from Johnny. She looked down toward the man who let her pass. "Aren't you going to stop me?! Aren't you going to do my brother's dirty work and lure an innocent man to his slaughter?!"

"Shut her up!" Johnny shouted.

But none of the men moved toward her.

She stared them down, one by one, swiveling around to defy any who might come near. "Aren't you going to be big men, now? Aren't you going to shut up one lone female?!" One of the men came toward her. She laughed at him, a mirthless laugh, her eyes blazing with contempt: "Well, now, and are you the one to be such a bully? You feel like a big man, do you, menacing one lone female?"

Sounds of discouragement came from the men around them. The man backed off. Johnny looked furious.

"Are you listening to her, then?! Are you willing to let the English kill us off one by one until there's none of us left?!"

"Johnny." A haggard-looking man stood up, throwing a bone onto a pile beside the fire. "There's enough, now."

"Yes." Paddy spoke from the entrance to the ravine, heads turning toward him, startled at the intrusion. "There's more than enough."

MaryKate ran to him. "He said you were ill."

KATHLEEN

"I know." Paddy stared at his brother for a long silent moment. "Come away now, MaryKate."

Johnny moved toward them. "She can't go."

"I'm taking her home," Paddy told his older brother.

"Did you hear me?" Johnny demanded.

"I've heard you all my life. And I've listened to you all my life. And I've done all you said. What has it gotten us?"

There were twenty pairs of ears listening to their exchange. Actuely aware of the eyes and ears all around, Johnny's anger escalated, filling him with a sense of urgency and sending him toward his brother.

Paddy saw him coming and raised his arms. "Get behind me!" he told MaryKate, preparing to defend himself from his brother.

But MaryKate moved between them, instead of behind Paddy, her small hands pushing Johnny back as he came nearer. "This has to stop!"

"There's no stopping between here and the grave!" Johnny said. "It's for shame, Patrick O'Hallion, that's what it is, that you can leave your brother in the lurch!" He stopped half a foot away from MaryKate. Brian came near, reaching for her.

MaryKate slapped Brian Flaherty's face hard, darting around Paddy's back and slipping up the narrow defile toward freedom.

"She's getting away!" Brian yelled, Johnny reacting, trying to shove past his brother.

Paddy pushed back, keeping Johnny from following MaryKate. Brian hit Paddy across the side of the head, the other men coming near, most of them confused. A few of them angry enough to menace each other. All the frustrations built up over decades and centuries of neglect, fear, hunger, and deprivation came welling up and pouring out from simple men who merely wanted to live their lives free from hunger and strife.

They listened to each other and used the anger of their neighbors to stoke their own, turning into a mob as Paddy slugged his brother-in-law, Brian, and stumbled past him, taking off after MaryKate.

"Get them! Get them back here, or my own family will be warning the son of a bitch!" Johnny came to his feet, all of them shoving each other in their push to get through the narrow defile, panic now mixing with their anger.

The Murphy cabin was on the absent Lord Cameron's land, at the far end of a tiny path that led only there. Harry's horse picked its way delicately across the weedy sod beside the priest's ancient trap, with Archie close behind.

"It looks deserted," Archie said.

"The men have gone on the public works—but maybe the women are about."

Harry reined in. Dismounting gingerly, he favored his wound as he moved. Halfway to the door, the smell stopped him. Behind him Archie's nose wrinkled. "What the bloody hell—"

Harry took out his handkerchief, covering his nose as he went the last few steps and pushed on the rotting cabin door.

The stench was overpowering.

The cabin was dark as night inside, no fire in the grate, the tiny windows begrimed. It took a minute for their eyes to adjust to the gloom.

A woman lay on tattered blankets on the floor near the cold fireplace. Beyond her were two children's bodies. Their emaciated skeletons were barely covered with skin, a few patches of limp hair still covering their skulls.

The three men were shocked into silence. A weak sound startled them, Harry moving closer.

"Don't touch it!" Archie said.

Harry reached for the bundled blanket near the woman's arms. Pulling it away from her, a baby stirred within the dirty bundle. Its eyes were blank, blinking once and then closing again as it mewled weakly. "It's alive," Harry said. "But the woman's gone."

"So are the others. What's that?" Archie saw movement in the dim light. "Are you sure the woman's dead? Her foot just moved." Archie started to reach for the blanket that lay across the dead woman's legs, and then jumped back. "Jesus, lover of my soul!"

"Sweet Mother of God." Father Ross crossed himself, starting to sink to his knees as a rat scurried away from one of her half-eaten feet.

"Don't!" Harry stopped the old priest. "It's not safe."

KATHLEEN

He grabbed the dirty blanket that held the half-dead child. Archie, swearing continuously, stomped the rat into the dirt floor, gagging at the sight.

Their eyes becoming accustomed to the darkness, they each became aware of movement around the floor, the dead bodies drawing rats.

Harry moved toward the rotted front door, shouldering his way outside and drinking in the fresh air in huge gulps. The baby lay motionless in his arms.

Father Ross blinked in the sudden sunlight, Archie following, still swearing. Anger and fear washed through him, turning his stomach. He gulped at the fresh air, his face pale.

"They say it's like this all over." Archie finally found his voice.

"How could the men leave them like this?!" Harry demanded.

"They've gone to make money on the government work, or they're looking for work in Cork or Dublin." Father Ross spoke quietly. "Trying anything to send money home."

Harry moved toward the horses, thrusting the dirty blanket toward Archie. "Hold this one until I'm mounted."

Archie reluctantly reached for the dirty blanket. "It's filthy."

"And so would you be. It's a miracle it's still alive."

"What are you to do with the child?" Father Ross asked.

"We'll take it to the doctor and see if it can be helped."

Archie watched his master grit his teeth and pull himself into the saddle. When Harry reached for the baby, Archie handed it up and then went toward his own horse.

"Maybe there'll be word of MaryKate when we get back."

Harry looked grim. "If not, we'll start again as soon as we've seen to the child."

They arrived back to find the stable deserted. Archie took the small bundle from Harry, reaching an arm to steady Harry as he descended.

"I'm all right!" Harry said testily.

"You're barely on your feet," Archie shot back, walking ahead to open the door.

The front hall echoed with their steps. "Wallace?" Harry shouted into the silence. "Wallace!"

KATHLEEN

The green baise door opened, and Wallace came toward them, his shirt sleeves rolled up, wet from the laundry water. "I'm sorry, Your Grace."

"Have you heard anything?" Harry demanded.

"Yes, Your Grace; the duchess sent them away and told them they'd have to bring an army with them if they came again."

Harry stared at the man. "What are you talking about, man?"

"Why, the authorities. They say there's a writ from the queen to take your land, Your Grace."

Archie felt his mouth drop open. Wallace glanced again at the dirty bundle in Archie's arms. "I'll take that laundry."

"It's not laundry. It's a child," Harry said, but did not explain. "Where is my mother?"

"Behind you," Elizabeth said, coming the rest of the way down the great front stairwell. "I thought I heard you say there was a child."

She stopped in front of him. Archie reached the dirty blanket out toward her. Elizabeth's nose wrinkled at the smell, but she took it in her arms. "What on earth have you been doing now, Henry?"

"Its brother and sister were dead, as was its mother." Harry looked toward Wallace. "Archie will tell you where. We've got to send men to bury them."

Archie interjected slowly: "It's not on your property, Your Grace. We don't have any right."

"Send to the owner. But if he does nothing, I shall."

Elizabeth's concern grew. "It may not be a good time, Henry. We've received a visit from the local constable saying that the queen has issued a proclamation against you for conspiring to help the rebels."

"Damn and blast. I've never conspired at anything in my life! Let alone rebellion! It's ridiculous," Harry told his mother. "Better get that child cleaned up and to the doctor before it dies in your arms."

She nodded to Wallace, who left quickly. "I'll get it clean linens," she said, starting back toward the stairs. "Is it a boy or a girl?"

"I don't know," he told her.

300

Elizabeth stared across the empty hall. "Why did you bring the child here?"

"I couldn't very well leave it there. Rats were eating its mother."

Elizabeth blanched. "Good God." She watched her son's set expression. "I'll see to the child until the doctor arrives."

~31~

Harry was upstairs, changing out of his stained clothing, when he heard sounds in the hall below and on the stairs.

Then he heard her voice calling out to Pugs.

His heart skipped a beat as he grabbed open his door, charging out into the hall half-dressed. MaryKate came running toward him, her cheeks tear-stained, her brother Paddy hesitating on the steps.

Harry saw nothing but MaryKate. He reached for her, pulling her close. "What happened?! Where did you go?! Why did you go?!"

"Johnny sent word Paddy had been hurt. But it was false. Oh, Harry, Johnny's gone mad, and his men with him!"

Harry held her close. Looking over MaryKate's shoulder, he saw Paddy staring at them.

Paddy watched his sister in the Englishman's arms. "They're out for blood. They may come here."

"Let them," Harry said grimly.

MaryKate pulled back a little. She looked shyly back toward Patrick, who was starting to move away. Harry stopped her, his hands gentle on her arms.

Then Harry stepped back, drawing her with him, into his rooms. "Let all the rest just be for a moment." She followed him, letting him close the door between them and Paddy. He stared at her. And then buried his face in her hair, drinking in the scent of her.

"I have to go," she told him quietly. "We both know that. I wanted to warn you. And to say good-bye to Her Ladyship."

"Amelia's gone."

"Dead?"

"Yes."

He pulled her closer, one hand on the small of her back, one hand behind her head, as he lifted her to his lips, only her toes still touching the floor.

She melted against his bare chest, trying to fight the feelings that were welling up within her. "I have to ready her for her burial," MaryKate said, tears streaming.

"She's being seen to. You don't have to—" he told her, his voice breaking. "I'm sorry, MaryKate, I'm so sorry."

"I have to leave here."

"Not yet!" He reached for her. And then let his hands drop to his sides. "I'm sorry. Whatever you wish." He watched her turn away from him, watching her reach for the door and walk outside into the hall. He wanted to grab her and beg her to stay. But she was already gone, the door closing between them.

MaryKate paused beside the closed door. She straightened her back, staring at Paddy defiantly, daring him to say anything. Tears trickled down her cheeks.

"MaryKate," the dowager duchess said from nearby. "There you are. I need your help."

MaryKate nodded. "Paddy, go to the kitchens and have a bite. Then you can help Wallace." She looked back toward Elizabeth.

"And you?" Paddy asked from the stairwell.

"I'll be down directly."

MaryKate walked into the duchess's rooms, stopping when she saw the tiny bit of human flesh on the bed.

Elizabeth glanced at MaryKate as they moved. "You look a sorry enough sight. Perhaps you'd best clean yourself up while you see to the child."

KATHLEEN

"Whose child is it?"

Elizabeth looked down at the tiny baby. "The priest said someone named Murphy—I'm not sure." She sighed. "Strange, isn't it? A new life in this house on this day of all days."

MaryKate looked down at the baby. "I'm told Lady Amelia is being seen to."

Elizabeth watched the girl. "You cared about Amelia."

"She taught me to read and write. I owed her a very great deal."

"And you care about my son?"

MaryKate bit her lower lip as she reached for the child. "I'll see to the child."

Harry was nearly dressed when Elizabeth tapped on his door. He strode toward it, opening it to reveal his mother. "Oh."

"I'm sorry I'm not who you hoped to see," his mother said.

He stood back, the hope in his eyes dying. "Hope is for fools."

"Yes, well, that's entirely possible. The queen's troops will be coming soon. You realize there will be trouble. You'll not be able to avoid them."

"It seems I can't avoid trouble on one side or the other." His expression darkened. "I've done no good in coming to Ireland."

"What did you do to so incense your neighbors and have everyone up in arms against you?" his mother asked.

"I tried to avoid having rats eating women's feet," he told her coldly.

She shivered. "I'll see to the child—a girl, by the way. The doctor said she's malnourished, but otherwise, she may have a chance. I've sent for a wet nurse."

"I doubt there's any to be had," Harry said.

"If not, the doctor's given a formula. What do you intend to do with her once she's well?"

Harry shook his head. "Father Ross said he would look after it."

His mother watched him. "It would seem you've done a great many things lately without thinking them through."

KATHLEEN

He watched her walk out, her words echoing in his ears.

MaryKate bathed the child in the kitchen, Cook helping with the large tin pan, testing the water with her elbow and hovering, giving instructions at every move.

Paddy sat at the table, finishing tea and biscuits, watching the two women fuss over the baby. Something crashed outside, making all three look toward the stableyard window.

Paddy was to his feet, heading for the kitchen door, his face grim.

"What is it?" MaryKate called out.

Paddy opened the door a little, peering out across the cobblestones. He closed it, looking back toward his sister. "There are men."

"Soldiers?" She breathed the word.

"No. Irishmen. It's probably Johnny, MaryKate. He won't let it end until he kills or is killed."

"Jesus, Mary, and Joseph." The cook was crossing herself.

MaryKate handed the baby into the woman's arms, the child turning a little, too weak to cry. "Take care of her; I've got to warn His Grace."

"MaryKate!" Paddy called after her, but she was already down the hall. Frustrated, he turned back to lock the door. "Where would that fella, Archie, be? And Wallace?"

"In the washroom, or the annex. The hospital, you know. Maybe with the doctor."

Paddy started for the hall to the front of the house.

"Why'd you bolt the door, then?" she called out after him.

"Whoever's here—they're not here for tea and biscuits."

Archie was coming in the front as Paddy came through the green baise door. "Are you friend or foe?" Archie asked.

"Neither. But I'm no murderer, either," Paddy replied.

"That's something, I guess," Archie told MaryKate's brother. "I've got to tell His Grace—" Up above them Harry descended the steps with MaryKate. Archie spoke when he saw Harry and MaryKate. "There's a bunch of unhappy-looking Irishmen milling about outside and more coming up

305

the hill. They all have spades and hammers and God knows what else."

Harry stared at MaryKate. "Wait, please!" Then he strode past them all to the front door, pulling it open before Archie could move to stop him.

Harry strode outside, onto the wide stone porch, stopping at the five stone steps that led down to the cobblestoned driveway.

Irishmen, somber and ragged-looking, were congregating near the stable, Young Tim among them. Others were trailing up the hill road. Scores of them gathered, with scores more, it seemed, behind them.

Harry spoke to Archie behind him. "You'd best get my pistols."

"You can't stand off a hundred to two."

"Three," Paddy said calmly, coming to stand beside Harry.

Surprised, Harry's eyes turned toward the young Irishman beside him. "Are you sure of what you're doing?"

"I'm sure of what I'm not doing," Paddy said. "I'll not be part of a lynching mob, no matter who or where."

Archie ran for the gunroom, grabbing pistols and extra shot.

The men did not come near Harry. None of them spoke to him. Young Tim hung back amongst the men nearest the stable, Harry staring at him hard. The boy looked away, unable to meet the duke's eyes.

Slowly the sounds of anger began to grow louder and louder, voices coming near, urging each other on. Paddy tensed beside Harry, who took one of the guns Archie had brought out and handed it over to Paddy.

Paddy was surprised. A grudging respect shone in his eyes as he took the weapon from the English noble.

The voices came nearer, the men coming around the side of the house.

Johnny was in the lead, Brian yelling at his side, urging the other men on.

MaryKate stepped out onto the porch, the Murphy baby in her arms.

"Get back inside," Archie told her.

KATHLEEN

"I'll have none of it," she replied sharply. She moved forward, standing beside Harry and her brother.

"You'll only make it worse," Paddy told her.

"Let them attack a woman and a child," she said coldly. Her voice rose, ringing out across the stableyard in the clear, cold air. "Let everyone see the brave men who will threaten women and children and sick people ill in the room beyond!"

Elizabeth came to the doorway. And then went outside, a pistol in her hand. "I've never shot one of these things. I hope I do it right."

Elizabeth's brow arched. She watched her son for a brief moment and then turned her attention toward the angry men who were nearing the stable door across the cobblestones from the Priory and where they stood. "There are quite a few. It seems you've upset everyone, Henry—the natives and your English neighbors alike. I fear you'll never make a diplomat."

Johnny O'Hallion saw his sister and brother beside the Englishman. "There they are! What did I tell you? The devil himself has beguiled them!"

One of the men near the stable door stepped out in front of Johnny, stopping him.

"Johnny O'Hallion, what do you think you're doing, then?"

"Morrison, I'm glad to see you boys are with us."

"We're not with you, Johnny."

"Then get out of my way! I'm here to teach this Englishman a lesson!"

"A lesson in what, then?" Morrison asked. Another man stepped forward from those near Young Tim.

"Johnny, it's a little off the beam you are, isn't it? You've no business here," the man said.

"Let's go down to the pub and lift one, Johnny," another man said.

The small group on the Priory steps stared at the scene before them as three dozen Irishmen stepped up, one at a time, between Johnny O'Hallion's angry little band and the English duke on the porch.

"Get out of my way, or you'll be dead, too!" Johnny yelled, brandishing a pistol.

KATHLEEN

"Is it killing your own, then, is that what you're after?" Morrison asked.

"It's none of your business!"

"Aye and it is that! My daughter is alive and at home, thanks to the English doctor and the English lord here, nursing her until she was well."

"It wasn't him—it was his wife, and he's killed her!" Johnny spat out the words.

"How dare you?!" MaryKate shouted toward her brother. "How *dare* you?!"

"Yes, and probably got you to pour the poison down her throat, being that soft-headed about him!"

MaryKate found Elizabeth's hand on her arm, squeezing it sharply. "Do not reply," Elizabeth said. "You'll only make it worse."

"But it's a lie!"

The men around Morrison shifted on their feet, Johnny staring from one to another. "Are you going to let us pass, then? Or do we fight you, too?"

"It's fight, Johnny O'Hallion," another voice called out. "You'll have to fight me, too."

"And me."

Voice after voice called out, the spades and hammers and tools in their hands gripped more tightly now.

"My wife's alive."

"My only son."

"We're eating on the money he gave back in rents."

"We're alive because of the grain he gives out free."

Brian pushed past Johnny. "There's no talking to fools! A little food given back, and you're all that grateful, are you?! Who *took* the food in the first place?!"

"The bloody English!" a voice behind Brian shouted, angry frustration spilling out, looking for a target. Any target.

"Not *this* bloody Englishman!" Morrison shouted.

"He's ruined my sister!" Johnny shouted his frustration.

"How *dare* you?!" MaryKate took a step forward, the Murphy baby in her arms. "How *dare* you accuse me of things you're not knowing?!"

"I've got eyes in my head! And whose bastard is that in your arms now?!"

308

KATHLEEN

"It's the Murphys' youngest," MaryKate said quietly. "The tyke's entire family was carried away by the fever and this one's alive because His Grace saved it!"

Horses' hooves pounded up the Priory Hill. "He's called the troops on us!" Johnny's men were turning, one of them running off around the side of the stable, trying to flee the soldiers who shouted for them all to halt.

Johnny's men were caught between soldiers behind and their own neighbors ahead. Johnny raised his pistol, aiming for Harry. "You'll be dead before they come!"

Harry raised his own, MaryKate shouting no to both of them. Harry stopped. Johnny pulled the trigger in the same instant Paddy moved in front of Harry to stop him. Elizabeth pulled MaryKate and the child toward the doorway as Johnny's bullet ricocheted against the stone wall, inches away from Paddy's head.

Johnny turned toward the soldiers, firing wildly, Brian grabbing the gun and reloading it as a soldier's bullet sang out past him and hit Johnny, sending him to his knees. As he pitched forward, his face hitting the dirt, soldiers ran near, surrounding his body. Paddy started toward his brother, Archie reaching to pull him back. "Stay back, or they'll shoot you, too."

Paddy jerked away from the little Welshman. "He's my brother!"

Archie whispered harshly: "There's nothing you can do for him now! He's gone and shot at the authorities!"

The soldiers moved cautiously through the crowd, herding up the men around Johnny, moving them toward the others who were back against the stable wall, some inside, others standing as still as statues, silent and watchful.

Paddy knelt down beside Johnny, startling a soldier who still kept his aim on the fallen man.

MaryKate saw the man begin to bring his gun up toward Paddy. She thrust the baby into Elizabeth's arms, running to throw herself between Paddy and the English soldier. "Shoot me, too, you coward!"

"Stop!" Harry's deep voice rang out, clear and cold across the courtyard. "Who's in charge here?" he demanded. "On whose authority do you trespass on my land?!"

KATHLEEN

A lieutenant turned away from the crowd of men near the stable doors. "On Her Majesty's authority!" he replied harshly, his eyes raking across Harry's countenance.

Harry stared the man down. "Then I assume you have that authority in writing."

"Yes," the lieutenant said, "we are charged with authority from the Crown to confiscate the grounds, desmesne, and estates being occupied by the Earl of Lismore, by order of Her Majesty, Queen Victoria."

The crowd surged, sounds of protest welling up, soft on the Irish air and then louder as the tenants realized why the soldiers were there.

"You can't be doing that!" an Irish voice called out.

"You have no right!" another said.

"Stand between them!" Morrison called. "Keep your hands at your sides, don't give them any excuses for shooting, now."

"Stay out of the way!" The lieutenant's voice rose above the scores of men who were pushing, slowly, closer and closer around the small contingent of English soldiers.

Harry walked forward, reaching for MaryKate and thrusting her toward Archie. "Take the women inside." He held his gun pointed downward, watching the soldiers beginning to raise theirs, intimidated by the crowd of surly-looking Irishmen. Archie and MaryKate reached Elizabeth's side.

"Just one moment!" Elizabeth's voice rang out, startling them all. Calmly, she handed the baby to Archie and moved past them, to her son. Harry put his hand back to stop her. MaryKate, pulling away from Archie, returned to her brothers as Elizabeth lifted her son's hand from her arm and squeezed it. She eyed the English lieutenant. "I am the earl's mother. I wish to see your orders."

The lieutenant hesitated.

"I'll not tear it up," Elizabeth told him dryly, "if that's what you're afraid of."

"I'm afraid of nothing," the soldier said stiffly.

"How unusual," Elizabeth murmured. Finally he handed over the parchment, eyeing her carefully as she quickly scanned it.

When she looked up her smile widened. "There's been a mistake."

"There's no mistake here," the lieutenant replied confidently.

"This document states that you are to confiscate the lands from the Earl of Lismore, by order of Her Majesty, and to hold them in trust for the lawful owner, the Duke of Exeter."

"So?" The man's voice was surly. If all the Irishmen around him had weapons, his men could be in serious trouble.

"I am the Dowager Duchess of Exeter," she told the soldier sharply. "And I am not accustomed to being spoken to in such a tone of voice!"

The lieutenant hesitated between anger and preservation of his rank. "If I gave offense, Your Grace, I am sorry. But Her Majesty's orders still stand."

"I quite agree," Elizabeth replied mildly. Hearing the angry murmur of Irish voices around her, her own voice rose louder. "And you are lucky to be able to discharge your duty so speedily."

It took the lieutenant a moment to put her words together. "What are you saying, Your Grace?"

"I'm saying that the duke is here. He already has possession of his properties."

Harry stepped forward, reaching for the parchment which his mother was handing toward him before the lieutenant could stop him.

"I have orders to confiscate this land!" the soldier told them.

"No, you don't," Harry replied. "You have orders to confiscate this land from the earl and to hand it over to the Duke of Exeter." He smiled tiredly at the thin English face beneath the stiff lieutenant's hat. "I am the duke." He watched the man's expression change. "The Fifth Duke of Exeter."

"That's impossible!" the lieutenant sputtered.

The press of unhappy Irishmen crowded closer at his words. A sergeant moved to his superior officer's side, speaking softly: "Sir, if this be true, we have no need to risk confrontation."

Elizabeth, the dowager duchess, still held the lieutenant's eye. He searched her expression, seeing the truth behind her gaze. He looked away from the small group on the wide stone porch, glancing around at the Irishmen who crowded close around.

"The duke of Exeter is in residence!" Elizabeth said more forcefully.

The lieutenant pulled his eyes away from the crowd. He glanced at Elizabeth and Harry, and then turned toward his men. "Stand down, men! Prepare to mount!"

Willingly, his men moved back, their firearms still in their hands, but pointed toward the ground now, away from the horde of men who stood in unmilitary rows between the Priory and the soldiers.

Paddy and MaryKate still knelt beside their fallen brother, as the soldiers hoisted themselves up into their saddles.

Elizabeth, Dowager Duchess of Exeter, walked back to Archie, reaching for the Murphy child.

MaryKate watched Johnny's closed eyes and silent mouth. He looked for all the world as if he were only asleep.

Paddy's voice broke: "It's over for him, MaryKate. It's all over. He's gone." And still she stared. "Stand up, stand up, girl. There's nothing you can do for him now."

Harry came up beside them, looking toward the quiet Irishmen all around. "Let's get him into the house."

"No!" Paddy's voice rang out. He straightened up, one hand to one knee as he pushed himself erect. He looked tired. "He wouldn't have wanted that. I'll take him where he belongs. I'll take him to his wife."

Men moved forward to help, muttering agreement. Harry reached to draw MaryKate back from her brother's corpse, his hands on her shoulders, drawing her up, away from the heavy body that lay crumpled against the cobblestones. "He meant well." Her heart broke as she spoke the words. "He meant well," she repeated.

"Meaning well isn't enough," Harry told her softly. "Come away, come away, Mary-Kathleen."

MaryKate spoke softly: "Somebody has to tell Sophie."

Harry led MaryKate to the porch toward where Elizabeth stood, watching. Harry stared into his mother's amber eyes. "We owe you gratitude," MaryKate told the dowager duchess sincerely. "I owe you gratitude."

"I did no more than was necessary," Elizabeth replied.

Harry looked somber as he helped MaryKate toward the

KATHLEEN

house. When they reached the wide stone porch, he looked back toward the silent Irishmen.

"Thank you," he told them sincerely. "I shall never forget what you tried to do for me. For all of us."

There was a long awkward silence that met his words and then several of the men began to speak at once, denying any special distinction, making a joke of what could have ended in tragedy for them all.

"Thank you," Harry said again, simply. He looked from one to another. His gaze stopped at Paddy. Handing MaryKate over to the dowager duchess, he turned back toward MaryKate's only living brother.

Paddy was lifting his dead brother to the saddle of a horse Young Tim had brought near. He stopped when he saw the English duke.

"We've no right to the horse," Paddy began defensively, but Harry stopped him with an upraised hand.

"You can have any bloody horse in the stable," Harry told MaryKate's brother, his eyes bleak. "I'd give anything I could to change what's happened here today," Harry said.

Paddy looked down. And then back up to face the Englishman. "Yes. Well, so would we all."

"I want to help," Harry said. "The family," he added.

"There's little enough that can be done now. What with a lawbreaker dead and a fugitive in the family," Paddy spoke matter-of-factly.

"There's America," Harry suggested.

Paddy started to reply and then stopped, watching the man who faced him, trying to gauge his intentions. "America's for those who have the passage to her," Paddy told Harry.

"You have passage to America," Harry said flatly. "There's no future for you here—not with all this to answer for. In America there's a new life to be had for the asking. And hard work."

"I've never said no to hard work," Paddy replied.

"Then you'll do well in the new country."

"But my family—"

"Your family will go with you." Harry saw Paddy hesitate and spoke into the silence. "As many as want to go, I shall pay their way."

313

Patrick O'Hallion gazed into the English lord's eyes. "Why?" he asked. The single word hung between them.

Harry took his time. "I want to," Harry replied finally. "I need to." His direct gaze met the Irishman's. "What has happened here is not your brother's fault. Or, if it is, it's not only your brother's fault."

Paddy thought about it. He watched the man Johnny had called an enemy. "No," Paddy said softly, "it's not only Johnny's fault—although it's full well his as much as many others."

There was an awkward moment of closeness between the two men. "I'll tell them what you've offered. A passage to America and all." Paddy watched Harry nod and turn, starting away, toward the main house. "And what of MaryKate, then?" Paddy called out.

Harry stopped and turned back to see Paddy staring at him.

"What of my sister, then?" Paddy asked again.

"She must do as she wishes." Harry felt a stricture round his heart, squeezing it painfully. "Whatever she wishes," he added before turning away.

Paddy watched the English duke walk through the old stone doorway, watched the great oak door close between them. He then turned back to help lift his fallen brother to the horse Young Tim brought forward.

Harry walked into the house to find his mother arguing with MaryKate. "You can't leave now, you're needed here!" Elizabeth was saying.

Both of them saw Harry in the same instant. Elizabeth came forward, the baby still in her arms. "Henry, you must reason with this girl!"

Harry looked past Elizabeth to where MaryKate was standing. "And what's this about?" he asked.

"I have to see to my family," MaryKate said. "Sophie and the children need me."

"Of course," Harry replied.

MaryKate, prepared to fight, took a moment to register what he had said. Then: "You mean it's all right?"

"If you go to your family? I would expect nothing less of you."

KATHLEEN

"Henry"—Elizabeth took a step nearer, laying one delicate hand on his arm—"this girl is a servant. In your employ. And, as such, is required to do her duty."

Harry stiffened. "You are wrong, madame," he told his mother. "This 'girl' is neither a servant, nor is she in my 'employ.' Her duties, such as they were, ceased when Amelia died. Any help she's given past that point is as a favor. It is neither paid for nor expected."

MaryKate watched Harry's countenance, trying to read it. "Thank you," she said quietly.

"There's no need to thank me," he told her. "My late wife hired you to perform various functions, which you have done admirably. You are of course welcome to continue nursing the annex patients if you so desire, and we can come to some kind of a financial arrangement. If you wish."

Elizabeth watched the girl try to read Harry's face, watched her turn away, casting one quick, furtive look toward Harry's mother.

"I'd best leave," MaryKate said. "I'll see to my family, and then I shall come back to help in the annex."

"Don't feel you must. There are others."

MaryKate watched Harry. "Would you rather someone else came to help?"

Harry stared at her, his eyes bleak. "Your brother's death is to some extent on my conscience. I cannot ask more of you. You have done your duty. To my wife. And to me."

MaryKate stared into dark eyes that were closed off. He had shut a door between them. He looked every inch a lord. A duke. A peer of the realm. He looked English.

MaryKate turned away. She walked to the door Wallace opened for her. Thanking him, her soft voice stabbed back across the hard marble hallway to where Harry stood, his back to her, listening to the sounds of her leaving.

When the door closed between them, he saw his mother staring at him. "You fool. I tried to help." Then she turned and walked into the library.

Harry looked down at his own booted feet. He felt the fool. And he did not know why. He wasn't even sure he wanted to know why.

Whatever he felt for MaryKate brought too much pain

along with it. He didn't want to acknowledge it. Didn't want to feel it. And so he thrust it away, determined to ignore it.

Outside MaryKate and Pugs caught up with Paddy and the horse that held the remains of her oldest brother. Paddy glanced at the tears that had dried down her cheeks and then looked ahead, down Priory Road. "So, you're back with the family, then."

"There's no place else I'm needed," she told him. Her voice was filled with the pain of accepting harsh reality. "I've been living in a dream."

"We have to tell Sophie," Paddy replied.

But Sophie already knew. MaryKate could tell when they walked into the cottage. Sophie turned, slowly, from the fireplace where she was boiling the last of the oats the Priory cook had sent down. She searched MaryKate's face and then looked past her sister-in-law to Paddy.

Then she looked down. "It's bad news, then," she said.

MaryKate came quickly forward. "It's not good, Sophie."

"I didn't think it could be," Sophie said. "Brian came running in, grabbing Ally and the wee ones and running out again without a word."

As Sophie spoke, her mother appeared in the doorway between the main room and the front bedroom. She stopped when she saw MaryKate and Paddy. "It's bad," the old woman said. There was no question in her tone. She coughed until MaryKate thought the old woman's lungs would burst.

"It's bad," Paddy confirmed. Then he looked toward Sophie. "Johnny's dead."

Sophie folded in upon herself. MaryKate moved quickly to break her fall, the two of them ending up in a heap on the clean-swept dirt floor of the small cabin as Sophie's mother grabbed the doorjamb, turning back to her bed.

MaryKate cradled Sophie close. "Let it be. It's all right, just let it be . . . let it be."

MaryKate repeated the simple words as Sophie's grief keened louder and louder into the cold night air.

Sophie sank to a three-legged stool by the fireplace, Paddy

coming near to hover above his sister and his sister-in-law, trying to help.

Betsy, young Johnny, and the rest of Sophie's children hovered together, hunkered down, near the fireplace, staring at their mother's grief with wide-eyed fear. Pugs padded over to them, flopping by Betsy's feet.

"What am I to do? What am I to do?" Sophie rocked back and forth, MaryKate holding her tight.

"It's going to be all right," Paddy tried to tell her.

"All right?!" Sophie's sobs punctuated the words.

"Shhh," MaryKate whispered. "We're here, we're all here. You're not alone."

Sophie grabbed MaryKate's hand, holding it tight. "You'll stay with me now?"

MaryKate answered quietly, "I'll stay."

Sophie looked with tear-filled eyes toward her children. "And what's to become of my wee ones now?"

"They'll be fine," MaryKate told her.

"America has all kinds of opportunities," Paddy said quietly. "We'll all do well."

"America?!" Sophie stared at Patrick.

"The Englishman's paying our way." Patrick looked pointedly at MaryKate. "*All* our ways."

"All our ways?" Sophie repeated, grabbing MaryKate's hand tighter. "America," Sophie said again.

"The sooner the better," Patrick told them.

"We can't leave until the funerals," MaryKate said.

"Yes, well, that shouldn't be long." Paddy saw Betsy's drawn face across the room. "Come to Uncle Pat, wee one." He reached out his arms, and Betsy ran toward them.

Folding her close he looked past her auburn curls toward her Aunt Kate. "We'll pay our last respects and then be off. Before any can stop us."

"None will stop us," MaryKate told him.

"Are you sure?"

"Yes."

"There's always the authorities," he told her. "And then there's you, yourself."

"No!" Sophie broke into their conversation. "MaryKate promised she'd stay with us! We need you!"

317

MaryKate rubbed Sophie's shoulders. "I know. I know. I'm here."

"And you'll stay."

"I'll stay," MaryKate said slowly.

Sophie stood up. "I'd better see to mum."

"Do you need help?" MaryKate asked.

"No, you've done enough up at the Priory. Mum'll be all right. She caught it nursing Meg back to health. I'll tell her about America. That will cheer her up."

MaryKate stood up. "I'd better take a look."

"Are you sure?"

MaryKate tried to smile. "I've done as much for strangers. I can do it for family."

32

JOHNNY'S FUNERAL was the next day, the same day as Lady Amelia's. Much to everyone's surprise, Father Ross officiated at both.

Harry would not let the Right Reverend Grinstead near Lady Amelia's corpse. There was talk, but all of it in whispers, that quickly stopped when Harry came near.

Crowds and crowds of people huddled near each other in the cemetery, many of them gaunt and hollow-eyed as they watched Johnny's casket being lowered into the winter-cold ground. All of them silent when the new duke came near.

Father Ross, hesitant at first with the sight of the English constabulary close to the gravesite, waxed eloquent as he warmed to the subject of Johnny's best points.

Harry stood a little apart, his expression somber.

MaryKate and Sophie both saw Harry at almost the same moment, MaryKate looking quickly away. When she looked back, he was gone.

Fingers of mist began to reach out across the valley, darkening the pale sunlight, leaving the land beneath gloomy and cold.

Lady Amelia's casket was lowered into the ground soon

KATHLEEN

after Johnny O'Hallion's. Crowds of Irish men and women came up the Priory hillside, crossing themselves and muttering their own silent prayers over Protestant and Catholic alike.

Harry stood alone, those who came to pay their last respects to Lady Amelia shying away from the silent man who stood nearest her grave.

MaryKate and Sophie stood with the children in the midst of other tenants. Sophie watched MaryKate gaze toward the tall man who stood alone and unspeaking, at the foot of his wife's grave. He looked stoical, his thoughts far away from the crowds around him.

Harry stared at the ground, thinking through the distant past to when he first met Amelia, to all the years that had led to the moment when he first laid eyes on Hugh Grinstead. And Johnny O'Hallion. And the cottage that now stood empty, the family gathered around the gravesite, the O'Hallion children drooping close to their black-garbed mother.

In Ireland Sophie would forevermore wear black. In her prime, her life still ahead of her, all would be forfeited to a grief she had no need of, a grief she did not deserve. There was no leeway and little pity in Ireland for the wives that were left behind.

Harry's eyes closed. He prayed to a God he wasn't sure existed to have pity on them all.

MaryKate saw Harry's eyes close. Her heart wrenched within her, and she moved away from her sister-in-law, never seeing the hand Sophie raised and then, slowly, dropped. MaryKate reached Harry's side. She reached for his hand, people nearby staring at them. His eyes opened, surprised to see her next to him. He tried to read her expression. "I'm all right," he told her.

"Are you?" she asked gently, earning a small smile.

Rain began to drizzle down from low-hanging clouds, the mourners scurrying for shelter.

Harry walked with MaryKate toward the cover of the side porch as Archie approached them. "There are people waiting in the front parlor," Archie said. "Government people," he added, seeing MaryKate's eyes widen. "I thought you should know."

KATHLEEN

Harry nodded. "I'll be there directly."

"I'd best be going, Your Grace," MaryKate said.

"Don't call me that!"

"That's who you are," MaryKate said quietly. MaryKate turned to see Elizabeth, the dowager duchess of Exeter, walking toward her as Harry went toward the parlor and the government men.

Elizabeth stopped in front of MaryKate, searching her face. "Are you back, then?"

"No, Your Grace. I came to pay my respects. And to say good-bye."

"Good-bye?" the dowager duchess asked the young Irish woman. "Good, because you would ruin him."

MaryKate blanched, feeling her heart constrict as the English woman's words reverberated inside her.

"I'm sorry, but it's the truth. Queen Victoria is in Dublin. Henry must make peace with her or stand to forfeit everything his family has—land, fortune and all. He can hardly be consorting with relatives of rebels."

"And does the queen think all her Irish subjects are the enemy?!" MaryKate demanded.

"Aren't they?" Elizabeth asked quietly.

MaryKate took her time answering. "If they are, it's none's fault but the Crown itself."

"Perhaps you should tell her so," Elizabeth challenged.

"Perhaps I should," Mary-Kathleen replied.

"If you do, think of my son. You'll not be helping his cause."

MaryKate spoke quietly, "I'll not hurt him."

"Good," Elizabeth replied. "He's been hurt enough, thanks to all of us. Myself included."

"I would never hurt him," MaryKate said.

"His entire future depends upon what you do now," Elizabeth said. She watched the Irish girl walk away.

Her son found her there a few minutes later. Alone. "What did you say to her?" he demanded.

"I think we should talk in more privacy," the dowager duchess told the new duke.

"I don't," he said curtly. "Whatever you said, Mary-Kathleen has gone."

"Hadn't she left already?" Elizabeth asked her son.

321

KATHLEEN

While he stared at Elizabeth, the last of the tenants and villagers were huddled under the stable overhangs, a cold rain pouring down all around them.

Elizabeth kept to her rooms for the next few days. Then, almost a week later, things changed. She called for dinner, as usual, in her rooms. Archie brought it himself. He stood in the doorway, hesitating, looking as if he wanted to say something. But in the end he left without a word. Elizabeth picked at her food, fingering a book, unable to concentrate upon it.

Later the sounds of revelry wafting up the great stone staircase woke her. Still in the fireside chair, still dressed, she stood up slowly, thinking she had dreamt the sounds. She began to ready herself for bed when laughter again filled her rooms. She was in her nightgown when she could no longer stand the loud voices and laughter. Reaching for her robes, she swept out into the upper hallway, the sounds even louder. She marched down the wide steps toward the sounds of revelry.

At the bottom of the steps she saw Archie standing near a door halfway down the long hall. The little Welshman looked toward her and then moved away from the closed door. When he reached the green baise door to the kitchens he looked back once, then disappeared down the back hall.

Flinging the doors to the billiard room open, she stood in the empty space between the doors, staring down the small group of English noblemen who turned to face her. Men who were ready to turn the queen against him now sat at his table. Drinking his port and playing billiards.

A hush descended upon the happy males, Elizabeth's eyes raking across the assembled group, lighting finally upon her son. "I need to speak to you," she told Harry.

He looked toward her, draining his glass, and reached for a decanter to refill it. "Yes?"

"Alone," she told him distinctly.

Harry took his time. He poured more port, but did not drink it. He picked up his billiard cue, but then threw it down, walking across the room toward and then past his mother. When he reached the hall, he waited for her. The

KATHLEEN

sounds of small caustic comments followed him, his friends urging him not to let her think she could order him about.

"Well?" he asked, his tone noncommittal.

"Not here." She walked toward him, closing the doors to the game room. Not waiting for a response, she headed toward a small back parlor.

Harry watched her and then slowly followed.

The tiny parlor was dark and cold. Elizabeth bent to light a lamp, Harry standing silhouetted in the doorway.

He came forward, reaching for the lamp, helping her.

"Queen Victoria is in Dublin," his mother began.

"Yes." He sounded disinterested. "You've already said."

"I received word from my Dublin solicitors regarding business I had there, and he mentioned the queen is already there—she will be in residence all month."

"So?"

"So you must go to her," Elizabeth said.

"Why?" Harry asked.

"Why?! How can you even ask?! To explain to her what all has happened!"

"It's not important."

Elizabeth heard the listlessness in his tone, saw his complete disinterest. "How can you say that? You could lose all."

"I've already lost all," he replied simply.

She searched her son's eyes. "Perhaps I understand," she told him, "more than you realize."

"Do you?" Harry asked. "Perhaps you do." But he still moved away from her. The alcohol in his system was already wearing off. The dullness it had allowed him for an hour was departing with it, leaving his nerves raw with pain and longing. "Was it worth it?" he asked his mother from across the room. He reached for the heavy velvet drapes, taking the dark green cloth in his hands and pulling it free of the braided ropes that held it closed.

Moonlight streamed in toward him, casting an eerie, stark light across his features. Behind him the gas lamp bathed his mother in its softer, golden glow. The rest of the small room was in deep shadows around them. His voice rose: "Was it worth it?"

"Yes," she replied quietly.

It took him a minute to digest her answer. "Would you do it all again?" he asked.

Elizabeth heard the pain under his words. She hesitated, and Harry turned back to see her face as she replied: "I did not choose it, Henry. I had no choices. My marriage was an arrangement between families—much as yours was. I met a man I could love. I didn't intend to, anymore than you have." She watched his expression change. "I did not want to leave you. But your father would allow nothing else." She watched her son. "I didn't really answer you, did I? Would I do it all again? Would I fall in love again? Yes. God forgive me, I would rather not live than live without knowing what love can be. I was not wrong about that."

"Perhaps Amelia would have agreed with you," Harry said.

"Amelia had her own problems, which she obviously did not allow you to help her with."

"How do you know that?" he demanded.

"I now know you," she told him simply. The dowager duchess reached out toward her son, walking toward the window, her eyes never leaving his. "I was wrong about part of it, Henry. I should never have left you behind."

"It's long past," Harry said curtly.

"Your father convinced me you would be better off with him. With wealth. And training for your station in life. I can see it was not enough. You needed love, too, Harry."

Harry heard a warmth in her tone that had not been there before. He heard her call him Harry.

"It's not important now," he said finally.

"Yes, it is. For we taught you to shut your feelings out. And you can't do it. You have too much of me in you."

"I can try," he said.

"Perhaps I was wrong about something else, too," Elizabeth told her son. "Perhaps you should go to her and bring her back. You may lose your inheritance, but that inheritance has not made you happy thus far. If you keep it and lose the one you care about—will it be enough? Will it be worth it?" When Harry didn't reply, she continued, "If you go to her and tell her the truth, you'll find out if she cares enough about you to accept you alone, without an inheritance, if necessary."

"And then?" he demanded.

"And then, if she will, you must face whatever life brings."

"Whatever life brings," Harry repeated slowly.

She watched him closely. He started to reach toward her, something stopping him before his hand reached hers. He let his arm fall back to his side. "Thank you," he said before he left the room.

Elizabeth sighed, listening to the sounds of the men in the rooms beyond, hearing Harry tell them it was time to leave.

When she went upstairs they were outside, calling for carriages and awakening Young Tim and their own grooms.

33

Harry urged Young Tim to hurry with the saddle. Or to get out of the way so Harry could saddle the black himself.

The boy yawned, rubbing his sleepy eyes and watching the duke finish saddling the black himself. The last of the duke's guests were clattering down the Priory Road. Walking into the stable, Archie demanded, "And where do you think you're going this time?!"

"I'm going to get her and bring her back."

"You're crazed. You've told me all week this was the only way. Now you change your mind."

"Yes," Harry said as he mounted the stallion.

"You'll wake them all!" Archie hollered. But Harry was already urging the horse across the cobblestones, letting the stallion have his head as he raced past the departing carriages, across the high fields, toward the river meadows below and the road to the O'Hallion cottage.

The fields were hung with mists, silvery when the moon came out from behind high clouds. Harry rode through the Irish night, the land silent around his horse.

Blighted fields awash with blackened, withered plants

surrounded the river meadows that were picked clean of green shoots, the poor eating every weed they could find.

It was a sad land, saddened by too much hardship and hunger, too little hope. Harry felt the sadness that permeated even the soft night air around him as he rode toward the O'Hallion cottage. And yet his heart raced with joy at the thought of seeing MaryKate.

Of bringing her back. She belonged with him.

No matter the cost.

The O'Hallion cottage was dark when he tethered the stallion to the narrow gate. He strode toward the door and raised his hand to knock, then hesitated, thinking of the children he would be waking. Thinking of waiting until morning. He couldn't. He had waited too long already. He knocked. And knocked. And knocked again.

There was no answer.

Silence, complete and empty, met his fist as he pounded harder on the door. "MaryKate—Mary-Kathleen!" he called out, willing to wake the entire family and the countryside beyond.

Frustrated, he turned the knob. The door opened, creaking on its rusty hinges. He stepped into a black hole of a room, his eyes taking a moment to adjust to the change in light.

After a moment the few rays of moonlight that fell through the tiny windows gave off enough light for him to look around himself.

The fireplace was stone cold, the room echoing as he called out her name.

Cold fear hit the pit of his stomach. He reached for the bedroom door, wrenching it open. No one was inside. The cottage was empty.

Anger mixed with fear and tiredness, spurring him on. He left the cottage and strode toward his horse. Mounting quickly, he rode down the narrow path, clattering up to the next nearest cottage and pounding on the door until an old man opened it. The man stared, bleary-eyed, at Harry.

"And who do think you are to be waking up honest, God-fearing—oh! . . ." He trailed off, recognizing the duke.

KATHLEEN

"Where are they? Where are the O'Hallions?" Harry demanded.

"Why, they've gone to America," the old man told him. "It's you, yourself, who's paying their ways, isn't it?"

Harry looked grim. "They've already gone?!"

"Yes. It's for Dublin they were bound, and the ship for America."

"Dublin," Harry repeated. He turned away, moving toward his horse. The old man closed the door, his wife looking up from their narrow bed.

"And what was that all about, then?" she asked her husband sleepily.

"For sure, all the English are crazed," the old man replied. "Himself, it was, who gave them the money to go!"

"Come back to bed," she told him, turning over. She was asleep when the old man finally made his way back to their bed.

Harry arrived back at the Priory to find Archie waiting for him. "She's gone," Harry told him. "MaryKate—Kathleen—is gone."

"Gone?" Archie stared.

Harry looked grim. "At first light we leave for Dublin."

"Dublin? To see the queen?"

"To stop MaryKate," Harry said and started away.

Archie followed him into the house. "And what if she doesn't want to be stopped?"

"She'll have to tell me that herself."

Elizabeth came to the door of her rooms when she heard her son's voice. "What's wrong?"

"She's gone to Dublin with the rest of them."

Elizabeth watched her son. "When do we leave?"

"I leave at first light."

"I'll be ready," she told her son.

"There's no need," he began, but she stopped him.

"Yes, there is need. You can't go to Dublin and not see the queen. I'll not slow you down, if that's your worry. I shall be ready as soon as you are."

He hesitated. And then spoke in a quieter tone. "Thank you."

"Don't thank me yet," she warned him.

328

KATHLEEN

"She has to come back," Harry said.
"And if she doesn't want to?"
"She has to want to."

They were on the road by seven that morning, Harry and Archie riding ahead of the carriage that held Elizabeth and their clothing. "Did you get the message to the priest?" Harry demanded of Archie.

"Aye, and he's as confused as I am. But he's waiting for you."

"Good."

He didn't speak again until they reined in at the Catholic church, Elizabeth leaning out to ask what was happening.

"I don't know," Archie told her. Harry was already inside the rectory, meeting the priest's startled gaze.

"You want what?" Brian Ross had Harry repeat himself.

"I want you to come with me to Dublin."

"But I can't, my parish—"

"I'll send you back in the carriage immediately. I'll give you anything you ask, but you must come and you must come now."

"What on God's green earth is going on?" Father Ross asked the Englishman.

"It would take too long to explain, but if you care for MaryKate, you'll come."

"Well and it will take you some time to be explaining just exactly that, Your Grace!"

"I want you to marry us," Harry told the rotund priest, who gave him a blank stare. "Me and MaryKate. If she'll have me."

Brian Ross finally found his voice. "You want me to—but you're not Catholic! Marry who?"

"We can talk on the way," Harry replied.

But they did not talk on the way. Father Ross found himself hustled to his room for a change of clothing, his housekeeper protesting all the way out the door as the old priest was bundled into the carriage across from the dowager duchess.

Harry was already on his way, Archie hard put to keep up as the carriage began to trundle toward Dublin behind them.

KATHLEEN

Brian Ross found himself staring at the duke's mother.

"Do you approve of what's going on, then?" he asked.

Elizabeth gave him a small smile. "Do you think it would matter whether I did or did not? Or any else? He was headstrong as a child. I see he hasn't changed."

Brian Ross shook his head. "I've never heard of the like. He's not even Roman Catholic—I don't know if it's even legal."

The Irish priest stared out at the countryside they were racing across as Young Tim whipped the horses faster, trying to keep Harry and Archie within view down the road.

They stopped only long enough to water the horses, to get a bite to eat, and to close their eyes for a few hours and then they were on their way again. Harry stopped at the public houses along the route, asking after the Dublin coaches, overtaking one they weren't on.

"There's a ship bound for America that leaves from Shannon next month," Archie said when they next stopped. "Do you think they went that way? It's closer."

"They'd not stay in Shannon for a month," Harry reasoned, hoping against hope he was right.

"You gave her brother carte blanche, right? He could use that to feed them until the ship came."

"She's gone to Dublin," Harry said.

"And if she's not?" Archie asked.

"Then I'll follow her to America," Harry told the Welshman.

Archie stared at the man he'd known since Harry had been in knickers. "I believe you would," Archie said.

They arrived in the outskirts of Dublin a day later, the clock just gone two in the afternoon. Elizabeth called out to her son, who rode back beside the carriage. "You can go on to the harbor if you like. Father Ross and I can make our way to Exeter House to wait for you."

"I sold Exeter House to pay for food and seed and all the medical supplies."

"I know," Elizabeth told him. "I bought it."

Harry stared at her. "I beg your pardon?"

"I had just arrived in Dublin when your orders came

through. Since you did not know of your father's death, I thought it simpler to buy it back, through my solicitor, than to explain long distance. I wanted to tell you myself about your father. And the fact that you had access to the entire fortune."

"You bought it?" he repeated.

"For you," she told him, smiling a little. "You can pay me back when you like."

"I'm not sure I even know how to repay you," he told her sincerely.

"Be happy," she said softly.

He looked away, a lump rising in his throat. He nodded, urging the black forward toward the harbor.

"I'll see you at home!" she called out after him. Elizabeth met the priest's eyes.

"They'll have to be raised Roman," Father Ross said. "The children," he added, seeing she did not follow him.

Elizabeth smiled. "If those two get together, I assure you I shall agree to their being raised anything that girl wants." She called out to Tim to turn down a side road, directing him toward Exeter Square and the great stone house that filled one end of it.

Dublin's docks were as busy as they'd been when Harry first saw them, months ago. Archie reined in beside him. "How are you going to find anyone in a place like this?"

"First we find the ship for America. Then we talk to the captain." Harry was already striding toward a nearby sailor. Archie watched them talk and saw the man point off across the docks.

They made their way to the ship the sailor directed them toward, Harry impatient with the crowds that slowed them down. Finally he dismounted, throwing the reins to Archie. "It'll be quicker to walk. I'll meet you at the bottom of the gangway!"

Archie threaded through the crowds of sailors and merchantmen, past towering piles of produce and grains. "It's a crime, this is," he muttered to himself, thinking of the dead and dying people all over Ireland, starving while all their food was shipped overseas.

* * *

KATHLEEN

Onboard the *Star of India,* Harry was shown to the captain's cabin.

"The captain will be right with you, Your Grace," the first mate told Harry, and then left him standing in the middle of the large cabin.

When the captain entered, Harry spun round toward him, his agitation apparent. "I need to find a family I am sponsoring to America."

"And you would be?"

"I am the Duke of Exeter."

"Oh!" The captain sprang to his feet. "I'm sorry, Your Grace. Would you care for something to drink or—"

"No," Harry spoke impatiently. "Just your records, Captain. I need to know if the O'Hallions are booked aboard your ship!"

"If they're leaving from Dublin this week, they're booked aboard." The man walked to his desk and opened a large log book, using his finger to page down the lines.

Harry came near, peering over the man's shoulder.

"I don't see the name, Your Grace. Could they be under another name?"

Harry thought of Sophie and her mother. "No. Well, some of them could, but I don't know the other name."

"There's a hotel at the end of the pier where some of the passengers for America are staying. They might know something there."

Harry hesitated. "If you hear of them, if they come aboard, send someone to Exeter House immediately. You will be well paid."

The captain smiled. "Of course, Your Grace. I'll watch for the name myself."

Archie saw Harry coming back alone. "And?" Archie asked.

Harry shook his head. "Would they be using another name?"

Archie shrugged. "They might, seeing as how their own isn't in good odor with the authorities."

"There's a hotel I have to check," Harry said grimly. Archie followed the duke, bringing the horses.

34

THE HOTEL WAS GRIMY, scores of families camped out in the lobby and the pub beside it. Children, dirty and half-clothed, huddled near their elders, their eyes wide as they watched the crowds around them.

Harry created a stir through the crowds, people drawing back away from the well-clad figure. Archie followed Harry, feeling the change in the listless people, hearing mumbled questions around them as men asked other men if they were the authorities. If there was to be a problem, they might not be allowed to leave for America.

Archie stayed close to Harry, who was oblivious to the sounds around him. The duke stopped at the front desk and spoke to the woman behind it.

"I'm looking for someone," he told her.

"We run a decent place here."

"A family known as O'Hallion. An old woman, two younger ones, a young man, and several children. Five children and one a babe in arms."

"I've not seen them," she said.

Harry leaned closer. "How would you know without looking? Look around you." His hand swept out toward the crowded floor. "There's ten that could fit that description that I can see from here!"

"A little quieter," Archie said. "You'll frighten them all and none will talk to us."

Harry hesitated. And then spoke to the woman. "It'll be worth your while to help."

She smiled then. "Oh, Your Lordship, in that case, I'm sure I can find something out. What did you say the name was now?"

They weren't there. It took Archie a long time to convince Harry they must go to the house. People were looking all over dockside for them. News would be sent to Exeter House. He wouldn't know they'd been found if he wasn't at home.

"You're not going to find them yourself," Archie told him over and over. Harry finally agreed, letting Archie lead him away, back toward the lovely green expanse of Exeter Square and the house he had thought was forfeited.

It was dinnertime when the butler announced a visitor. Harry was out of his chair and into the hall right behind the butler.

In the hall a constable stood, his hat in his hands. "Begging your pardon, Your Grace, but I understand you're looking for an Irish family named O'Hallion."

"Yes," Harry said.

"Well, now, there's a queen's warrant out for O'Hallion men, you see."

"Where are they?"

"Well, now, as I was saying, there's a Paddy O'Hallion we've picked up—if that's any help."

"*Where* is he, man?!" Harry thundered at the constable.

"Harry," Elizabeth said, coming up behind her son. "There is no need to be discourteous." She smiled at the startled man. "I'm sure the constable is more than ready to take you to them."

"To him, then," the constable said. "I don't know about the others."

"I'll follow you," Harry told the policeman.

"Visiting hours—"

334

KATHLEEN

"Damn and blast visiting hours!" Harry thundered. "I have to see the man immediately!"

Harry strode to the front door, the butler opening it a fraction of a second before Harry reached for it himself. He stopped on the steps outside, turning back to wait, impatiently, for the constable and Archie to catch up.

The constable told the sergeant behind the worn wood desk that His Lordship wished to see the prisoner, Patrick O'Hallion.

"*His Grace* wishes to see," Archie corrected the man, seeing the sergeant give him the once-over.

"It's against regulations," he began.

"Many things are," Harry said flatly.

"What is your relationship to the prisoner, Your Grace?" the sergeant asked.

"He is one of my tenants. What is he accused of?" Harry demanded.

"There's warrants out for all O'Hallion men."

"There are only two, unless you count small children," Harry told the man, staring him down. "John O'Hallion is dead and Patrick has committed no crimes."

"You're sure of that, Your Grace?"

"Yes, I am," Harry said flatly.

The sergeant hesitated. He was unused to having English nobility standing as character references for Irish peasants. "You want to see him?"

"I want to have him released into my care," Harry replied.

"That's up to the magistrate in the morning court."

"Get him here," Harry said.

"I can't do that."

"You can and you will. Or you will contact your superior officers until you find one that can." Harry loomed over the desk, the sergeant irritated but also intimidated by Harry's manner.

"I don't know what I can do," the sergeant told them all. But he went through a narrow door behind his desk, closing it firmly.

Archie looked around the dark walled room. "There's a

KATHLEEN

bench of sorts." He looked back at Harry. "This could take a while."

Harry was eyeing the constable who waited with them. "It had better not."

The sergeant was back within minutes, but it took three quarters of an hour to get the magistrate away from his dinner table long enough to explain the situation.

It took a moment more for him to stalk to his study and sign the parchment form, swearing all the while at the constable who stood waiting, miserably accepting the judge's ill temper.

Paddy walked through the narrow door behind the sergeant's desk, blinking a little as if he'd come from a darker place. He stopped when he saw Harry and Archie.

"We're here to take you home, lad," Archie said. "Or at least as far as Exeter House."

"Where are the others?" Harry asked.

"Outside, then, shall we?" Archie asked pointedly.

Harry, with bad grace, complied. He waited until they were all settled inside the carriage before he asked again.

"She doesn't want to see you," Paddy said.

"They have to eat. They have to have a roof over their heads until the ship sails," Archie put in quickly. "And if the police keep snapping you up, then where will they be? You won't know what's become of them. And what if they sail without you? Or worse yet, don't sail waiting for you."

Paddy hesitated. "She saved money, she said. We wouldn't need yours. But everything's so expensive in the city."

"Where is she?" Harry asked quietly this time.

"I'll show you," Paddy answered finally.

Paddy led them to a pub with rooms attached, three doors down from the hotel Harry had been sent to earlier.

People were huddled all over the place, poor people with the life gone from their eyes. Their clothing, what little they had, was threadbare and worn. The children's little arms and legs were no more than sticks in several of the family groups Harry and Archie waded through behind Paddy.

KATHLEEN

They ended up in a tiny hallway. Paddy knocked at a pocked door and opened it. The room was empty.

"What the hell!" Paddy stared at the empty room.

"Where *is* she?!" Harry demanded, grabbing Paddy by his worn coat lapels.

"Easy there," Archie said.

"I left them here!" Paddy was truly alarmed.

Unwillingly Harry released the Irishman, his hopes plummeting. "We have to find her."

A small dog's high-pitched bark intruded on his words, and then ran toward the English duke, barking happily, jumping up toward his doeskin-clad knees.

Harry glanced down and then grabbed at the dog, lifting him high. "Pugs! Where *is* she?!"

"Unless you've taught him English, you'll have to let him down to find out," Archie told his employer tartly.

Harry, unwillingly, let the dog go. "Show me, boy, show me where she is."

Pugs raced down the hall and scratched furiously on another door.

Sophie's mother opened the door, coughing. Tears welled up in her eyes when she saw Paddy. She reached up to hug him. "We were afraid you wouldn't find us after they moved us." Then she saw the others. "Saints preserve us. What's gone wrong now?"

Inside the room Pugs scampered toward MaryKate, who turned toward the door. "What is it?" She came nearer, seeing Harry at the same moment he saw her.

"MaryKate," he said as he took a step nearer.

"No." She stepped backward, going back to where Sophie was washing the children, a bowl of cold water and a damp rag her only tools.

"Come home with me," Harry said, ignoring the others who were crowded into the tiny room.

"There's no good talking about any of it," MaryKate replied.

"Marry me," he said.

Shock drew in Sophie and her mother's breath at the same precise moment. Paddy stared at the Englishman as if he'd gone insane. Archie sighed.

MaryKate did nothing. She stood as she had, one hand

holding Sarah's hair, the other holding the brush. She stood stock-still until Sarah asked why her aunt had stopped combing.

MaryKate looked down at the girl and began to methodically comb through her long fair hair.

No one spoke. Harry watched MaryKate, his eyes never leaving her face. Waiting.

"Well, now," Archie said into the silence, "is everything ready for this boat ride then?"

Sophie looked toward him. "As ready as we'll ever be," she told him, walking nearer the door, trying to ignore the tall English lord who dwarfed the rest of the people in the room. "Betsy, Johnny, come away, come away now."

"Where are you going?" MaryKate demanded.

"To get a little air."

"At this time of night?" MaryKate asked.

Sophie stared at her sister-in-law. "Mary-Kathleen O'Hallion, the rest of your life is at stake here. I suggest you listen to the man. I've asked a lot of you. Maybe more than I should."

"Don't be crazy!"

"I hope I'm not, but"—Sophie smiled a little—"I don't think I've ever seen you so scared before."

MaryKate turned away. "I'm not scared."

"Come along, then, the rest of you. So Aunt Kate can say her good-byes. Or whatever." Sophie shooed her children and her mother out the door. "Give them a bit of peace. Come along, Paddy?" Paddy hesitated and then followed. Archie was the last to leave.

Looking back he spoke before he closed the door: "Don't be talking all night, now; I didn't get me supper yet."

Harry stood where he was, waiting for MaryKate to turn toward him. When she did he saw tears glistening in her eyes. He reached toward her, but she stiffened at his touch. And then let him draw her near.

"You'll lose everything," MaryKate said.

"I may." Harry looked deep into her eyes. "Does that matter to you?"

"Of course it matters!"

Harry hesitated, afraid of what he might hear from her lips. "Tell me how it matters," he asked finally.

"You'll never forgive yourself for not doing your duty. I know you by now, Harry." She said his name again, softer, his lips coming down to stop her words.

His touch ignited something within her breast that warmed her and spread fire through her veins, her senses coming alive.

His lips were claiming hers, reason suspended somewhere far away from the reality of touch and taste. She tried to be sensible for the two of them, tried to tell him of his mother's words, but the words caught in her throat, his arms pressing her closer against the length of him.

"We mustn't," she said when she could finally catch her breath. "You can't do this."

"Why? Why can't I?"

"You are an English duke."

"Yes. I am. And as an English duke I can do anything I wish."

"And the queen?" MaryKate asked.

Harry hesitated. He held her at arm's length, studying her. "I may lose all—we could easily become paupers. You should know this now." He watched her expression slowly change. Astounded when she began to smile. "Are you aware of what I'm saying?"

"You're saying you want me."

"I'm saying I want to marry you. If you'll have me."

She lost her smile. "You'll lose everything you have, won't you?"

"You said that didn't matter," he reminded her.

"It doesn't to me. But you've no understanding of what it's like to be poor. It will matter to you."

"Not if I have you," he told her. "I've lived without love. Living without wealth is much easier; however, I have no right to ask you to share a life that may be destitute."

"Oh, Harry, we'll never be destitute, not if we have each other."

"Is that yes? Will you stay with me? Will you marry me?"

Her eyes were shining. "Say that again, please?"

"Will you marry me? Will you be my duchess, if only for a day?"

KATHLEEN

"Yes, oh, yes!" She laughed joyously. "An Irish duchess! Even for one day, that will be a memory!"

"And then?" he asked her. "And then will you be content with just plain Harry Hanover?"

She spoke slowly, "I love just plain Harry Hanover."

"Oh, Kathleen, Mary's Kathleen." He pulled her closer.

They held each other, content just to be close in each other's arms.

Archie had the common sense to knock before he stuck his head in the door. "I hate to spoil your conversation, but there's a little matter of tired kiddies out here. And an audience with the queen in the morning, Your Grace."

Harry released MaryKate. "We'll all go back to the house tonight. Your family can't very well stay here."

Sophie heard his words. "Oh, we couldn't!" She was dumbstruck.

"Now's not the time to try to reason with him," Archie told Sophie pragmatically. "He's not listening. Neither of them is." Archie looked back to where MaryKate and Harry stared at each other.

"I'd best help with the children," she told Harry. "You might as well, too," she added. Seeing his startled expression, she smiled softly, handing him one tired child as Sophie brought them back in. "Come along, then, we'll get some proper tea in a little while."

Archie stared at the duke of Exeter, a sleeping child in his arms. Archie grinned at Harry's grimace. "All right, all right, let's get to it, then." They started toward the lower reaches of the two-story building as Archie ran on ahead.

"Archie, where are you going?!" Harry called out. "You can help, too."

"I am helping. They'll never all fit in the one carriage!" Archie turned back to grin toward Harry. "Your Grace has a *much* bigger family now."

"I don't know why I put up with you," Harry grumbled, the child stirring in his arms.

"Nor I you," Archie replied complacently.

"Is he all right?" Sophie asked Harry.

"What?" Harry stared at the woman. "The child?" Harry

340

KATHLEEN

looked down at the babe he held. "Yes." He looked back toward the mother.

"He'll do fine," MaryKate told her sister-in-law.

They arrived back at Exeter House to find the dowager duchess waiting up for them, her concern turning to shock when through the front door trooped a motley assortment of Irish women and children.

The butler looked from one to the next, and then to the young thin woman who came toward him. "If you'll show them to a room, we'll get the children to sleep. Then I'll make us some tea," MaryKate told the man.

He looked quickly over at the new duke. And then at Elizabeth. "I shall see to your tea, miss," the butler told MaryKate when he found his voice. "This way, please," he said to them all, starting for the stairwell, a tired group of bedraggled-looking children helped up the steps by mother, grandmother, and aunt. And a very proper butler.

Elizabeth saw her son watching MaryKate climb the stairs. "Have you adopted them all?"

"And if I have?" he responded defensively.

The dowager duchess shrugged delicately. "Perhaps you should take them to see the queen. All of them."

Harry stared at the mother he barely knew. "Are you being facetious?"

His mother spoke calmly, "The queen is very much a family person. She loves children. You might do your cause great good by bringing the family to her. At this point they are merely a name. A name attached to rebellion. She might see herself that such is not the entire case. But before you see her, I suggest you make your situation legal."

"Legal?" Harry asked.

"Our little queen is a wonderful lady, but she is very particular about morals. She likes people to be married before they even kiss."

Harry stared at his mother. And then, slowly, grinned. "She must have had a few things to say to you."

"Many," Elizabeth said, smiling back at her son, "which is one of the reasons she'll have no patience with my son."

Harry thought about what she had said. "What would you suggest?"

341

KATHLEEN

"I'd suggest you wake the Irish priest and tell him you need a ceremony before you bed her tonight."

"Mother!" Harry's shocked tones resounded around the room.

"He's retired to his room for the night, but I'm sure all the commotion above has kept him awake," she said blandly. "And then again, after all, he *is* responsible for her soul, is he not?" Elizabeth looked innocently at her son.

Harry, for the second time in the last few minutes, and the second time in his life, grinned at his mother.

The sight warmed her heart.

The children's high-pitched querulous voices chattered away up above them. Harry's gaze drifted toward the ceiling. "It sounds good, doesn't it . . . children's voices in the house."

His mother spoke softly. "Perhaps you will soon have your own."

"I'm not sure I would be a good father."

"Or perhaps you will be the very best of fathers. Having known the lack of love." Elizabeth looked down and then reached out, almost blindly. "Please listen to me, Harry. I have no right to speak, but I am your mother and I must try. Even this late. Your father loved you as much as he was capable of loving anyone. He wanted the best for you, which is why he kept you close. He wanted you safe, and he felt you were safer with him."

"And was I?"

"Probably," she told him.

"Where is your . . . paramour?"

Elizabeth took a moment before she answered. "His name was William. He was a good man, caught in a bad situation, Harry. He never willingly hurt anyone in his entire life. He died five years ago."

"Five years—and you never came back."

"No. I did not feel I had the right," Elizabeth said quietly.

Harry sighed. "Perhaps none of us ever has the right to do anything. Perhaps we must simply do what we feel and hope someone responds."

Sudden tears glittered in Elizabeth's eyes. "You are a son anyone would be proud of."

Harry turned away. "Hardly."

KATHLEEN

"I had them hold dinner for you," Elizabeth said after a moment.

"I'll have something as soon as MaryKate comes down."

"She'll not run away this time," Elizabeth said. "Harry, you don't have to worry. At least not about that." She watched Harry start away. "Where are you going?"

"To wake the priest," he replied.

The dowager duchess smiled, watching her son until he was out of sight. Then she rang for a maid. "Port," she said, when the girl came in, stifling a yawn.

"Port, Your Grace?" The maid was surprised.

"Port," Elizabeth said. "And lots of it, please. This is going to be a long and arduous night."

35

"I DON'T UNDERSTAND," Father Ross told Harry. He drew his nightshirt closer, hugging his sides in the chill night air. The fire in the guest room grate had gone to embers, the night winds outside seeping coldness through the walls. "You have to be married tonight because you're seeing the queen on the morrow?"

"Precisely," Harry replied. "Get dressed."

Harry started out. The old priest was still shaking his head when Archie looked in. "Need anything gotten ready?" Archie asked.

"Is there insanity in his family?" Brian Ross asked.

Archie grinned. "Depends on your definition," he said, and closed the door.

Sophie's mother was wondering the same thing in the room the liveried butler left her in. The old woman looked from her daughter to MaryKate. Young John was holding the baby, rocking him to sleep. His eyes, large and somber, followed the conversation.

"Does anyone here understand what is happening, then?" the old woman demanded.

KATHLEEN

"Mother, it's not our business," Sophie said.

"I think it's daft," Paddy told MaryKate flatly. "I'll not stand in your way, but I think it's daft."

"I have something to say," Young John spoke up, his voice thin with youthful soprano. He saw the adults look toward him, surprised. Young John rarely spoke. "What you're all talking about. Does it hurt my mother?" There was no immediate answer, the adults still staring at him. "I'm the man of the family now, what with my father gone." He couldn't bring himself to say dead. "I'm responsible for my mother and the small ones."

"Your uncle is here to help, too," Sophie said quickly.

But Paddy was smiling. He walked toward the boy. "Yes. You are. And we need your help. All of us."

Young John stood taller, the baby still in his arms.

"It's not to do with your mother, boy," his grandmother told him. She looked toward MaryKate. "But it will never work."

Mary-Kathleen turned away from the old woman's dark eyes. And then turned back, staring directly into her unforgiving gaze. "You may be right."

"Well, then," the old woman said.

MaryKate spoke gently: "It doesn't matter."

The old woman shook her head impatiently. We've all been young, once, haven't we?! I'm trying to save you from disgrace and worse. These people aren't our own—they'll never accept you. Not really. And then what? What of when he's grown tired of you?! What then?"

Sophie shook her head at her mother, trying to get her to stop. "He wants to marry her, Ma."

"So he says. I'm wise to the ways of the world," the old woman said ominously.

"Ma, stop it!" Sophie spoke harshly, looking quickly toward Mary-Kathleen. "It's *none* of our business."

"I think it is!" the old woman told her daughter. "She's family!"

"Don't talk about me as if I weren't here!" MaryKate said sharply.

"And the children are here!" Sophie added.

"You should be talking to him, if you have something to

345

say," Paddy said. "I know MaryKate. Once her mind's made up, it's too late to talk to her."

Sophie's mother hesitated before moving to the door. "Then I'll find someone else to talk to!"

"He'll never talk to the likes of us!" Sophie said.

"*She* will!" her mother replied. And was gone.

In the hallway Sophie's mother hesitated, her willpower dissolving into the rich carpets and oil paintings that surrounded her.

At that moment Elizabeth came up the stairwell, slowing when she saw the elderly Irish woman, dressed in black widow's weeds and standing as if she were the angel of death in the middle of the upper hall.

"Do you need something?" Elizabeth asked, more out of good manners than any real concern. Her patrician upbringing kept her from feeling close to the woman who stood before her—an Irish peasant with whom she had nothing in common.

"I think we should talk. Your son has turned Mary-Kathleen's head."

"Has he?" Elizabeth said archly. "Or has she turned his?"

"It will never work," the old woman said.

"I told Mary-Kathleen that," the dowager duchess told the Irish peasant woman.

"And?" she asked finally.

"Mary-Kathleen agreed," Elizabeth said quietly. "She left. That very day."

"And your son came to get her!"

"Yes. He did. With my blessings."

The old woman stared at Harry's mother. Elizabeth was not that much younger, although she looked from a different generation with her coiffured hair and immaculate silken clothing. "I don't understand."

Elizabeth smiled suddenly. "Would you like some fresh-brewed Earl Grey?"

"Yes, I would."

"Good," Elizabeth said, as if something had been settled. "We'll talk over a good cuppa."

The dowager duchess's rooms were in the front of the

huge house, overlooking the moonlit square. Dublin, outside the nighttime windows, was dark and still in the late hours before midnight, a few lamps glimmering in the distance, carriage wheels hitting the cobblestones of Exeter Square now and then, a late carouser home to his family.

Upstairs in the large stone mansion at the end of the square an unlikely twosome had a very late tea. The dowager duchess of Exeter, English to her fingertips, rich before she was born, sat across from the only daughter amongst nine sons, of an Irish fisherman who had never had enough money to buy a bit of land.

Elizabeth poured. "Help yourself to the sugar and cream."

"Thank you, Your Grace."

"I think we can dispense with titles at this juncture." Elizabeth stopped, looking toward the other woman. "I'm sorry, I don't even know your name."

"It's Bridget, Your Grace."

"And I'm Elizabeth, Bridget. Now. What are we to do with our children?"

Bridget stared at the woman across from her. "I'm sure I don't know."

"I think we should let them see to themselves," Elizabeth said firmly.

A knock at the door brought Archie inside, looking toward the two women. "I'm to tell whoever cares that we're about to have a wedding in the front parlor—the more witnesses the better, His Grace says."

Elizabeth stood up: "We could hardly refuse such a romantic invitation, could we, Bridget?" Elizabeth turned toward the small Irishwoman who stifled a cough and stood up.

"Hardly," Bridget replied stoutly.

"We shall be down directly," the dowager duchess told her son's retainer.

Downstairs Father Ross stared at MaryKate, whom he had know since birth, and the English duke of Exeter, who had waltzed into their lives and turned the parish upside-down.

KATHLEEN

"You're both sure about this," the Irish priest began dubiously.

"Yes," Harry said clearly. Then he looked down at MaryKate, who looked the old priest in the eye.

"Yes, Father. Very sure." She spoke quietly, her words warming Harry's heart and convincing the priest.

"All right," the old priest said testily. "Well, then, get your witnesses in, and let's get you two squared away with God. Our good queen you shall have to see to yourselves!"

Harry looked deep into MaryKate's eyes. "That we shall, that we shall. Together."

While Harry and Mary O'Hallion's daughter, Kathleen, pledged themselves to each other, Queen Victoria and her Prince, Albert, slept the sleep of the innocent in Dublin's Government House. Beyond all temptation and earthly cares, they dreamt of each other and of more kindnesses the fates would bestow upon their most worthy, most pious, majesties.

When morning's first rays of light reached out toward Dublin City, Her Majesty's servants were waiting to do her early bidding. The soft scent of the queen's favorite lavender permeated bed and rug and tablecloths as Victoria awoke to a new day.

And the news that the rebel lord, the Earl of Lismore, newly made Duke of Exeter, awaited Her Majesty's pleasure in the audience room below.

"I shan't see him!" Victoria exclaimed to her husband over her morning tea and toast.

"Eat more, my love," Albert urged his wife.

She smiled shyly. "I am such a small person, I would become a washtub if I ate all that the servants brought me. I want to please you, Albert. I want to be like the paintings of the masters." She blushed at her forwardness, her husband coming near to reach for her tiny hands, kissing them delicately. "Only for you, beloved," Victoria ended softly.

"You are my liege lord and my dreams come true," Albert told his wife. "And I know the way to serve you is to help you see what is best for your people and to help you make them live up to what is best for them and the realm you inherited, thanks be to God."

The diminutive queen looked up at her handsome husband. "I can't imagine what I should have done if you had not come into my life. If you had not loved me."

He straightened up, smiling. "There would have been others to guide you."

"But none such as you," she told him sincerely.

"Perhaps not, but God, in His infinite wisdom, saw fit to give you into my charge."

Victoria reached to kiss his hand. "And I need your help with my cousin Harry. He's married into that rebel O'Hallion family. Without my consent, as well you know."

Prince Albert frowned, his handsome head bent forward toward the tiny woman who was his wife and his queen. "With lesser monarchs, he would already be incarcerated in the Tower of London."

A trace of doubt wrinkled the queen's smooth, pale forehead. "Have I been too lenient, Albert?"

"All the dispatches from Ireland say the family is of the worst sort. Lower class and rebellious against your rule."

Victoria considered his words. "Yet cousin Harry has always been a particular favorite of mine."

"Entirely understandable," her husband conceded graciously. Victoria might rule England, but Albert ruled Victoria and both of them knew it. "Your uncles, including his father, were not the best examples of Christian virtues."

The queen sighed, her well-endowed bosom swelling with the effort. Her husband looked down upon her, proud of how eager she was to do right. "You, yourself, are an exception to the libertine ways of your family. So we must allow your cousin the benefit of the doubt."

"You are the wisest man alive," Victoria told her husband. "I shall talk to him myself. But I want you near."

"I will always be near, my sweet."

Queen Victoria sighed again. But this time a smile accompanied the sigh, her eyes soft as she gazed up at the handsome giant who was her very own Prince Charming.

Two hours later the young queen was ushered toward a large chamber three floors below her private quarters. Behind an intricately carved walnut screen within the audience chamber, Prince Albert was already positioning himself.

KATHLEEN

Ready to listen, and to counsel his wife later, Albert relaxed back and waited.

The diminutive Victoria swept into the room. She moved more slowly when she saw children in front of her. Beyond the children two young women, and an older one, watched their queen move forward. Harry stood near the door.

Queen Victoria stopped where she was, looking toward her tall, dark cousin. "I was expecting only my cousin, the new duke of Exeter."

"Your Majesty," Harry bowed low, "I hoped to present my wife and my family."

"To what purpose?" the queen asked.

"So that you may meet your subjects, Your Majesty," Harry replied.

There was a very telling pause. Finally, Victoria herself broke it. "Then introduce me."

"Yes, Your Majesty. May I present my wife's widowed sister-in-law, Sophie, her children, and her mother, Bridget. They are on their way to America." Harry watched his cousin Victoria as he spoke. "They wished to meet you before they were forced to leave the land they were born in."

"Forced? By whom?" Victoria demanded imperiously.

"By none but God, Himself, Your Majesty." Sophie surprised herself by speaking up at all. She trailed off into silence, her cheeks burning red.

"My daughter means the blight," Bridget said into the silence that greeted Sophie's words. "None else."

"Ah, the blight," Victoria said. "It is a terrible legacy. A curse upon this island."

"And curable," Harry said.

The queen looked toward her cousin. "Curable? My ministers say it is not. They say it is inevitable."

"Then they have no imagination. And less interest in helping the Irish."

Victoria watched her cousin closely. "Some things are beyond our intervention."

"Some aren't," Harry replied.

The queen gauged her cousin. Her gaze drifted toward the ornate screen Prince Albert sat behind. Then she turned

350

KATHLEEN

toward the children Sophie and her mother were trying to keep under control.

The baby in Sophie's arms began to cry, distracting Victoria. She looked toward the Irish woman and then walked nearer. "Why is the baby crying?"

Sophie stared at the English queen. Finding her voice, she spoke over the lump in her throat, "He's teething, Your Majesty. That is, I mean—" Sophie faltered, not knowing what to say.

"Have you tried camphor?" Queen Victoria asked.

"Oh, yes, Your Majesty."

The two women bent their heads over the small crying child as Harry drew MaryKate aside.

"What is it?" she asked. "What is happening?"

"I think the queen is beginning to realize your family is just that. A family. Not rebels. Merely people trying to live their lives like any others."

Beyond them the ornate screen stood sentinel, Prince Albert behind it, listening.

The diminutive queen turned toward Harry and MaryKate. "You may withdraw," she told them. "I shall assess the situation."

Harry bowed, withdrawing. MaryKate, beside him, curtsied and then straightened, staring the queen in the eye for one brief instant before she also withdrew.

Behind Harry and MaryKate, Sophie, her mother, and her children prepared to follow, leaving the queen, their liege lord, behind.

As they left, Victoria herself reached out toward the baby in Sophie's arms. "Let me know if he does not respond." At Sophie's look Victoria continued, "My own had the worst teething you've ever seen."

Sophie smiled softly. "I suppose there's not so much difference between us all, then."

"Perhaps not," the queen of England said.

Sophie hesitated. "The duke, he never did one thing you'd be ashamed of."

The queen watched her Irish subject. "You're sure."

"Yes," Sophie replied earnestly. "He made us all see that the English weren't all evil." Sophie realized who she was talking to and blushed scarlet.

351

The young queen smiled. "I must admit I have no soft feelings for the Irish. They are a people who give me trouble beyond measure. But, as for you and your family, I warrant, I see more than an enemy of the realm. Therefore, the duke of Exeter's request is granted. You have free passage to America."

Sophie started to reach for Victoria's hands. And then stopped, realizing. "Thank you, Your Majesty."

Prince Albert came out from behind the wrought screen after the last of their subjects had left. Victoria went toward him, smiling. "And?"

Albert stared down into her smile and her anxious eyes. Then he smiled, her eyes lighting with happiness at the sight. "I think none could have handled the situation better," he told her. "I doubt any of them ever were conspirators. They are not the type."

Victoria beamed. "My sentiments precisely!"

The duke of Exeter's carriages drew up in front of Exeter House, disgorging Harry and his new wife from the first carriage, her sister-in-law, nieces, and nephews from the second carriage.

At the door Patrick greeted them, his brow creased with worry. "And is it all all right, then?" he demanded of Sophie.

"Yes. And they were right in not having you come. She might not have seen you the way we do."

"And what did she see, then?" Patrick demanded.

"A teething baby," Sophie replied, "and people who are leaving for America."

Harry saw his mother waiting at the top of the stairs. He bounded up the steps, hesitating for a moment beside her. And then reaching to hug her.

"Thank you."

Elizabeth fought back tears, her arms going around her full-grown son for the first time in thirty years. "There's no need to thank me." She tried to speak over the lump in her throat.

"I would never have taken the children with me. You should have seen her with them! You could see her soften."

Elizabeth's eyes glittered with unshed tears as she smiled

KATHLEEN

up at her tall son. "It helps to know the person you are dealing with, even when she's a queen."

"Especially when she's a queen!" He laughed, the sound warming his mother's heart. "She didn't say a word about confiscation. We've done it. We've done it! My God, somehow we've won through!"

Father Ross opened the door to his room, peering out into the hall. "What's happened now?" he asked, bleary-eyed.

"A miracle!" the duke of Exeter roared.

Father Ross shrugged. "Ah and is that all, then—miracles may be strange to you Protestants, but Catholics don't wake up their households because of them."

"It's broad daylight!" Harry told the priest.

"And whose fault is it I had no sleep last night, if not yours?" Father Ross demanded. "I'm sure to expire of exhaustion if I don't get some soon."

"Father Ross, I'm sorry—truly!" Harry grinned, letting go of his mother and sketching a bow toward the little priest. "Go back to bed, please. We'll not disturb you further." Harry turned to look down the stairs at MaryKate's family. "You all should get some rest. We all should." His eyes searched out MaryKate. "Kathleen?"

MaryKate stood near young Johnny. She looked up toward the man who was now her husband.

"Come here." Harry captured her eyes and wouldn't let go of them. "Come to bed, wife."

MaryKate blushed. She could feel eyes all around her as she walked, slowly, forward, toward the stairs. And her husband.

MaryKate lifted her skirts, her eyes still on her husband, ascending the steps that led toward him.

When she reached his side, he captured her hands within his own, drawing her away from the stairwell toward the double doors that led into the ducal suite.

The suite was decorated in shades of deep red, burgundies, and clarets covering walls, floors, chairs, and tables.

The huge mahogany bed was draped in claret velvet, cream-colored embroidery edging the satin sheets.

Harry still held MaryKate's hands, drawing her toward the bed.

"It's midday," MaryKate said.

353

KATHLEEN

"Yes, it is," Harry replied.

She watched his eyes. "What are we going to do?"

"We're going to make love," he told her.

"Now?"

"Now."

"They'll wonder where we are."

"They'll know where we are," Harry said. He dropped his hands. Staring at her. "I want you to undress."

"Undress?"

"Yes." He stood in front of her, watching her blush. A warm glow suffused her cheeks and spread down, across her body, as she reached the bodice of her gown, fingering the first button and, slowly, unbuttoning it.

She stopped.

"Kathleen," Harry called her name softly.

"I've never done this," MaryKate said softly.

Harry reached for the next button. Unbuttoning it. Then he stepped back. Waiting.

She reached for a button, slowly releasing it, more of her white shift showing beneath the open bodice of her gown.

"Step out of the gown," Harry prompted.

MaryKate reached to lift one shoulder and then the other out of the emerald satin gown she had worn to Lady Amelia's party so many weeks ago. She held the top of the gown in her hands and then, slowly, let it drop to her waist.

"MaryKate," Harry spoke her name, "I want you to want me."

"I do," she answered softly.

"Show me," he said. "Show me."

MaryKate watched Harry. She reached to her waist, taking hold of the emerald satin and sliding it down, past her hips. It pooled around her feet, a dark green froth on the floor beneath her thin cotton shift.

36

"Take off your shift." Harry's voice came from deep within his throat.

MaryKate watched him. She reached for the left strap, raising it and letting it fall down past her shoulder. She touched the right strap, her chemise falling toward the rise of her breast, slipping down slowly, one pink nipple exposed. And then the other.

MaryKate's eyes never left Harry's. She saw his eyes widen, saw the hunger, the need, that welled up within him, spilling out his eyes.

Her chemise was to her waist, ivory skin gleaming in the wintry daylight that filtered through the heavy velvet drapes. The curves of her body as her breast narrowed to her waist were exposed to his gaze.

Then she stopped, her hands falling to her sides.

"Why do you stop?" His voice was gruff.

She didn't reply. He took a step toward her and then another, standing in front of her. His eyes fell to her bare breasts. She turned her back, waiting for the touch of his hands.

When it came, his hands closed around her bare shoul-

355

ders, making her shiver. He stood still for a long moment before he relaxed his hold. He ran his hands lightly across her shoulders and down her arms. The tips of his fingers grazed the sides of her breasts, making her shiver the more.

His hands came back up her arms and then, slowly, traced down her back, to the tiny back buttons that held the skirt of the thin white shift closed. Her eyes closed as his large fingers worked clumsily at the delicate buttons, freeing them one by one.

The soft cotton slid down her slender hips, Harry's hands reaching to cup her bare hips, the lace of her borrowed garter belt and the stockings that came to the tops of her thighs. He reached to unsnap the stockings, slipping off the garter belt as he turned her around, watching her closed eyes until they opened. He leaned to kiss her lips, his arms straining around her bare body, lifting her to her toes and then off her feet, the length of her naked body held close against him.

"Kathleen," his breath came in ragged bursts, matching her own. He reached an arm down around her legs, lifting her high and carrying her to his bed. Her arms clung to his neck, releasing him slowly as he straightened over her, staring down at her face. And then, slowly, letting his eyes travel from her lips down the length of her body.

Slowly, standing above her, he began to undress, throwing off jacket and vest, cravat and shirt. Bare to the waist, he reached toward her right leg, taking the top of her stocking and rolling it down her calf, off her narrow foot. She moved under his touch, one hand reaching to stop her, to keep her still as his other hand reached for her left stocking, leaving her naked against the red velvet coverlet.

MaryKate reached up to his face, gently bringing his lips back to hers. The touch of his lips jolted through her, liquefying her bones. He found her ear, nibbling at the edge, his tongue reaching inside, her body reacting, her lips searching out the side of his neck, kissing him shyly and then losing her shyness, biting little bites as he moved against her.

He reached to pull off the rest of his clothes, MaryKate helping, her hands tracing patterns against his flesh, feeling him shiver at her touch, and then strain to be nearer.

KATHLEEN

"Harry, oh, Harry," she moaned against him. Harry reached to trail kisses down her breast, his lips finding a nipple and pulling it into his mouth. MaryKate surged against him, her hands digging into his sides. He reached a hand to part her legs, feeling her resistance and then feeling her let go as he rolled over, on his knees between her legs, bending still to kiss first one breast and then the other.

His lips trailed downward, MaryKate moaning softly. Harry's own breath came out more sharply, his tongue dipping into the hollow of her belly button and then, slowly, moving toward her thighs. She strained against him, unused to the feelings he brought welling up within her. He moved to kiss the inner side of her thigh, but MaryKate sat up. Her arms reached to stop him, to pull him up toward her mouth.

"No . . . no . . ." He whispered the words, his arms reaching up to lay her back down. His mouth touched the soft mound, biting at auburn hair. She drifted in clouds of pleasure, her body cradled by softest velvet, her hands reaching out to her sides, grasping the silken satin of the sheets. Harry's hands traveled the length of her body, teasing nipples, trailing fingertips along the sides of her thighs as his mouth moved, slowly, lower.

Her back arched when his tongue reached between her thighs. Harry cupped a hand under each of her buttocks, reaching gently to pull her thighs farther apart, lifting her toward his mouth.

"Harry, no . . . no . . . you . . . ohhhhhhhhhhh . . ." Her words ended in a sigh, his tongue touching softest lips and reaching to nibble at the tiny point of flesh that sent spasms of pleasure surging through her, hardening her nipples as his own flesh responded.

He fought his own desire, restraining himself as her hands fluttered around his shoulders, her fingers widening as she touched the back of his head, closing around locks of his dark hair, little sounds escaping her lips.

He kissed her deeply, her fingers tightening, pulling on his hair, bringing him up to her breast as her hands reached down his body. Her legs moved against his, her body reaching up toward his, grazing the hardened flesh he was fighting to control.

KATHLEEN

His body shivered, thrust against hers, not wanting to lose the feelings.

Then, their bodies fused. She surged against him, his flesh entering her, the shock of their sudden coupling melding them into one being, arms, breath, heartbeats, bodies. In their uniting, they lost the rest of the world, reality far away.

Here, in the center of the universe, she felt him move within her, invading her further, drawing back only to thrust, ever deeper, her body molding around him.

She felt tremors build within them, unsure where hers began and his ended, reacting to his every movement as he brought them closer to the edge of the universe.

"Oh, God, MaryKate, God, I need you so much." His voice was ragged, her arms tightening around him, her body convulsing with his words. He poured forth within her, sending them over the edge, lost within each other.

He moved to his side, bringing her with him, their bodies still melded together.

"I love you so much." She was cradled in his arms, whispering into his ear.

He pulled back a little, tipping her chin to look deep in her eyes. "MaryKate, Mary's Kate. You make me so happy."

"Do I?"

"Don't you know you do?"

"You've never told me," MaryKate told her husband.

"I've never been good with words."

"You've never even told me you love me."

He stared at her. "Don't you know it? Can't you feel it?" He watched her. "MaryKate, I've loved you since you sent me tumbling into the mud."

"I?! I sent you?! You were the one racing like a mad Englishman through the countryside!"

"Are you arguing with me?" he asked her.

"I—I—" Her voice softened to a whisper. "No."

"Good." He kissed her cheek. "Because I have other plans for us today, and tonight, and tomorrow, and forever." He punctuated each whispered word with a kiss, his lips drifting across her body. "Kathleen, my own darling. Kathleen mavourneen."

* * *

KATHLEEN

Hours later, night fell gently outside the velvet-draped windows of Exeter House. The dowager duchess found herself teaching the card game Patience to Sophie's mother while Sophie and her children sat in front of the library fireplace, listening to Patrick O'Hallion spin tales of what they would find in the new land.

A grandfather clock began to chime seven as the English butler opened the hall door, announcing dinner.

Johnny looked toward his mother. "Should I go fetch Aunt Kate?" he asked.

Sophie blushed. "No."

"But she doesn't know he's sending our presents with us to the New World—what we won! She'll want to know he kept his promises."

"Leave off, John Patrick," his uncle Paddy told him.

"Why?" He stared at his mother's scarlet cheeks. "Is something wrong with Aunt Kate?"

"Nothing's wrong with your aunt," Elizabeth answered him from across the room.

"Where is she?" Young John asked.

"None of your business," his uncle told him gruffly.

"Isn't she coming to America with us, then?" Betsy asked.

"No, she'll be staying here," Sophie told her daughter.

"Part of the year," Elizabeth corrected. "They'll have to spend part of their time in London. Now come along to dinner."

Johnny's grandmother chuckled. "Not to worry, Young John, your Aunt Kate is exactly where she wants to be."

"And what will she be doing there?" Johnny asked.

"What?!" His mother nearly screeched the word.

"What's she to do in England?" Young John repeated.

The dowager duchess looked toward the young boy, restraining a smile. "I rather imagine she will be helping her husband bring Ireland's plight to the right ears. Perhaps helping to rebuild your country."

"Oh." He thought about it. "And is that what she's doing now?" he asked the adults around him as they walked toward the hall and the dining room beyond.

There was a moment of shocked silence as they left the library.

KATHLEEN

And then laughter filled the hallway, rising up the staircase toward the ducal chamber as solemn children watched laughing adults.

Betsy leaned toward Johnny. "What are they laughing at?" she asked him.

"Come along," her mother called, still smiling. "Come along, then. You're much too young to have it be any of your business. Your grandmother is right. Aunt Kate is exactly where she wants to be."

And she was.

Jude Deveraux

America's favorite historical romance author!

The James River Trilogy
___ COUNTERFEIT LADY 67519/$4.50
___ LOST LADY 67430/$4.50
___ RIVER LADY 67297/$4.50

Enter the passionate world of the Chandler Twins
___ TWIN OF ICE 50049/$3.95
___ TWIN OF FIRE 50050/$3.95

The Montgomery Saga Continues
___ THE TEMPTRESS 67452/$4.50
___ THE RAIDER 67056/$4.50
___ THE PRINCESS 67386/$4.50
___ THE AWAKENING 64445/$4.50
___ THE MAIDEN 62196/$4.50

POCKET BOOKS

Simon & Schuster, Mail Order Dept. JRT
200 Old Tappan Rd., Old Tappan, N.J. 07675

Please send me the books I have checked above. I am enclosing $_____ (please add 75¢ to cover postage and handling for each order. N.Y.S. and N.Y.C. residents please add appropriate sales tax). Send check or money order—no cash or C.O.D.'s please. Allow up to six weeks for delivery. For purchases over $10.00 you may use VISA: card number, expiration date and customer signature must be included.

Name _____

Address _____

City _____ State/Zip _____

VISA Card No. _____ Exp. Date _____

Signature _____ 388-05

The Best Historical Romance Comes From Pocket Books

- ☐ **BRYARLY** Jacqueline Marten .... 63522/$3.95
- ☐ **FALLING STAR** Elisabeth MacDonald ..... 66798/$3.95
- ☐ **FLETCHER'S WOMAN** Linda Lael Miller .. 66443/$3.50
- ☐ **FORBIDDEN LOVE** Maura Seger .... 64154/$3.50
- ☐ **GLORY IN THE FLOWER**
  Jacqueline Marten .... 62719/$3.95
- ☐ **HONOR'S SPLENDOUR** Julie Garwood ... 63781/$3.95
- ☐ **JASMIN ON THE WIND**
  Mallory Dorn Hart .... 62303/$4.50
- ☐ **PASSION MOON RISING**
  Rebecca Brandewyne .... 61774/$3.95
- ☐ **REBELLIOUS LOVE** Maura Seger .... 64367/$3.50
- ☐ **SOMETHING WONDERFUL**
  Judith McNaught .... 62719/$3.95
- ☐ **SONGBIRD** Linda Shaw .... 45474/$3.95
- ☐ **TAPESTRY OF PRIDE** Catherine Lyndell 62328/$3.95
- ☐ **THE LION'S LADY**
  Julie Garwood .... 64360/$3.95
- ☐ **THE TROUBADOUR'S ROMANCE**
  Robyn Carr .... 61708/$3.95
- ☐ **TO PLUCK A ROSE** Elsa Cook .... 64368/$4.50
- ☐ **TROPIC GOLD** Carol Jerina .... 64361/$3.95
- ☐ **WANTON ANGEL** Linda Lael Miller .... 62197/$3.95
- ☐ **WINDS OF ENCHANTMENT**
  Jan McGowan .... 64307/$3.95
- ☐ **MOONFIRE** Linda Lael Miller
  62198/$3.95
- ☐ **WARY HEARTS** Marylyle Rogers
  65879/$3.95

POCKET BOOKS

**Simon & Schuster Mail Order Dept. HRS
200 Old Tappan Rd., Old Tappan, N.J. 07675**

Please send me the books I have checked above. I am enclosing $_____ (please add 75¢ to cover postage and handling for each order. N.Y.S. and N.Y.C. residents please add appropriate sales tax). Send check or money order—no cash or C.O.D.'s please. Allow up to six weeks for delivery. For purchases over $10.00 you may use VISA: card number, expiration date and customer signature must be included.

Name _____

Address _____

City _____ State/Zip _____

VISA Card No. _____ Exp. Date _____

Signature _____ 89-05